THE TAMING OF
DR ALEX

BY
JOANNA NEIL

THE MAN
BEHIND THE BADGE

BY
SHARON ARCHER

MILLS &
BOON

THE TAMING OF
DR ALEX DRAYCOTT

BY
JOANNA NEIL

First published in Great Britain 2011
by Mills & Boon, an imprint of Harlequin (UK) Limited,
Eton House, 18-24 Paradise Road, Richmond, Surrey TW9 1SR

© Joanna Neil 2011

ISBN: 978 0 263 88589 7

Printed and bound in Spain
by Blackprint CPI, Barcelona

Dear Reader

It takes all sorts to make a world, doesn't it? Some people are driven to make a success of their careers to the point where they lose sight of what really matters. Others are serene and laid-back, taking life as it comes and never getting overly concerned about anything.

This set me to thinking. What if two such people met and struck sparks off one another? How could a relationship ever work between them—especially if neither of them was looking for anything permanent?

And that was exactly the problem that confounded Callum and Alex when they met and clashed in the A&E department.

Alex had so much to cope with after adversity had struck her family, so she wasn't in any mood to tread softly around anyone who didn't agree with her attempts to reorganise the department, despite the fact that she was trying to save it from closure.

Would Callum be the one to break the ice and show her what it was to be a warm, loving woman?

With best wishes

Joanna Neil

When **Joanna Neil** discovered Mills & Boon®, her life-long addiction to reading crystallised into an exciting new career writing Medical™ Romance. Her characters are probably the outcome of her varied lifestyle, which includes working as a clerk, typist, nurse and infant teacher. She enjoys dressmaking and cooking at her Leicestershire home. Her family includes a husband, son and daughter, an exuberant yellow Labrador and two slightly crazed cockatiels. She currently works with a team of tutors at her local education centre, to provide creative writing workshops for people interested in exploring their own writing ambitions.

Recent titles by the same author:

BECOMING DR BELLINI'S BRIDE
PLAYBOY UNDER THE MISTLETOE
THE SECRET DOCTOR

CHAPTER ONE

'Look how many strawberries I picked,' seven-year-old Sarah announced, coming into the kitchen. She placed a wicker basket on the table, filled to the brim with fruit. 'There's loads,' she said, her blue eyes bright with excitement. 'Can we have some for breakfast?'

Alex looked at the lush fruit. 'Yes,' she murmured, 'of course…and as there's such a lot, perhaps we ought to take some round to Mrs Marchant next door? I've noticed she's usually up and about at this time of the morning.'

Sarah nodded. 'I'll go, if you like.' She smiled. 'I like Mrs Marchant. She's kind…but I think she must be quite old, you know, or poorly? She always looks a bit tired and sometimes she says she has to go and sit down for a while…but she's always nice. She gave me some toffees when I took the magazine round there yesterday.'

'I want to take the strawberries,' five-year-old James chimed in, his eyes lighting up at the mention of toffees. 'You went last time.' He glared at his sister and began to tug at the basket.

Sensing impending disaster, Alex intervened. 'We'll all go,' she said, taking hold of the basket and moving it from harm's way. 'Now, finish your breakfast, both of you. We don't have much time before we have to leave for school.

And you need to go back upstairs to your bedroom and find your PE kit, James.'

'I don't like that bedroom,' James complained, scowling at Alex across the kitchen table, a lock of brown hair falling across his forehead. 'It's too small. Why can't I have the room with the window seat?'

'Because we talked about this…' Alex murmured. 'And you chose the one that looked out over the orchard.' She inspected the contents of his lunch box and then clipped the lid in place.

'So?' He hunched his shoulders. 'That doesn't matter, does it? I changed my mind. I can swap with Sarah.'

'No, you can't.' His sister batted that one away before the idea could take root, her fair hair quivering with indignation. 'I want the one where I can see the garden… I chose it…and I picked the colours and Auntie Alex has already started painting the walls for me. So it's mine.'

'Perhaps we can rearrange the furniture in your room to make it better for you,' Alex said, glancing at James. She pushed his lunch box into his school bag and closed the zipper. 'I made you egg mayonnaise sandwiches, and there are cracker biscuits with ham and cheese. And don't forget to screw the lid tight on your drink bottle when you use it, or we'll have another mess in your bag like the one we had last week.'

'I don't like egg maynaze.' James's chin jutted and his grey eyes took on a mutinous glint.

Alex held back the sigh that had started to build up in her chest. She raised dark brows. 'You told me it was your favourite.'

He gave her a disdainful glance. 'That was yesterday. Today I like peanut butter.'

'Well, I'm sorry about that, James, but I really don't have time to start over.' Alex flicked back her long chestnut hair so that it settled in a gentle flurry across her shoulders, and handed him the bag. 'We have to get you and Sarah to school, and I have to go to work.' She checked her watch. 'Do you remember what I told you? This is my first day in the new job, and I need to be at the hospital on time.'

'Will you be in trouble if you're late?' Sarah's anxiety sounded in her voice. 'Mummy said she always got an ear bending from the boss if she wasn't at work for nine o'clock.' She frowned. 'I think that must hurt a lot. I wouldn't like it if it anyone pulled my ears.'

'How could that happen to Auntie Alex?' James said in a scornful tone. 'She's the boss. She can do what she likes.'

Alex smiled. 'Not exactly, James. There are several bosses in my department…but the fact is, if you're in charge you need to lead by example…show people the right way of doing things…so it's even more important that I get there on time.'

Sarah's face still bore a worried expression, so she added gently, 'Ear bending just means the boss would talk to your mother about where she was going wrong.'

'Really?' Sarah's blue eyes brightened. 'Well, I think he must be sorry, anyway, 'cos he sent Mummy some flowers. There was a card, and it said, *Get well soon.*'

She frowned again, and Alex gave her a hug. 'We all hope for that, Sarah. At least your mum and dad are in good hands. They're being looked after by the very best doctors.'

For once, James had nothing to say, and Alex sent him a quick, thoughtful glance. He seemed to be coping well enough in the aftermath of his parents' accident, but she suspected his newfound belligerence was all tied up with what had been going on in his life this last few weeks. She would have to keep a keen eye on both children for the foreseeable future.

A few minutes later they left the house and went next door. It was a minute or so before Jane Marchant answered Alex's knock, but when she did her smile was welcoming and she invited them inside.

'We can only stop for a minute or two,' Alex said, following her neighbour into the neat, pine kitchen. 'We just wanted to bring you these strawberries, and to make sure that you're all right.'

Jane stared at the fruit, her mouth dropping open in awe. 'Just look at that fruit—so ripe and juicy.' Her eyes glimmered with appreciation. 'I'll enjoy those with my tea—and I could make a lovely strawberry sponge cake. You'll have to come and share it with me.' She looked at the children, who nodded with enthusiasm at the suggestion. 'Thank you for this,' she said, embracing all three of them with her smile. 'It was very thoughtful of you.'

'Just don't go overdoing it,' Alex warned her. 'I know what you're like when you get started with the baking. I've been worried about you just lately, especially after that dizzy spell you had the other day. Are you still getting the headaches?'

Jane nodded. 'But you don't need to worry yourself over me, love. I'll be fine. Like I said, the doctor's been trying me with different tablets to see if we can calm things down. I probably just need to take things more slowly, that's all. I've perhaps done too much in the garden. I've been trying to tackle the weeds—you know yourself what a job that can be when you have an acre or so to look after.'

'I do.' Alex's lips made a downward curve. 'I'm still wondering what possessed me to take on that rundown house next door, with its dilapidated orchard and all those outbuildings.' Her mouth flattened. 'It just seemed like a good idea at the time.'

'I love it,' Sarah said. 'The garden's all wild and raggedy, and there's lots of fruit bushes all tangled up. And there's masses of strawberries…' she made a wide circle with her arms '…just spreading out all over the place.'

'It's like a jungle,' James put in, ignoring Alex's faintly amused groan. 'We can play explorers, hunting the bad people.' He began to make swashbuckling moves with an imaginary sword.

Sarah looked at Jane once more. 'I can help you with the garden,' she offered. 'Any time you like.'

'Thank you, sweetheart.' Jane beamed at the little girl. 'You're a treasure. Alex must be so happy to have you with her.'

'It's true,' Alex agreed. 'Both she and James have been good as gold, helping with the move.' She frowned. 'But as far as your tablets are concerned, I'm not so sure that they're doing the job.' She glanced at Jane. Her neighbour was in her early sixties, a slender woman with brown, wavy hair and pale features. As Sarah had pointed out in her innocent way, she didn't look at all well. 'I really think you ought to go back to your doctor and ask him to do some tests to find out if there's a specific cause of the high blood pressure that might have been overlooked—especially since you're having other symptoms, like the back pain and the muscle spasms.'

Jane looked doubtful. 'I really don't like to bother the doctor any more. I've already been back several times and he's doing what he can to keep everything in check.'

'Even so,' Alex commented, 'as a doctor myself, I think your symptoms need to be looked into a bit more. I worry about leaving you on your own during the day while I'm at work. Is there no one in the family who can come and look out for you?'

Jane shook her head. 'There's only my nephew. We're very close—in fact, he's more like a son to me. His parents, my brother and his wife, are out of the country, working on various projects.' Her features softened. 'He's such a lovely young man. I think the world of him…and he comes to visit whenever he's able. We often talk on the phone. I'm sure he'd do anything for me, but I know he's busy and I don't want to burden him with my problems.'

Alex's brows drew together. 'Maybe you should think twice about that—after all, he'd want to know if you were ill, wouldn't he?'

'Of course, but it won't come to that. I'll be fine. Besides, he has enough troubles of his own to deal with right now…' She pulled a face 'There's to be some kind of audit at work, apparently, and he has to figure out how to keep the chiefs off his back. He says they've appointed a new manager to whip the department into shape, and the last thing he needs is some busybody poking his nose into all the corners to see how they do things and then use it against him to turn all his carefully organised systems upside down.'

Alex's eyes widened a fraction, and she let out a small breath. Managers were never popular. 'I see what you mean…he does seem to have a lot on his plate at the moment, doesn't he? But I think you're more important than any of that. I wonder if he could find time to help occasionally…with the garden, maybe?'

'Oh, he does what he can.'

James was beginning to show signs of restlessness, wandering about the room, peering at all the fine porcelain plates and glassware on display. He ran his fingers over the smooth lines of a ceramic cookie jar and then began to reach for a chicken-shaped timer, intent on examining its flamboyant red comb and wattles.

'I think it's time we made tracks,' Alex murmured, stopping to give Jane a quick hug. She'd only known this woman for a couple of weeks, but already it was as though they'd been friends for a lifetime.

'Let's go,' she said, handing Sarah her school bag. 'With any luck we'll get to school before the first whistle goes.'

Jane went with them into the hall. 'See you later,' she said.

'I don't like school,' James began as Alex shepherded them out through the front door. 'Mrs Coleman won't let me do painting. She made me sit in the reading corner instead. I don't like reading...'

He was still complaining as Alex bundled them into the car. 'It's a shame you're not happy, James, but it's nearly the end of term, you know, and you'll be able to look forward to the summer holidays.' She glanced at him. 'Fasten your seat belt. You know, if you want to paint, you have to remember to keep your brushes to yourself and resist the temptation to daub the other children. Mrs Coleman said she'd explained it to you. Perhaps you could tell her that you'll be sensible if she'll let you have another go.'

'Yes—well, I don't like her, either.' James clamped his lips together and squinted at the road ahead through narrowed eyes.

Alex checked that Sarah was safely installed in the back seat with a good space between her and her brother, and then drove towards the school. It was about a mile away from the house, along a winding country lane, and the drive was a pleasant one, though even that was not enough to calm her increasingly stretched nerves.

Had she taken on too much, making the decision to

look after her brother's children? In itself, it shouldn't have been too difficult, but alongside the new job at Oakdale Hospital, and adding in the fact that she'd had to move to Somerset to be close to where they used to live, the stress was beginning to pile up. Her once calm and orderly life had been turned upside down. Everything was chaotic.

Not that there was much she could do about any of it. The car accident that had injured her brother and his wife had wreaked havoc with all their lives.

'Bye,' she said when they arrived at the school. 'Take care. Be good.' She kissed the children and hugged them and then watched for a minute or two as they met up with friends and went to stand in line for their teachers.

Then she headed back along the main road to town and her new place of work. The hospital was a few miles inland from the sea, and she drove towards it now, past the soft, rolling hills of the Quantocks, their slopes richly carpeted with heather and occasional dark oases of green woodland.

At the hospital, she parked in her designated place, and then made her way to the A and E department. She pulled in a deep breath, straightened her shoulders and walked into the main reception area. This was a new challenge, a difficult task that she'd been assigned, and she would need to have her wits about her. She was a little apprehensive about what lay in store, but she was determined to make the best effort she could.

Her first impression of the unit was a pleasant one. Everything seemed relatively calm in there. The treatment rooms were occupied, with patients being tended by medical staff, and the whiteboard showed the status of admissions and stage of treatment.

Across the room, a doctor was standing by the desk, chatting to nurses, until, after a moment or two, he noticed

Alex and came over to her. He was good looking, long and lean, immaculately dressed in dark trousers and a white, self-striped shirt, finished off with a muted tie in a pale shade of blue.

'Hi, there,' he said. 'Can I help you? I guess you're not a patient, or you'd have been directed to the waiting room.' His voice was easy on the ear, deep and well modulated, and there was a warmth about him that made it seem as though he was genuinely interested in her. He had black hair, cut short to frame his angular features, and his eyes were a vivid blue, alert and enquiring.

'That's right. Yes, thank you, I'm looking for...' she checked his name badge '...Dr Brooksby.' She smiled. 'I believe I've found the very man I want.'

He laughed. 'Well, that's not something I get to hear every day...but more than welcome, all the same, coming from someone who looks as good as you.' His glance shimmered over her, taking in the tailored, dove-grey suit she was wearing, with the pencil-slim skirt and the jacket that nipped in at her slender waist. His gaze came to rest on the burnished, silky swathe of her hair, lingering there for a while longer than was absolutely necessary.

'Anything I can do for you, you only have to say.' His manner was open and friendly, his blue eyes quizzical, inviting her to offload any worries or problems she might have.

'That's very kind of you.' She let her glance roam fleetingly around the department. 'I must say, it's good to come to an A and E unit and find the atmosphere so relaxed and easygoing. That must be quite unusual, or perhaps I've come at a particularly quiet time? Either way, I imagine your bosses must be pleased with the way you run things around here.'

'You'd think so, but actually they're bringing in new

management. And as to being quiet, it only appears that way—we've just finished dealing with the aftermath of a road accident, and now we're taking a breather and making the most of things…before the new manager comes along to sort us out and tell us where we've been going wrong.' His mouth made a rueful slant. 'Sorry to offload that way. It's a sore point. He's supposed to put in an appearance some time today so we're all on tenterhooks.'

A small ripple of dismay ran through her. This was definitely not going to be an easy ride, judging by his comments. 'Oh, I see.' She reflected on what he'd said for a second or two, before venturing, 'Maybe he'll find that everything's perfectly in order?'

'What a refreshing idea.' He gave a wry smile. 'Unfortunately, I very much doubt it. He's a bean-counter, sent to trim us to the bone. This is the NHS, after all.' He pressed his well-shaped lips together briefly. 'Enough of my problems, though. What can I do for you, Miss…?'

'It's Dr,' she answered carefully. 'Dr Draycott. Alex.'

He stared at her, his mouth dropping open a little until he recovered himself. 'Alex Draycott?' he repeated, cautiously.

She nodded. 'That's right.' She studied him. 'You look as though you're taken aback by that. Is something wrong?'

Slowly, he shook his head. 'No, not at all. It's just that… well…you're a woman.'

She smiled. 'That's very observant of you.'

He was still staring, and she prompted gently, 'Is that likely to be a problem for you?'

'Uh… No, of course not. It's just that, well, Alex is a man's name, isn't it? We were expecting a man.' He frowned, looking at her in a slightly accusatory fashion.

'And I thought you were maybe a relative concerned about one of our patients.'

'I'm not.'

'No, I see that now.' His frown deepened. 'So you're the new doctor/manager who's come to join the unit?'

She hesitated. 'Um…bean-counter was how you put it, I think.' She gave him a wryly amused look, her grey eyes taking in his obvious unease. 'It's odd how defensive people become whenever managers arrive on the scene, isn't it? And it's totally unnecessary, you know—after all, we're all in this together, aren't we, working for the greater good of the hospital? I have a job to do, but it doesn't have to put us at odds with one another.'

'Doesn't it?' He appeared sceptical. 'Perhaps you aren't aware that your reputation has gone before you? We've all heard how you wielded the axe at your last hospital. There were job cuts and ward closures.'

She sent him a quick look, her grey eyes troubled. 'Sometimes, no matter how you try to preserve what's already in place, it becomes impossible in the end, if budget restrictions are too tight. But in all fairness to me, I did manage to keep the department open, I kept the job losses down to natural wastage, and I put new measures in place so that some patients could be tended to elsewhere.'

'You didn't stay around, though, did you, once your job was done?' His blue gaze was flint sharp. 'Was that because you found the atmosphere suddenly less friendly?'

The attack was swift and unexpected and Alex felt a knot tighten in her stomach. 'I left for personal reasons,' she said, a catch in her voice. 'It was nothing to do with the job. My circumstances changed, and my contract had come to an end anyway. I chose not to renew it.' Even the memory of that time, when she had first heard about her brother's accident, was enough to make the blood drain from her face.

He studied her thoughtfully, and perhaps he realised that he had touched a nerve, because he said softly, 'I'm sorry. That was uncalled-for on my part. Put it down to tension, if you will. We're all a little on edge here, uncertain about what the future holds for us and for the department. Of course, you were just doing your job.'

He laid a hand lightly on her elbow. 'Perhaps I should take you along to the doctors' lounge and offer you a cup of coffee? It was thoughtless of me not to suggest it before. It's just that your arrival threw me off balance for a minute or two. We weren't expecting you until later this morning.'

'No, I realise that…but I thought it would be as well to come in early and get the feel of the place.'

'I expect I would have done the same,' he said, leading the way along the corridor to the lounge. 'I think you'll like it here. Everyone's very friendly, and we work well together for the most part. The only real problem is the one that faces all hospital trusts. We're struggling with budget deficits and the department is under threat of being closed down. Dr Langton, the chief executive, has been warning us that it's a possibility.'

Alex frowned as they entered the room. 'I was appointed by the board to try to make sure that doesn't happen.'

His mouth made a wry twist. 'Well, let's hope you can work wonders. It's a difficult job you've taken on, and in some ways management can turn out to be a poisoned chalice. Not many would want to do it.'

'I suppose not.' She was thoughtful for a moment or two. 'But in all the years I've worked as a doctor, I've come across things that aren't working as well as they should, and over time I began to think that perhaps if I went into management, I might be able to make a difference.'

'You've obviously put a lot of thought into it. For myself, I prefer hands-on medicine one hundred per cent of the time.'

'And I'm sure that must be the reason you've done so well for yourself. I've heard nothing but good things about you, from the occasional article in the press and the medical journals, as well as from Dr Langton. You've been at Oakdale for some time, haven't you?'

'Yes, for several years. I came here originally as a registrar and then I was offered the post of consultant. I love it here…it's like a home from home for me.' He grinned. 'Mind you, I think medicine's in my blood. It's been there ever since I was a child, pretending to be an army surgeon to my wounded toy soldiers.'

She laughed softly, trying to imagine him as a youngster. 'I can see you in my mind's eye,' she said, 'bandaging your action figures. Though I expect most boys wouldn't bother too much with those who'd been invalided out.' Still, even James had made a crutch for a toy soldier that had lost its plastic leg, painstakingly taping the wooden stick to its hand.

He made a wry smile. 'Maybe not.' He went over to the coffee machine to one side of the room and poured hot liquid into two mugs. 'Do you take milk and sugar?' he asked, and she nodded.

'Both, thanks.' She sniffed the air appreciatively. 'That smells good.'

He nodded. 'It's one thing I look forward to around here. Decent coffee.' He waved her to a chair. 'Have a seat and make yourself comfortable.' He came to sit close to her and swallowed his coffee, savouring the taste and taking a moment to relax. 'So, tell me about yourself,' he said quietly, his glance moving over her and coming to rest briefly on the smooth shapeliness of her long legs. 'From what I heard, you've moved here from Herefordshire? I suppose that means this job must have had some special appeal for you?'

'I thought it would give me the best of both worlds, the chance to work in paediatric emergency, which is what I like doing best—it's what I specialised in—and at the same time it allows me to take on a managerial role.' She clasped her cup in both hands, feeling the comforting warmth spread slowly through her. 'But the main reason I'm here is because I have family who have settled in Somerset.'

'Your parents?'

She shook her head. 'My brother and his family. My parents do have a home here, but they're away at the moment, because of my father's job. He's a troubleshooter for an oil company, so he tends to travel a lot.'

He gave a brief smile. 'That's something we have in common, then. My parents have always travelled far and wide, as far back as I can remember.' A fleeting sadness came into his eyes and she studied him thoughtfully for a moment or two. Had that been a problem for him?

'Perhaps I've been lucky,' she murmured. 'My parents were always there for me while I was growing up. It was only when I started work as a doctor that they began to travel further afield.' She would have liked to ask him about his family, but something warned her that this might be the wrong time to do that. She didn't want to blunder into areas that might cause problems, especially on her first day. Perhaps when she knew him a little better…

'It must have been difficult for you, uprooting yourself,' he said. 'Did you manage to find a place of your own, or are you renting while you look around?'

'I thought about renting. Back in Herefordshire I'd taken out a lease on a flat, but it ran out—another reason why it seemed feasible to make the move to Somerset. I planned to do the same down here, but then I saw this big, old house on the market, going for a song, and I decided to snap it up. It was purely an impulsive action—not like me at all, but something about it appealed to me. Of course, the reason it was going so cheap is because it needs a lot of work...' She pulled a face. 'And the owner wanted a quick sale.'

'But things are working out fairly well for you, overall?'

She nodded. 'I think so. I hope so.' She drank her coffee and looked around. 'As I see it right now, though, my biggest challenge is going to be this job. According to Dr Langton, the hospital is deep in debt and the accident and emergency department is at risk. I want to do all I can to keep it safe, but it means taking some measures that might not be all that popular.'

She braced herself. 'In fact, I think I ought to make a start on getting to grips with the job right now—it's been good to spend a few minutes in here, and I appreciate you taking a break and having coffee with me, but perhaps now I should start to familiarise myself with the way things work around here.' She glanced at him. 'Mr Langton suggested you might be available this morning to give me an insight into the way you run things—where and when you use agency staff, for instance—and perhaps you could let me see your drugs list, so I can gain some idea of expenditure in that area?'

He frowned. 'Are you sure you want to do that on your first day? Wouldn't you prefer to take a general look around and get to know some of the staff? I'm sure they're all anxious to meet their new colleague.'

She nodded. 'Of course, and I want to meet them, but I don't want to intrude on them while they're busy. I'll definitely make time to introduce myself to them through the course of the day. For the moment, though, I think it would be better if I were to spend time with you…going through the workings of the department.'

'Hmm…yes…' He seemed to be distracted all at once, and glanced at the watch on his wrist. 'Unfortunately, I have an emergency to attend,' he said, getting to his feet. 'So I'm afraid you'll have to forgive me. Maybe we could get together some other time?'

She frowned. 'But I understood that you would be free from clinical duties this morning for a couple of hours. Is that not so?'

He nodded. 'But then this emergency came up…a thoracic injury, flail chest. He should be coming back from Radiology any time now.'

Alex stood up. 'But I was really hoping to make a start…'

'Of course. I appreciate that, but, you know, I don't actually have the figures you want right at this moment…you've caught me on the hop a bit there, and I really do have to go and check on my patient.' He gave her an encouraging smile. 'Perhaps it would be best if you go and find our registrar. He'll help guide you around the department. Ask him anything you want to know. He'll be only too happy to help you.'

'But I…' Alex gazed at him in confusion.

'I'm sure you'll soon have all the information you want.' He laid his hands on her shoulders, his grasp gentle, his fingers warm and strong, causing a ripple of heat to flow through her. It was odd, but all at once, as he held her, she became strangely conscious of her femininity. It was confusing. She was so used to taking charge, of being in control, and yet with just one simple act he had made her overwhelmingly conscious of his powerful masculinity.

'Take time to ease yourself into the job,' he said. 'It will all work out, you'll see.' Then he smiled, his blue eyes homing in on her face, taking in the faint line that creased her brow and the look of uncertainty that hovered around her eyes and mouth. 'You'll be fine, Alex,' he murmured. 'It's good to have you here.'

Then he released her and strode briskly away, leaving Alex to stare after him in a bewildered fashion. Somehow, she couldn't help thinking he was fobbing her off, albeit in a kind and gentle manner, and if he was an example of what she might expect from the staff here, it was clear she was in for a tricky time from the outset. His easy charm had befuddled her senses and she was finding it hard to come to terms with that. It knocked her off track, and she wasn't used to that at all.

CHAPTER TWO

'It can never be easy, can it, seeing your loved ones this way...even if you're a doctor?' The nurse was sympathetic, sensing Alex's distress. 'All I can say is that your brother's condition is stable at the moment. I hope that might be some comfort to you.'

'It is. Thank you.' Alex dragged her gaze away from the hospital bed. It was heart-rending to see her younger brother lying there, looking so fragile. He was deathly pale, his hair dark against his pillow, various tubes and drains coming from his body, and there were cables linking him to monitors. Ross, who had always been so vigorous and who could be relied on to brighten any room with his presence, was just a shadow of his former self.

'It was a nasty accident,' the nurse added, 'and there was a considerable amount of lung damage because of the broken ribs he suffered. That's why he's still on the ventilator, but he's receiving pain medication, so at least he should be fairly comfortable.'

Alex nodded. 'I know you're all doing everything you can for him.'

The nurse made a note of Ross's heart rate and blood-oxygen levels. 'Have you been to see his wife? I know she was badly injured, too.'

'Yes, I make a point of looking in on her every day. The

doctors are treating her for a laceration to her liver, but they found there was some damage to her kidney as well. She's been through surgery, and she's in much the same situation as Ross, reliant on tubes and drips and monitors. Even so, she's fretting over the children.'

'I'm sorry.' The nurse laid a hand on Alex's arm. 'It must be very worrying for you, especially with the youngsters to consider. I think it's good that you've been bringing them in to see their parents, though.'

Alex sucked in a deep breath. 'Better for them to see what's happening, I thought. Otherwise their imaginations might cause them to worry even more. Their grandparents will be coming over at the weekend, so that should help to cheer them up a little.' Her mouth flattened. 'My parents have found it hard, being so far away when it happened. But they've worked out a schedule so that one or other of them will be over here to spend time with Ross for a good part of the week.'

'You said they were working abroad, is that right?'

Alex nodded. 'My father works for an oil company. It's a really difficult time for him right now, but all he can think about is Ross.'

'That's understandable.'

Alex spent a few more minutes by her brother's bedside until she finally had to acknowledge that time was getting on. She had taken a late lunch, but now she needed to go back to work. Reluctantly, she made her way to the ground floor of the hospital, heading for A and E.

Things were no easier in that department, either. Her work colleagues were uneasy, doubtful about her intentions in her role as manager, and worried regarding their job security.

Alex tried not to let it unsettle her. She would try to put their minds at ease, and she would do the best she could for the department. After all, she was her father's daughter, wasn't she, strong, determined, willing to put in every effort for a cause she felt to be worthwhile? And in these difficult times keeping the A and E department viable and open for business was surely the best outcome for everyone?

Today, though, she was here in her role as doctor, and now she glanced at the whiteboard as she walked over to the main desk. 'Katie, I'll take the three-year-old with fever in treatment room two.'

'Okay.' The triage nurse handed her the child's admission notes.

Alex headed for the treatment room. As she had told Callum, landing this job had given her the best of both worlds—management took up fifty per cent of her time, and working as a consultant emergency paediatrician took up the rest.

She glanced at the triage nurse once more as she passed by the desk. 'Is Dr Brooksby about?' She'd been on the lookout for him all morning.

Katie hesitated, tucking a strand of glossy black hair behind one ear. 'Um…last I saw of him he was in Resus.'

'Hmm.' Alex had already checked, and he certainly wasn't there now. 'Thanks, Katie. I'm sure I'll manage to hunt him out.'

She found him a minute or two later in the treatment room next to hers. He was checking an ECG printout, while at the same time assuring his patient that he was in safe hands.

'You've had a minor heart attack,' he told the middle-aged man lying on the bed, 'but we have things under control now. The medication should help to open up your blood vessels, and things should soon start to feel a lot easier. Just keep pulling on the oxygen.'

He glanced across the room as Alex put her head round the door. 'So there you are,' she said. 'I'm glad I've run into you at last. I've been searching everywhere for you.'

'What it is to be popular,' he murmured, winking at his patient. He adjusted the settings on the medication pump and checked the drip. 'What could be better than having a gorgeous young woman seeking you out?'

Alex pulled a face. He obviously knew how to charm the birds out of the trees. 'I know you've a lot on,' she murmured, 'but I really need you to go over the drug expenditure figures with me some time soon—and I noticed your casualty cards aren't up to date. We need to get them filled in so that we can check waiting times.'

'Yes, of course.' He nodded agreeably. 'I've been working on it. We always try to fill these things in on time, you know, but it can get pretty frantic around here, and it isn't always easy to keep up with the admin paperwork.' He sent her an engaging smile, inviting her to agree with him, his blue gaze shimmering over her so that she found herself unwillingly caught up in his masculine magnetism and his easygoing manner.

'Yes, well…um…' She blinked. It was thoroughly disconcerting, the way he managed to tip her off balance. What was she thinking? She made an effort to pull herself together. 'Maybe we could get together for a few minutes as soon as you've finished here and go through a few of the items we need to get to grips with? I'll be next door in the paediatric bay, working with a patient.'

'Sounds like a good idea. I'll see what I can do.' He was totally relaxed, completely unfazed by her request.

'Good. That's encouraging.' She slanted him a brief,

searching glance. 'See you in a few minutes, then,' she murmured.

She left the room, with a friendly nod to the patient, who was looking much better than he had done a short time ago, and went to see the toddler next door.

The infant was lying on a trolley bed, clearly feeling too wretched and uncomfortable to be held in his mother's arms. A nurse was cooling him by holding a damp cloth to his forehead, but as Alex entered, she went to step aside.

'That's all right, Charlotte,' Alex said. 'You go on with what you're doing. I'm sure he'll feel much better for it.'

Alex smiled at the boy's mother. 'Mrs Stanhope, I understand Tom has been poorly for several days?'

The woman nodded. 'It's horrible to see him like this. He won't eat, he keeps being sick, and now he has a temperature. I'm really worried about him.'

'Of course you are.' She looked at Tom. 'The poor little chap looks really miserable.' She spoke gently to the boy. 'I'm going to try to make you feel a bit more comfortable, Tom,' she murmured, 'but I need to listen to your chest first…and maybe look at your tummy. Is that all right?'

The toddler looked uncertain, his lower lip trembling, and the nurse attempted to distract him by producing a teddy bear from a basket at the side of the bed. 'Look,' she said, 'Teddy's feeling poorly, too. His tummy hurts.'

Tom's eyes widened and he gazed at the toy, putting out a hand to feel his silky fur. Alex sent the nurse a grateful glance and gently began her examination. When she had finished, she said softly, 'That's all done now, Tom. You were very brave.'

The boy clutched the teddy to him. 'Teddy hurting,' he said. 'He feels sick.' Suddenly all the colour left his face and the nurse promptly moved forward with a kidney dish, holding it in place as he began to retch.

Alex went to sit next to the child's mother. 'We tested Tom's urine earlier,' she told her, 'and it looks as though he has a urinary infection of some kind. It's quite possible that his kidneys are inflamed, so I'm going to start him on a course of antibiotics. I'll give him the first dose by injection so that it will start to act quicker, but the rest we'll give by mouth.' She glanced at Charlotte and gave instructions about the medications. 'And that includes something to ease the pain and bring down his temperature.'

'Thank you.' Mrs Stanhope seemed anxious. 'How long will it be before he's better?'

'It could be two or three weeks... I feel we should admit him to hospital so that we can keep an eye on him—I know that's probably worrying for you, but we have to make sure we deal with this properly, right from the start, and of course that way he'll be on hand when we get the results of his urine culture back from the lab.'

Mrs Stanhope nodded. 'It's all right. I just want what's best for him.'

'That's good. I'll make the arrangements.' Alex stood up and went back to her small patient. 'Just a tiny jab,' she told him, preparing the antibiotic injection. 'It will all be over in a second or two.'

A few minutes later, she left the infant and his mother in Charlotte's capable hands, and went to look for Callum. He was nowhere to be found, not in any of the treatment rooms, or in Resus, or even out by the ambulance bay. She checked the quadrangle where staff sometimes took a breath of fresh air between seeing patients, but he wasn't there either.

She frowned. 'Any sign of Dr Brooksby?' she asked Katie as the nurse walked towards the reception area.

'None at all.' Katie shrugged lightly. 'I expect he's gone back to Resus.'

Alex suppressed a sigh. 'Not to worry,' she said. 'I dare say I'll catch up with him sooner or later.'

Katie nodded. 'That's how it is down here, unfortunately. Everyone's so busy.'

Alex's mouth made a flat line. Busy or not, they all had to work together to help streamline the department, or before too long the trust board would be calling for closures. One way or another they had to find time to co-operate with her. 'If anyone needs me, I'm heading over to Pathology,' she said.

She would take Tom's sample over to the lab herself for culture, and ask if the results could be hurried up. Once they knew the bacterial culprit, they could choose the most appropriate treatment for the child. The wide-spectrum antibiotic she had used was a catch-all for the most likely bacteria, but given the severity of the infection it was possible that they needed to use something more specific to counteract it.

She walked into the lab a few minutes later, shooting a quick glance around the room. Over to one side, by the workbenches, she saw a by-now familiar figure huddled over a rack of test tubes.

'So here you are,' she murmured, after handing over the specimen to the lab technician. 'I never would have thought to find you here, Dr Brooksby.'

He straightened, turning to look at her. 'I'm checking on some samples I sent for testing. I want to see how things are coming along, you know.'

'Really?' She inspected the label of the sample he was studying. 'Since when were you working with the staff on the geriatric ward? Was your patient sent there from A and E?'

He frowned. 'It's the wrong sample,' he said. 'My patient's elderly, but not geriatric.'

She sent him a cautious look, her grey eyes doubtful. 'You wouldn't be deliberately trying to avoid me, would you, Dr Brooksby?'

'Callum, please. Now, why on earth would I want to do that?'

'That's what I'm wondering. Only I was under the impression we were going to meet up in the treatment room a while ago. Didn't you agree to that?'

'Of course—though I believe what I actually said was that it was a good idea, which is not necessarily the same thing as saying I'd be there. You can't guarantee anything in the hectic atmosphere of the A and E department.' He searched among the papers in a wire tray and grasped one in triumph. 'Found it,' he said. He held it up to her. 'My patient's results.'

She stared at him in frustration. 'Why is it that I have the feeling you're playing games with me?' she asked. 'You haven't actually completed the drug lists, have you? Or tried to catch up on filling in the waiting times on your casualty cards?'

He leaned back against the workbench, his long legs crossed at the ankles. 'Actually…uh…no, you're right. I haven't.' His mouth made a rueful shape. 'As I said before, I'm much more of a hands-on medic than someone who concentrates on keeping his paperwork up to date.'

His gaze ran over her, appreciation lighting his eyes as he took in the shapeliness of her figure outlined by her classically styled dress. 'I know you want to get on with updating your numbers and counting the financial cost of everything, but is it so essential that it's done right this minute? You've only been here a short time. Surely you need to take some time to settle in? And how about giving everyone a bit of leeway? Give them a chance to get used to the idea of you being around. That way people would be so much more on your side.'

She sighed. 'That would be so satisfying, wouldn't it... just to let everything hang easy for a while, gain a little popularity and then sit back and enjoy the ride?' There was amusement in her tone. 'I hardly think that's going to happen.' Her grey glance meshed with his.

'You don't?' He frowned.

'I don't. Why do you imagine I was brought in here? The executives were hardly going to appoint a pussycat to monitor things, were they?' She didn't wait for an answer. 'The hospital budget is badly overdrawn and the trust has to make drastic cuts if the services the public want and expect are to survive.' She drew in a deep breath. 'So that's where I come in. I have the task of auditing the department to find out where savings can be made...and if I don't come up with the right answers, the whole emergency unit is at risk—so it's not just my job on the line, but those of everyone who works here.' She studied him. 'You do understand that, don't you?'

He lifted his shoulders. 'Of course I do...it's just that I don't see why you can't hold fire for a while. The trust has been overspending for years—a few weeks isn't going to make much difference to the grand scheme of things, is it?'

She shook her head, causing her chestnut curls to swirl and shimmer under the overhead lights. 'That's where you're wrong, I'm afraid. I have to report back to the board at the end of each month. They aren't going to look kindly on me or the department if I show them an empty file.'

He watched the cloud of burnished hair drift and settle. 'You realise, don't you,' he countered, 'that the board will do what it wants, no matter what facts and figures you manage to produce? If they're set on closing the department, then ultimately that's what they'll do. They just need you to give them the firepower.'

She regarded him steadily. 'Well, I don't think that way about it at all. I believe that I can make a difference. I believe we can make savings in lots of ways. In fact, going on my experience with a young patient this morning, I've decided I want to start a separate audit into the treatment of children with urinary infections…let's see if we can't cut down on the number of ultrasound scans, and choose our drugs more wisely, so that we're not prescribing expensive ones where generic drugs will do better.'

She warmed to her theme. 'It's just a question of devising the forms for people to fill in whenever they treat a child—and at the end we'll collate all the information and see what savings we can come up with.'

He looked at her, aghast. 'Good grief, woman…don't you have enough to do without getting started on audits that aren't even part of your remit?'

'But it all comes down to the same thing in the end, don't you see? Savings are at the heart of everything.'

He relaxed, beginning to smile at her. 'I can see why you got the job…and I have to admire your persistence. You're so full of energy and enthusiasm—but there's more to life than work, you know. Where do you find time in all that for a social life—that thing called 'fun'—boyfriends, and so on?'

His glance drifted over her. 'You're a very attractive woman, and I'd have thought men would be queuing up to ask you out. Yet from what I've heard you don't have a significant other, you don't join the staff at the local pub—or even share lunch breaks with them. Isn't there something missing from your life?' His gaze became thoughtful. 'Or perhaps you've been hurt…' he said softly. 'Maybe someone let you down?'

She stared at him blankly for a moment or two. So he thought she was attractive? He'd said it before, but even so, it gave her a warm, fuzzy feeling, hearing him say it again. But as to the rest, when did she have time to socialise? Any spare time she had at work was spent on visiting her brother and his wife, and after work she needed to take care of the children.

'I see the hospital grapevine has been busy,' she murmured. 'Is nobody's life private around here?' She frowned. 'Though I could say the same for you. Snatches of gossip I've heard tell me you don't ever settle to a relationship— fear of commitment is how they put it, I think.'

He laughed. 'I don't see fear coming into it. Life's too short, and I'm having a good time just as I am—being footloose and fancy-free. Why would I want to change things?'

'Why indeed?' She smiled wryly. 'And much the same goes for me. I'm far too busy to even contemplate getting involved with anyone right now. Let the gossipmongers make of it what they will.'

'And they will, believe me.' He studied her. 'Why don't we fox them all and make a date for dinner—this evening, maybe? You should take time out, let yourself unwind a little.'

Unwind, with him? The thought had a dizzying effect on her. 'Thanks, but I really can't do that right now.' All the same, she conjured up a vision of the two of them together, taking a walk in the moonlight after a romantic meal at a restaurant, and all at once heat began to pool in her abdomen.

She couldn't let the idea take hold. It was impossible. She wasn't about to get involved with anyone, especially him, a man who seemed so laid back he made it seem as though she was positively racing through life in contrast.

Anyway, she had far too much on her plate. The children relied on her to be there for them, her family life was chaotic, and, besides, he was simply trying to divert her, possibly even disarm her into the bargain, wasn't he?

His gaze flicked over her. 'That's a shame. Maybe some other time, then? I'm sure you'll feel all the better for a little rest and relaxation.'

She had the idea this was something he wouldn't give up on easily. 'I'll feel a whole lot better when I have your drug expenditure forms laid out on my desk,' she retorted swiftly. 'Along with a list of agency staff employed by the department over the last three months.'

She ignored his muffled groan as she made her way to the door. 'Any time in the next twenty-four hours will be fine.'

She was still debating how best to deal with Callum Brooksby when she made her way home later that day at the end of her shift. He was a thorn in her side, a devious, happy-go-lucky, aggravating man who gave the impression of being as difficult to catch as thistledown. Every time she had him within her sights, he somehow managed to whisk himself away, out of reach.

'Look what we've found,' Sarah said excitedly, greeting Alex as she went to collect the children from her neighbour's house later that day. Sarah led the way into the kitchen. 'Auntie Jane showed us how to collect honey from the beehives in the orchard. We've been putting it into jars. It smells of flowers.'

Alex sniffed at the glass pot Sarah thrust under her nose. 'So it does,' she said. 'I expect the bees have been visiting the apple blossom and the bramble bushes. That should make for good fruit later on in the season.'

She looked at Jane, who was standing by the fridge,

looking pale and tired. 'You've been busy. Are you sure you should be taking on all this work? I feel bad enough that I'm asking you to watch the children for me.'

'Oh, I like having them around. Anyway, I volunteered to have them after school, and it's no trouble to collect a bit of honey.' Jane smiled. 'I expect you had no idea what a wealth of treasures you were gaining when you bought the property next door. Of course, I didn't let the children go near the hives when I collected the honeycombs, but they loved seeing the end result. They were fascinated.'

'It tastes funny,' James said, screwing up his nose. 'Yuk.'

'I like it,' Sarah said happily. 'We had some on pancakes and they were scrumptious.'

'It sounds as though you had a lot of fun.' Alex watched the children as they carefully spooned the golden honey into scrupulously clean jars. Jane sat down by the table and let them get on with it for a while.

'How have you been feeling, Jane?' Alex asked, giving her a long, thoughtful look. 'Have you been back to see your doctor?'

'Not yet.' Jane shook her head, and at Alex's small murmur of protestation she added, 'I know...I keep putting it off, and I shouldn't, but what's he going to do for me but give me more tablets? Nothing's working, so I might as well put up with things as they are.' As she spoke, she absently rubbed her back. 'The only that really gets to me is this pain, but I suppose I can take painkillers for that.' She sighed. 'But I guess that's old age creeping up on me.'

'I don't think so, Jane. I think it's something that needs to be investigated.'

She might have said more, but there was a brief tap on

the kitchen door just then, and a moment later it opened, as a visitor stepped into the kitchen.

Alex pulled in a sharp breath.

'Hi, Aunt Jane,' Callum Brooksby said, going over to Jane and giving her a hug. 'How's my favourite aunt?'

'Oh, it's so good to see you,' Jane said, smiling. She looked at him with genuine affection. 'I was hoping you'd come round.'

He nodded. 'I know I've left it a little bit longer than usual. It's been a busy time lately, what with work and overseeing the builders at home.' Then he straightened and looked around, interested in seeing who had come to take tea with her.

His gaze met Alex's and they both stared at one another in shock.

'Alex?'

'Callum?' She blinked.

Callum frowned, his dark brows drawing together in a straight line. 'What on earth are you doing here?'

'I...I bought the house next door,' she said, stumbling a little over the words, still in shock. 'That's how I came to know your aunt—she's been good to me, looking after the children while I'm at work.'

'Children?' His expression became incredulous as he turned his attention to James and Sarah, happily spilling honey over the scrubbed pine table and the assembled jars. 'Good grief.' He looked back at Alex. 'I don't know you at all, do I?'

Jane looked from one to the other, a puzzled expression on her face. 'So you two have met before this?' She frowned. 'Of course, it must be the hospital—it didn't occur to me. I knew you were in Paediatrics, Alex, and, Callum, you're in Emergency, but of course you must meet up on occasion.'

'All the while, Aunt Jane,' Callum agreed, a look of wonder coming over his face. 'We work in the same department.'

Alex was still trying to get over the shock. She studied him carefully. 'So you're the nephew?'

His head went back. 'Nephew? Why, who's been talking about me?' He looked at Jane, a glimmer of amusement coming into his eyes. 'It has to be you, doesn't it? You've only told her good things, I hope?'

'As if I'd do anything else,' Jane answered cheerfully.

Callum put an arm around her in a gesture of affection. 'She practically brought me up,' he told Alex. 'She's been like a mother to me.'

Jane patted his hand.

'Auntie Jane, can we go and play in the garden?' James asked, coming over to her and beginning to tug on her skirt.

'Yes, of course.' Jane's glance ran over him, and a line indented her brow. 'Perhaps we'd better get you cleaned up a bit first, though.'

James looked down at the honey trails that streaked his T-shirt. 'It's all right,' he said. 'I can do that.' He pulled his shirt up to his mouth and began to lick the sticky patches.

Sarah pulled a face. 'You are so gross,' she said in disgust.

'Why?' James responded, astonished. 'Am not.'

Callum began to laugh. 'Was I ever like that?' he asked his aunt, and she nodded. 'All the time.' She turned her attention back to the boy. 'I'll get a cloth.'

'No, don't do that. I'll see to everything,' Alex said, intervening when Jane would have stood up. 'You stay there and rest. You've done enough for one day.' She helped the children to wash their hands, before sending them outside, and then she began to clear up the mess on the kitchen table.

Jane tried to lend a hand, gathering up spoons and honeycombs, but Alex gently took them from her. 'You're already hurting,' she remonstrated softly. 'Let me do it.'

Callum frowned, looking at his aunt. 'What's this about you hurting? Is it your back again?'

Jane nodded. 'It's nothing for you to worry about,' she said. 'I'll be fine.'

'Hmm. Why don't you go and sit down in the living room, and I'll bring you a cup of tea? I'm sure you'll be much more comfortable in there.'

His aunt smiled. 'You're probably right. What a good idea.' She looked from one to the other. 'Anyway, I expect you young things have plenty to say to one another.'

She left the room, and a moment later, still frowning, Callum began to help with the clearing up. He placed sticky jars on the drainer, and flicked the switch on the kettle.

'I still can't get over seeing you here,' he said, looking at Alex. 'It's a small world, isn't it?'

'It certainly seems that way.'

He began to prepare a tray, setting out a cup and saucer, along with a plate of home-made biscuits. He smiled as he peered into the cookie jar. 'She's always loved baking,' he said, helping himself to an oat biscuit. He offered the jar to Alex. 'She let me help her when I was a child, but I'm not sure my efforts were all that brilliant. They tended to be misshapen, and a bit cracked around the edges.'

'Much like mine, then,' Alex said, helping herself to a biscuit, and they both chuckled. She looked at him, trying to imagine him as a child, mixing cookie dough or playing outside in the long garden. 'You said she was like a mother to you...does that mean you lived here with her?'

He nodded. 'For a good deal of the time, anyway.' He looked around. 'I love this house. It feels like home to me. In fact, I love the whole area.'

'And your parents? Where were they?'

'Mostly abroad, either in Africa or South America. I didn't see a lot of them in my teen years because they were off working on projects to improve the health of the underprivileged children out there. Things are much the same nowadays.'

'That must have been difficult for you.' Her grey eyes were sympathetic. She remembered how sad he'd been when he'd first mentioned his parents. 'You must have missed them.'

'I suppose so.' He frowned. 'But my aunt and uncle made up for it. They gave me a decent home life and showed me what it was like to be part of a loving family. Until then, nothing had ever been stable. My parents were always busy, working all hours, and we moved around constantly. There was no chance of putting down any roots.'

Alex was sad for him. He'd obviously not known what a loving family was like in his earlier years.

'You were lucky, then, that your aunt was able to take you in.'

'Yes, I was.' He poured tea into the cup. 'I'd better go and check on her, and take her the tea.'

Alex glanced at him and hesitated a second or two before saying, 'You know she's having problems with her blood pressure, don't you?'

He nodded. 'It was diagnosed some time ago. She's been prescribed a number of different medications over the past year or so.'

'Yes, that's what she said. But it seems to me that whatever her GP's giving her isn't working, and I suspect that's because he hasn't yet found the root cause of her problem.

I'm wondering if she ought to have some tests done at the hospital. She's suffering from a number of symptoms that need to be investigated…headaches, dizziness, pain in her back.'

A line etched itself into his brow. 'Her doctor's been taking care of her for years, though. She trusts him, and it's no easy thing to get her to go along to see anyone else.'

Alex's mouth flattened. 'Even so…I don't see how she can go on this way. She doesn't look at all well. Something needs to be done. In fact, I feel really guilty that I took her up on her offer to look after the children. It worries me that I'm putting too much on her.' She pulled in a deep breath. 'And I don't believe she's coping too well with the house and garden either. The weeds are beginning to overtake the borders, and it's all much more than she can manage.'

Callum gave Alex a perplexed stare. 'I mended the fence and tidied up the rockery a couple of weeks ago.'

Alex finished wiping the table with a flourish. 'I'm sure the stress of keeping up with the maintenance is taking a toll of her. Is there any chance you could arrange a more regular schedule? Find a local gardener who will come along and tidy things up, perhaps?'

He didn't say a word for a moment or two, but simply studied her as though he was deep in thought.

'You're very good at this sort of thing, aren't you?' he said at last, a note of wonder in his voice.

'This sort of thing?' She frowned. 'I'm afraid I'm not following you.'

'Organising people…deciding what needs to be done. I get the strongest feeling that not only am I being audited at work, but now you're taking stock of how I conduct my personal life as well.' He turned his blue gaze on her. 'I'm obviously done for. Maybe I should give in, here and now?'

Alex felt warm colour fill her cheeks. 'Well, that would be a good idea,' she said, giving a self-conscious laugh. 'That would make things easier all round, wouldn't it?'

He gave a wry smile. 'You'll find I don't surrender that easily.'

CHAPTER THREE

'I'M ALL done disturbing you, angel,' Callum murmured as the two-year-old girl fretted and tossed restlessly on the bed. 'No more horrible needles and stethoscopes and all that palaver.' He adjusted the medication drip, and then drew an ink line around the perimeter of the reddened area on the infant's leg. 'Let's hope that rash starts to shrink very soon,' he commented to the nurse who was assisting him. 'We'll make arrangements to admit her.'

He gave his attention back to the child. 'I think you'll be feeling a lot better before too long. I'm going to come back later to take a look at you, and I hope I'll find that nasty red area is beginning to disappear.' He carefully adjusted the bedcovers around the child, and gently brushed away the flaxen curls that massed around her hot cheeks. 'Just you go to sleep and let the medicine do its work. We'll have you right as rain in no time at all.'

Alex stood in the doorway of the treatment room, following his movements as he briefly checked the monitors. She had slipped into the room quietly, not wanting to disturb him, so he hadn't realised she was there, and for a moment or two she was able to watch him at work, undisturbed. It gave her a fascinating glimpse of the man behind the professional mask, and though she felt guilty at not announcing her presence, the compulsion to feast her gaze on him somehow overcame everything else.

He might well be a constant source of frustration to her where her budget schedule was concerned, but there was no doubting his commitment to the patients in his care. And even though paediatrics wasn't his specialty, she could see he had a sure instinct for dealing with children. This wasn't the first time she'd seen him tending to a youngster in A and E. It was clear that he had a genuine concern for his young charges, and the tenderness that she saw in him as he leaned over the cot brought an unexpected lump to her throat.

It made it all the more difficult that she had to confront him right now, but she had a job to do, regardless, and so she stiffened her shoulders and quietly claimed his attention. 'Might I have a word with you, please, Callum?' she said.

'Uh-oh…' Callum glanced at her, and then moved away from his young patient's bedside, giving final instructions to the nurse before walking towards the door where Alex waited, chart in hand. 'I've heard you use that tone of voice before…' he said under his breath, as he went out into the corridor. 'Quiet but insistent.' He frowned. 'It generally means I'm in trouble of some kind.'

'Not at all,' Alex murmured, following him and adding sweetly, 'You're obviously developing a persecution complex of some sort.'

He nodded, a faint grin tugging at his mouth. 'True. Funnily enough, it seemed to happen right about the time you joined the department.'

She tilted her head to one side. 'Guilty conscience, perhaps?'

He shook his head. 'Not true. I'm innocent as the day… at least, I think I am.' He glanced at the chart she was carrying. 'I expect that's one of mine, or you wouldn't be here. So what have I done this time?'

'It isn't just you,' Alex said in a sympathetic tone. 'I'm not singling you out. Please don't think that. I'm checking everyone's lab work to see if we can cut down on unnecessary testing…and here, looking at yours, I find you've ordered blood cultures, urine samples, swabs, to name just a few, for one small patient. Are you sure all these are really needed? Apart from the cost, we're laying a great strain on the laboratory facilities.'

He put on a stern face. 'If I hadn't needed them, I wouldn't have ordered them.'

'For a simple fever?'

'For a not-so-simple fever. The child was burning up, there was the beginning of a rash, and I suspect an insect bite of some sort that has led to a generalised infection which could lead to septicaemia.' He studied her. 'Do you really expect me to treat my patients without the proper diagnostic tools in place?'

'Of course not.' She smiled. 'I'm just checking, that's all. There's nothing wrong in making sure everyone keeps efficiency and cost awareness in the forefront of their mind, is there?'

He gave her a sour look. 'I'd appreciate it if you would take your checks elsewhere. I'm a consultant, remember, like yourself. I didn't get to this position by not knowing what I'm doing.'

'And I'm not suggesting otherwise. I see no reason why you should be so uptight about the situation,' she commented in a soothing tone, trying to placate him. 'We all want to do our best for our patients, and all I'm saying is that it's only natural that sometimes we might be a little over-zealous in our efforts.'

'I was not being over-zealous…I was being thorough.

The child needs admission to hospital and treatment with an intravenous antibiotic. And if that doesn't meet with your approval, then I'm afraid it's too bad. That's how it's going to be.'

She put up a hand as though to ward him off. 'I'm not stopping you from doing anything. All I'm saying is that we all have to be responsible and think carefully about the tests we order. It's easy to slip into lax ways when you're not the one counting the cost. Unfortunately, that's down to me, and ultimately I have the job of making sure everyone complies with the new, stringent measures.'

He gave her a long look. 'It never ceases to amaze me how very single-minded you are. Don't you ever relax and watch the world go by without wanting to leap on its back and wrestle it into shape?'

She gave him a bewildered glance. 'I've a job to do. What do you expect?'

'I expect you to take a breather every once in a while.' He checked the gold watch on his wrist, and as he moved she noticed the sprinkling of dark hairs that ran along his bare forearm. His shirtsleeves were rolled back, to show an expanse of skin that was lightly bronzed. His arms were muscular, his wrists strong, giving the impression of overwhelming masculinity, and for a second or two she felt a sudden tide of awareness that surged throughout her body and left her momentarily breathless.

He began to speak again, his voice cutting into her thoughts, and she reluctantly dragged her gaze away. It was strange, these weird sensations of being out of control that had afflicted her of late. She wasn't used to feeling this way. Perhaps she was overworked, stressed, and the sheer amount of changes that were taking place in her life right now was making her unduly sensitive.

'It's getting late,' he said, 'and I don't suppose you've

had a break since lunchtime. I certainly haven't. Why don't we take a few minutes to go and get a cup of coffee—in my office, perhaps?'

She shook her head. 'I'm sorry,' she answered abruptly, struggling to get a grip on herself, 'but I don't have time. I have to finish this data chart by the end of my shift, and I'm already running late.'

'We could use the time to go over the budget cuts you had in mind,' he suggested silkily, a glint coming into his blue eyes. 'Of course, if you'd rather leave it until another day, that's fine by me.' He started to turn away.

Alex was suspicious of his sudden apparent willingness to work with her, but his offer was one she could hardly refuse, was it? 'Uh…maybe I was a little hasty. I dare say I could spare a few minutes, since you appear to have had a change of heart.'

'Change of heart? Me? I've always been happy to go along with your suggestions.'

She gave him a withering look. 'Let's not push it, shall we?'

He laughed softly, and stopped for a moment to sign off his patient's treatment chart before dropping it into a tray on the reception desk. 'Are there any casualty cards for me to fill in?' he asked the girl behind the counter.

She checked, but then a moment later shook her head. 'Seems you're all up to date,' she told him.

Callum gave Alex a smug glance. 'See?' he said. 'Didn't I say I was only too happy to work with you?'

She made a wry smile. 'I heard you'd shut yourself in your office and barred all callers after your shift yesterday so that you could catch up with things.' He hadn't been in the best of moods, by all accounts. 'Amazing what a little gentle badgering will do, isn't it?'

He huffed, and gently but firmly took her by the arm, and ushered her into his office. He shut the door.

'Oh my!' she exclaimed softly, looking around. 'You've done well for yourself, landing a prize room like this, haven't you? It's much bigger than mine.' She gazed out of the large, Georgian-style window onto a wooded landscape to the side of the hospital. 'What a beautiful view.' After a moment, she turned back to face him. 'I'd find it really hard to work in here—I'd be so distracted by that lovely scenery.'

'I was going to say, hands off,' he said thoughtfully, 'but maybe we should do a swap—it might help to slow you down a bit. I've never met anyone before who was so driven—well, maybe one, but she was an exception, like you.'

'You'd give up your room for me?' She seized on his words and stared at him, wide-eyed, ready to tease him mercilessly. 'What a lovely idea.' She gazed around the room once more, her glance taking in the glass-fronted bookcase and luxuriously upholstered leather chair. She ran her fingers lightly over the polished surface of his desk. 'I could really see me making myself at home in here.'

'Yes, so can I.' He watched her float dreamily about the room, stopping only to perch on the corner of the desk, draping herself possessively over it, one hand flat on the shiny top, the other resting lightly on her hip, her long legs crossed at the knee and showing a hint of creamy thigh. He looked at her abstractedly for a moment or two and appeared to be struggling to pull himself together.

'On second thoughts, forget it,' he said, going over to the other side of the room and setting out a bowl of sugar on the worktop. He retrieved a small jug of cream from the fridge. A coffee jug had been simmering gently on its base since they'd entered the room, but now he lifted it and began to pour the liquid into two mugs. 'I can just imagine,' he added in a droll tone, 'once you get yourself established in here, you'd be so invigorated you'll end up doing twice the amount of work you're doing now.'

She chuckled. 'You think so?'

'I know it.' He waved her to a padded leather chair by the side of the desk, and pushed the mug of coffee towards her. 'Help yourself to cream and sugar.'

'Thanks. Mmm…this is good.' She sniffed the aroma appreciatively and then went to sit down. 'Much better than the stuff in the machines out there.' She waved a hand towards the corridor outside and then frowned. 'But I'm a little concerned about your opinion of me. Where did you learn to be so mistrustful?'

His mouth quirked. 'At my mother's knee. And through dealing with people like you who prod and poke and instigate changes until what was once a smooth-running organisation becomes a mere sliver of what it was before.' He lifted his mug to his lips and swallowed the hot coffee. 'What is it that makes you so focussed and determined?'

She shrugged lightly, adding cream to her coffee and stirring it slowly. 'I suppose I've always had a strong work ethic. It probably comes from my father. He believes in hard work, sticking to a task—for him there's no such word as "can't". He says there's always a solution and we have to keep going until we find it.'

'And you live by his rules, even now, even though you're a grown woman, with a mind of your own?'

'Why wouldn't I?' She met his gaze full on. 'It seems a reasonable enough philosophy to me. Besides, I've worked hard to get where I am today, and I'm not about to let it all slide. I always wanted to be a doctor…ever since I was little and I saw my friend being struck down by appendicitis, I knew it was the career for me. Now I've reached the point where I can see things that would be better for being changed, and I'm glad I'm in a position to do something about it.'

He sighed. 'Lord save us from a woman on a mission,' he murmured, his gaze sweeping over her. 'Does it never occur to you to stop for a while and look at things from someone else's viewpoint?'

'Like yours, you mean?' She shook her head. 'I've a feeling you think everything can stay the same, and you go ploughing on, regardless of the warnings from all around you. There'll come a time when the plough will break down and there will be no money to replace it. What will you do then?'

'Get a spade and start digging.' He frowned, studying her closely. 'I must say you seem to be very clinical in your attitude, and strangely unemotional.'

She shrugged. 'Someone has to be.' She took another sip of her coffee and looked him over. His dark hair was a perfect foil for his rugged good looks and his eyes had that quality of being able to see right into your soul. It was disturbing, to say the least.

'Anyway,' she said, 'I've noticed the same work ethic in you. You put in a lot of hours, you're very dedicated to the job, and you must have been ambitious to get as far as you have in this profession. There aren't too many consultants around who are in their mid-thirties.' Her glance ran over him, gliding over the strong line of his jaw, coming to rest on the firmly moulded mouth that hinted at hidden sensuality. Dreamily, she wondered what it would be like to kiss him... Then she brought herself up sharply, veering away from the errant path her thoughts would have taken her. What on earth was wrong with her?

'I suppose that's true.' He looked at her oddly, as though he was trying to fathom what was going on in her mind, and a wave of heat ran through her body. Heaven forbid he should work it out!

'So what made you decide to become a doctor?' she asked. 'Are your parents in the same line of work? You said they were working with underprivileged children.'

He nodded. 'In a manner of speaking, they are. They're part of the World Health Organization, so mostly their work involves organising medical care. They generally manage to collaborate with one another on various projects.'

'So I guess you don't see much of them?'

'That's true. Of course, they come home on vacation, and they have a fairly generous span of time off, but they're dedicated to what they do, especially my mother. The job is very important to her.'

He gave a faint smile but didn't comment any further, and Alex was prompted to ask, 'Would I be right in thinking your mother is the other person you know who is "driven", as you put it?'

'I guess so.' He pressed his lips together briefly. 'She's a very fierce believer in getting things done. Once she sets her mind on doing something, it becomes the be-all and end-all…there's no stopping her. Of course, that's great, if you've a project that needs to be up and running, but it doesn't bode well for anyone who would hanker after a cosy home life.'

'Like you?' She was frowning a little, wondering what it must have been like for him as a young child to live with parents who were constantly travelling the world. 'I expect you must have seen more than your fair share of countries.'

'That's right. I always went with them in the beginning, but there came a time when I was due to start my secondary education, and I wanted stability. So that's where my aunt and uncle came in…although my uncle passed away a few years ago. My parents kept in touch by phone and email—we even have a video link set up now.' He smiled. 'My mother was anxious about leaving me, but Aunt Jane is a home bird and she more than made up for any sense of loss I might be feeling. My uncle and aunt didn't have any children of their own, and so I think they were glad of the chance to look after me.'

'She's a lovely woman,' Alex said. 'I took to her straight away—and the minute she saw that I had children she offered to help out. I still feel anxious about letting her take that on, especially with the school holidays coming up soon...but she seemed like a godsend at the time.'

He nodded. 'Strange, that,' he murmured. 'I'd no idea that you had children.' He stood up then to go and fetch biscuits from a cupboard on the wall. 'We have bourbons, sandwich creams, plain, ginger...' he said, rummaging through the various packets. 'Or there are fruited tea buns left over from yesterday afternoon.' He pressed the packaging to test their freshness, and his features lit up. 'They seem fine. Would you like one?'

She grinned at his boyish pleasure. 'Thanks, that would be great.'

He set them out on plates, and added a selection of biscuits. 'I'm starving,' he told her with a hint of apology. 'My lunch was interrupted today—an emergency cropped up. It's always happening—that's why I keep a stash of goodies on hand in here.'

He came to sit back down, and pushed a plate towards her before biting into a tea bun. 'You'll be pleased to know that I made an appointment for my aunt to see a specialist friend of mine—I managed to arrange it for next week, so we should soon know the score about what's causing the high blood pressure. Like you, I've been worried about her.'

'I'm glad you did that.' Alex smiled, and he looked at her, almost as though he was seeing her for the first time, his gaze lingering on her features for a while.

Then he seemed to pull himself together and said cautiously, 'As I said, it was a bit of a shock to find that you had children. It must make things difficult for you, doing a high-powered job like this one and still having to maintain a family life.'

'It isn't easy, I grant you.' Alex took a bite from the remaining bun, and chewed thoughtfully for a moment or two. 'First there was the move down here to Somerset, that was an ordeal in itself, for me, at least, and it was a bit of a challenge for the children, having to settle into a new house.'

He glanced at the fingers of her left hand, and then frowned. 'And your husband? I don't see a ring. Are you and he divorced…separated?'

'Neither. I've never been married.' She finished off the bun.

He drew in a deep breath and looked faintly puzzled. 'But the children's father…'

'Is in hospital. He's my brother.' She took pity on his bewilderment and went on, 'He and my sister-in-law were involved in a bad motorway accident. They were travelling back from a reception organised by his firm when it happened, so, in one way, perhaps it was fortunate that they were on their own in the car. The children were staying with friends.'

'I'm so sorry, Alex.' He reached for her hand, covering it with his palm. 'That must have been a terrible shock for you.'

'Yes, it was.' She tried not to think about the way his gentle touch evoked warm ripples of sensation and sent them coursing along the length of her arm. 'I suppose, in the end, I'm just thankful that they survived. It was bad, but it could have been worse.'

'Yes, it could. But at least the children were safe. I suppose that became the immediate priority.'

She nodded. She was finding it hard to concentrate with his long fingers clasping hers. It was a gesture of comfort and support, and it made her feel good inside, as though he was letting her know he was there for her and that she need not be alone in all this. It had been a long while since she'd felt that way.

'There was no one to look after the children, and Beth was desperate that they shouldn't go into care, so I stepped in. I love my family and I want to do the best for them.'

'Of course you do.' He frowned. 'So what was the reason for you buying the house?' he asked in a puzzled tone. 'Didn't they have a place of their own?'

'They did. They'd all moved into rented accommodation some six months ago when Ross took up a new job in the area, but the lease expired and the landlord didn't want to renew it. So I had to look for a place with enough room for all of us.'

He shook his head. 'It sounds as though you had a hefty task on your hands. I can't imagine having to juggle all those problems at once. You must have worked wonders to hold it all together.'

She gave him a faint smile. 'I don't know about holding it all together. Sometimes I worry that I've taken on too much, especially with the house. But at least the children were already settled at school. That was one less problem to sort out.' Her brows drew together. 'All I have to worry about now are the school holidays. I'm going to have to sort out some full-time care for them. I don't want to ask Jane, because she seems so unwell.'

'That's true, but I'm sure you'll find someone very

capable and willing to look after them. Obviously it will be better if it's someone you know.' He frowned. 'And this job must be an extra worry for you. You've taken on a big responsibility.'

She sighed. 'Yes, but I'm sure things could work out well if we just put our heads together and try to sort things out...' she sucked in a breath '...which reminds me, weren't we going to discuss those budget cuts?'

'It's true, we were.' He straightened up, reluctantly sliding his hand away from her. Then he swallowed the remains of his coffee and glanced down at his pager. 'But it appears that I'm wanted in Resus.' He glanced at her. 'Sorry to have to break things up, but I must go.'

Alex stared at him. 'I didn't hear your pager go off.'

'No,' he said, 'you wouldn't. I set it to silent alarm.' He showed her the text message that was displayed on the pager's screen and then gave her an encouraging smile. 'But not to worry, perhaps we can do this another day? I'll come up with all the figures you want, I promise. Meanwhile, why don't you stay here and finish your coffee? It's been good to see you relax for a while. I'm sure a little longer will do you the world of good.'

He stood up and made for the door, and Alex was filled with frustration as she watched his disappearing back. It seemed that all her efforts to get the job done were fated where he was concerned.

CHAPTER FOUR

'IF ONE more ball goes flying over the fence into next door's garden, I shall stop you from playing football out there.' Alex abandoned her battle with the ancient Aga and went to remonstrate with James in the garden. 'Auntie Jane has better things to do than to keep throwing them back, and sooner or later you're going to damage something.'

'Oops.' The warning came too late. James pulled a face as his favourite football went sailing over the fence and was followed a second or two later by an ominous thudding sound. 'I didn't mean it,' he said, with a bemused expression. 'It was an accident.'

Alex sighed. 'You'd better go round there and apologise,' she told him. Turning to his sister, she said, 'Will you go with him, Sarah, please? Find out if there's been any damage. I have to stay here and keep an eye on the pizza in the oven.'

'Okay.' Sarah took James by the hand and led him away.

'Why do we have to go?' James complained. 'I didn't do it on purpose. I just tapped it and it went over.'

'Yeah, like always,' Sarah said. 'That's 'cos you keep trying to see how high you can kick it.'

'No…I was just aiming for the goal. You wanna see how Rooney does it,' James said, warming to his theme. 'See how they did it in the match on telly? You have to run and shoot, get it in there quick.'

'Yeah, but they lost the game,' Sarah pointed out in a blunt tone. 'Didn't do them any good, did it?'

'Well, they'll do it next time.' James scowled at his sister as they went out of the back gate.

Alex could still hear them bickering as they walked along the path to her neighbour's property. A wave of guilt swamped her. There was no doubt about it, she ought to have gone with them, but there was just so much to do… lunch to prepare, laundry to finish, ironing, and that was before she made a start on tackling the endless round of decorating that was needed to spruce up this old farmhouse property.

And now the Aga was playing up. The pizza, which should have been cooked several minutes ago, was still pale looking, and Alex guessed that meant she would soon be paying out for a new thermostat for the oven.

She left it to bake some more and started to gather together the ingredients for a salad. And what of the football game that had gone wrong out there? Was she going to have to fork out for damage to Jane's property as well?

The children came back a few minutes later. 'Auntie Jane made us a cake,' Sarah said excitedly, bursting into the kitchen.

'Goodness! A reward for causing her all that trouble? Auntie Jane must be a saint.'

'It's all covered with strawberries and cream.' James was licking his lips in anticipation. 'I'm hungry,' he said. 'Can we have some now?'

'After you've eaten your lunch,' Alex murmured.

'Isn't that just typical of adults?' a familiar, deep voice commented, and Alex was startled to see Callum follow the children into the kitchen. 'There are never any goodies to be had till after the main course, are there?' He peered around the door. 'Is it all right if I come in?' His glance slid warmly over her, moving from head to toe and taking in her slender shape, outlined by the snug-fitting jeans and the stretchy cotton top she wore.

'Of course.' She studied him in return, flummoxed for a moment, seeing him here, in her kitchen. He looked good, dressed in casual clothes, dark chinos teamed with a loose cotton shirt, a strong contrast to the smart, formal suits he wore for work.

She waved him to a seat by the table. 'Come and sit down.' She frowned, and then added hesitantly, 'I was just about to serve up lunch. You're welcome to stay and eat with us, if you like.'

He smiled, seeming surprised by the invitation, and she was back-footed all over again by the way the smile softened his angular features. 'Are you sure? Thanks. That would be great…if you're positive it's no trouble?'

'None at all…though I won't guarantee the state of the pizza.' She frowned. 'It started out with all the promise of a healthy, home-made meal, but it's a bit of a sorry effort now, given that the Aga's putting on a go-slow.' She took the pizza from the oven and set it out on the worktop.

Callum studied it. 'Looks fine to me. Lovely golden melted cheese…with ham, tomato and salami… Definitely a winner.' He sniffed the air appreciatively. 'Smells good, too. This reminds me of being in my aunt's kitchen when I was young. Lots of lovely baking smells.'

'Talking of which…' He held out a large, round plastic container and placed it on the table. 'Aunt Jane asked me to give you this…it's her famous Somerset pound cake. Apparently it's a mix of butter, sugar, flour and a whole basket full of eggs.' He grinned. 'I can tell you from experience that it's a mouth-watering concoction, anyway.'

Alex looked at the cake. 'It's wonderful,' she said. 'She's too good to us—we really don't deserve it after the trouble we've been to her. I've lost count of the number of times the ball has landed in her vegetable patch—and last time it went over, we heard this awful thud…was anything broken?'

He shook his head. 'The shed took a strong hit, but it's a solid, sturdy piece of workmanship. She says not to worry about it.'

'That's easier said than done. I'd be getting stressed out if the neighbours kept doing it to me.'

His mouth made an odd quirk. 'Yes, but you seem to be constantly under pressure, what with work and keeping up with this place. Aunt Jane tells me you're finding all sorts of problems here—you need to have some of the roof tiles replaced, she says. That must be a hassle you can do without.'

'And the rest.' She pulled a face. 'I didn't realise this place needed quite so much work, when I took it on.' She glanced at him as she set out plates on the table. 'But you must be having problems of your own—didn't you say you had builders working on your house? It was why you hadn't been able to get around to seeing your aunt, you said.'

'That's right. I was having work done on the garage and in the garden. The work's all finished now, though. Obviously, it was nothing compared with what you have to do here.'

Alex nodded. 'I keep asking myself why I bought this place.' She broke off to tell James and Sarah to go and wash their hands at the sink. 'Originally, I'd no intention of buying such a rambling place, but it sort of drew me in… It looked like a dream house, with its lovely, honey-coloured Somerset stone and the sloping roofs at all angles, and once I set eyes on it, I was hooked. I've never owned a house before…I've always lived in small, rented accommodation. Nothing else seemed necessary.'

'But suddenly you wanted to put down roots?'

She nodded. 'I think so. I don't know why. I really don't know what came over me. Up to now, I've been so busy with work that I didn't need anything more than a place to rest my head. Then I came here…' She frowned. 'Perhaps I thought it was time for a change. I had visions of this old farmhouse being lovingly renovated, and the orchard bursting with fruit—a kind of rural paradise, if you like.' She grinned. 'Now I'm beginning to wonder if I might have bitten off more than I can chew.'

Callum opened his mouth to answer, but he was interrupted by a horrible clanking and groaning sound coming from the water pipes as the children turned on the kitchen tap. No water came out.

'Where's the spanner?' James asked, his face serious as he began to hunt around in the cupboard underneath the sink.

'Isn't it there?' Alex frowned. 'I must have moved it. Look on the shelf by the fridge.'

Callum looked from one to the other, clearly puzzled. 'He's not going to try to fix it, is he? Surely he's too young?'

'Nah…it's easy,' James told him, putting on his man-of-the-house expression. He found the spanner and bent down inside the cupboard, concentrating deeply on the task in hand. Then he gave the pipe a couple of hard whacks. 'Try it now,' he instructed Sarah.

She did as he told her, and obligingly water spurted from the tap.

Callum watched in wonder. 'I'm impressed. Who needs a tradesman when you can do it yourself?'

Alex's mouth curved. 'It is annoying, though,' she said.

'The water pipes creak and groan and make an almighty noise a lot of the time. I'm going to have to do something about it, because one of these days banging on the pipe just won't do the trick.'

The children finished washing and came to sit at the table. 'I love pizza,' James said, trying to cram a whole portion into his mouth at once.

'That's great, but slow down,' Alex warned him. 'I don't want to see you choking on your food.'

James grinned amiably, and he and Sarah compared slices before James began to show his sister how to make faces with pieces he arranged carefully on his plate. 'You just cut it with your knife, like this,' he explained.

Alex turned her attention to Callum. 'So how is Jane?' she asked. 'I looked in on her this morning, but it seemed as though she'd been overdoing things again. Her cheeks were very flushed, and I guessed her blood pressure was up. Has there been any news from the hospital?'

'Yes, I talked to the specialist yesterday, and I gave her the news this afternoon. She said it was okay to let you know the result.'

'And that is?'

'She has Conn's syndrome. It's very rare, and that's perhaps why it wasn't picked up before, but the CT scan showed a tumour on her adrenal gland. It's causing the gland to produce too much aldosterone, and that's pushing up her blood pressure.'

Alex pressed her lips together briefly. 'That must have come as a huge shock to her. Is she all right?'

'I think so. She went to lie down for a while, but she seemed to take it well enough.'

'And what about you? How do you feel about it? It must be a real worry for you.'

His mouth straightened. 'I'm not sure. Generally these

things turn out to be benign, so I'm trying to stay calm about it. I tried to paint a positive picture for my aunt, too… but she's a hardy woman, generally. I think she'll be all right. Things don't normally knock her back for long.'

Alex pulled in a quick breath. 'I'll make sure to give her any help and support she needs,' she vowed. 'When will she be having the surgery? Is your friend going to operate?'

He nodded. 'He said he'd do it next week. One of his patients postponed, because of unexpected travel plans, so he'll fit my aunt in then.'

'That's brilliant news. She's healthy enough otherwise, isn't she, so there shouldn't be any problem?'

'Let's hope so.' He helped himself to salad, and then sent a cautious glance in the children's direction before asking quietly, 'How are your family doing? You said they were involved in a nasty accident and they must already have been in hospital for quite a while.'

Her eyes clouded. 'It's going to take some time before they're back on their feet. Ross is still on a ventilator, but Beth is doing a little better. Even so, there were broken bones that need to heal, as well as the internal injuries.'

She shot a look at the children. Thankfully, they were both still engrossed in seeing who could make the best pattern with what was left of the pizza. Sarah had added cherry tomatoes to her effort, along with a curved slice of red pepper for a mouth, and now she pronounced that she had made the best face.

'She has curly hair, too,' she said proudly, showing off the adornment of pasta spirals.

James pursed his lips. 'Faces are easy,' he said. 'I'm making a tractor.'

'Oh, is that what it is?' Sarah squinted at his effort,

tilting her head sideways so as to see it from a different angle. 'You need some salami rings for the wheels.'

'Yes, but I ate them,' James said, frowning. He inspected her plate. 'Can I have yours?'

'No, you can't.' Sarah moved her plate out of reach when he would have swooped with his fork, and Alex closed her eyes fleetingly.

'Try eating your food instead of playing with it. And when you've finished, you can go outside and play on the swing for a while. Get rid of some of that energy,' Alex said to both of them.

'I want to play football,' James said, his grey eyes challenging her.

'No more football today,' she answered. 'We talked about that.'

'Well, then, why can't we go to the seaside instead? You keep saying we'll go, but we never do.'

'Yes, but we've only been here a few weeks, James, and we've been busy. There's been a lot to do, moving in here and getting everything shipshape.'

'It isn't a ship!' James retorted, his brows shooting upwards. 'I want to go to the seaside.' He glowered. 'Mum would have taken us.'

Alex hid a groan, and Callum's mouth twitched a fraction. 'They know how to hit where it hurts, don't they?'

'Too right they do.' She glanced at the children, but by now James was making another attempt to steal salami from Sarah's plate, and she decided it was time to intervene.

She picked up James's plate and held it aloft. 'Have you finished with this?' she asked. 'Do you want me to put this out for the birds?'

James scowled, but shook his head.

'All right, then. Eat up. Any more messing about and I'll take it away, and then there'll be no strawberry cake.'

Both children began to eat, and Alex gave a faint sigh. 'They're like this all the while,' she told Callum, with a shake of her head. 'I don't know how their mother used to cope. I feel as though I'm run ragged half the time, sorting out their disputes.'

'I expect she lets them get on with it,' he said, smiling. 'By the time you've come around to playing referee, they'll have moved on to something else.'

'That's true enough,' she said with a laugh.

He glanced at the youngsters, who had begun to argue over which one of them had more cheese than the other, and added softly, 'Of course, James does have a point about the seaside, you know. To a child, a day can seem a long while to wait for something, let alone several weeks—and the coast is only a few miles from here.'

A small line creased her brow. 'I know I should have taken them—it's just that the weekends are so full, and they haven't really mentioned it much.'

'Perhaps they were waiting for you to arrange it. Anyway, I can't help sympathising with youngsters who want to spend time at the seaside...especially when their parents aren't around to take them there.'

'I know.' She frowned. 'I kept thinking we'd wait until I have some time off from work, in the summer holidays. As it is, I have a mass of work to do here. I'm halfway through painting the living room, I have to do something about the blocked-up chimney in the dining room, and the kitchen cupboards need stripping down to bare wood so that they can be restored to what they once were. And that's not counting the roof tiles that need replacing and the plumbing that needs to be fixed. I just don't know when I'm supposed to do all this.'

'Later,' he said. 'All those things can wait. You need to get your priorities sorted out.'

'Do I?' She made a soft sound of exasperation. 'That's easy for you to say, isn't it? You're not involved. As far as I can tell, everything's going smoothly for you, and all you have to do is make sure your aunt is safe and secure.'

'Maybe, but I'd like to do what I can to help you. I'm sure we can find a solution.'

'What do you mean?'

'I mean how about I take a look at the plumbing, while you clear the table and get everyone ready for a trip to the coast? I know a lovely little cove not far from here, where the children can fish in the rock pools.'

'Yes!'

'Yes!'

Alex looked round in astonishment as James and Sarah both shouted gleefully, whooping with delight. 'Say yes, Auntie Alex...please say yes.' Sarah turned pleading blue eyes on Alex, and James's face was lit up with joyful expectation.

Alex was stunned to find that they had both been listening to her conversation with Callum. She turned to him. 'Now look what you've done.'

Callum's expression was bland. 'Who? Me? I didn't do anything. I just offered to try and fix the taps for you. If you want me to leave it, that's fine by me.'

'No, no...Auntie Alex, don't let him leave it...' Sarah was beside herself with dismay. 'You keep saying how you're going to...knock that pipe into next week if it doesn't stop playing up. Now you don't have to. I know he can fix it for us...or at least he can try.'

'And then we can go to the seaside,' James finished.

'Yeah!' They both added the chorus.

Alex melted at the sight of the children's eager faces.

'I don't see how I have any choice.' She looked at Callum and gave a faint shake of her head. 'There are a thousand and one jobs I should be doing, but now it looks as though I'll be spending the afternoon by the sea.' She gave him a mischievous look. 'Maybe you could help out in other ways,' she suggested with a wry smile. 'Perhaps you'd like to come and do my laundry while you're about it, and mop the floors?'

His mouth twisted. 'Sorry, but I don't do domestic. I come from a household steeped in tradition—Aunt Jane did all the homely things, and my uncle ran the show from his study. He always had lots of advice on how things should be done...but leave it to the women, he used to say.'

Her mouth curved. 'Well, let's hope at least you can fix the plumbing,' she said. 'That would be a definite bonus.'

He nodded. 'I'll need a carrier bag and a sponge of some sort if you have one?'

She stared at him blankly. 'Those aren't the usual plumbing tools, are they? I can offer you spanners, a wrench, hammers...pliers or grips...'

'A carrier bag and sponge will be just fine, thanks... and some plastic adhesive tape if you have it.'

She frowned. 'Okay.' She studied him briefly. 'Are you quite sure you know what you're doing?'

He nodded. 'I hope so.'

She went to fetch him what he needed, and then sent the children upstairs to get ready for their outing. 'You'll need a spare set of clothes in case anything gets wet,' she told them. 'And you'd better hunt out your swimsuit and trunks.'

'Seaside! Yay!' James ran up the stairs, followed

swiftly by Sarah. 'Can we take the fishing nets?' he called back.

'I'll get them,' Alex told him. She stopped to think about that for a moment or two. Last time she'd seen them, they'd been at the back of the shed, along with buckets and spades from previous years...years when they'd gone with their parents to spend time by the sea, digging in the sand and making spectacular sandcastles, with moats and drawbridges, and all sorts of embellishments made from shells and pebbles that they'd found lying about. She'd seen the photos, and heard all about it from Ross and Beth.

The memories brought sudden tears to her eyes. How could she ever hope to replace all that love and commitment, even for a short time? Would things be the same for them ever again?

'Are you all right?' Callum was looking at her oddly, and Alex blinked, trying to stem the tears that threatened.

'I'm fine,' she said, her voice a little choked. 'I was just thinking about Ross and Beth...it caught me unawares. I suppose I've been a bit wound up lately, trying to work out how to deal with everything.'

He wrapped his arms around her and drew her close. 'You're bound to feel that way,' he said softly. 'So much has happened in such a short time.' He ran his hands over her shoulders, her back, gently soothing her.

'I'm just afraid I've let them down.' Her voice faltered. 'It's as though I've been suffering from tunnel vision lately, trying to form order out of chaos. I've concentrated so hard on dealing with day-to-day life...it all seemed so important at the time.'

He rested his cheek against hers. 'Perhaps it was the only way you could cope. But what really matters is that they should be happy. You can't make up for this awful thing that has struck down their parents, but you can do something to help the children.'

She nodded. 'You're right. I know you're right.'

He smiled. 'Anyway, you could do with a break yourself. It's time to step off the treadmill—so, if you'll pass me the sponge and tape, I'll get on.'

He carefully released her, easing back from her a little, and she took a moment to get used to being on her own once again. She missed his warm embrace. She missed his closeness.

But she needed to pull herself together, so she went to find the things he needed.

She handed them to him a minute or so later, and then watched curiously as he placed the sponge inside the carrier bag and taped it firmly beneath the outlet of the tap.

'First we switch on the cold tap,' he said, 'then the hot. Wait for the gurgling to stop… then turn off the hot tap.' He waited a moment or two, leaving the cold tap running, and then abruptly removed the bag and sponge. Water spurted out.

'We'll try that one or two times more,' he murmured, 'and see if it does the trick. It's just an airlock that's causing the trouble.'

A minute or two later, the water was running freely, and Alex watched and marvelled. 'Thank you for that,' she said. 'I would never have guessed it was something so simple. I can see I'm going to have to get myself a book on how to fix things around the house…or find a decent internet site that explains everything in layman's terms.'

'As opposed to having a man around the place?' He sent her an oblique glance, a smile playing around his lips. 'Are you sure you wouldn't prefer your own handyman on the premises?'

Her mouth curved. 'Are you putting yourself forward for the job?'

'Oh, yes.' His glimmering gaze skimmed over her. 'With perks, of course...'

'Oh?' She looked at him warily. 'And they would be?'

'Well, let's see...you could pay me with tea and pizza, or maybe a slice of strawberry cream cake...'

'That sounds reasonable enough,' she said with a smile. 'I think we could manage both of those.'

'Hmm.' He dried his hands on a tea towel and then turned to face her once more. 'Though there are other far more interesting ways I could think of.' His gaze lingered on the pink fullness of her mouth, and she simply stood there for a moment, lured by the sheer invitation in those incredible blue eyes and wondering what it would be like to be kissed by him. Somehow he was so close that it would only take a breath of movement, and his lips would be touching hers. She felt heady with the intensity of the moment, lulled by the spell he was weaving around her.

'James wants to take his snorkel and flippers,' Sarah said, coming into the kitchen at that moment. 'I told him we're not going swimming, but he won't listen. And he thinks we're going to take the dinghy and his wooden boat as well as the beach ball.'

Alex came back down to earth with a bump. She gave Callum one last, cautious glance, and saw that his mouth had curved into a resigned smile. 'Tell him the beach ball and his wooden boat are fine,' she said, trying to keep her voice on an even keel. 'And we'd better get a move on if we're to have plenty of time at the beach.'

She turned to Callum, breathing in deeply to calm herself. 'Will your aunt be okay while we're out? It seems like the wrong time to leave her.'

'I'm sure she'll be fine. Martha from across the way is coming over to visit her this afternoon, so at least she'll have company. Anyway, she knows to ring me if there's a problem...but I'll go and have a word with her right now, and then we'll set off.' He paused a moment, then added, 'You might want to ask Martha about looking after the children during the school holidays, if my aunt's going to be out of action for a while. She used to foster children, so I know she'd like the opportunity.'

'Really? That's great. I'll talk to her about it.' She marvelled at his thoughtfulness. She'd been trying to work out what to do for the best, and he had come up with a solution. Having him around was turning out to be a boon.

'Good. And as to what we were saying before...I'll come round and give you a hand with some of the jobs you have to do around here. I'm quite handy with a paintbrush and I'm not too bad on fixing roof tiles either. Between us, we should soon have this place looking good.'

'Oh...that's really thoughtful of you.' The words left her on a soft breath of surprise and, impulsively, she reached out to touch his arm. 'That's a wonderful offer, but you don't need to do that. I took it on, and it's my problem. I'm the one who should deal with it.'

'I don't see it as a problem. I see it as a project. I'll be really glad of the chance to help you renovate this place on my days off. It'll be good to have something to do that's completely different from work at the hospital.' He smiled as he walked towards the door. 'And it will give us the chance to spend more time together.'

She stared at him in shock, stunned by his offer. Did he really want to spend his weekends with her?

By the time he came back from Jane's house, they were all ready to set off. James was wearing his super-spy slim-line shades, and Sarah had her favourite drinks bottle with the curly plastic straw.

Callum drove along the main road towards the coast, pointing out the various landmarks along the way. Soon, the rolling hills of the Quantocks gave way to Exmoor's rugged landscape, with majestic headlands, towering cliffs and beautiful bays. The sea was a perfect blue.

'I thought we'd stop at a little cove near here,' he said, as he turned the car onto a road leading towards the sea. 'It's sheltered by the cliffs, so you can get some shade from the sun, and when the tide's out, as it is now, it leaves behind lots of pools where you can find baby crabs.'

He parked the car and looked back at James. 'Did you bring a bucket?'

James nodded, holding up a huge blue bucket, shaped like a castle. 'For the crabs,' he said.

'Good. A boy after my own heart,' Callum said. He glanced at Sarah. 'Are you all right with crabbing? Not squeamish, are you?'

Sarah shook her head. 'But Auntie Alex isn't too keen. She doesn't like their little pincers.'

He laughed. 'I might have guessed.' He sent Alex a sympathetic look. 'Not to worry. You can collect shells and seaweed instead, if you like.'

'Thank you so much,' Alex answered, her tone dry. 'I can't think of anything I'd like more.'

He nodded. 'You will, once you get the hang of this "taking things easy" exercise.'

'Of course I will,' she murmured. 'I have vague memories of it, from when I was in my teens, I think.'

'What it is to be focussed,' he said softly. 'Is your career really the be-all and end-all of everything?'

They climbed out of the car, unloading rubber rings, a huge beach ball, the bag with towels and a change of clothes, and another bag with camera, drinks bottles and assorted paraphernalia.

'Do you remember good times by the sea with your parents?' Alex asked Callum as they walked down the cliff path to the sand below.

'Some,' he said. 'But mostly I went with Aunt Jane and my uncle. They'd let me bring a friend along, sometimes a couple of friends, and we had some great times.' He looked around. 'This was a favourite haunt.'

She nodded, looking around for a place where they could settle down when they reached the sandy beach. 'I can see why. It has everything you could want.'

She handed out buckets and spades, and the children set to work, digging in the sand. 'I'm going to make a fort,' James announced, 'with battlements and a moat.'

Alex gazed out over the sparkling waters of the Bristol Channel, and then looked back at the cliffs, layered with strata of shale, and blue, yellow and brown limestone. 'This place is fantastic.'

'It is,' Callum agreed. 'I used to hunt for fossils in those rocks. It was great fun.'

'I can imagine.'

They spent the next hour digging in the sand and fetching water from the sea so that James and Sarah could complete their grand castle. That done, they set off to explore the cove, treading carefully over flat rocks and peering down into rocky inlets where the tide had washed up all manner of seaweed and sea creatures.

James filled his bucket with baby crabs, while Sarah collected shells, looking for perfect specimens. 'I want to take them to the hospital to show Mum,' she said.

Alex watched as they padded over the damp sand. Callum bent to look at James's latest find, and the two males engaged in a deep discussion about how the creature moved and whether it could live out of water. Then Callum turned to Sarah and admired the perfectly intact cockle-shell she had discovered.

He was good with both of them, Alex acknowledged. He spoke to them quietly, interested in everything they had to say, and every now and then his gentle laughter floated on the air.

Eventually, they returned to the sandcastle where they had started off, and Alex hunted out drinks from the depths of one of the bags. Satisfied after quenching his thirst, James wanted to go down to the water's edge to paddle in the surf.

'Okay, but stay where I can see you,' Alex told him. 'No further than that wooden marker.'

Sarah went with him, and Alex watched their progress, anxious in case they should wander too far into the water.

'It's a safe beach,' Callum told her. 'They'll be okay... and we'll both keep an eye on them.'

She nodded. 'This is really lovely, being out here. It seems so long since I last sat on a beach and looked at the sea. I didn't realise how much I missed it.'

'Didn't you take holidays?'

She shook her head. 'I haven't done recently. Somehow I just don't seem to have found time for a proper break these last few years. I've been studying for specialist exams, taking on high-profile jobs and generally letting myself be swamped with work.'

'I suppose you must get an adrenaline buzz from all that, otherwise you wouldn't do it.'

'Maybe.' Her eyes clouded. Why was it that her life's work suddenly seemed nothing compared to these stolen moments in a sandy cove where the only sounds were the gentle swish of the sea lapping at the shore and the call of the gulls overhead? What had she been missing all these years?

Callum leaned back against a rock and studied her with a quizzical expression. 'And where do men friends fit into all this hard work and dedication to the job in hand? You said you were too busy to be involved with anyone right now, but there must have been someone in the past?'

'Maybe.' She wasn't going to fill him in on her skirmishes with romance, and anyway it seemed odd to say that no man had ever featured greatly in her life. There had been opportunity enough, if she'd wanted to take it, but somehow no one had ever lit that spark in her that would make her fall head over heels in love. There had been good men, rugged men, men who'd made her laugh and promised her the world, but none had made her want to give up her career or turn her back on ambition. Perhaps there was something wrong with her. Perhaps she was expecting too much.

'I see…dark secrets, eh?' Callum tilted his head on one side to study her. 'I heard there was a doctor in Men's Surgical who lost his heart to you for quite a while. A couple of years, at least, but it was unrequited love, people said. They say you think more about the job than you do about your love life.' His glance meshed with hers. 'That's quite a challenge for any man.'

'Is it?' She saw his gaze drop to her mouth, and felt a sudden flood of heat in her abdomen. 'I don't know what to do about that, because the truth is I mean it when I say I don't have time for a relationship right now.' Her mouth made a brief quirk. 'Heavens, I don't even have time to do my ironing. At this rate, the children will be wearing crumpled T-shirts to school in the morning.'

He laughed. 'I don't suppose anyone will mind. You'll be the only one who notices.' He leaned over her and smoothed back a tendril of hair that had fallen across her cheek.

'Maybe. But that's the problem I'm wrestling with, isn't it? I notice all these things and I care about them, and I want to put them right. Not T-shirts so much, but generally taking care of the children and making sure everything runs smoothly.'

'It could be that these things aren't so important as you imagine.'

'But they matter to me.'

Perhaps that was the reason none of her relationships had worked out right in the past. She had her own set of priorities, and the men she had known had without fail wanted to override them with their own concerns. Callum was probably much the same.

She gazed out to sea, to where the children were splashing one another and jumping with each wave that rolled onto the shore. 'The tide's coming in,' she said. 'I think we'll have to make a move.'

'Yes.' There was a note of regret in his voice. 'I think you're probably right.'

CHAPTER FIVE

'YES, I understand perfectly, Dr Langton...we're looking for cuts right across the board.' Alex frowned. 'Of course, you realise, don't you, that it isn't as simple as cutting back on nursing staff and putting the cleaning contract out to tender? Either of those measures could mean that the emergency department will function less well.' Alex adopted a gentle, coaxing tone. 'I was hoping rather that we might make savings through using low-priced generic drugs and altering practices within the unit so that we're more cost-efficient.'

Dr Langton shook his head. 'My dear, that simply won't be enough. From the figures you've shown me, those measures will take far too long to bring results. Unfortunately, this job's all about tough decisions. We need to do something now...and reducing staff numbers is top priority, along with putting a stop on any new equipment being ordered. Some departments are quite irresponsible in thinking they can demand all the latest equipment...we simply don't have the budget for it.' He frowned. 'Make sure they know that in A and E, won't you? Out of all the departments, that one has the highest expenditure for the last six months.'

'I've already done that,' she said. 'I've put a stop to any new orders.'

'Good.' He gave her a benign smile. 'We need to show the board that we've made dramatic headway at the next meeting...but I know you can pull this off, Alex. I've every faith in you.'

Alex nodded. 'I'll do my best. At least with all these measures in place we should be able to keep the A and E department up and running. I've looked closely at the figures and everything seems to be on course.'

He nodded. 'That's what it's all about.'

She left the chief executive's office a short time later, deep in thought, and made her way to A and E. Things were going from bad to worse. Right from the beginning, this day had started out wrong.

First of all she had visited Ross and Beth, only to find that her brother had suffered a setback. His breathing had deteriorated, and the doctors were worried about an infection in his lungs. They were initiating more tests and thinking about changing his medication...all of it bad news. How was she to explain things to the children? And on top of that, this was the day that Jane was having surgery to remove the tumour on her adrenal gland...one more thing to play on her mind.

For now, though, she tried to concentrate on the job in hand. She didn't have to look too far to find the culprit behind some of the so-called irresponsible ordering that had annoyed the chief executive.

Callum was determined that A and E should have the best equipment for the job, and although he was aware that the budget was restricted, he'd been determinedly pushing for those things he felt necessary.

And as for staff cuts, those wouldn't go down well at all, would they? It was a disturbing situation. Even though Dr Langton was the boss, she couldn't help thinking he was being short-sighted in ordering them.

'There you are…I'm glad you're back from your meeting,' Katie greeted her as she entered the unit. 'We've a three-year-old in treatment room two—he has a foreign body in his ear, and so far Dr Henderson hasn't been able to remove it. The boy's getting quite distressed, and his mother's becoming agitated, too. Dr Henderson's tried irrigation and now he's having a go with forceps. He doesn't like to admit defeat and he's doing his level best, but I think it's a difficult one for him. He asked for a second opinion.'

'Okay, I'll go and see the boy. It's not easy dealing with youngsters when they're fractious, and it's amazing how deep into the ear canal they can push things.' She glanced at Katie. 'Is there a nurse assisting?'

Katie shook her head. 'No, everyone's busy at the moment, but I could go along if you like. I've finished here for the moment.'

'That would be great, if you would. He might need help to calm the infant.'

Callum came up to the desk as she was speaking. He looked purposeful and energetic, as though he meant business, immaculately dressed in dark trousers, a navy-blue shirt and a subtly patterned grey-blue tie. He was so different from the casually dressed man she'd spent time with on the beach, and yet either way he managed to set her pulse racing.

'Did I hear you talking about Simon Henderson's patient—the three-year-old who thinks it's fun to stick things in his ear?'

Alex nodded.

'I would have had a look at the boy myself,' he said with a frown, 'but I have a patient waiting—I suspect she's had a mini-stroke.' He gave Alex a smile that warmed her through and through. 'You've just come from seeing Dr

Langton, I take it? What was it today? Cut back on the use of surgical gloves and paper towels and make do with cheap coffee in the staff lounge?'

She shook her head. 'No, nothing like that. I'm afraid it was much more serious.' She hesitated. He probably wasn't going to like what she had to say, but she gave him a wry smile and tacked on, 'As far as you're concerned, it means ordering any new equipment is definitely off limits for the foreseeable future.'

His brows drew together. 'I might have guessed. Still, let's look on the bright side—that can't apply to stuff already on order.' He pulled a face. 'I don't suppose there's any news on the transcranial Doppler ultrasound machine I requested, is there?'

Alex sucked in a breath and laid a hand lightly on his arm as though to soften the blow. 'Callum, you know as well as I do that it's not a piece of equipment that would normally be used in the emergency room. You're setting your expectations way too high in this economic climate. You don't have a chance. You know the board won't sanction any undue expenditure.'

Perhaps it was a mistake, touching him. It made her recall all too vividly the way they had sat close together on the beach. A wave of nostalgia hit her. Those few short hours had seemed like stolen moments, and she longed to experience them all over again...but it seemed as though she was wishing on a moonbeam. Her life was complicated enough, without hankering after something that was out of reach. And she and Callum had nothing in common, did they? Their personalities were totally different, and even at work they managed to clash. She let her hand drop to her side.

He laid an arm around her shoulders and looked into her eyes. 'That's as maybe, but refusing to even look at it shows a complete lack of forward thinking on the part of the board.' He grinned. 'I'm pretty sure you could sweet-talk them into changing their minds. With the right diagnostic equipment in place we could save several days of waiting for test results. That way, we could avert imminent strokes, and by taking quick action we could save the hospital money by not having to keep patients in hospital for long periods. You could say it's false economy to avoid having one.'

Alex's mouth made a crooked shape. 'You could say that, and I can see your point, but I'm not at all sure Dr Langton will be convinced by that argument. He's not into long-term solutions right now. All he wants is to see immediate cost-cutting.' She liked having his arm around her. It might not mean anything…it might simply be his way of trying to wheedle her into doing what he wanted, but it still felt good.

'Hmph. So I guess all this means you won't be putting a rush on my order for another bedside X-ray machine, will you?'

She shook her head. 'You already know the answer to that one. No, I won't…not for the foreseeable future. I did warn you.'

He nodded. 'It's as I thought…but it's a very misguided attitude. The repair bills for the one we're using are getting beyond a joke.' He was thoughtful for a second or two, before adding mischievously, 'And I suppose I'm right in thinking there's going to be a bit of a wait for my new ECMO machine?'

Alex laughed out loud at that. 'An extracorporeal membrane oxygenating machine at around a hundred thousand pounds with running costs? I should think so, Callum. That's a very expensive pipe dream.'

His mouth twitched, before turning down at the corners

in mock dismay. 'But one we could do with—after all, we're near the coast, and drowning is just one other way in which a patient might need bypass support for the heart and lungs. Children have been known to recover from drowning in cold water, and with one of those machines on hand to gently warm their blood supply, their chances of survival would be so much greater.'

'I'm with you all the way on that one,' she acknowledged with a smile, 'but it isn't going to happen, I'm afraid. Why don't you get back to the real world and go and save your mini-stroke patient from imminent disaster by giving her the standard treatment?'

'A couple of aspirin, you mean, while I wait for the MRI scanner to be freed up—not likely to be very soon, given the waiting list—or until I can gain access to CT in a few days' time, given that the patient isn't on the critical list?' He made a face. 'A transcranial Doppler ultrasound machine would have given me an accurate diagnosis in a fraction of the time.' He sighed, releasing her, and Alex immediately felt the loss of his comforting arm around her. 'What it is to be working in modern medicine.'

He went on his way and Alex watched his confident stride. How was it that he had found his way into her affections so easily? She had always been careful about the men she let into her life, and yet he seemed to have invited himself, and was completely at ease.

She made an effort to shake off these distracting thoughts, and hurried along to see Dr Henderson's patient in the treatment room.

She could hear the child squealing before she even reached the room, and when she pushed open the door and looked inside, she saw a tearful, red-faced infant rubbing his eyes with his knuckles and glowering at the unfortunate junior doctor. Dr Henderson had relinquished the forceps and was trying unsuccessfully to pacify both the child and his mother. Katie was doing all she could to divert the boy's attention, offering him toys to cuddle and talking to him in a soothing voice, all to no avail.

'Poor Harry,' Alex murmured, going over to the boy after introducing herself to his mother. 'Is your ear hurting?'

The boy stopped sobbing long enough to nod and stare at her. 'Oh, dear, I'm sorry about that,' she said softly. 'This has all been a bit too much for you, hasn't it? I think we'll give you something to calm you down a bit, and then you'll feel much better.'

She turned to the boy's mother. 'Sometimes these foreign bodies in the ears can slip much further down than we can easily reach and it's obviously troubling him now—but not to worry, I'll give Harry an injection of a sedative and something for the pain, and then we can try again, using suction.'

The woman nodded. 'Thank you. I hate seeing him this way. It's really upsetting.'

'Of course it is. Do you know what it was he put into his ear?'

'A wooden bead. I've told him time and time again not to put things in his ears. He wasn't supposed to play with the beads, but his sister got them out, and he was straight in there. He's into everything these days, like a tornado around the house.'

'It happens a lot, especially with boys,' Alex said in sympathy. She shuddered to think about all the things James got up to... Beth had told her about the time he'd dismantled his toy car and swallowed the button battery. That had meant a swift visit to A and E after it had stuck in his throat.

She prepared the injection and gently explained to the

boy what she was about to do. 'Just a scratch,' she said, signalling with a nod of her head to Katie, who was ready to divert him with a toy train.

They waited for the injection to take effect, and when Harry finally appeared to relax and began to take an interest in the toys, Alex showed him the light on the otoscope and explained to him that she was going to use it to look in his ear. 'It's a bit like a torch,' she said.

He seemed happy to go along with that. 'I'll seek out the position of the bead, Simon,' she told the young doctor, 'and then I'll introduce the catheter through the otoscope and apply suction.'

She reached for the catheter that was attached to a wall suction device and after a few fraught seconds carefully located the object that was lodged deep in the child's ear canal. A short time later, she withdrew the catheter along with the bead, which she dropped into a kidney dish. 'There you are,' she told the boy. 'All done.'

Harry's mother smiled, and Simon looked relieved and embarrassed at the same time. 'I hate having to remove these things,' he admitted under his breath. 'It can be such a tricky procedure, and the children are always fractious. You make it look so easy.'

'It just takes practice,' she said lightly, adding with a grin, 'From now on, we'll make sure to give you all the cases that come in when you're on duty.'

Simon looked horrified. 'You don't mean that?'

'Well, maybe one or two…just so you get used to doing it,' she said in a cheerful, placating tone. 'Don't worry… you'll always have help on hand.'

He grimaced, but seemed resigned to his fate, and a few minutes later she left him with the mother and child, and started back towards the main desk.

'Alex…' Katie called her name and fell into step beside

her. 'I heard you telling Callum about Dr Langton putting a stop on ordering new equipment. Is that all he's asking for…along with the cost-saving measures you've already put into place?'

Alex shook her head. 'I'm afraid not, Katie. He thinks we should cut staffing levels.'

'By staff, you mean nurses, don't you?' Katie's brow furrowed.

'Yes, but I don't want you to start worrying about that just yet. I'm not planning on making any cuts amongst the general staff. I'll see what I can do by stopping all agency work to begin with. That should make a big difference.'

Katie was still concerned. 'But it will make our jobs harder, too, won't it? How are we to cover for people who are off sick, or cope when we're inundated with patients in A and E? What if we have a major incident to handle?'

'I'm sorry, Katie, I do understand what you're saying, but I'm afraid that's the way it has to be. We're going through hard times. There just isn't enough money available to cover everything.'

'It's worrying.' Katie frowned.

'Yes, it is. But I promise you I'll do everything I can to keep things running as smoothly as possible. If you have any major problems, let me know and we'll see if we can find a way around things.'

Alex talked to Katie for a little while longer and then went to find her next patient. She worked solidly for the next few hours, and when she had made some headway through the mass of patients on her list, she stopped and stretched her aching limbs and began to think about lunch. Perhaps now that things were a little quieter in the waiting room, it would be a good time to go and grab something to eat. Maybe she could even drop in on Jane for a few minutes, to find out how she was doing.

She left the department, and walked towards the delivery bay close by the open quadrangle where staff sometimes took their lunch. She caught sight of Callum there, talking to a man in uniform while he cheerfully signed a paper attached to a clipboard. She brightened a little. Perhaps they could have lunch together.

She went over to the two men, nodding towards the deliveryman before turning to look directly at Callum. 'Hi,' she said. 'I wondered if we might have lunch together?'

'Ah… there you are,' Callum said quickly, pulling in a sharp breath. He seemed to be distracted by her sudden appearance. 'That sounds like a good idea…though I thought you might already have gone for lunch by now. You're a bit later than usual, aren't you?'

'Yes, I had a heavy workload.'

'Ah.'

She frowned. His manner was definitely a little odd, and she was beginning to wonder why he was so preoccupied. She looked around, wondering what it was that the man in uniform was delivering. Behind him, on a trolley, half-sheltered by the two men, was a huge package, as big as a man and twice as wide. Then it occurred to her that something highly suspicious was going on.

'This looks interesting,' she murmured, peering behind them to glance at the box once more. 'Is this something I should know about? Is this something that's destined for the A and E department?'

'Um…yes,' Callum answered quickly, 'but it's nothing at all for you to worry about.'

'Isn't it?' She lowered her voice, turning away so that the deliveryman wouldn't hear. 'We weren't expecting any deliveries, were we? I thought we'd agreed that any order for new equipment was to go through me first of all?'

'Yes, yes…that's quite true, but everything's in order,

so you don't need to worry about it.' He moved her gently to one side, while at the same time saying to the man, 'I'll leave you to take it through to the department, then, Jim. You can leave it where we arranged.'

Jim nodded and Callum turned his attention back to Alex. 'Actually, I'm glad I bumped into you. I was thinking of going up to see Aunt Jane after I've eaten. Do you want to come along? She should be out of the recovery room by now.'

'Yes, of course, I planned to do that, but...' She looked around to see where Jim was taking the package, but the man had disappeared along with his trolley. She frowned. Callum was clearly trying to distract her. 'You're up to something, aren't you?' she said, her gaze thoughtful. 'I specifically said no new portable X-ray machine was to be ordered, and yet somehow you've managed to go behind my back and acquire one.'

'What makes you think it was an X-ray machine?' he said in surprise, raising dark brows. 'All I could see was plain brown packaging.'

'With the words, *Radiology equipment* written in black ink along the base,' she retorted in a laconic tone. 'I suppose you thought you'd sneak it into place while I wasn't looking, and make out it was the one we already have. Did you really think I wouldn't notice the difference?'

He winced. 'Something like that.' He looked her over. 'There's no getting anything past you, is there? You're like a hawk, keeping a beady eye on everything, ready to swoop without warning when you see something you don't approve of.'

'Is that so?' Unaccountably, his description of her stung, and she said crossly, 'Perhaps I wouldn't have to be like that if it wasn't for people like you...haven't you just shown yourself to be a devious, underhanded, sneaky kind of a man who has absolutely no respect for rules and regulations?' Her eyes narrowed on him. 'How could you deliberately flout the new policy that way?'

'I didn't.' He gently placed a hand beneath her elbow and started to lead her towards the quadrangle and the corridor that led to the hospital restaurant.

It was yet more diversion tactics, but she wasn't going to let him wriggle off the hook that easily. 'Didn't it occur to you that I would see the invoice? Or were you hoping to sneak that past me, too?'

He appeared to be giving it some thought. 'I suppose there was always the chance I'd get away with it, for a week or so at any rate. But you must agree with me that the old machine needs a thorough overhaul…it's always breaking down at inopportune moments and then we have to wait for the main X-ray room to be clear for use. And some patients are in too bad a way to be moved, so a bedside X-ray is really convenient…as well as quick and safe.' He looked at her closely, his gaze sweeping over her taut features. 'Surely you understand why I did it?'

She looked at him in frustration. 'Of course I understand, but you know as well as I do that things are tight around here these days and we have to be extra-careful with spending. But you don't seem to care about that. Why else would you spend money we don't have?'

He opened his mouth to answer and she cut him short. 'No, don't answer that. I'll tell you why. You did it because you thought you could get away with it…because that's the kind of man you are, a law unto yourself, totally oblivious to the wider picture, to how your actions will affect everyone else, let alone having any regard for the kind of example you're setting. As long as you get your own way, nothing else matters, does it?'

His dark brows rose. 'Phew!' He whistled softly under

his breath and stared at her, his eyes widening. 'I didn't realise you had such a negative opinion of me. Are you quite sure there isn't anything you left out?'

'Oh, I'm sure there's more where that came from,' she said tersely. 'Give me time, and I'll come up with a list.'

He absently nodded agreement. 'I thought you might...' He studied her. 'I'd no idea I could rouse you so much... you're usually so calm and in control. You never lose your cool. It's what everyone says about you...you don't show what you're thinking. You just get on with the job and deal with everything and everyone efficiently, without any kind of sentiment.'

He studied the quick rise and fall of her chest, his glance roaming over her tense figure, drifting down over the cotton pin-tucked blouse she wore, with its self-coloured buttons, and the slim-fitting skirt that gently skimmed her hips and ended at the knee, to show shapely calves.

'Perhaps things are different now, though,' he murmured. 'Nothing's quite going the way you want it to now that Dr Langton's intervened, and you're having to fight to keep everything in order. You seem quite flushed with the exertion.' Light glimmered in his eyes. 'It makes a very appealing picture, you being all pink and agitated. I'm not at all used to seeing that, though I have to wonder why you're getting yourself so worked up...I might even say passionate...about what you imagine I've been up to.'

'I'm not getting myself worked up.' She ground the words out through her teeth and sent him a stony look. 'I'm just pointing out the error of your ways.'

'Yes, I appreciate that. But I'm still intrigued. This is so unlike you. You never vent your spleen, no matter how provoked you might be.' His expression was quizzical, his glance trailing over the firm jut of her chin and coming to rest on the soft fullness of her mouth. 'I wonder if you'd have reacted the same way if it was any other colleague who had been implicated?' He shook his head. 'Somehow, I doubt it. I have the notion that I'm the only one who can bring out such strong feelings in you.' His eyes glinted. 'Now, there's food for thought.'

She pulled in a shocked breath. 'That's complete nonsense.'

'Is it?'

They went out through the glass doors and into the deserted quadrangle. From here, they would be able to reach the restaurant, which was situated just beyond the dense screen of trees and herbaceous plants.

Alex was deep in thought. He was talking rubbish, wasn't he? Of course she wasn't getting herself all stirred up about him...it was the situation that disturbed her, wasn't it? It couldn't be that he had managed to fire up some spark that lay dormant within her...could it?

She couldn't fathom it out. Why *was* she so het up? Was it really true that he, alone, was able to provoke her to such a wild and deeply emotional response, one that started up in the very core of her being? Surely not? The idea was unthinkable. She sent him a surreptitious glance, at the same time giving an imperceptible shake of her head, as though she was trying to rid herself of the notion, but just at that moment he turned towards her and caught her troubled glance.

'Thinking it over?' he asked, an amused note coming into his voice. 'You're having doubts, aren't you?' He reflected on that. 'Perhaps we should put the theory to the test.'

She looked at him suspiciously. 'What do you mean?'

'I mean, maybe we should find out just how deep your feelings go.' He placed a hand lightly under her elbow, and before she realised what he was doing, he had managed to manoeuvre her into the shelter of a privet hedge. 'Perhaps you're not so cool and unemotional as you make out, and it's all welling up inside you, but you just don't know how to handle those instincts that you've buried deep down.'

She shook her head. 'You're way off beam. Why would I...?' Her voice trailed off in uncertainty as his arms gently slid around her waist.

'Why would you get yourself into a state over me?' he finished for her. He drew her close, so that the softness of her breasts was crushed against the hard wall of his chest and her legs encountered the pressure of his strong thighs. 'Well, let's see now...could it be that you're not quite as immune to normal, human emotions as you think you are?' He lowered his head so that his mouth was just a breath away from hers, and Alex suddenly found that she couldn't think straight any more. She knew that she ought to pull away from him, but although her head told her one thing, her treacherous body was telling her something altogether different. His hands were warm on the gentle slope of her hips and she was discovering that she liked the feeling.

'I don't know what happened to me, why I reacted the way I did,' she said cautiously, trying to keep herself on an even keel. She hesitated, doubts clouding her brain. 'I don't know what came over me.' She frowned, confusion settling on her, so that she was torn between wanting to berate him for his misguided actions, and yet, at the same time, she was conscious of her own shortcomings holding her back and undermining her confidence. And all the while he was holding her, setting her senses on fire with his gently stroking hands and somehow managing to befuddle her wits.

'It's not surprising you feel this way,' he said in a soothing tone. 'You're stressed and overworked. You've taken on far too much...your brother and his wife are seriously ill, you have the children to care for, the house is a work in itself, and on top of all that, you have a difficult job to do. You shouldn't blame yourself. Anyone would bend under the strain.' He ran his hand over the length of her, letting it glide slowly over her back, her hip, her thigh. 'But I can make things easier for you. I can show you how to forget your worries for a while.'

He rested his cheek against hers, his hand lightly caressing her, smoothing over the small of her back, and drawing her into the shelter of his body. 'You just have to let me help you.'

For some reason, she didn't even think of resisting, wanting only to lean into him and take comfort in his nearness...and that was strange, because no man had ever had quite that effect on her before this. Perhaps he sensed that inherent need in her, because after a moment or two he moved even closer, brushing his lips over hers and delicately testing the soft contours of her mouth.

Involuntarily, her lips parted, tantalised by his sweet exploration, and she gave herself up to his kiss, loving the way he moulded her to him and wrapped his arms around her. Somehow, just by holding her and cherishing her this way, he made her feel that she was all woman. For just these few moments she felt utterly feminine and desirable, and she realised that it was a feeling that she had lost over these last few months. She had been so bound up in her work, her problems, that she had forgotten there was more to living than being an automaton. It had taken Callum to bring her to life and show her that she couldn't stay locked up in her ivory castle. Why was it that she let her work and the chaotic demands of family and household chores rule her everyday life?

'Alex?' He lifted his head and looked down at her, reaching up with his hand to smooth away the creases that had formed on her brow. 'You're thinking again. I can feel you thinking… I thought we'd established you should take time out from that?'

'I…I don't know…I didn't realise…' She could feel herself tensing up all over again. 'That's all very well for you to say, isn't it? You seem to sail through life without worrying about anything. I'm the one who has to explain to the bosses when things go wrong. I'm the one who has to come up with answers. I can't just cast it off as though it's nothing.'

He sighed, leaning his head against her forehead. 'This is about the X-ray machine again, isn't it? There's no way you're going to relax until you've resolved it in your mind.'

'You know me so well, don't you?' It was a question tinged with regret. Why couldn't she simply let go, and cast her worries to one side?

'Would it help if I told you that it isn't a new machine?' He frowned. 'It's a reconditioned model—what they euphemistically call "pre-loved". And as to the money to pay for it, I've been raising funds for some time now, through various fun runs and dinner dances, raffles and so on. Now we're reaping the rewards.' He ran his fingers through the silk of her hair. 'So you see, you had no reason to worry. I didn't go against you. In fact, I told you that in the first place.'

'Oh!' She looked at him, aghast. 'And you let me go on…'

'And on…' He chuckled. 'I'd have stopped you, but it occurred to me that you needed to get it off your chest. You've been wound up for days, weeks. All you think about is the job, cost-cutting, and whether or not everyone is toeing the line.'

She stiffened. 'But that's what I'm here for. It's the reason I was set on.'

'But you're not alone in any of this. I'll be there for you. I'm working with you, not against you. I appreciate how difficult the job is for you, and I'll do whatever I can to help you. Together we can sort this out. Believe me.'

She closed her eyes briefly. She wanted to believe him. But in the past those men she had thought she could rely on had always let her down. They didn't want to know about the hassles of the job. All that mattered to them was to take life as it came and if things went wrong, so be it.

She couldn't live like that. She wanted to relax and enjoy life, but she couldn't let it toss her about on a whim, like flotsam and jetsam on a beach. Somehow, if it was in her power, she wanted to make a difference.

Could she trust him? Those few moments of inner peace, when he had held her in his arms and shown her that another side to life was possible had been so fleeting. Deep down, she recognised that they were two different people, opposites in every way, and yet she was drawn to him, as though by some invisible, magnetic thread.

Now she was more confused than ever.

CHAPTER SIX

'Do you think Mummy will like this?' Sarah asked, adding petals made out of red tissue paper to the flowers that decorated the front of the card she was making. 'It's a vase, see, with lots of flowers in it.'

'I'm sure she'll love it,' Alex said, admiring her efforts. 'It's very pretty, and I know your mother loves flowers.'

'I made a sailboat picture for Daddy,' James put in, waving his card in the air. 'He likes boats. He takes me to sail mine in the brook sometimes.' He frowned, his grey eyes troubled, and Alex wondered if he was thinking about those special times spent with his father, which had come to an abrupt end after the accident.

'You're right, it's perfect for him…and we'll put it on his bedside table at the hospital, so that he can see it as soon as he's feeling a bit better.'

'He's really poorly, isn't he?' Sarah's eyes clouded, and Alex wished there was some way she could comfort her. The children missed their parents and as time went on it was becoming more and more difficult for her to soothe their worries. 'The nurse said he wasn't well enough to see us. She said he had to rest.'

'When are we going to see him again?' James asked. 'I want him to come back home. I want Mummy to come home.'

'I know… It's very difficult for both of you, isn't it?'
Alex laid her arms around the children's shoulders as they
stood close to one another by the kitchen table. 'But your
mother is getting stronger every day, and perhaps it won't
be too long before she's able to come home.'

'And Daddy?' Sarah's gaze was almost pleading and
it wrenched at Alex's heart not to be able to give her the
answer she wanted.

'I don't know. The doctors and nurses are doing what
they can to make him more comfortable. We just have to
wait, and hope that soon he'll be stronger.'

James's bottom lip trembled, but he didn't say anything
more, and Alex gave him a hug. 'Why don't you finish
making your cards for Auntie Jane?' she suggested. 'If
you can finish them off in the next few minutes, before I
drop you both off at Martha's house, I'll be able to give
them to Jane when I go in to work today.'

'She's going to be home soon, isn't she?' Sarah brightened a little. 'You said she had her operation and she was
all right.'

Alex nodded. 'She just has to stay in hospital for a
couple of days, so the doctors can make sure she's healing
up nicely.' Jane's operation had been done with minimally
invasive surgery, which meant that the surgeon had made
several small incisions and used a laparascope to help with
the procedure.

'I don't want to go to Martha's,' James grumbled, his
bottom lip jutting. 'I want to stay here with you.'

She knelt down and put her arms around him. 'But I
have to go to work, James. You know that, don't you?'

'Yes, but I want you to stay at home. I want you to stay
here, with us.'

Alex shook her head. 'I'd like to do that. I wish I could,
sweetheart, but it just isn't possible right now. I have to

go to work to earn money so that I can pay all the bills. I'd love to stay here with you, but I can't.' Alex frowned. 'Anyway, I thought you liked being with Martha? You have a good time at her house, don't you?'

James didn't answer, but Sarah said quietly, 'She's okay. She takes us to the park—but it's not the same. We like it here with you. The only thing better would be for Mummy and Daddy to come home.'

Alex kissed both of them, wanting to comfort them and reassure them at the same time. 'If I could wave a magic wand and make it happen for you, I would, but for now, we all have to make the best of things.'

She got to her feet and glanced at the table, littered with glue sticks, cards and coloured tissue paper. 'Like I said, if you want me to give the cards to Auntie Jane, you'd better get a move on, because we have to leave here in twenty minutes.'

She arrived at the hospital some time later, feeling harassed and dejected. James had begun to play up as she'd dropped him off at her neighbour's house, and it had taken all her ingenuity and powers of reasoning to soothe him and help him to settle down. It also meant that she was a few minutes late for work, and that added to her stress levels, leaving her flustered.

'We're short-handed,' Katie told her as she made her way to the main desk. 'The waiting room's full and we don't have enough nurses to cope with the workload. Charlotte's off sick, and Simon Henderson is away on a course.' She shook her head. 'I don't know how we're going to manage things.'

'I know it's difficult, but we'll just have to keep going as best we can,' Alex told her, giving it some thought. 'Unfortunately, I can't bring in any locum doctors, and we won't be using the agency nurses any more. It means that your job, triage, is more important than ever, because we'll probably need to allocate nurses to the most serious cases. Waiting times will be stretched, of course, but there's nothing we can do about that in the circumstances.'

Katie sighed. 'We'll do what we can.'

'Thanks, Katie. You're all very good at what you do, and I'm just hoping that you'll be able to keep things together for as long as possible.'

She took a moment to glance at the status board. An infant was coming in by ambulance…something else to turn up her stress levels a notch. Very young, sick children were always a source of concern.

'Did I hear something about waiting times?' Callum came over to the desk. He placed a chart in the tray and picked out another one, just as Alex reached for a file. Their hands brushed against one another, sending small explosions of sensation to rocket through Alex's arm. She sucked in a breath. Why was it that her senses went on overdrive every time he came near? She stole a glance at him, but looked away when his gaze met hers. It didn't help that he always looked so good, either. Her heartbeat had quickened and there was a strange ache starting up inside her. He was way too distracting. He wore dark trousers and a shirt that moulded his body and showed off the flat plane of his stomach, hinting at the vital, energetic man within, a man who was always on the go and kept himself totally fit.

'Waiting times are getting longer,' Katie said. 'It's the budget cuts coming home to roost.' She moved away, heading towards the treatment room.

Callum's brows drew together. 'There's no easy answer, is there?' He glanced at Alex, who was trying to clear her head of errant thoughts by attempting to concentrate on her work schedule and make some sense of it. She was not going to let herself get worked up about him. It was her hormones that were bothering her, nothing else. 'No,' she said. 'The problem is, we need more money, not less.'

She frowned at her work schedule. How was she going to pull in her clinic time as well as take in another meeting with the executive board? Dr Langton seemed to forget that she had other priorities when he called these impromptu gatherings. And in the meantime, would it help to cheer up the nurses if she bought in pizzas and cookies to keep them going through the busy times when they weren't able to get away for a proper break? It was surely worth a try. She made a mental note to phone the local take-away food shop to arrange delivery.

'You look a little flushed,' Callum said, sending her a thoughtful glance. 'Is it the staffing problem, or something else? I saw you come flying in here a couple of minutes ago as though the hounds of hell were at your feet.'

Alex made a helpless gesture with her hands. He was looking at her so intently and she wanted so desperately to be close to him. She was trying not to think about the way he had kissed her not too long ago, or about the way it had felt to be wrapped in his arms.

'It's the children, mostly,' she murmured, 'James and Sarah. It's very worrying. They're both finding it difficult to cope with their parents in hospital, and I don't know what to tell them now that Ross has taken a turn for the worse. I'm becoming really anxious about him. And now that school has broken up for the holidays they're saying that they want me to be there for them.' She gave a sigh. 'I feel as though I'm being torn all ways.'

'There's no perfect solution to any of those, is there? Given a choice, I suspect children are always going to want their parent or guardian close at hand...but in this day and age even in the best of circumstances I guess it isn't always possible.'

She shook her head. 'No, it isn't. I've been thinking about it, and maybe I'll try to get them enrolled in some play activities over the next few weeks. That might help to distract them a bit.'

'Good idea. That could work out well.'

A siren sounded in the distance, and they both turned towards the ambulance bay. 'This must be the two-year-old we've been expecting—the one with the high temperature and vomiting,' Callum said. 'Would you be able to work with me? I've a feeling we'll need your skills as a paediatrician with this one.'

She nodded, walking briskly alongside him. 'Do we know anything about her condition? The GP sent her to us, didn't he?'

'That's right. Apparently, she had chickenpox a few weeks ago, and since then she's been going rapidly downhill. She's been generally unwell, lethargic and showing signs of irritability. Her mother complains that she's gone off her food over the last few days, and now she's very poorly.'

They hurried to greet the ambulance technicians, who were wheeling the child into the department. 'This is Rachel Vernon,' the paramedic said. 'She's two years old. She had a couple of seizures in the ambulance, so we've given her medication to control them, but her condition's still unstable. There are signs of neck rigidity and photophobia.'

Callum nodded grimly. 'Thanks,' he said, taking over and accompanying the infant into the treatment room. He gently began to examine the child while Alex talked to the girl's parents.

'It's bad, isn't it?' the father said, his face taut with

anxiety. 'She looks so ill. The GP said it might be meningitis.'

'It's a possibility,' Alex agreed. 'Meningitis means that the meninges, the brain's protective covering, are inflamed, but I'm concerned that the seizures are a sign that there's inflammation within her brain, too. We'll do tests to find out exactly what's causing her problems, though, and in the meantime we'll give her supportive treatment.'

She tried to reassure the parents that they would do everything possible to help their child. Then she turned to Callum, wanting to know the results of his examination.

'It's possible we're dealing with a viral infection,' he said, 'but if that's the case, it's more serious than usual. This little girl is very sick.' His expression was sad as he looked at the infant, but there was something else in his eyes that Alex had learned to recognise, a growing determination, perhaps, that he would do his utmost to pull the child through this distressing illness and get her back on her feet once more. He straightened. 'I'll get a CT scan done as soon as possible.'

Alex nodded. 'I agree. I'd recommend antibiotics as a cover, until we know what we're dealing with, along with medication to bring her temperature down and control her pain, and something to stop the vomiting. And we need to do a lumbar puncture as soon as she's stable.' A lumbar puncture would show them whether they were dealing with a bacterial or a viral infection, and once they knew the nature of it, they would be able to choose the most appropriate treatment.

He nodded and briefly addressed the nurse who was assisting. 'I'll give the child a corticosteroid to control the inflammation, along with an anticonvulsant, and at the same time we'll set up an EEG so that we can monitor any more seizures. Later on we may need to start an infusion of mannitol to control any rise in intracranial pressure. In the meantime, we'll take blood for testing, and I'm going to ask the lab to get back to us urgently with the results.'

'Okay, I'll organise a trolley.' The nurse hurried away to prepare the equipment.

Some time later, when they had done all they could to safeguard the child and make her more comfortable, Alex and Callum spoke once again to the parents, before finally turning their attention to their other patients.

'We'll look at the possibility of doing a lumbar puncture in a few hours,' Callum said. 'It all depends how well she responds to the initial treatment.'

'Waiting's always difficult,' Alex said, frowning. She could see that he was worried about his small patient, but their options were limited right now. They were doing everything possible to control the infection, but until they knew exactly what they were dealing with, they were working in the dark. 'Given that she's just suffered a bout of chickenpox, it's quite likely that we're dealing with a viral source...the abnormalities on the EEG certainly seem to point that way, but without the lab tests we can't know for sure.'

They both went their separate ways after that, treating a variety of patients who had come in with all manner of problems from fractures to worrying chest infections.

Around lunchtime, Alex met up with Callum again as she was suturing a gash in a child's hand. He put his head around the door of the treatment room, and said quietly, 'Rachel hasn't had any more seizures since we last saw her, so I'm thinking we might do the spinal tap after lunch. Right now, though, I'm going up to see my aunt... I thought you might want to come with me as soon as you're free. I'll be in the staff lounge, grabbing a bite to eat.' He gave her a knowing wink. 'I heard some good fairy had pizza sent in, along with baguettes and cakes and other goodies.'

Her mouth curved. 'Just give me a minute to finish up in here.' She glanced at her young patient a short time later. 'That's it…we're all done, Lewis. The nurse will put a dressing on the hand for you, and then you're free to go home with your mum.' She smiled. 'You've been very brave,' she added, presenting him with a teddy-bear badge and a page to colour, and he left the room with a beaming smile on his face.

She found Callum in the lounge, tucking into a bacon-filled baguette. 'These are good,' he said, munching appreciatively. 'You want to try one?'

She nodded. 'Perhaps I will.' She could see from what was left in the boxes that her gesture had gone down well with the staff. Katie and a couple of the other nurses on their lunch break were tucking in.

'There's a rumour going around,' Katie said, swallowing the last dregs of her tea and rinsing her cup at the sink. 'People are saying that Dr Langton will use the reduction in staff as an excuse to cut down on the emergency department's hours.'

Alex frowned. 'I haven't heard anything like that. When I told him that we were on budget to keep the department up and running, he agreed with me.'

Katie made a face. 'I wonder how much we can trust him. My friend worked at a hospital where he was an executive some time ago. He closed her unit down and transferred the services to the city hospital several miles away.'

Callum was thoughtful for a moment or two. 'I suppose, with the cuts in place, he could say that we don't have the people to man the unit, and therefore we'll no longer be able to provide a twenty-four-hour service.'

Alex's eyes widened. 'That isn't going to happen here. I'm making these changes for the good of the department. I'm not going to stand by and watch the A and E unit be disbanded.'

'Well, I thought it only right to warn you.' Katie made her way to the door. 'But thanks, anyway, for the food. It helps a lot. There's nothing like a full stomach to give people a boost.'

Alex watched her go out into the corridor, followed by the other nurses, leaving them alone in the room. Could there be some truth in what Katie had said? She brooded on the subject for a moment or two before going over to the table and picking out a slice of pizza.

'Try not to worry about it,' Callum said, studying her taut features. 'You're doing the best you can. I don't see how you can do any more.' He gave a crooked smile. 'As it is, you're like a whirlwind at the best of times, coming up with all these ideas for savings, starting new practices and setting up new audits. Since you arrived, no one's really had time to gather breath.'

'Oh.' The word came out on a faintly shocked exhalation. What was she to say to him? 'Is that really how you see me?'

'I think you believe in getting the job done. You don't think about failure…and that's a good thing.'

'Is it?' She nibbled at the pizza. 'Right now, if there's any truth in what Katie says, it looks as though failure's staring me in the face. It seems that whatever I do, Dr Langton will try to close us down.'

'But we won't let that happen, will we?' He smiled at her. 'I've been thinking about what you said—about the hospital needing more money, not less. Perhaps there's a way we can make that happen.'

'Oh?' She was intrigued. 'I'm not sure how we could

do that, unless we offered paid services of some sort.' She finished the pizza and wiped her hands on a serviette.

He nodded. 'That's exactly what I was thinking. Maybe we could rent out facilities that aren't being used, if not full-time, then on a part-time basis…like the theatres and the scanner, for instance.'

She thought about it. 'You're right,' she said, her mouth curving. 'And maybe we could rent out some of the outpatient facilities that aren't used at weekends. That way, we could perhaps have a GP-run minor injuries unit to take some of the strain off A and E.'

'See? You're getting the idea.' He came and put his arms around her. 'I told you I would help.'

'And you have, brilliantly.' She tilted her face up to him, glad to have him hold her and keep her close. 'I could put those suggestions to the board. It would make such a difference—it's a whole new way of thinking.'

He ran his hands along her arms. 'So maybe now you'll be able to think less about work, and more about getting some much-needed rest and recuperation along the way. I was thinking of maybe a trip out somewhere…an afternoon in the hills, or a few more hours by the sea, or perhaps we could drive out to Cheddar some time?'

'Oh, what bliss.' She smiled up at him. 'You make it sound so tempting. And I did have such a good time the other day. It was so lovely to walk with you over the rocks and then sit with you and watch the waves break on the shore.'

He dropped a kiss lightly on her mouth, making her whole body tingle with pleasure. 'Then we'll do it again, soon.'

He moved away from her as the door opened and one of the junior doctors came in. Alex drew in a quick breath. How had she let herself be tempted into such a situation at work of all places? All sensible thoughts seemed to go out of her head the moment Callum touched her. Emotionally, she was all over the place at the moment, and it was so unlike her to be this way. What was happening to her?

Perhaps it was simply that she was of an age to be settling down and having children of her own. Up to now, she had bypassed that route, but thinking about it, a distinct pang of loss ran through her.

For an instant, as she tried to imagine how things might be, she could see herself quite clearly with a family of her own, living in the beautiful, sprawling, mellow house with the orchard and acres of land. Subconsciously, hadn't she chosen it because it was a place where she could put down roots?

She thought about it some more. All the children in her surreal vision would not be like her, she was sure of that. They would take after their father, a man who was laid-back, carefree, taking life as it came…the complete opposite of her…

It was odd how these images clamoured to be seen, showing her two sides of a coin, almost as though she was fighting a battle within herself, and she tried to shake off the strange feelings that were assailing her. What was wrong with her? Perhaps she'd been overdoing things. That had to be the explanation.

Callum cut in on her thoughts. 'Perhaps we should go and see Jane while we have the chance?' he suggested.

She nodded, draining the last dregs of her coffee. 'She should be feeling a bit better by now, I expect.'

'Let's hope so. It's been twenty-four hours since the tumour was removed, and by all accounts the surgery went well. Her blood pressure is settling down nicely, too, according to the nurse on duty.'

'It all sounds positive, at any rate.' They left the lounge together and made their way up to the ward.

'It's good to see both of you,' Jane said with a smile as they entered the room. It was a small bay, with four beds, and she was sitting in a chair by the window, looking out over the hospital grounds. For the moment, she was the only occupant. 'The others have gone to the day room,' she told them, 'except for one lady, who's having physio.'

She caught her breath as she spoke, as though she was in pain, and began to rub absently at her side. Alex frowned. 'Are you all right? How are you feeling?'

'I'm okay,' Jane answered. 'A bit bruised, I think. It's gone a bit purple-looking around here.' She waved a hand vaguely over her upper abdomen. 'It hurts when I breathe, but that's probably only to be expected after the surgery.'

Callum was instantly alarmed. 'May I see? Has the doctor been to look at you since the operation?'

'Yes, dear.' She patted his hand, and allowed him to check the bruising. 'I went to have an ultrasound scan this morning...' She paused to gather her breath. 'I think they were just checking everything's all right. They didn't say much to me about it. The technician said she has to send the results to the doctor, and I'll be seeing him again, later today, apparently.'

Callum stood up, tension evident in his whole body, and Alex understood his reaction perfectly. The purple bruised area was not what they should have expected to see. 'Why wasn't I told about this?' he asked, almost as though he was talking to himself.

'I'm telling you now,' Jane said.

'But the medical staff should have kept me informed.' He shook his head, frowning. 'I must go and find out about this. I need to know what's going on. Excuse me. I'll be back in a little while.'

He left the room and Jane sighed. 'Oh, dear. Now there's going to be trouble.'

'I'm sure he'll be very thoughtful in how he goes about things.' Alex gave her a reassuring smile, keeping her own anxieties about Jane's condition to herself. Jane was looking worried, and perhaps the best thing she could do was wait until Callum returned with details of what was actually wrong before she made any comment.

'He loves you dearly, you know,' she said. 'He won't rest until he knows you're up and about and feeling strong again.' She gave her the get-well-soon cards the children had made for her. 'And you've made a lasting impression on James and Sarah, too.'

'Bless them. These are lovely.' Jane looked at the cards, Sarah's bright with a basket full of paper flowers, and James's a mouth-watering design of a delicious-looking cherry cake.

'James is looking forward to you being home and filling the house with the smell of baking,' Alex told her. 'He says it's the best thing in the world. Of course, to be fair to him, his instincts aren't entirely selfish. He's really fond of you…but he just loves your cooking, too.'

'Oh, he's a treasure.' Jane chuckled. 'He does so remind me of Callum when he was a youngster. He was always up to something, and he could wind me around his little finger when he wanted.' She paused to rest for a while, lightly rubbing at the ache in her side. Then she glanced at Alex and said, 'So, how are things with you? Are you managing with the children? I know it must be difficult for you, especially with your brother taking a turn for the worse.'

'We're coping,' Alex said. 'Martha's been a great help. I'm really glad you put us in touch with each other.'

'Well, I knew you would need some help.' Jane was quiet for a moment, studying her features. 'Something's wrong, though, isn't it? I could tell as soon as you walked in. You're not yourself. Is it the job? Or Callum? Have you two been fighting?'

'Me...fight with Callum?' Alex gave a self-conscious laugh. 'Heaven forbid! I'd never win... I thought I was strong-minded and on the ball, but he runs rings around me without even trying.'

Jane was very perceptive. Nothing much escaped her, did it? Even when she was ill. 'I think he feels I'm a workaholic.' She gave a faint sigh. 'I don't see how I can do things differently. I was given a job to do, and I'm getting on with it as best I can.'

'Ah, well, you shouldn't mind him too much. Most likely, he's speaking from personal experience there. His feelings go way back to his childhood, and it was always a bone of contention for him that his mother was so often away from home. Of course, she had an important job to do. He always understood that, and she always tried to make up for it once she was back with him. I dare say he has mixed feelings about the whole business of career women. I think that's why he's never settled down. I have the feeling he was put off by his parents' way of life—he saw how the idea of parents and family could go wrong and he doesn't want to risk that for himself.'

Alex frowned. He'd told her once, some time ago, that he preferred to be footloose and fancy-free, and she'd taken it to mean that it was just a temporary state of mind. But perhaps the hospital grapevine had it right after all...he was afraid of commitment.

Callum pushed open the door just then and came to join

them. He was still frowning. 'I just had a word with the doctor,' he said, going over to his aunt and sitting down beside her. 'It's nothing to worry about, but the reason you're feeling so uncomfortable is that during the keyhole surgery the space for manoeuvre was limited, and it seems that one of the instruments caused a blood clot to form on your liver. It's building up slowly, and that's why you're feeling so uncomfortable.' He glanced at her to make sure that she understood what he was saying.

Jane was puzzled. 'Are they going to do something about it? Or will it go away on its own?'

'The surgeon's going to drain it for you this afternoon, in an hour or so. He's going to come and talk to you about it in a while. It's not a difficult procedure, and he'll do it with the aid of the ultrasound monitor to guide him. He'll anaesthetise the area and give you a sedative, so you won't feel anything, and afterwards you'll be much more comfortable.'

'Oh, I see.' Jane fell silent after that, but there was tension in her shoulders, and Callum gave her a gentle hug. 'I'll stay with you throughout the procedure, if you like. I'll be there to make sure everything's all right.'

'Are you sure you'll be able to do that? Won't you be too busy with your work in A and E?'

'You're more important to me than my work,' he said simply, putting his arm around her. 'If it will make you feel better, then I want to be with you.'

She nodded, and relaxed a little, some of the stiffness leaving her shoulders, and Alex guessed she was more worried than she appeared. She wanted Callum to be with her. He was a comfort to her, and she thought the world of him, as though he was the son she never had. Watching them, Alex almost envied them their closeness. He thought the world of his aunt, and Alex could see that it was a bond that would never be severed.

They stayed and talked to her for a little while longer, and then Callum said reluctantly, 'We have to go back down to A and E to look in on a little girl, but I'll be back with you before you know it. Don't worry about anything.'

'I won't.' She clasped his hand as he lightly kissed her cheek, and then she waved them to the door. 'Go and see to your work,' she said. 'I'll be fine.'

Callum didn't say anything as he and Alex went down to the emergency department. Alex wanted to talk to him, she even opened her mouth to ask him how he was feeling, but he shook his head, cutting her off. His features were shuttered, as though he was working something out within himself, and she just had to accept that this was the wrong time, that she would be intruding if she pushed him to speak.

Just a few minutes later, they worked together to prepare the little girl for the lumbar puncture. She was still very poorly, and Alex was anxious to see that they made the procedure as painless and unobtrusive as possible for her.

'We'll give her a sedative first,' Alex told the nurse, 'and it would be better for her if her mother could come and be with her.'

The nurse nodded. 'I'll make sure we have some toys on hand in case we need to distract her.'

As soon as everything was in place, Callum injected the girl with anaesthetic around the area where they were to do the spinal tap. He waited for it to take effect, and then inserted a needle to withdraw some of the spinal fluid.

Alex labelled the vials and gave them to the nurse to take to the lab. 'We need the results urgently,' she told her.

Once they had finished, they made sure that Rachel was sedated enough so that she would lie still for the next hour or so. Callum checked her medication and made certain that everything was in order, before finally checking his watch.

'I should go,' he said, glancing at Alex. 'Would you take over for me while I'm away?'

'Of course,' Alex said quietly as they left the treatment room. 'You're worried about your aunt, aren't you?' She frowned. 'It's not a difficult procedure, to remove the haematoma, you know. I'm sure she'll be all right.'

He nodded. 'I'm not really concerned about that side of things.' His expression was bleak, his mouth flattening a little as they walked along the corridor. 'It's just that she has always been so strong in every way. Up to now, she's always been there for me whenever I needed her, she would look after me and comfort me when I was ill as a child, and now that the positions are reversed it hurts to see her looking so frail.'

His eyes darkened. 'She won't give any sign that she's worried or upset, but I know that deep down she's afraid and uncertain. And who can blame her? To think that these last few years she's been suffering all these symptoms of high blood pressure and I did nothing about it. I let the doctor go on treating her with tablets that were doing no good whatsoever. I should have spotted that something was wrong sooner and arranged for her to have tests.'

Alex laid her hand on his, causing him to come to a stop by the lift bay. 'As things turned out, you couldn't have done any more than you did,' she murmured, running her fingers along his arm in a gentle caress. 'It was normal procedure to treat her with medication in the first instance, and none of the tests would have shown the presence of a tumour until this late stage. Her condition is really very rare. You can't blame yourself.'

He wasn't convinced. 'You're very sweet, Alex,' he said softly, lifting a hand to gently cup her face. His fingers traced the line of her cheekbone and slid along the angle of her jaw. 'Thank you for trying to make me feel better... but I'm okay, you know. I can handle it. I just have to make sure that she knows I'll be there for her, come what may.'

The lift doors swung open, and they parted company as Callum headed back up to his aunt's ward. Alex turned away to go and seek out her next patient. She could still feel the light touch of his fingers on her cheek, and somehow that made her incredibly sad, and at first she didn't know the reason for that. Perhaps it was because it made her yearn for what she could not have.

Because there was no way she could allow herself to fall for Callum, was there? So far, he hadn't shown that he was the kind of man who was ready to settle down, and for her part, there was far too much going on in her life right now for her to even think of getting involved.

Why, then, was the temptation so irresistible? Right now was the worst possible time for her to be even thinking of starting a relationship, especially one with a colleague...and yet there was no getting away from the fact that she was filled with a longing that couldn't possibly be assuaged.

CHAPTER SEVEN

'It's good to see you finally taking time out to relax,' Callum said, sitting down on one of the comfortable patio chairs that Alex had set out on the raised wooden decking just beyond the back of the house. It stood amongst landscaped gardens, with rustic arbours and pergolas that were covered with rambling roses.

'I don't recall you giving me much choice,' Alex said grumpily. The sun was shining down on them from a clear blue sky and she was overheated and becoming conscious that she would have done better to wear a cotton skirt with her loose, sleeveless top, rather than her jeans. 'One minute I was repairing the boundary fence, and the next you'd taken over and sent me to make cold drinks.' She was still hot with indignation at being moved bodily out of the way and relegated to the kitchen. She had one day off this weekend to get things done, and he had come along and thwarted her plans.

'You have to admit, though, you weren't getting on too well, were you?' Callum gave her an amused look. 'If I hadn't stopped by to pick up some fresh clothes for Aunt Jane, you'd still be struggling with it now. Anyway, before that you were busy in the kitchen making goodies to take into hospital for her—that was very thoughtful of you, so I figured the least I could do was to help you out.'

He'd already helped her out a good deal over the last few days, coming along to fix the tiles on the roof and lend a hand with the painting. 'Well, I felt it was the right thing to do. She was looking so much better yesterday, so I thought she'd be in a mood to appreciate some cookies. And the children enjoyed helping to make them.' She could hear their voices now, coming from the orchard as they played amongst the trees that were burgeoning with fruit.

He nodded. 'I was worried about her, but everything went well, and it's beginning to look as though she'll make a full recovery. And the tumour was benign, so that was the best news of all.'

'Oh, it was such a relief to hear that. Now all she has to do is rest for a couple of days and then with any luck she'll be able to come home.'

'Let's hope so.' He looked at her, his mouth making a crooked line. 'That might work for you, too,' he said. 'You've been looking quite stressed lately, and I can't help feeling that you could do with some days off.'

'Well, don't hope for too much, because it isn't likely to happen.' She shook her head. They both knew they were miles apart when it came to the demands of her job. 'Though I suppose in the end I *am* glad you came along and stopped me today,' she admitted with a rueful smile. 'That fence has been bothering me for ages, and I was struggling a bit with the wood, where it had rotted.'

'Well, there are new planks in position now, so everything's secure and looking good once more.' He gazed around at the colourful, flower-filled garden and then looked beyond it to the meadow that bordered the apple orchard.

'You certainly picked a gem when you bought this place,' he said on a thoughtful note. 'And all your hard work is paying off at last. You've tidied everything up, the garden, the orchard…and after a lick of fresh paint the house looks like a beautiful, rambling old cottage. It's like something on a picture postcard, with the wisteria round the door and the natural stone wall with the plants growing in the crevices.' He frowned. 'And yet I bet you hardly have time to sit back and enjoy it.'

Alex was wistful. 'I certainly haven't until now. When I took it on, I wasn't at all sure I was doing the right thing— it was rundown and I knew it would be difficult to sort out, but I couldn't help myself—something told me it had potential.' She nodded towards him. 'You're right, it has been hard work, but with your help, we're gradually restoring it to its original state. Things are beginning to come together now really well.'

'I've been surprised how much I've enjoyed helping out.' He smiled. 'I think house renovation could become a new hobby for me.'

'You're certainly good at it. The old inglenook fireplace in the lounge looks great after being spruced up. I hadn't realised the house held so many treasures.'

She lifted the jug from the centre of the table and started to pour out glasses of chilled Sangria. Ice cubes clinked and mingled with slices of melon, apple, orange and lemon. She handed him a glass.

'Thanks.' He took a sip of the bright red liquid, and savoured the taste on his tongue for the moment. 'This is good,' he said, shooting her a quick glance. 'Is there some subtle ingredient I don't know about?'

'That depends on how you usually make it,' she answered. 'I put in red wine, orange juice and ginger ale, and then topped it up with fruit. I added a few cinnamon sticks, too.'

'It's delicious.' He peered at the slices of apple. 'It won't be too long before you're harvesting your own apples,' he mused. 'Have you thought about what you'll do with them? From the looks of things there are going to be masses.'

She shook her head. 'Apart from eating the dessert apples and making pies with the rest? No, I haven't. Though I suppose I could look into the whole business of cider making. At one time it was made here, on the premises, apparently, in all those old outbuildings.'

He smiled. 'And that will mean even more work for you. You're a glutton for punishment, aren't you? I suppose you wouldn't even consider the easy option, selling them to the local shops, would you?'

'I don't know.' She shrugged. 'Maybe. Though the idea of cider making is sort of intriguing—and it's what Somerset's all about, isn't it? So if I did decide to have a go at making my own, I would be part of it, wouldn't I?'

She leaned back in her chair, studying him through her lashes. He was probably right in what he was saying. It was in her nature to take on too much. As it was, she had been working frantically from early that morning, trying to catch up with her chores, baking and then tackling some of the repairs to the property, and it had taken Callum's determined efforts to make her stop. That had annoyed her. She had a limited time scale, and she'd been so intent on getting everything done, on ticking all the boxes and making sure things were in order, that when he had inter-vened she had put up a strenuous fight, only to lose out.

She was fast discovering that in his casual, unconcerned way he was every bit as strong-willed as she was. He was her opposing force, the common-sense counterpart to her frenetic power hub.

And yet, for all that, in the end, she was thankful for these few moments of peace and tranquillity that he'd given her. For all her misgivings, she felt better for sitting here, letting the sun warm her bare arms, and she had him to thank for that.

She liked the fact that he was close by, too, sitting back in his chair appearing calm and perfectly relaxed. And he was as heart-stoppingly good-looking as ever. He was dressed in casual clothes, stone-coloured chinos and a dark cotton shirt that emphasised his broad shoulders and brought out the intense blue of his eyes...eyes that were looking at her now and making her go hot all over. It was strange how just with a look he could make her heart quicken and cause the blood to surge through her veins like wildfire.

The sound of children's voices cut in on her reverie. 'We want to pick flowers for Mummy and Auntie Jane,' Sarah shouted up to her from the garden. 'Can we cut the sweet peas down by the fence?'

Alex stood up and went over to the deck rail. 'That's okay,' she said. 'Just make sure James is careful with the scissors.'

'I will.' Sarah's fair curls quivered with excitement. 'We want to decorate some flower baskets. Can we use the ones out of the greenhouse?'

'Yes, that will be fine. I'll help you with them later.' She'd have to, otherwise the sweet peas would probably end up bedraggled, with broken stems and crushed petals, and the flower basket displays would be haphazard and lopsided.

Callum came to join her by the rail. 'Flower baskets?' he queried. 'They won't be content with anything so simple as a bunch of flowers, then?'

She smiled. 'You don't know these children, do you? They don't do anything by halves. Next thing, I'll be sorting out flower-arranging plastic foam and helping them create something special in a wicker basket. They're always coming up with ideas for something or other.'

He laughed. 'They obviously take after you. Perhaps it runs in the family. Is your brother as doggedly determined and resourceful as you?'

A shadow touched her features. 'He was,' she said quietly, 'until he had the accident.' She shook her head. 'I just don't know how he's going to come through it. I don't know what to say to the children any more. I try to shield them from what's happening, but all the time I'm afraid for the worst.'

He put his arm around her. 'I'm sorry. That was thoughtless of me. You must be sick with worry.'

'I'm okay.' Her tone was flat. 'I'm just trying to take things one day at a time.'

'I suppose that's all you can do for now.' He held her close, letting his head rest against hers. 'You amaze me, Alex, the way you get on and cope with life. You don't let anything faze you for too long, do you? You have this marvellous ability to forge ahead and get through things, no matter what.'

She gave a faint smile. 'Some people simply say I'm stubborn and don't listen to reason, but that I keep on going regardless.'

He shook his head. 'I don't see it that way. I have nothing but respect for the way you deal with everything that comes along. Given what you've had to cope with, I suspect a good many women would have given up by now and settled for the easy life…a rented property, an undemanding job, keep the children quiet with videos and a selection of DVDs…but you've done the opposite. You've grabbed life head on and given it a good shake. I think that's remarkable.'

'I'm glad you think so,' she murmured. 'I just wish I

felt as strong as you imagine I am. For myself, most of the time, I feel bewildered, lost, under pressure, a little scared about what's to happen.'

He drew her into his arms and held her close. 'You don't have to feel that way,' he said softly. 'I'm here for you. Remember that. I'll do whatever I can for you.'

She lifted her face to him. He looked as though he meant it, as though his words were heartfelt, and it warmed her to think that he would want to be by her side in this, to help her through it. It was comforting to feel that she could rely on him to take some of the burden from her. 'Thank you,' she whispered. 'That means a lot to me.'

His head lowered a fraction, until his lips gently brushed hers, and in the next moment he was kissing her, slowly, with infinite care, as though she was the most precious thing in all the world. Alex gave herself up to that kiss, revelling in the feel of his long body next to hers, loving the way his hands moved over her and lightly shaped her body.

This was more than just a kiss. It was an expression of tenderness, of warmth, of wanting to take care of her, and yet, soon, it became much more than that. There was a growing passion, a sudden heated desire that started as a flicker and developed into an all-consuming blaze.

He deepened the kiss and his body moved to pressure hers, almost as though he would meld with her and claim possession. His breathing became ragged, and Alex clung to him, wanting more, overcome by the frenzied outpouring of sensuality that had overtaken both of them.

'I want you so much, Alex,' he said in a roughened voice. 'You drive me wild with wanting you. Somehow, when I'm with you like this, it's all I can do to hold back. You've put some kind of spell on me. I don't know what it is that you do to me to make me feel this way.'

She cupped his face with her hands, and then slid them down over the hard wall of his chest. She felt the same way. She wanted him, and it was an overpowering feeling, something that she'd never felt before with such intensity.

'This is madness,' she murmured huskily, her breathing coming in quick, short bursts. 'We're worlds apart, you and I.' But it was a madness that devoured her all the same, one that took over her soul. She returned his kisses with feverish abandon, running her hands over his arms, his shoulders, wanting more than this, needing him to show her that he cared enough to be there for her for ever. She was stunned by the intensity of her feelings. She had never before felt this way about any man.

It was an earth-shattering moment of realisation for her. Because, for all their differences, and despite all her guarded emotions, she realised she was falling for him. How had it happened? She was filled with doubts. Was it simply an overwhelming desire that had crept up on her out of the blue? She didn't know. She couldn't tell. She had never experienced anything like it before.

'Auntie Alex, come and see how many flowers we've collected.'

James's childish voice registered on Alex's consciousness like a bolt of electricity. It startled her and pulled her back into the reality of where she was and what was going on. She stared up at Callum and laid her fingers shakily against his chest.

'I have to talk to them,' she said in an unsteady voice. 'I have to see to the children.'

She eased herself away from him, and he let her go, reluctantly, watching her as she turned to look over the deck rail once more. 'You've been very busy, haven't you?' she managed, trying to keep her voice even. James's grey eyes were bright with enthusiasm, and Sarah was bursting with energy and eager to get on. The children had filled both baskets with the delicate flowers, more than enough to make a couple of gift presentations. 'Take them into the house and put the stems in some cold water in the sink. I'll be there in a minute or two.'

James nodded gleefully and ran off towards the house, leaving Sarah to follow.

'Are you all right?' Callum wound his arms around her once more and looked at her cautiously.

'I don't know,' she said. It was one thing for her to be taken up with the heat of the moment and to have given way to her emotions, but what was really going on inside his head? How did he actually feel about her? 'I feel a bit strange to be honest. I'm not sure I understand what just happened… I think I need to get my head straight.'

He smiled ruefully. 'That goes both ways, I guess. I can't say I was expecting to feel the way I do. Perhaps it's the midafternoon sun that's getting to both of us.'

She frowned, trying to gather her thoughts together. Was he regretting what he'd said just a few moments ago and trying to find a way out? Perhaps it was just as well that they'd been interrupted.

'Maybe.' She looked at him, her gaze troubled. 'I should go and see what the children are up to,' she said.

He nodded acknowledgement of that, and slowly released her. 'I know.'

She added hesitantly, 'Do you want to stay and have some tea with us?' She wasn't altogether sure how she would cope, having him close by for the rest of the afternoon. She was already overwhelmed and confused.

He shook his head. 'I think I'd better go,' he said with some reluctance. 'I promised I would take some clean nightwear into hospital for my aunt, along with a few bits and pieces she asked for, magazines and so on.'

'Okay. You could take the cookies in to her, if you like.'

'Will do.'

She saw him off a few minutes later, feeling sad to see him go, as though she was losing something special. Then she went back into the house and tried to push those thoughts aside and give all her attention to the children. She spent the rest of the afternoon making flower baskets with them. With any luck, they would stay fresh until they could take them along to the hospital.

'Can we go and see Mummy tomorrow?' Sarah asked. 'I want to see if she can come home soon.'

Alex nodded. 'I have to work, but Martha said she would take you there. She wants to go and see Auntie Jane.'

Alex's weekend break came to an end all too soon, and she was left feeling frustrated at not having achieved all she wanted, as well as being slightly out of synch. There were never enough hours in the day to do everything that was necessary, and it left her irritable and out of sorts. Perhaps the workload was beginning to get to her.

Worrying about her brother didn't help the situation. She pulled in her visits to Ross, Beth and Jane first thing next morning, before she started work, and that only added to her anxieties. Ross was in a bad way. He was breathless, breathing fast and he was complaining of chest pain.

'We're going to get an X-ray of his chest,' the nurse on duty told her. 'And, depending what that shows, the doctor might order a CT scan. There was a lot of trauma to his chest, initially, but after surgery we thought he was on the mend. This is a complication he could do without.'

Alex nodded. 'Will you let me know what happens? I'll be down in A and E, but you can page me at any time or use my mobile number.'

'I will.'

Things were no more settled down in the emergency unit. In fact, when Alex walked towards the department a few minutes later, she found her way to the main doors was blocked by a throng of news reporters, all shouting questions towards a small group of doctors and nurses.

'So how do you feel about the threatened closures?' one man asked. He thrust his recording device towards Katie, who was obviously the spokeswoman for the nurses.

'I believe it will do irreparable harm to patients,' Katie told him. 'They will be diverted to the new hospital some fifteen miles away, and that means treatment will be delayed for precious minutes. People who live locally are being denied the services they need.'

The reporter turned to the others and began asking more questions. 'Why is the board considering making this move?'

'It's all about budget cuts,' Simon Henderson answered. 'The hospital is running out of money.'

Alex worked her way to the fringes of the group. 'What's going on here?' she said urgently, keeping her voice low as she drew Katie to one side.

'Oh, you won't have heard, will you? You weren't here.' Katie frowned. 'Dr Langton's threatening to close the A and E department down at night. He laid the plans out in a circular he distributed to the staff late yesterday. He thinks we can save money by staying open for fewer hours, but it makes us think that will just be the beginning.'

'Is it actually going to happen, or is it just a threat?' Alex was bewildered by the news. 'Why have the press been called in? How did they get to hear about it?'

'As soon as we read the circular, we thought they should be kept informed. Maybe if the public know that their emergency department could be lost to them, they'll be able to influence the hospital board and persuade them to drop their plans. That's what Callum believes, anyway. He thought our idea of bringing in the press was a good one.'

'Callum? He's part of this?'

'Very much so.' Katie nodded. 'He's over there, speaking to a journalist from one of the nationals.'

Alex pulled in a sharp breath. 'I'll go and talk to him.'

Involving the press was a bad move, bad for everyone. It meant that people would be tense and antagonistic and much less likely to listen to reason, and it would probably irritate the members of the board and cause them to react in a negative fashion. This whole thing was wrong.

She turned to look back at the reporters as Callum's voice suddenly sounded loud and clear. 'If Oakdale's services are moved to the new city hospital, lives could be put in danger. We have to fight this. Asthmatics, patients with heart conditions or kidney disease—all these could suffer if they have to travel long distances for emergency treatment. This is a bad policy. It will be a bad day for the people who live locally if this plan is allowed to go ahead.'

Alex's expression was bleak as she watched him. He had the attention of everyone present. They were hanging on his every word, eager to capture his thoughts and take the story back to their newsrooms. How could he do such a thing without talking to her first? He knew how hard she'd worked to keep the unit viable by making savings, and he knew how much it meant to her to succeed.

She moved towards him, only to be waylaid by one of the reporters who read her name badge and thrust his tape recorder towards her. 'You're one of the managers here, Dr Draycott? What do you have to say about the proposed closure?'

She took a deep breath. 'I'd say that's all it is…a proposed measure. Nothing has been decided, and there are other options still to be considered. We've already made substantial changes to ensure the smooth running of the emergency department, whilst still being able to work within a limited budget—but there are other steps we can take. It's my opinion that services should continue to be provided here at Oakdale, and I shall be talking to the members of the board with suggestions as to how we can do that.'

The reporters threw a barrage of questions at her, but she stepped back, saying briefly, 'Excuse me, please. I have to go to work. As soon as there are any detailed announcements, please be assured you'll be the first to hear them.'

She pushed through the main doors and went into the A and E department. She pulled in a deep breath. How could she have been pushed into defending her ground like that? How could Callum have let it happen?

'You stood your corner well, back there,' he said, coming up alongside her a minute or so later. 'It must have come as a shock to you, to walk into that.'

'It certainly did.' She sent him a troubled glance. 'Why on earth would you want the press involved? And how do you imagine I feel, when you know how hard I've worked to keep things running smoothly? It's as though you've pulled the rug out from under my feet. You know Dr Langton can't make a move without the approval of the board—this was all unnecessary. I'd expected more from you. I'd hoped you would support me.'

'I do support you, and if you'd been here yesterday I would have brought you in on what we were planning— but, believe me, Dr Langton would have gone to the press sooner or later. As soon as we saw the circular, we realised he'd reverted to his old style. It's what he did when he worked at the other hospital, and we felt we had to gain the upper hand, one way or another. The new hospital building in the city is his pet project. It's beginning to look as though he has no loyalty to Oakdale. He thinks services should be centralised and that's what he's pushing for.'

'But Dr Langton doesn't have the final say in this.' She frowned. 'He's just one member of the board, and if the rest of them disagree he'll have to go along with the majority decision. You're all assuming it's a done deal. It isn't, and I'm just so disappointed that you could throw away everything I've done as if it was of no account, and that you have so little faith in me.'

'Alex, you're putting the wrong interpretation on this. It isn't that we don't appreciate what you've done. You've done your very best in a difficult situation. But going on past history, Langton is a law unto himself. He's totally single-minded, and once he's decided on something, he's not easily diverted.'

'We'll have to see about that, won't we? All I know is that you kept me out of the loop and went ahead without talking to me. I feel so let down.' She started to move away from him, her shoulders stiff, her whole body tense.

'This isn't about you, Alex, or the way you've done your job.' He caught up with her and laid his hands on her shoulders, his grasp warm and firm. 'It's about Dr Langton and his policies. You're overreacting.'

She was stunned by his comment. 'You think I'm over-reacting?' She shook her head. 'How exactly would you expect me to react? You're handing Dr Langton a pub-licity coup—how do you think he's going to respond to this? He'll bring out all the arguments for placing the new foundation hospital at the centre of things. Oakdale will become yesterday's news. Well, let me tell you—that's not going to happen if I have anything to do with it.'

'Alex, you need to listen—'

'No, I don't think so.' She started to walk briskly away from him, and didn't stop when he called after her. She was going straight up to Dr Langton's office to deal with this matter at its heart.

'I'm sorry, but Dr Langton is not seeing anyone at the moment,' his secretary told her when she walked into his office a short time later.

'I believe he'll see me.' Alex walked across the room and knocked on the inner door. Then she opened it and went in.

'Alex…' Dr Langton was startled.

His secretary followed Alex into the room. 'I'm sorry Dr Langton…' She hesitated, appearing flustered. 'I told her that you were busy and not free to see people this morning.'

'It's all right, Natalie.' He waved her away. 'You can leave us alone…just hold my calls for a few minutes, will you?'

Natalie withdrew, shutting the door behind her, and Dr Langton sent Alex a cautious look. 'You seem upset, my dear,' he said. 'Is there something I can do for you?'

'Yes, I'm upset.' Her glance ran over him. 'And, yes, there is something you can do for me. Perhaps you can explain to me why you've circulated plans to close down the A and E department without even consulting with me first of all. Wouldn't it have been a professional courtesy to keep me informed of what you had in mind? And perhaps you can tell me why are you even considering closure when there are so many alternatives available to us?'

'Ah…so you've heard about that?'

'Oh, yes. There's a gaggle of press outside the main

doors, all clamouring for information, and I was caught up in it without having any warning or knowledge of what it was all about.'

'The press?'

'The press,' she confirmed. 'Did you not expect word to get out?'

'Well, maybe not so soon...'

'The thing is, Dr Langton, I feel you should have kept me informed of your plans regarding A and E. You put me in a difficult position, having to defend management strategies. As I understand it, you think we can cut down on the hours that the department is open and gradually divert services elsewhere. Am I right in thinking that way?'

She waited for him to answer.

He cleared his throat. 'Ahem... It does seem to me that the community might be better served if services were more centralised. I felt that by putting out a circular we might put forward the ideas for change and at the same time gauge the reaction of the staff.'

'But you didn't consult with me first. I'm saddened that you didn't feel able to share your ideas with me—it might have saved a lot of distress if you'd done that—because unfortunately your circular has upset a lot of people.'

'I would have included you, of course, my dear, but the timing seemed right, with the board meeting coming up shortly. It was all a bit rushed, I have to confess, but I think the board members will most likely agree with my proposals.'

'Yes, it was rushed. And as you've said, the whole matter still has to go before the board. I have to disagree with your notion about the outcome. I don't believe the closure of the A and E department, at night or permanently, is a foregone conclusion at all. And I do feel that there are still so many proposals to lay before them so that they will think twice about any reduction in the A and E services.'

He spread his hands in an open gesture. 'Of course, you're entitled to your opinion. I know you've worked tremendously hard, but we have to think of these things on a larger scale. We have to think what would best serve the wider community.'

Alex's mouth firmed. 'We also have to think of the local community. Oakdale has a great reputation for being one of the best hospitals around, and its A and E unit is second to none. I won't see it obliterated in order to justify the expense of a foundation hospital. A good many people who live around here owe their lives to this emergency department, as do the tourists who come to the area every summer. Believe me, Dr Langton, I won't stand by and see it fall by the wayside.'

She left his office in a flurry of determination. After all the meetings she'd had with him, all the different ways she'd come up with to pare down expenses, he'd turned his back on her and gone his own way. Well, he would regret that. The board would hear of her ideas for boosting the hospital budget and there would be no more going through Dr Langton first—he hadn't been considerate enough to consult with her. Instead, she'd email her suggestions to them and follow them up at the next board meeting. She was on good terms with the other executive members and she would see what they had to say about all this.

She was still disturbed by the whole business when she went back to her office in A and E. She sat down at her desk and rattled off a round-robin email, pressing the 'send' button just as Callum knocked on her door and walked in.

'Is it safe for me to come in or are you likely to throw

things at me?' he asked, making a show of protecting himself with his hands.

'I don't find any of this the least bit funny,' she said in a dry tone.

'No, actually, neither do I.' He glanced at the computer monitor. 'I should say, though, it might not be wise to send off emails while you're upset.'

'Are you saying you don't trust my judgement?'

'I didn't say that.' He came and perched on the edge of her desk and she shot him a cool glance. 'I'm just warning you, that's all,' he murmured, 'in case you might do something you come to regret.'

'I don't regret any of my actions. Perhaps Dr Langton will think things through, though, after my visit to his office.'

Callum winced. 'You've been to see Dr Langton?'

'I have.'

'Was that wise?'

'I've no idea. It felt pretty good to me at the time.' She sent him a thoughtful glance. 'Have you come here to discuss my actions, or are you looking for a rundown on the latest management diktats and offerings?'

He frowned. 'And what would they be?'

She braced her shoulders. 'Here, I have a list. Perhaps you'd like to give me your opinion.' She pushed a piece of paper across the table to him. 'From now on, the pharmacist is going to pass to me any requests for prescription drugs that don't fit the criteria of generic or are expensive where cheaper versions are available. No more trying to sneak around the protocol and think it won't be noticed.'

He had the grace to look uncomfortable at that and she gave him a wry smile before going on. 'Another change that's about to happen—the cleaning contract was put out to tender, and a new team will be starting next week. I'm hoping everyone will do their best to make them welcome. And the cafeteria and restaurant likewise—they are being operated under new budgetary restrictions. But I'm sure people will find the meals just as nutritious and satisfying as before.'

She hesitated briefly, letting her words sink in. 'So, what do you think?'

He studied the paper in silence for a moment or two, and then said flatly, 'And those are just the tip of the iceberg. There are several more items written down here.'

'True.'

He raised dark brows. 'I hardly know what to say. I think you're formidable…like a steamroller.'

'Well, that's good, isn't it?' She made a fleeting smile. 'I think I'm quite pleased about that.'

His mouth twisted. 'It wasn't intended as a compliment.'

She shrugged and made a face. 'Perhaps it's all in the eye of the beholder. Was there anything else I can help you with?'

He put up his hands as though to ward her off. 'I don't think so. I can see that you're not in an altogether receptive mood, and I guess this is quite enough for me to be going on with.'

He left the room and Alex slumped back in her chair. She stared at the door long after he had gone. She felt as though all the air had left her body, and now she was thoroughly deflated.

She was utterly alone. The one man who had promised to support her, to be there for her, had gone and left her to her own devices. It all came down to a question of loyalty, didn't it? And it was beginning to look as though that was something that was distinctly lacking in their relationship.

CHAPTER EIGHT

ALEX stayed in her office for another half an hour, ostensibly dealing with managerial tasks, until the sounds of activity beyond her door intruded on her and drew her back into the mainstream of activity. She started working her way through the list of paediatric admissions, and when she was satisfied that their treatment was under way and all the necessary tests had been done, she went over to the reception desk.

'This has just arrived with the latest batch of lab reports,' Callum said, passing her a sheet of paper. He looked at her cautiously, as though trying to assess her mood. 'It's the test results for young Rachel.'

'It's about time,' Alex acknowledged. 'When I checked on her in the assessment ward first thing, she was still very poorly. The antibiotics don't seem to have done much to help, but at least her temperature's down and she's had no more seizures.'

He nodded. 'According to this report she has viral meningitis and encephalitis, but at least now we can start her on antiviral medication. I'm proposing to use acyclovir.' He gave her a wry smile. 'Does that meet with your approval, or will the pharmacist be blacklisting me?'

She scowled. 'Let's not resort to childishness, shall we?'

His mouth twitched. 'Sorry, obviously you need a little

longer to get yourself back in the right frame of mind. Maybe coffee would help?'

'Or perhaps getting on with the task in hand would do the trick.' Her grey eyes flashed with renewed vigour. She wasn't going to let him ply her with coffee and coax her into submission. 'Isn't there a patient waiting in treatment room three? A small child, so I guess that's probably one of mine.'

He nodded. 'I looked in on him earlier, and sent him for an X-ray. He should be back from there by now.'

She shot him a quick glance. 'Do you want to keep this case?'

He shook his head. 'I have to see a cardiac patient. Anyway, I'd better not get any more involved with young Kyle. His parents were bickering about the ruination of their holiday... I could feel myself getting hot under the collar at their attitude, so perhaps it would be better if you take over. I wouldn't trust myself not to say something untoward.'

Alex was astonished. 'Hot under the collar—you? That doesn't sound like the man I know. You're always calm and relaxed, no matter what happens.'

'Not this time. In fact, I may already have gone too far.'

She gave a wry smile. 'It looks as though we're both having one of those days.'

He nodded, and threw her a quick glance. 'It must be something in the air.' He picked up a chart. 'But, seriously, you have a different way of looking at things, and maybe you'll manage the situation better. Perhaps I could look in on you later, and see how things are going?'

'Okay.' She was glad to be able to get back to work. It was what she knew best, and while she was with her patients at least she didn't have time to think about annoying administrators or wonder about how Callum managed to get under her skin and cause her emotions to ebb and flow like mercury.

Her patient was a young boy, six years old, tousle haired, with tearful blue eyes. A nurse had placed a supportive sling around his arm, but he looked thoroughly miserable.

'I don't know what we're doing here,' his father told her. 'There's nothing wrong with him. He just had a bit of a fall, that's all. He should have been looking where he was going, and then he wouldn't have tripped over. Anyway, he's done it before, and he's been fine afterwards. His mother's mollycoddling him, insisting on bringing him here.'

'A bit of a fall that has left him unable to use his arm,' Alex remarked in a blunt tone. 'I believe that's something that needs investigating.' She glanced at the boy and saw that a single tear was sliding down his cheek. 'And I have to ask you to think carefully about what you're saying, Mr Dunbar,' she added quietly. 'Your son is obviously very upset. I'd prefer we keep things calm and try to soothe him as best we can while we find out what is wrong.'

'More mollycoddling.' He strode across the room and stood by the window as though to distance himself from proceedings.

Alex went over to the boy. 'Hello, Kyle,' she greeted him. 'I'm Dr Draycott, and I'm going to have a look at you and see what we can do to make you feel better.' She gave him a reassuring smile. 'Has the nurse given you something for the pain?'

He nodded. 'She gave me some tablets.'

'And are they helping?'

'Yes, a bit.'

'Hmm.' She gently examined his arm, frowning when

she discovered she couldn't feel the distal pulse. It was possible that a major artery was being constricted. 'There's quite a bit of swelling there,' she said, 'so I think we'll give you some medicine to help bring that down. Just excuse me for a moment, while I go and find a nurse to organise it.' Once the inflammation had settled down, it was quite possible that the pulse would be restored. If not, she would have to apply forearm traction as an emergency measure.

Katie was with another patient, but she agreed to bring the medication as soon as she had finished. 'I'll be with you in a few minutes,' she said. 'We're rushed off our feet here.'

'I know. I appreciate what you're up against.'

Going back to Kyle, she found his father pacing the room impatiently. 'We've been here for hours,' he complained.

Alex checked the waiting-time log. 'An hour and a half, to be exact,' she murmured. 'And in that time Kyle has been assessed by the triage nurse, looked at by a doctor, received painkillers and has been to Radiology for an X-ray.'

His mouth flattened. 'We were supposed to be setting out to meet up with relatives,' he said, 'my brother and his wife and their children. We were already late to begin with. They're coming all the way from London. Can't you just give him some more painkillers that we can take along with us? He's got his arm in a sling. Why do we have to hang around? What's the problem?'

Alex brought the image of the X-ray film up on the computer monitor. 'There's the problem,' she said, pointing to an area of bone around the elbow. 'It isn't very clear on this film, but I believe it's what we call a supracondylar fracture. These things can be quite complicated, and need careful attention.'

She examined the boy once more, worried that there might have been damage to nerves in the arm, or vascular injuries. She looked up as Katie came into the room, and smiled in acknowledgement before turning back to her patient. 'I'm going to ask another doctor to come and take a look at you, Kyle,' she said gently. 'He's a doctor who knows all about bones and joints and how to put them right.'

Kyle's father made an explosive sound of exasperation. 'Another doctor? What's going on here? You're a qualified doctor, aren't you? Or aren't you capable of deciding what to do about it yourself? It's not that difficult, is it? He's always falling over or getting into scrapes. It's never anything serious. It's just how he is. He's clumsy.'

Kyle's bottom lip began to tremble, and tears washed his eyes once more. Alex stood up. Enough was enough. 'I can see this is a trying time for you, Mr Dunbar,' she said, 'so I'm going to ask you to leave. Kyle is obviously upset and I'm afraid your attitude is not helping. Perhaps you would care to go and get a cup of coffee in the waiting room just across the corridor?'

'No, I wouldn't.' He glowered at her.

'No? Then I'm afraid you leave me no option but to call Security and have you removed,' she said, stepping closer to him and speaking quietly so that Kyle would not hear. 'Your son is in a great deal of discomfort, he has a broken elbow, which may require surgery, and I need to be able to concentrate on my work. I'm sure, when you've had time to think things over, you'll come to realise that your child's health and well-being is far more important than you being late for a meeting.' She studied him for a moment or two. 'So, have you made your decision? Which is it to be? Do I call Security?'

He face was a rigid mask as he turned away from her

and walked briskly out of the door. He didn't even look back to see if his wife was following.

'I must apologise for my husband,' Mrs Dunbar said, hurriedly. She was a thin, fair-haired woman, with blue eyes and features that closely resembled those of her son. 'He's been under a lot of pressure lately, but I'm sure he'll calm down before too long. A whole lot of things have gone wrong today, and he's a little uptight about this meeting with his brother and his family. They haven't seen each other for some time.' She gave Alex a quick look. 'I hope it's all right if I stay?'

'Of course. I'm sure Kyle will be glad of it.'

Alex went over to the phone at the side of the room to call for an orthopaedic surgeon to come and look at Kyle's arm. Katie was smiling, and as she came alongside her to prepare the boy's medication, she said softly, 'That was very well done, Alex. You and Callum must be two of a kind. The only difference is that Callum wasn't going to call Security, he was going to do the job himself until the man backed down.' She shook her head. 'It makes you wonder why some people bother to have children.'

'That's true.' So Callum had squared up to him? She couldn't imagine him doing anything so aggressive. It was so unlike him.

Alex went back to her young patient. 'It looks as though you've broken a bone in your elbow, Kyle,' she told him, 'and things are a bit out of place there, so a doctor needs to put them right for you. I think what will probably happen is that Mr Adams will come along and fix things for you. He'll give you something to make you go to sleep, so that you won't feel anything while he does it.' She looked at him. 'Is there anything you'd like to ask me?'

He shook his head. 'I don't think so.'

'Okay.' She turned to his mother. 'What about you, Mrs Dunbar? Do you have any questions?'

'Only one, really…do you have any idea how long will it be before his arm is better?'

'I couldn't say for certain…it really depends what Mr Adams, the surgeon, makes of it…but it's a longish job. It could be up to twelve weeks before function is restored, and overall it might take six months before things are completely back to normal.'

'Oh, dear.' Mrs Dunbar put an arm gently around her son. 'Not to worry, Kyle. Everyone's going to take good care of you here.'

'But Dad doesn't believe me.' Kyle hiccupped and chewed at his lower lip, still distressed. 'He thinks I'm making it up.'

'And your dad's going to be very sorry when he realises that you've really hurt your arm.'

Callum came to see how things were going some time later when Mr Adams was making his assessment.

'Luckily, he's had nothing to eat or drink for a few hours,' the surgeon said, taking Alex and Callum to one side after he had spoken to Kyle's mother, 'so I'll see him up in Theatre in about half an hour. And we'll admit him for observation. I don't foresee any problems, but you never know with these things.'

'Thanks,' Alex said. 'I'll make the preparations.'

She left the room with Callum some time later, leaving the boy in Katie's capable hands.

Callum checked his watch. 'It's getting late. Shall we go and get some lunch? There's nothing urgent going on here, and you look as though you could do with getting away from the hospital for a while.' He glanced at her. 'You're a bit pale, and I guess being here isn't helping very much. I know a pub not too far from here where they do a great lasagne—their honey-glazed ham is delicious, too. What do you say?'

She thought it over, but prevaricated. 'It sounds good, but I'm waiting for news about my brother. He took a turn for the worse this morning, and I want to be on hand in case they get back to me.'

He sucked in a sharp breath, his blue gaze running over her features. 'Alex, I'm sorry. You didn't say a word... I wish you'd told me, instead of trying to cope on your own. What is it...his lungs? You said the doctors thought he was fighting an infection, didn't you?'

She nodded. 'But I think this is something more. The nurse said they were worried about him. She's going to let me know if there's any news.'

His mouth firmed. 'This is all the more reason for you to get away for a while. I think you've had about as much as you can handle for one morning. The pub is only a ten-minute drive away. We'll come back the instant we hear anything.'

'And what about A and E? Oughtn't we to stay around?'

'You're entitled to a proper break. There's another consultant on duty, plus the registrar, and in any case, we can be reached by phone. Katie will let us know if she hears of anything major coming in. Besides, you're not even supposed to be on clinical duty this afternoon, are you? This is one of your management days, isn't it?'

'Yes, it's true.' She sighed. 'You know, I think you're right, I could really do with getting away for a while, but I can't help thinking it would be unwise to leave the hospital grounds right now. At the same time, I feel as though I'm on a roller-coaster ride, going up and down and round and round, and now, all of a sudden, I just want to get off.'

'Then that's exactly what you'll do.' He took hold of her

arm and led the way along the corridor to the main doors, stopping off on the way at the main desk to tell the clerk where they were going. Alex felt a strange sense of relief that he was taking charge.

They walked out to the car park. 'You're positive it isn't far away?' she said, a frown creasing her brow.

'I am.' He held open the car door for her, and she slid into the passenger seat, leaning back against the soft leather upholstery, relaxing in the sheer opulence of this luxurious vehicle. It even smelled new, and she closed her eyes and breathed in the subtle fragrance of expensive leather and wax polish.

They drove for a while through the Quantocks, past heather-clad moorland and rolling hills, where sparkling streams meandered by scattered villages and small hamlets. Soon they reached a charming country inn, and Callum drew the car to a halt on the forecourt.

'It's lovely,' Alex said, stepping out of the car and gazing around in wonder. 'Just look at that open countryside. It's so peaceful.'

'I thought you'd like it. Come inside, and we'll see if we can find a table by the window. The service is pretty good here. You don't usually have to wait too long for your meal.'

Alex chose seared breast of chicken wrapped in bacon and served with a tangy sauce, creamed potatoes and vegetables, while Callum opted for the lasagne.

'They make the sauce for the lasagne with red wine, tomato and Italian seasoning, as well as onion and mushrooms,' he told her. 'It's delicious.' He dipped a fork into the lasagne and offered it to her. 'Here, have a taste. Tell me what you think.'

He slid the food into her mouth and she savoured it for a moment or two, conscious all the while of his gaze centred on the ripe curve of her mouth before it moved along the slender column of her throat.

'Mmm…you're right, it's lovely.' She sent him a quick, mischievous glance. 'You just did that to make me doubt my choice, didn't you?' She made a weighing action with her hands. 'Chicken and bacon on the one hand…lasagne on the other… What to do…what to do?'

'You've changed your mind?' He smiled. 'That's all right, I'll swap you, if you like. It really doesn't matter to me.' He began to push his plate towards her.

'No…no, really, I was just kidding.' She held up a hand to stop him. 'Keep it, please. I'm perfectly happy with what I've chosen.' She sent him a quizzical glance. 'Trouble is, you're not used to seeing me in a teasing mood, are you? You see me as straightforward, always concentrating on work. I expect you think I'm not capable of letting my hair down.'

He shook his head. 'I don't know about that. I think you could be absolutely fabulous at letting your hair down, given half a chance.' His eyes glinted, his gaze moving slowly over her, taking in the smooth line of her dress that clung where it touched. His glance lingered. 'That's definitely something I'd love to see…but unfortunately I get the feeling it's highly unlikely.'

Alex felt her cheeks flush with heat. She could imagine spending time with Callum, getting close to him, experiencing the thrill of being in his arms, knowing the touch of his hands on her body…but she was coming to realise that she wanted much more from him than just a passionate fling.

It had never happened to her before. There had never been anyone who had made her feel this way, but now she knew she wanted a relationship that would last.

But where Callum was concerned, wasn't that just a

flight of fancy? She couldn't help feeling that in the long term she simply wasn't his kind of woman. He would never choose to spend his life with a career woman. His soul mate would be someone who was relaxed and tranquil, someone who could share his philosophy on life, instead of a woman who caused him problems on a daily basis.

'The trouble is,' he said, bringing her back to the present with a jolt, 'you never have time to simply be yourself.' He tasted the lasagne and was thoughtful for a moment. 'There are always too many demands on you…like this morning, for instance. You were plunged into that press conference out of the blue, and that's probably why you—'

He broke off, and Alex finished for him. 'That's probably why I reacted the way I did this morning.' She gave an awkward smile. 'I'm sorry about that. You were just doing what you felt to be right.'

'Still, it's perhaps just as well that we showed Dr Langton we wouldn't let him get his own way without a fight. He'll keep pushing it.' Callum paused, his fork halfway to his mouth. 'Anyway, what did you say to him? Did you ask him about the circular?'

She nodded. 'I told him that I had some proposals of my own to put before the board.'

'Good.' He frowned. 'In fact, just before we came away, I heard he's organising a meeting with the board for tomorrow to bring it to a vote. That could turn out to be a turning point for all of us…but with you there to back our cause, I imagine we stand a better chance.'

'Maybe. Though, going on what we talked about the other day—renting out services, and so on—I've already put forward some money-spinning suggestions to the board in the emails I sent out. They won't be popular with everyone, but I'm hoping they'll at least have time to think about them.' She took a sip of her iced drink, a pure fruit juice topped up with lemonade. 'It all depends whether they agree with my way of thinking…but either way, I don't see how we can do any more.'

He curled some creamy strands of cheese around his fork. 'We could try to get a licence to run a lottery. That should bring in quite a bit of money for the department, and there are always raffles to be run every now and again. I'm on the fundraising committee and we have some good people who are willing to put in a lot of time and effort for the cause.'

'They get results, too, judging by the new portable X-ray machine we've just acquired.' Her mouth curved. 'You're not at all what you seem, are you? You appear to be quiet and unassuming and altogether laid-back, but one way and another you achieve an awful lot behind the scenes, don't you? I'm thinking about the way the doctors and nurses look up to you and respect your decisions…and then there are those seriously ill patients you manage to edge higher up the waiting lists, not to mention the way you handle the press.'

He made a dismissive movement with his hands. 'What's the point of being in high places if you can't manipulate the odds from time to time?'

She chuckled and finished off her chicken and bacon, laying down her knife and fork.

'Would you like dessert and coffee?' he asked, and she nodded.

'Oh, yes, please. I've had my eye on the toffee pudding they have in the glass-fronted display case over there. And coffee would be great, thanks.' She toyed with her serviette while he called the waitress over to take their order.

'I'll have the apple pie,' he said, handing the girl the

menus. She nodded, giving him a dimpled smile, and he responded with a gentle curve of his lips.

Watching them, Alex felt an immediate, involuntary stab of jealousy. The force of it shocked her to the core. What was wrong with her? Why did it matter that he smiled at a girl in a restaurant? She frowned. The truth was, she was beginning to care for him deeply, but how could she ever compete with all those pretty girls who knew how to take life as it came and simply enjoy being around a good-looking, easygoing man?

She didn't know how to be his type of woman. She was here with him now, enjoying a wonderful meal in a romantic country inn, and hadn't she spent most of the time talking about work?

Callum glanced at her, a small line indenting his brow. 'Is everything all right? You look anxious all at once.'

'I'm fine.' She tried to get a grip on herself. He was too perceptive by half and it wouldn't do to have him know what she was thinking. 'I'm glad you brought me here,' she said. 'It's good to be able to relax and enjoy the comfort, and the great food, as well as to look out over the hills. It just makes me wish I could do it more often. Of course, it's difficult with the children.'

He nodded. 'You could always bring them with you... except I don't suppose you'd be able to relax too much, knowing how those two get into everything.' He sent her a crooked grin. 'They certainly keep you on your toes.'

'True.'

He shot her a quick look. 'You must be really pleased with the way things are shaping up at home. The trees in the orchard look healthy and strong, and it looks as though it will be a good crop. But I still can't imagine how you settled on such a place. I could see you in a small, executive-type home, with all the mod-cons, something easy to manage, with no fripperies, but I've never picked out a rambling farmhouse with acres of land, in a month of Sundays.'

'You see me living a very orderly life, don't you?' She smiled. 'I must say, nothing's been straightforward these last few months. Far from it. I've had to come to terms with a whole new way of life, but I've found that I'm actually enjoying the farmhouse side of it. It's the one place where I feel contented. I think the children are happier for being there, too.'

'Where will they live when your brother and his wife come home from hospital? Didn't you say they used to rent a place before the accident?'

'That's right. Ross had relocated because of his job, and was renting while he looked around for something suitable. I expect they'll do the same again.'

She studied him. 'But what about you? I haven't seen your house, but I imagine you living in something like a barn conversion, with lots of books and a plasma TV and music centre.'

He laughed. 'Completely wrong, I'm afraid. I have what they call a studio apartment not too far from the hospital. I don't need anything grand, because it's just me living there. It's basically open plan, with a mezzanine floor where I have my bed…and my books. There are definitely lots of books.'

'And the building work you mentioned a while back?'

'I had the garage extended, and a wall built around the back of the garden. It's only small piece of land, but it goes with the apartment, and I wanted to keep it secluded.'

She shook her head, trying to imagine how he lived. 'That's not at all what I expected,' she said. 'You drive a fantastic car, you wear expensive, beautifully tailored clothes, and I expected your house would be equally grand.'

He shrugged. 'When I bought it, some years back, I didn't see the point in owning anything more than a bachelor pad. Not that it's under par in any way... I've been told it has the wow factor that everyone goes on about these days. But the fact is, I was young and I didn't see any reason to settle down, start a family and so on. I suppose I looked at the way my parents lived their lives and decided that maybe marriage and commitment weren't for me. My parents were never in one place for long and, no matter how they tried, they weren't able to look after me properly.'

'Not all families are like that.'

'No.' He winced. 'But you see those like the Dunbars, where everything is supposedly normal and yet beneath the surface there are all those tensions bubbling away...a father who thinks more of his own agenda, rather than caring for his son. I wonder sometimes if they're representative of a good many families. I don't know. I just see so many broken relationships, children left without steady parenting, and it makes me think that's not the sort of thing I would want for myself.'

Alex didn't comment on that. She didn't know what to say. Instead, she dipped her spoon into her toffee pudding and let it rest there for a moment or two. Callum had said he didn't want marriage or commitment—or at least, that's how he had felt when he'd first bought the apartment, and yet she'd come to realise that those were the very things she wanted. All these years, she'd been relaxed about how she viewed relationships, but things had changed. She'd met Callum, and she'd discovered that for her, it was all or nothing.

If he was still keen on the bachelor way of life, it seemed that she had been right to be cautious about getting involved. Trouble was, it was way too late for that now.

CHAPTER NINE

'OH, GOOD, you're back.' Katie greeted Alex and Callum as they walked into A and E after spending their lunch break. 'Your niece and nephew arrived a few minutes ago with your neighbour, Alex—she said her name was Martha. I'm afraid the children are a bit upset—they've been asking for you. I suggested they might like to wait in the staff lounge. I thought it would be a bit more comfortable for them in there.'

'Thanks, Katie. That was thoughtful of you.' Alex's heart had started hammering, going into alarm mode at the news, but she tried to stay calm as she asked, 'Do you happen to know what they're upset about? Is it my brother?'

Katie nodded. 'I think so. It sounds as though he's in a bad way and they weren't expecting to see him like that. The nurse didn't realise they'd gone in to see him until it was too late.'

Alex took a steadying breath. 'I'll go and see if I can smooth things over. Thanks again, Katie.'

'You're welcome. I found them some paper and coloured pencils, and one or two toys to try to keep them occupied for a while, but I don't think they can settle to anything.'

Alex nodded. 'I knew I should have stayed here,' she

said under her breath. 'I just knew something would go wrong.'

Callum laid a restraining hand on her arm. 'Don't start blaming yourself,' he advised her. 'Take a deep breath and stay calm. You had lunch, nothing more, and they've only been here for a few minutes. You can't be at everyone's beck and call every minute of the day. They'll come through this. You'll all come through it.'

'I'm all right.' She was beginning to feel increasingly agitated. 'I must go.'

'I'd like to come with you. Is that okay? I might be able to help in some way.'

She nodded, and they hurried along to the staff lounge.

They found Sarah in tears, sitting on one of the sofas, while James was trying to keep a stiff upper lip but was unable to disguise his shaky, ragged intakes of breath. He looked at Alex with bewildered eyes, not really knowing what was going on but sensing the tense, unhappy atmosphere in the room.

'I feel terrible about this,' Martha said, coming to meet Alex. She was a sensible woman, middle-aged, with gently waving brown hair and grey eyes that were troubled. 'I'd no idea Ross was in such a bad way or I'd never have taken them to see him.'

'What happened?' Alex tried to suppress her anxiety, wanting to stay calm and composed for the sake of the children. 'Did the nurse tell you what was going on?'

Martha shook her head. 'She wouldn't tell me anything about his condition, because I'm not a relative.' She lowered her voice. 'But he looked terrible…pale, with beads of sweat on his face, not breathing properly. He was very weak.'

'Daddy couldn't talk to me,' Sarah said, the tears welling

up in her eyes and spilling over. 'He couldn't sit up in bed or do anything. And the nurse had to help him lean back against his pillows.' Her voice began to wobble. 'I tried to talk to him, but he couldn't answer me. His mouth moved but nothing came out and then the nurse put a mask on his face.' She began to sob.

Alex went to sit down on the sofa between the two children. She put her arms around Sarah and held her close. 'I'm sorry you had to see your dad looking so poorly,' she said softly. 'I know the doctors and nurses are doing everything they can to make him better.'

Sarah's sobs became louder. 'But it's not working.'

Alex hugged her, and laid an arm around James's shoulders, squeezing him gently. He, too, had given way to tears. 'Have you been to see your mother?' she asked.

James nodded. 'We gave her the flower basket.' He pulled in a shuddery breath. 'She said she thought it was lovely.'

'That's good, isn't it? You know, she's doing so well, I expect she'll be coming home soon. You'll like that, won't you?'

'Yes. She said she'd be home in a few days. She wants to come and live at your house for a bit.' He looked up at her. 'Can she?'

'Yes, of course.' She glanced at Sarah to see if any of their conversation had managed to divert her, but the little girl was locked into a cycle of misery.

'I think I should take them home,' Martha said quietly. 'They wanted to stay here and see you, or we would have gone earlier.'

'I know. Thanks, Martha.'

Sarah turned tear-drenched eyes on Alex. 'I want you to come home with us.'

'I'll come in a little while, Sarah.' She glanced at her

watch. 'I have to finish my shift here, just another couple of hours, and then I'll be home with you.'

It wasn't what she wanted to hear, and Sarah started to cry all over again.

Callum went down on his haunches beside her. 'You know, Sarah,' he said in a quiet voice, 'your mother wouldn't want you to be upset like this. She'd want you to be strong, so that you can take care of your little brother. He doesn't really understand what's going on, but if he sees you being all grown up and getting on with things, it will be better for all of you.' He paused, waiting to see what effect his words were having on her. 'Maybe you could go home and start preparing a room for your mother. Put some flowers in it, perhaps make up a fruit basket, or make something for her that she'll enjoy when she comes home.'

'Like a little box for her rings?' James's eyes lit up with enthusiasm. 'We did some paper curling at school...we could make a lid with some decorations on it.'

'They call it quilling, I think,' Martha said. 'I've some coloured paper we can use. Shall we go home and give it a try?'

James nodded, wanting to go right away and get started, but Sarah was still reticent. 'I don't want you to stay at work,' she said, looking earnestly at Alex. 'I want you to come home with us.'

Callum stood up, laying a gentle hand on her shoulder. 'She won't be long.'

'I'll be there before you know it,' Alex told her. 'Go home with Martha now, and I'll follow in my car. I won't be long, I promise.'

They left a few minutes later, with James full of ideas about the box he was going to make and Sarah still subdued. Alex watched them go and then, as the strength drained out of her body, she reached for a chair and sank down into it.

'You know, you could have gone with them,' Callum murmured. 'You don't have to stay here, and it's obvious they need you. Sarah must have been very shocked by what she saw, and she clearly needs reassurance—perhaps that's something only you can give her. Martha's doing her best, but she isn't a relative. The children have already gone through the distress of knowing their parents were injured in a road accident, and now this is an added stressor.'

'Do you think I don't know that?' She resented his implied criticism. 'Do you imagine all I ever think about is work? I want to be with them, I want to make all this go away, but I can't.'

Perhaps she had been too sharp in her retort, because his head went back a fraction, light flaring in his blue eyes, his mouth making a straight line, and she was instantly conscious of the fact that he was only trying to help. The last thing she needed right now was to get into an argument with Callum.

'I have to go and see my brother and find out what's gone wrong,' she said. She felt as though she was caught up in the middle of a whirlwind. These last few months had been a nightmare and she was about at the end of her tether. Her brother was dangerously ill and she needed to go to him. He was her priority right now.

'Of course you do.' He frowned. 'But I don't think you should be on your own right now. I want to be there with you.'

A feeling of relief shot through her at his understanding. She gave a faint, almost imperceptible nod, and they left the room together.

When they arrived at the intensive care unit Alex found that her brother was every bit as ill as Martha had said.

'He looks so much worse than he did this morning,' she said in a whisper, and Callum laid a comforting arm around her shoulders. It was plain to see that Ross was in a bad way. He was deathly pale, and the constant bleeping of the monitors around him warned of a galloping heart rate and a worrying lack of oxygen in his blood.

'We've been doing tests all morning,' the nurse told her, 'but Dr Allingham looked at the CT scan a little while ago and said he has a pulmonary embolism. I was just about to page you.'

Alex pulled in a shaky breath. A blood clot on the lung was a dreadful diagnosis. Depending on its severity, it could mean the difference between life and death, and, judging by Ross's condition, this was the worst news she could have received. A blood clot in one of the main arteries could cause his circulation to fail, and the damage to his lungs would mean he couldn't get enough oxygen to his tissues.

'What is Dr Allingham going to do?'

'He started him straight away on anticoagulants, and he's prescribed thrombolytic therapy. It will take a while, of course, but he's hoping that we'll see initial results within the next twenty-four hours. After all Ross has been through, he wants to reserve surgery as a last option.'

'I can understand that.'

She looked at Callum, her eyes bright with tears, and he said softly, 'They're doing everything they can for him. At least they've found out what's wrong, and now they can do something about it.'

'I know.' It didn't make it any easier to bear, though. Who could say if the medication would work quickly enough? Anticoagulants would thin his blood and prevent any more clots from forming, while the thrombolytic therapy would begin to dissolve the clot, but this was a race against time.

Callum gently drew her head down into the crook of his shoulder, and she nestled against him for a moment or two, absorbing the comfort he offered. Tears trickled down her cheeks, but she was soothed by his steady support. He was strong and reliable, and by being with her right now he was showing her that he cared about her and her brother.

After a while she managed to gather herself together. She glanced at the nurse. 'I'd like to stay with him for a while, if that's all right?'

The girl nodded. 'Of course.'

She stayed with Ross for a few minutes, talking to him even though she couldn't be sure that he heard her. She told him how Beth was becoming stronger, day by day, and how the children were looking forward to him coming home. 'You've always been a fighter, Ross,' she said softly. 'You can do it. You can get through this.'

When she was ready to go, she walked with Callum to the car park. 'I could drive you home,' he said, but she shook her head.

'I'll be all right. Thank you for staying with me.'

'I wanted to be with you.' He hesitated. 'Maybe when your brother is better and things are going more smoothly for you, we could spend some time together…maybe take a trip somewhere. I think it will do you a world of good.'

She nodded. 'Maybe.'

The children were quiet when she picked them up from Martha's house and took them home. James, being younger, was vaguely aware that something bad was happening, but it wasn't at the forefront of his mind. He could be distracted fairly easily. Sarah was much more difficult to handle. She was a sensitive, loving child, and intelligent enough to recognise that her father was in great danger.

She'd always been Daddy's girl, and this was hard for her to take in. She knew there was a chance that he might not come through this latest setback.

'Shall we do some baking?' Alex suggested when they were back in the farmhouse kitchen. 'I thought we might make an apple-and-blackberry pie and take it round to Auntie Jane. She's only just home from hospital, so she's not up to doing very much for herself yet. I expect she'd be glad of some home cooking.'

Sarah nodded, and James went to fetch the pastry board and rolling pin. 'I love apple-and-blackberry pie,' he said. 'Do you think we'd better make two?'

'Definitely. That's a very good idea.'

By keeping them busy, Alex managed to calm them down over the next few hours, but she wasn't at all sure how she was going to handle things the next day. Instinct told her she should stay home with them, but she was supposed to be on duty at the hospital and Dr Langton had called a crucial meeting for the afternoon.

'Are you going to work today?' Sarah asked her at breakfast next morning. Her expression gave nothing away, but she didn't quite look Alex in the eye, and there was the merest flicker of a glance from under her lashes as she tried to gauge Alex's response.

Alex hesitated. 'I thought I'd stay here with you,' she said. 'We could go and see Auntie Jane this morning, and perhaps we might plant those dahlias for her—the ones that she bought before she went into hospital. And of course there will be a lot of weeding to do.'

'Yay! I want to do that,' James said, cramming a piece of buttered toast into his mouth.

Sarah relaxed visibly, her shoulders sloping as though a great weight had been lifted from her. She came over to Alex and gave her a hug. 'Can we phone Mummy later today? I want to tell her about the room we're getting ready for her and Daddy. She said Gran and Grandad were going to visit her this afternoon, so I might be able to talk to them as well.'

'Okay. That sounds like a good idea. It's good that your gran and grandad have been able to come to see them, isn't it?'

Sarah nodded. 'They said they wanted to see me and James as well. Grandad said his job was all done and they were coming back to stay at their house in Somerset.'

'That's good news, isn't it? I expect they'll come and see both of you very soon.'

In the meantime, Alex was still in a quandary about work. She wasn't sure what she was going to do about Dr Langton's meeting, but the least she could do was to warn Callum that she wouldn't be there. She called him after she had rung the hospital for an update on her brother.

'I'm going to stay at home with the children today, and probably tomorrow as well,' she told him. 'I think it's for the best.'

'I wondered what you would do,' he said. 'Is everything all right? Are they okay?'

'They seem to be,' she said. It was good to hear his deep voice. It was somehow reassuring, as though he was close to her even though the miles separated them. 'They're a lot more settled, having me here with them. Things are probably a lot better all round this way. Dr Langton seems to think so, anyway. That's the impression I had when I spoke to him on the phone a few minutes ago. I get the feeling he's pleased I won't be there to spike his guns.'

'Hmm. How do you feel about that?'

She was quiet for a moment. 'A bit deflated, really, and anxious because I might be letting people down. But I don't see any way round the situation. Sarah's not saying very much, but she's on the verge of tears a lot of the time, and what she's not saying is speaking volumes, if you know what I mean.'

'Yes, I think I do. I can understand why you've chosen to stay with them. As to the meeting, it's a pity I'm not on the committee, or I could stand in for you and state your case. Let me give it some thought, and I'll see if there's some way we can get round it.'

'Thanks, Callum.' She didn't think there was anything much he could do, but she was glad of his offer to help. He was without exception caring and thoughtful, ready to step in where he was needed, and she was coming to realise that he was someone she could rely on in her darkest hour.

'I'm happy to do what I can,' he said. 'Is there any news about Ross?'

'Only that his condition is much the same. At least he isn't any worse. I haven't told Beth yet. I didn't want to worry her, and I'm hoping Sarah won't say anything when she phones her this afternoon. I'd sooner tell her if and when he appears to be on the mend.'

'That sounds reasonable enough to me. Keep your chin up. Just remember I'm here for you if you need me.'

'I will. Thanks.' She was sad when he cut the call, because she wanted to go on hearing his voice. It filled the empty void and made her feel that she was not alone, just for a few minutes. She wanted to be with him.

In truth though, wasn't she kidding herself? He was concerned about her and he was offering to help, but what did he really feel about her? Yes, he was caring and sympathetic, and he had shown her that he would be there for her, but how deep did his feelings go? He might be attracted to her, but that might be as far as it went.

And who was she to complain about that? Wasn't that how she had viewed things, to begin with? Her career meant everything to her, and there had never been much time for anything else. She had been reasonably content. There had been no one who might have persuaded her to set it all aside…until now, until she had met Callum. He had proved himself to be a man apart from all others. He was quiet, strong and steady, and he had tried to show her how to take herself less seriously.

And perhaps his efforts had achieved a result. After all, she had changed over these last few months. Perhaps looking after her brother's children had shown her a different way of life, had taught her that home and family could take precedence over ambition.

She sighed. Musing on all this wasn't getting her anywhere. For now, she had to put aside her thoughts about Callum and concentrate on the children. They needed her, and she ought to be keeping them occupied instead of standing here wool-gathering.

'We need the gardening tools,' she told them, calling them back into the kitchen a few minutes later. 'Gardening gloves, forks, trowels and the bag of plant food out of the greenhouse. We'll need compost, too.'

'I'll get the food,' James said. 'Sarah can bring the tools.'

'I'm not carrying all that lot on my own,' Sarah complained, scowling at her younger brother. 'You can help.'

'Nah.'

He threw her a mutinous, cheeky glance and ran off, leaving Sarah to say crossly, 'He's always doing that. Daddy says he… Daddy said—' She broke off, biting her lip to stop it from trembling, and Alex put her arms around her and gave her a hug.

'I'll help you with the tools. I'll talk to James in a little while—just as soon as I manage to catch him,' she said.

They spent the morning with Jane, planting dahlias in

her sunny border, while she sat in a garden chair and offered them cold drinks from an iced jug.

'You look so much better than you did a while ago,' Alex told her, coming to sit beside her and take a break for a while. 'Has your blood pressure settled down yet?'

Jane nodded. 'Yes, it has. And I'm healing up nicely, too, so I'm beginning to feel as though I'm on the mend at last.'

'That's really good news.' Alex took a long swallow from her glass. 'That was a bit of a scare you had, back in the hospital, wasn't it? I know Callum was worried about you.'

'He's a good man. He's always looked out for me, and made sure that I was getting on all right.' Jane was quiet for a moment or two, and Alex guessed she was thinking about the way he had helped her over the years. 'I know he has a difficult job to do at the hospital, and sometimes he has a lot on his mind, with all the worries about patients, and so on. He cares about people, you see. And I know he's concerned about these threats to close the unit down. He said he'd written to the board members, telling them of the risks to patients if services were to be transferred to the city.'

'Has he?' Alex was surprised. 'He didn't mention that to me.'

'No, well, I think he feels you have enough to cope with already. He didn't want you worrying about what he was doing and saying.'

Perhaps he had been put off by her reaction when he'd gone to the press. Alex made a face. It was her own fault that he didn't confide in her. Just lately she had been edgy and out of sorts, and who could blame him for going it alone?

Still, he'd offered to try to sort something out before

the meeting this afternoon. Would he be able to come up with anything? She wanted to put her views to the board, and it would have been much better to do that in person rather than through an email that some members might not even have read.

She took the children back home an hour or so later. 'Why don't you go and play in the orchard for a bit while I make lunch?' she suggested.

'I want to stay here, with you,' Sarah said quietly. 'I don't want to play. Do you think Daddy is all right?' Her voice quavered. 'I heard the nurse say that he might not make it without an operation.'

Alex frowned, and Sarah hurried to add, 'She didn't know I was there. She was talking to another nurse.'

Alex studied her thoughtfully. She had been clingy all morning, not wanting to stray far from her side, and that made her realise that it was probably a wise decision she had made to stay home with her. What was it Callum had said? The children needed a relative at a time like this. 'I'm sorry you heard that,' she said. 'It must have been upsetting for you, but the nurse said she would ring me if there was any news about your father—if he had taken a turn for the worse. Even so, I'm going to phone her now, to find out what's happening. After that, you can talk to your mum, if you like.'

Sarah nodded. James took himself off to the garden to play on the old rope swing, and Alex dialled the hospital number. Best to do it now, and hopefully put Sarah's mind at ease, along with her own.

'There's been no major change,' the nurse told her, 'but his blood oxygen level has risen very slightly. Dr Allingham thinks that could be a good sign, but he says Ross has quite a way to go yet.'

'Thanks.' Alex relayed the news to Sarah. 'It means we

still have to wait and see, but at least it's not bad news.' It was difficult to know how to handle this kind of situation with a young child. She didn't want to be negative, but at the same time she didn't want to fill Sarah with false hope. The consequences of that could turn out to be disastrous.

She left Sarah talking to her mother and grandparents a few minutes later, and went into the kitchen to prepare a salad for lunch. Her mobile rang as she was slicing peppers, and she wiped her hands on a towel and went to answer it.

'Hi, there,' Callum said, and her heart warmed at the sound of his voice. 'How are things? Are you managing all right with the children? Are they coping?'

'James is fine,' she answered, 'but Sarah's finding things difficult. We just rang the hospital to see how Ross was doing and there's been no real change as yet.'

'These things take time. At least they've made the diagnosis and started to act on it. A good many pulmonary embolisms go undetected until it's too late.'

'I know.'

'And how are you? Are you bearing up?'

'I'm okay.' She wasn't going to tell him how she really felt, her worries about her brother or her fears for the children's well-being. For the moment, it was enough for her that he had called. His voice was deep and soothing, like a balm to her overwrought senses.

If only he could be here with her right now. Suddenly, she wanted to see him, to be with him. She wanted to have him hold her and reassure her that everything was going to turn out all right. Just being in his arms would have given her the strength to go on.

'How about you?' she asked. 'Your aunt said you were

concerned about what was going on at the hospital. She said you'd written to the board.'

'That's true. I thought it might help. Actually, I've been thinking about the meeting this afternoon, and I've a suggestion to put to you. You don't have to consider it...you might have other plans, or you might want to walk away from it all, given that you've so much on your plate right now.' She could hear the frown in his voice. 'Though I think you should know that most of the staff appreciate how hard you've worked ever since you started the job and they're all behind you in this.'

'I'm glad about that. What was it you wanted to ask me?'

'It occurred to me that you could still take part in the meeting if we set up a video link. I could fix it from the hospital end—it would give me an excuse to be in on the meeting if I have to monitor the link, so I could maybe add my twopenny worth to anyone who cares to listen. And anyway the executives have asked for one or two representatives from non-board members to be present— and you could set up the software and web-cam on your laptop from your end.'

She thought about it for a while. Having Callum take part in the meeting was another bonus point. 'It sounds feasible, but I don't know how well it would go down with the board if Sarah or James were to come and interrupt every few minutes.'

He chuckled. 'That's one of the hazards of working from home, I suppose. You could always bribe them to keep quiet with fizzy pop and cookies. Not very politically correct, but quite effective at times, I'm told.'

'Yes, you're probably right.' She came to a decision after a second or two. 'I dare say I'll think of something. Will you let me know when you've organised it at your end?'

'I will.' There was a smile in his voice. 'Thanks, Alex. I owe you one.'

'Let's just hope it goes well. I'll do my best, but I can't promise anyone will listen.'

He rang off, and Alex went on with her preparations for lunch, trying to think of ways to keep the children amused while she attended the virtual meeting.

'How about you look through the DVD collection and choose something to watch while I'm talking to the people at work?' she suggested, taking the easy way out. 'I really need you to promise not to interrupt me unless it's something very important. Do you think you can do that?'

'Yeah…if we can watch space aliens,' James announced eagerly.

'Space aliens are rubbish,' Sarah told him. 'We should watch the one about the animals who escape from the farm.'

'Nah…that's a girly film. I'm not watching a girly film.'

Alex intervened. 'You have five minutes to choose something you both agree on,' she said briskly, 'or I'll choose for you.'

Half an hour later, she was seated at her desk in the study, talking to the hospital executives. Callum's image appeared on her computer monitor, almost centrally on her screen, and it was a huge comfort to her to be able to see him, even if he was not there with her in the flesh.

'You already know of the many savings we've made in the A and E department,' she said, addressing the board in general. 'We've gone almost as far as we can down that route. Perhaps the time has come to think of the situation from another angle.'

'Another angle?' one of the executives challenged her. 'What are you suggesting?'

'I think we could look at ways to bring money into the hospital.'

He frowned. 'And how do you propose to do that?'

'There are some areas that are underused for one reason or another. I'm suggesting that we could rent out certain wards and theatres to the private sector. There's also the scanner—it isn't used from six o'clock in the evening unless there is an emergency—and it seems to me that's another opportunity for us to earn income from the private sector. Fee-paying patients will benefit from having treatment out of hours, and the hospital will gain by getting a badly needed cash boost.'

'This is the NHS,' Dr Langton said dismissively. 'The principle has always been that it is free for those in need of medical help. NHS treatment and private medicine don't mix. The two are incompatible.'

Alex nodded. 'I know some people find the idea of private medicine unpalatable. I've always believed in the principle of the NHS, that treatment should be free for everyone who needs it. But the private sector serves a purpose for those who don't want to wait to see a specialist or be put on a long waiting list for surgery, and in these days of cash-strapped hospitals perhaps this is the time for radical thinking. A good many hospitals have already gone along this route, with great success. With the money earned from the private sector, we could keep the department open and make changes that would benefit other areas of the hospital.'

Callum intervened. 'I think Alex is right. With extra money we could streamline some of the services we already offer and make them more efficient. We could set up a minor injuries unit to be run by nurses and a doctor—maybe a GP—and we could add a new mini-stroke unit, which would have a preventative role and eventually save patients from progressing to major problems—which in themselves would cause further strain on our limited resources.'

The discussion went on for another hour before Dr Langton drew the meeting to a close.

'Thank you, everyone,' he said. 'Obviously, a lot of points have been made here today, and they will need some consideration. I suggest that the executive board meets again tomorrow to make its final decision.'

Alex gazed at the screen. She had done what she could and now they simply had to wait for the result.

Callum's glance meshed with hers. His expression mirrored her thoughts, saying, 'That's it for now. There's nothing more we can do.'

She looked for something extra in his eyes, something that would show her a hidden message, perhaps, a hint that he wanted to be with her…but there was nothing. He simply turned away as one of the executives began to speak to him, and a few minutes later the video link was cut.

CHAPTER TEN

ALEX wandered aimlessly about the house next day, trying to decide which job she ought to do next. Nothing appealed to her or filled her with enthusiasm. The trouble was, she didn't feel inclined to do anything. All she really wanted was to talk to Callum, to hear his voice. Better still, she would have liked to be with him.

She reached for the phone before she could change her mind. 'Hi, Callum,' she said. 'I hope you don't mind me disturbing you at work. Are you busy?'

'Alex...' She could hear the smile in his voice. 'You can call me at any time. In fact, I was about to call you myself. It's quiet here just now...no major accidents, just a waiting room full of the walking wounded. Of course, we're all waiting for news of the board meeting, but we won't get that until a little later.' Then he added on a concerned note, 'Anyway, how are you? Are you all right?'

'Yes, I'm fine. I just...' She let the words trail off. Perhaps it had been a mistake to call him—she never made the first move with any man, and she was acting completely out of character—but for once she had thrown caution to the wind. 'I'm on my own here,' she said, 'and I just wanted to talk to you for a while...not about anything in particular.'

'You're on your own? How did that come about?'

'My parents came over just before lunch and took the children out for the afternoon.'

'That's brilliant,' Callum said. 'You must be glad of the break.'

'Yes, it's lovely for the children to be able to go out with their grandparents. The thing is, Mum and Dad are back here to stay now, in Somerset, and they say they'll be around to help out from now on...which is great news. I just wasn't expecting it and, to be honest, I'm not used to having the place to myself. I'm feeling a little strange...a bit lost, somehow. I know that must sound odd.'

'It doesn't sound odd at all to me. You've been through a difficult time lately, and you're used to working at full stretch.' He chuckled. 'It isn't every day you get the chance to play hooky.'

'No.' She smiled. 'I suppose not.'

He sobered. 'Is there any news about Ross?'

'Yes,' she said brightly. 'They say they're cautiously optimistic. His oxygen levels are better and his breathing is a little easier. Actually, I was thinking of going in to see him in a while.'

'That's a good idea. It will cheer you up to see him looking better.' The smile was back in his voice. 'Maybe I could go with you? I could come and pick you up, and then we can play hooky together?'

She laughed. 'But you're at work...are you saying you're going to take time off? That isn't like you.'

'No, it isn't,' he agreed. 'But I have a half-day owing to me, and it seems to me that this is as good a time as any to take it. Besides, I want to make sure that you're all right.'

'I am, thanks.'

'Good. Well, perhaps after you've been to see Ross, we

could go out for the afternoon and make the most of the sunshine. What do you say?'

'I'd like that…if you're sure you can get away.'

'I can. I'll come and pick you up in half an hour.'

She was glowing inside when she cut the call a second or two later. She looked around. It was only just dawning on her that everything she'd done, all the loving care she'd poured into this place was for nothing if she didn't have Callum by her side. And now her dreams were coming true because he was on his way home to her.

The doorbell rang some half an hour later, and she hurried to answer it.

'Hi,' Callum said, as she pulled open the door. He rested a hand against the doorpost and gave her an engaging grin.

She couldn't stop the smile from spreading across her face. 'I was half-afraid you would change your mind,' she said. 'I thought if an emergency cropped up you'd have to stay at the hospital.'

He shook his head. 'We've enough people on duty to cover this afternoon.' He sniffed the air. 'Is that coffee I can smell?'

'Yes, come in, and I'll get it for you.'

He followed her into the kitchen. He looked like perfection to her, long and lean and totally masculine, wearing dark trousers that moulded his long legs and a cotton shirt that was open at the neck to give a glimpse of lightly bronzed skin.

She passed him a mug, and he sipped the hot liquid as he glanced around. 'It's very quiet in here without the children. I don't know whether that's a good thing or a bad thing. I think I could get used to the sound of their banter.'

'Me, too. I've loved having them around.'

'Still, it gives us the chance to slip away, doesn't it? After we've called in at the hospital, I thought we might take a trip to Cheddar Gorge and see the sights if you want?'

She nodded, her spirits soaring. 'I'd like that.'

'Good. Maybe we'll have lunch when we get there, and then take a wander around the place? I don't know how you feel about exploring the caves, but the whole area is beautiful.'

'So I've heard.' It didn't really matter to her where they went. Just being with him was enough for now.

They called in at the hospital a short time later. Ross was still being given supplemental oxygen, and he was breathing faster than normal, but he was propped up against his pillows and he was able to talk to them, which filled Alex with hope.

'It's good to see you, Alex,' Ross said, taking his time with the words. His grey eyes were filled with warmth. 'I feel we owe you so much, Beth and I.'

'No, you don't.' She glanced at the monitors, glad to see that the readings were coming down to a more normal level. She could hardly believe that this was the man who had been so near to death a couple of days ago. 'I'm just so happy to see you looking so much better than before. Has Dr Allingham been in to see you today?'

'Yes, he came just about an hour ago. He seemed pleased.' He rested for a few moments, leaning his head back against his pillows, a lock of brown hair falling across his brow. Alex looked at him with affection. 'He said there was a chance I might go home in a couple of weeks if I go on making progress. I'll have to carry on with the medication for a few months, but he thinks I'll be able to build up my strength better at home.'

'That's brilliant news.' Alex gave him a hug. 'I told Beth

you could all stay at my house until you find a place of your own. You haven't seen it yet, but I know you'll like it. There's plenty of room. It's an old farmhouse I bought, with extensions that have been added on over the years.'

'Thanks for that, Alex. You're a treasure.' He glanced at Callum, who was standing quietly by her side. 'I don't think I've seen you before, have I? You must be someone special... Alex is very cautious about who she lets into her life.'

Callum smiled. 'Yes, I've begun to realise that over this last couple of months. It hasn't been easy, getting to know her as well as I'd like.'

'Well, just as long as you do right by her. I love my sister. I don't want to see her hurt.'

'I'll take good care of her, you have my word,' Callum said.

Alex sent him an uncertain look. That sounded as though he meant it. Did it mean he was planning on staying around, being part of her life?

They left her brother a few minutes later so that he could get some rest. 'Sarah will be so happy when she hears the news,' Alex said as they walked out to the car park.

Callum nodded, laying a reassuring palm on the small of her back. 'You must be relieved. Perhaps now that your mind's at ease you'll be able to relax and enjoy the rest of the afternoon.'

'Definitely,' she said, looking up at him and drinking in his features. For the first time in ages she felt as though life held some very real promise.

Suddenly, the quiet was disturbed by the bleeping of Callum's phone. His mouth flattened. 'Sorry about this,' he said, gently releasing her so that he could answer the call.

He spoke to the person on the other end of the line for

a minute or two. 'Thanks, Katie,' he said after a while, and Alex looked at him curiously. Why would Katie be phoning him?

'It's good news,' he said, cutting the call and putting his phone back into his pocket. 'The board has posted its decision—the A and E unit is safe. They're going to follow some of your suggestions to bring in money from outside. And it looks as though my mini-stroke unit is a go, as well.' He grinned. 'You realise, don't you, Miss Bean Counter, this means I'll probably get my Doppler ultrasound machine after all?'

'Oh, Callum, that's great news.' She flung her arms around him. 'I hardly dared hope they'd go for it.' Then she leaned back a fraction and looked him in the eyes. 'Bean Counter?' she said, lifting a brow. 'Is that going to be my title for evermore?'

'Hmm. I'll have to think about that. Maybe we could change it for something else.'

'I should hope so.'

He smiled. 'Perhaps we should be on our way. I'm starving, so I think we should find a place to eat first of all.' He pulled open the car door for her. 'I know this great place just as you come into Cheddar.'

'Another one? How come I don't know these places?'

'Probably because you've had your nose to the grindstone for way too long. It's high time you learned how to loosen up and enjoy life.'

'And you'll show me how to do that?'

'Oh, yes.' His blue gaze travelled over her, his eyes filled with promise. 'I'm making it my very next project.'

He set the car in motion, and headed for the main road that would take them towards the Mendip Hills and on to Cheddar. Alex watched as the landscape changed from gentle slopes to rugged hills and deep gorges. It felt strangely as though she was travelling towards some new destiny, but perhaps that was due to the sheer excitement of being with him on this glorious afternoon, free as a bird for once. She wasn't going to think about the future, she decided. She was just going to take life as it came.

They stopped at a pretty, stone-built inn, made colourful with window-boxes full of flowers and hanging baskets spilling over with bright surfinias and trailing silver-leaved ivy.

'We could sit outside, if you like,' Callum said, leading the way through the inn and showing her the gardens through the open glass doors. There were bench tables set out in a courtyard that had been decorated with foliage plants and tubs of scarlet begonias. Beyond that were landscaped gardens, where flowering shrubs bordered a wide sweep of lawn.

'Yes, please, that would be lovely.' She could feel the sun warm on her bare arms, and on her legs where her light cotton skirt flowed delicately and skimmed her calves.

For his meal, Callum chose fillets of sea bass, served on a bed of roasted vegetables, whilst Alex went for a pork steak, topped with an apple-and-cider relish, and finished off under the grill with Cheddar cheese.

'They make the cheese just along the road from here,' Callum murmured, as he watched her spear the topping with her fork. 'Have you heard the legend about how it came to be made?'

'No, I haven't.'

'Well, apparently a milkmaid left a pail of milk in one of the Cheddar caves, and returned some time later to find that it had turned into a tasty cheese. Whether that's true or not, I don't know, but even today they mature the cheeses in Gough's Cave, wrapped in muslin cheesecloth.

They say the tangy taste is due to the rich grazing pastures around here.'

'So if we visit Gough's Cave, we'll see them?' She thought about that. 'And probably smell them.'

He chuckled and lifted his fork to taste the succulent fish. 'Among other things, yes.'

Some time later, full up and satisfied after a meal that had been finished off with fresh fruit salad and liqueur coffees, they set off in the car once again. Alex was relaxed and happy. Her only niggling desire was that Callum should put his arms around her, but of course he wouldn't do that. They were in a public place…and she couldn't help wishing that they could be somewhere else where they could be totally, utterly alone.

He sent her an oblique glance as they drove along the road towards Cheddar. 'You're very quiet. Is everything okay? You're not worried about your brother, are you?'

'No, I'm fine. I'm sure he's going to be okay. I'm having a great time. It's just good to be out here under a perfect blue sky, and it's taking me a while to get used to it.' It wasn't like her to be this way…hung up on getting close to a man…but Callum was different. He was gentle and thoughtful, and it was totally restful, being with him.

They were opposites, though. He was good for her, but was she good for him? She'd always been ambitious, following her career, and by all accounts that was the kind of woman he would rather steer clear of in the long term.

It was some half an hour later when they reached Cheddar Gorge. The scenery was spectacular, and Alex marvelled at the ravine, and its sheer-sided cliffs, cut out of ancient limestone. The banks were rich with greenery, and there was the occasional crop of wildflowers here and there, adding tiny patches of colour.

'Have you been here before?' Callum asked as he parked the car.

She shook her head. 'I've heard all about it, though. They say it was formed by a river some three million years ago, and then the Ice Age came, and after that the meltwater carved out the gorge.'

'I think that's probably right. Shall we go and take a look at Gough's Cave? It's the biggest one, and it's well worth seeing.'

'It would be a shame not to, while we're here.'

'Good.' He clasped her hand in his and she felt the thrill of his touch glide along her arm like a ripple of warm silk. They walked to the cave and went inside, and before long Alex was marvelling at the weird and wonderful formations that had been brought about by water dripping through the limestone over millions of years.

It was awe-inspiring. In one chamber, impressive stalactites were reflected in a pool below, giving an impression of a village perched on a mountain top. In another chamber, huge stalagmites reached high up into the roof and water droplets were reflected in the cavern's lights so that they sparkled like crystal.

Alex shivered slightly in the cool atmosphere, and Callum immediately took off his light jacket and wrapped it around her, drawing her close. 'We can't have you getting cold,' he said. 'We don't want you ending up like the man they found in here, do we?'

Alex was shocked. 'What man? What happened to him?'

Callum laughed softly. 'He was young, apparently, and he was buried here some nine thousand years ago. His skeleton was found intact, and they've even managed to extract DNA from his tooth cavity, to show that he still has relatives living in the area.'

'You're joking!'

'No, it's true, believe me.'

She smiled. 'That's some family history—if you were searching for your ancestors, you'd hardly expect to go so far back, would you?'

'You wouldn't.' He held her close, walking with her back through the caves, until they emerged out into the sunlight once more.

She handed him his jacket. 'Thanks for that,' she said. She was reluctant to let it go. It had been warm from his body, and it had bought her nearer to him than she had been for what seemed like a long time.

He slung it over his shoulder, holding it with one hand, while he clasped her fingers with the other. 'Shall we walk by the river for a while?' he suggested.

'Yes, that sounds good.' She looked up at him. 'Somehow, I don't want the day to end. I know it must, eventually, but it's been so good, I want it to go on and on.'

He laid his arm around her shoulders. 'That's how I feel, too, and I think it's done you a world of good. You needed a break after all that's been happening. You certainly look better for it. There's colour in your cheeks and your eyes are sparkling.'

They walked towards the fields and the river, taking their time, ambling along and enjoying the lushness of nature all around them. By the riverside, Alex spotted a kingfisher searching for prey in the water, and further on there were two white egrets, shuffling their feet in the shallows.

It was glorious and so peaceful, and they stopped and sat for a while on the grassy bank in the shade of a broad oak tree, watching the sunlight playing over the water.

Callum eased himself closer to her. He looked at her,

his gaze wandering over her features, over the smooth line of her cheekbones and the soft curve of her cheek. Then he bent his head and dropped a kiss on to her soft mouth, surprising her and starting up an array of tingling sensations that ran from her lips right down to the soft centre of her abdomen.

'Oh,' she said huskily. 'What was that for?'

'Just because.'

'Because what?'

'Because it was something I just had to do. Because your lips are soft and inviting and it's all I can do to resist you.' His fingers caressed her cheek. 'Because I've been wanting to do that all day.'

'Oh.' She was finally speechless. She gazed up at him, loving the feeling of being close to him, of having his long body mesh with hers.

His blue eyes glinted, his gaze trailing over her as though he would absorb her features into his memory.

'It's been great to see you looking so relaxed. We'll have to find more opportunities to take time out and explore different places together. I want to spend a lot more time with you.'

'Funny, that…I was thinking the same thing.'

He nodded. 'It doesn't matter where…the beach, meadow walks, your place or mine…just as long as we're together.'

She smiled at him. 'It's what I want, too.' She was quiet for a moment. 'Strange, isn't it, that I've never seen your place? I was beginning to wonder if it was some kind of sacred bachelor pad…your very own sanctuary.' Her expression became wistful. 'You more or less said that's what you intended when you bought it.'

His mouth made a crooked shape. 'People change. I changed…at least, I changed when I met you.' His glance flicked over her. 'I'm not alone in that, am I? Hasn't the same thing happened to you? You used to live in a rented place, and then you came down here and bought that rambling old property. I always wondered why you took it on, especially at a time when you had so much else on your plate. I think your subconscious mind was telling you that you needed to settle down, to be part of a family unit, and that house would be the one place where you sensed could be truly happy.'

'You think so?'

'Mmm-hmm. Though it's going to be a little more crowded than you expected, quite soon, from the sound of things, when your brother and his wife move in with you. I think it's great that you're doing it, but are you going to be happy with that?' He tugged her closer to him as though he needed to feel the softness of her curves against his taut, masculine body. His hands stroked the small of her back, moving over the swell of her hips.

'I think so.' She snuggled up against him, cherishing the moment. 'I want to see Ross and his family reunited, and they need somewhere to stay while they recover from their injuries. Beth's come on by leaps and bounds, and I'm sure she'll soon regain her strength. I think Ross will take a little longer, and he needs to be perfectly fit before they can go house-hunting...unless Beth does it for them. At least his job is being kept open for him. The company wants him back.'

Callum smiled. 'That's good.' He lowered his head to hers and kissed her once again, taking his time, exploring the softness of her lips, moving against her as though he couldn't get enough of her.

Alex was in seventh heaven. This was way more than she could have hoped for, to have him kiss her and hold her and make her feel that she was everything to him just then. She ran her hands over his shoulders, his arms, trailing her fingers over the length of his spine.

'That feels so good,' he murmured, his voice roughened as he dragged his mouth reluctantly from hers. 'But every time I hold you I think it's not nearly enough. I want us to be together.'

She gave him a cautious look from under her lashes. 'I'm not sure what you're asking.'

He laid his cheek against hers. 'Do you think you might want to move in with me for a while, once Ross and Beth are settled in your house? I know my apartment is a bit small, after what you're used to, but we can at least be together, alone, private.'

She hesitated, drawing back a little and laying her palms flatly against his chest as she looked up at him. 'You're suggesting we live together?' Was he saying he wanted just a casual fling, no strings attached? Her spirits plummeted. She wanted so much more than that.

He nodded. 'Just until Ross and Beth find a place of their own. I mean, I really like the children, and it's great having them around, and I'm sure I'll get along fine with your brother and his wife…but I really would like to have you to myself for a while. I know it's a lot to ask of you, but once they find their own house, I can put my apartment on the market.'

She frowned. 'Why would you want to do that?'

'Like I said, I've changed. Why would I need a bachelor apartment any longer? I've fallen in love with a woman who has the perfect family home. We could spend a lifetime together there.'

Her mouth dropped open a little. 'Is this your way of telling me that you love me?'

He nodded. 'I do love you, Alex. We're like two opposite halves, but we fit together so well. I just know we could make it work…if you would agree to be my wife. After all, you said you didn't want to be Miss Bean Counter, didn't you? Mrs Brooksby has a nice ring to it, don't you think?'

A soft sigh escaped her. 'I thought you were asking me to move in with you, for us to live together without any kind of commitment.' She looked up at him, her expression quizzical. 'I thought you said you never felt the need to settle down, that marriage and commitment weren't for you?'

He nodded. 'That was all true…until I met you. Then after that everything was different. It took me a while to realise what was happening. I couldn't believe that I'd fallen for someone who was so strong and career minded—the very opposite of what I thought I wanted—but you showed me that you know instinctively what's more important. You showed it when you came down to Somerset to look after Sarah and James, and you showed it again when you took the time off work to be with them. I know things are going to work out just fine for us, Alex.' He looked at her intently. 'I just need you to tell me that you love me too, and that you want me as much as I want you.'

'I do.' She gave a soft sigh. 'I never knew that I could feel this way. I never met anyone who could make me feel the way you do. You're so calm and relaxed, you don't let things throw you, and you know exactly how to cajole me into seeing what really matters. And at the same time you're single-minded and so good at what you do. You're the perfect man for me…the only man for me.'

She tilted her face to his and kissed him tenderly. 'I love you,' she murmured. 'More than anything in the world. And I'd love to be your wife and move into your apartment…' her mouth curved '…just as long as we get back to the farmhouse as soon as possible.'

He breathed a sigh of relief. 'That's just wonderful. For a long while, I've felt as though there was something missing from my life, but now I feel complete. Just as long as I have you, life will be everything I ever wanted.'

'Funny, isn't it?' she said softly, reaching up to kiss him once more. 'That's exactly how I feel.'

THE MAN
BEHIND THE BADGE

BY
SHARON ARCHER

First published in Great Britain 2011
by Mills & Boon, an imprint of Harlequin (UK) Limited,
Eton House, 18-24 Paradise Road, Richmond, Surrey TW9 1SR

© Sharon Archer 2011

ISBN: 978 0 263 88589 7

Harlequin (UK) policy is to use papers that are natural, renewable and recyclable products and made from wood grown in sustainable forests. The logging and manufacturing process conform to the legal environmental regulations of the country of origin.

Printed and bound in Spain
by Blackprint CPI, Barcelona

Born in New Zealand, **Sharon Archer** now lives in County Victoria, Australia, with her husband Glenn, one lame horse and five pensionable hens. Always an avid reader, she discovered Mills & Boon as a teenager through Lucy Walker's fabulous Outback Australia stories. Now she lives in a gorgeous bush setting, and loves the native fauna that visits regularly… Well, maybe not the possum which coughs outside the bedroom window in the middle of the night.

The move to acreage brought a keen interest in bushfire management (she runs the fireguard group in her area), as well as free time to dabble in woodwork, genealogy (her advice is…don't get her started!), horse-riding and motorcycling—as a pillion or in charge of the handle-bars.

Free time turned into words on paper! And the dream to be a writer gathered momentum. With her background in a medical laboratory, what better line to write for than Mills & Boon® Medical™ Romance?

Recent titles by the same author:

BACHELOR DAD, GIRL-NEXT-DOOR
MARRIAGE REUNITED, BABY ON THE WAY
SINGLE FATHER: WIFE AND MOTHER WANTED

*My thanks to lovely friends
Anna Campbell and Nikki Logan,
and especially Rachel Bailey, for listening
and for the chance to bounce around ideas.*

And always my thanks to Glenn!

CHAPTER ONE

TOM JAMIESON reached into the cabin of his four-wheel drive and slotted the handpiece of the police radio back into its cradle. He straightened, stripped off the yellow reflective safety vest and tossed it on the passenger's seat. The perspiration that had made his black T-shirt cling had begun to cool. Flexing his tired shoulders, he ran a hand over his face and felt the stubble rasp across his palm. It had been a long day and a longer evening but, for all the frustration, it had been oddly satisfying.

He smiled wryly as he listened to frogs croaking in a distant chorus. His city colleagues wouldn't believe the action that made up his average working tasks these days.

He breathed in a deep lungful of fragrant eucalyptus, the clean tangy oils still heavy in the air after a hot day. In the nearby trees, a lone magpie chortled, its diurnal senses confused by the brightness of the full moon. The gentle night sounds and scents gathered around him like a cloak of serenity.

Coming back to Dustin had been the right choice for him.

In the paddock beside him, a dozen bovine silhouettes munched contentedly on the pasture in their temporary new home. Moonlight gleamed off the black hides of the now-sedate Angus yearlings. A far cry from the fractious cavorters that had led him and his helpers on an hour-long chase along the roadside.

He shifted, reaching for the vehicle door. Time to go home, get out of clothes that carried the aroma of cowpats and get clean. His stomach growled.

Shower. Food. Sleep. In that order.

A set of approaching headlights stabbed the night to form a weird hazy glow in a patch of low-lying mist. Tom glanced at the clock on the dashboard. Nearly one in the morning. An odd time to be travelling into Dustin on a Sunday night. He watched with reluctant curiosity as the car drew nearer.

A few seconds later, he recognised the shape of the small car. He frowned as his heart thumped hard.

Kayla Morgan.

Dustin's new doctor.

And currently the woman he fancied more than common sense dictated—especially given that she barely acknowledged his existence.

As the car zipped across the end of the side road where he was parked, Kayla's pale face was illuminated briefly in the side window. She glanced his way and for a second her eyes seemed to look right at him. His hand lifted in an automatic salute even though he doubted that she'd looked long enough to see him let alone identify him. Pretty much par for the course with their social interaction to date. He huffed out a self-mocking snort.

He, on the other hand, noticed every minuscule detail about her. From the top of her honey-blonde head to the cheeky pink-tinted toenails that peeped out of the sandals she'd worn to the hospital barbecue when she'd first arrived in town two months ago. Even her eye colour…he'd never been fanciful about eye colour. Irises were blue, brown, green, hazel—standard cop's vocabulary. But not when it came to Kayla. Nope. She looked straight through him with eyes the colour of polished pewter.

She made him want things more in keeping with the old Tom Jamieson. The live-hard, play-hard party animal. The man he'd been before a bullet had stopped him in his tracks a little over two years ago. His near-death experience, the time in hospital and then the months of rehabilitation afterwards had forced him to reassess his priorities. Made him realise he wanted to go home to his roots, build his future there.

Start a family.

To do that he needed a wife and he knew what he was looking for. A down-to-earth woman, someone loving and generous. Someone with a sense of humour.

Not someone like Kayla. She was a city girl through and through. Polished perfection, dressed to the nines, designer labels, never a hair out of place. Positively stingy with her smiles.

Cool, reserved, fastidious.

For all that his brain knew what he *needed*, his body *wanted* otherwise. Kayla made him want to howl, beat his chest, risk potential frostbite to get close to her. He didn't much like this glimpse of his old self. That harder, hungrier, edgier man who wanted nothing more than to get Kayla Morgan into his bed…even when she flicked her unusual silver eyes over him as though he was invisible.

He frowned as he yanked open the car door and slid behind the wheel. What the hell was she doing in Dustin anyway, besides upsetting his equilibrium? He knew the short answer. She was working at the hospital and ultimately filling in as a medical locum for Liz Campbell's maternity leave.

But what had made her want to come all the way out

here, to his country town, when she so obviously didn't belong?

And now she was returning after another weekend in the big smoke. Had she been getting a fix of civilisation, something to sustain her for her sentence in rural purgatory? Or did she have a man tucked away down there?

Someone happy to have a long-distance relationship with her?

Someone as controlled and contained as she was?

An image leapt into his mind. Male hands other than his touching her, sliding over that perfect, creamy skin. He cursed under his breath.

Jaw set tight, he slammed the vehicle door. The fangs of unrequited lust sank deep. He was slowly going crazy.

After clipping the seat belt, he reached for the ignition key.

An unholy shriek of brakes sliced through the air, the brutal noise cutting off the gentle murmurs of the mellow night. For a split second, Tom froze. Then, pulse rocketing, he jerked his head towards the sound. In the distance, a strange light show played erratically across the vegetation. Yellow beams dipped and spun like out-of-control searchlights. A moment later, everything stopped with a sickening crunch of metal.

Kayla!

A shaft of icy dread pierced his gut. With a quick, hard rev of the engine, he accelerated down the short stretch of gravel road to the intersection and spun the steering-wheel in the direction of the now stationary lights. His vehicle leapt forward as the tyres gripped the sealed road.

God, what would he find? The thought of that feminine perfection injured—or worse—appalled him.

His low beam cut through the thickening wisps of pale fog. The small jelly-bean-pink car was sitting diagonally across the middle of the road. It looked whole but perhaps the damage was on the other side.

On the driver's side.

He was still too far away to see clearly inside the vehicle, to see if there was any movement. He leaned forward over his steering-wheel, as though that would somehow help his vision.

A moment later, her car moved, headlights swinging around in a U-turn.

He swallowed, shaken by an abrupt wash of relief that left his joints momentarily water weak.

Kayla was all right, the car was whole.

Her headlights kept moving and for the first time Tom noticed a dark blue sedan with its bonnet crumpled against the trunk of a gum tree.

Her car stopped with the beam of lights trained on the wreck.

He positioned his vehicle across the lane to block any oncoming traffic, emergency lights flashing and his headlights adding to the brightness of Kayla's. Her door opened and she scrambled out. He yanked on his handbrake and uttered a pithy curse as she ran towards the wreck.

What was the woman doing? The scene needed to be secured before she went charging in. They'd had no rain for weeks. Fire danger at the moment was extreme. Hot exhaust, long grass. A recipe for disaster.

As Tom threw open his door, a man's guttural cries echoed in his ears.

'Help me! Somebody. Please. Please.'

Fire extinguisher, woollen blanket and torch in hand, Tom ran to the front of the crumpled bonnet. The sweetly nauseating tang of petrol fumes filled his sinuses. In his peripheral vision, he was aware of Kayla swinging the driver's door wide.

'It's all right, we'll look after you,' she said, loudly enough to cut through the man's groans. She sounded firm, confident. Trustworthy. 'What's your name?'

'A-Andy.'

Charred grass smouldered and, even as Tom scuffed dirt into the blackening area, a flame flickered to life in the dry leaf litter around the trunk of the tree. Crisp twigs crunched beneath his boot as he stamped out the fledgling fire. He spread the blanket strategically to smother the tinder dry fuel.

'Hello, Andy. My name's Kayla. I'm a doctor.'

With one ear on Kayla's conversation, Tom shone his torch into the engine cavity beneath the buckled bonnet. No obvious hot spots or smoke at this stage but that could change in an instant.

'You're going to be fine.' Her soothing voice continued. 'We'll look after you now.'

Tom placed the extinguisher on the ground within easy access then strode to where Kayla was crouched at the open driver's door. She'd positioned a cervical collar around the victim's neck and was shining a small pencil-slim torch-light into the man's eyes.

Tom leaned low and growled at her, 'This scene is not safe.'

'Then please organise it for us, Sergeant.' She sounded pleasant but remote. Her attention was fixed on her patient and she didn't look up.

Tom smiled grimly as he braced his hand on the top of the door and reached across her towards the steering column. At least she knew who he was. 'I have organised it, *Doctor.*'

'Well done.' The casual, dismissive praise rankled as he watched her twist further into the car and dig her hands down either side of the man in front of her. 'Any pain anywhere, Andy?'

'M-my ankle.' The slurred words were accompanied by a belch of stale alcohol. Tom could smell it even though he wasn't directly in its path. Kayla didn't flinch.

'Okay, I'll have a look.'

Tom gritted his teeth as his fingers found the key in the ignition. It was in the off position. 'We need to get Andy out. *Now.* There's—' His train of thought dried up abruptly as Kayla shifted to the right and the bare skin on her shoulder brushed the sensitive skin of his inner arm. Electricity sizzled along his nerves, making his fingers fumble with the car key. He forced his thoughts back into line. 'Kayla, there's petrol vapour, a hot exhaust, tinder-dry grass. The danger of fire is extreme.'

She glanced around at him then and gave a quick, short nod. 'Of course. I understand. We need to move him.'

Instead of shifting back, as he'd expected, she leaned further into the car. Tom tightened his lips to stop himself from yelling at her. She was doing her job, and doing it well, but that didn't stop him wanting to pull her out of the car, get her to safety.

'Andy, can you move your legs?' Not by the tiniest quiver did her voice betray any concern.

'No.' The word was more of a moan. 'It hurts.'

By the time Tom strode to the other side of the car and wrenched open the passenger door, Kayla had her arm pushed down into the well beneath the dashboard.

'Can you feel that, Andy?'

'Y-yes.'

'Where am I touching you?'

'Leg. Shin.'

'That's great.' She withdrew her arm and shone her pencil torch into the cramped space.

Newspaper crinkled under Tom's knee as he knelt on the seat and leaned across to reach under the driver's seat.

'Be careful,' Kayla said sharply. A heady mixture of whisky fumes and her light, spicy perfume assaulted his nostrils. 'There's glass from a broken bottle.'

'Thanks.' Tom winced at the gravelly catch in his voice.

'Andy's legs are caught under the dash. Apart from his ankle pain, there's no other obvious injury but visibility isn't great. I can't tell if he's trapped or just wedged forward with the seat.' She looked up, her wide eyes on a level with his for a breathless second. 'We can't shift him until we can straighten his legs and see. Before we try to move him out of the car, I'd like to try and shift the seat back so I can assess any lower limb damage properly.'

'Shift the seat. Right.' Tom drew in a lungful of air when her eyes swivelled back to Andy.

'Can you wriggle your toes for me, Andy?' she said, calmly carrying on with her examination.

'Y-yeah.'

'Are you allergic to any medications?'

'No.'

'Do you take medication for anything? Diabetes? Heart condition?'

'N-no. Need something for the p-pain.'

'Okay. You're doing great, Andy. I'll get you something for your pain now.' She turned away for a moment then was back with a vial and syringe in her hands. With the slender capping sheath clamped between her teeth, she filled the syringe. Tom blinked. He'd seen the paramedics use the same technique countless times. But somehow Kayla's even, white teeth performing the familiar action was unbelievably sexy.

As she plunged the needle into Andy's leg, Tom shook

himself mentally and reached across to grope for the lever under the driver's seat. 'I'm going to move the seat back as far as I can, Kayla.'

'Sure.'

He jiggled the lever. Nothing. Applied more pressure. Still nothing. The angle was awkward. He moved further forward, closer to Kayla. Closer to her evocative female scent. *Concentrate*. He braced his knee uncomfortably on the handbrake and yanked directly upward.

The chair slid back with a jerk. Andy moaned.

'Sorry, mate,' said Tom.

Kayla was there in an instant. 'Where is your pain, Andy?'

'Ankle. Still.'

Tom edged back outside. The deadly petrol fumes were stronger. They had to hurry. He clambered in behind the driver's seat. 'I'm going to lower the seat so we can take him out through the back.'

He wound the reclining mechanism with quick flicks of his wrist. 'Nearly ready to move him?'

She nodded, her mind obviously on the job as her voice sounded distracted when she spoke to him. 'Just let me make sure both his legs are free.'

There was a small popping noise.

'Hell.' Tom was moving as a terrifying whoosh followed. 'Kayla! Get out! Now!'

He scooped up the fire extinguisher, pulling the pin as he ran to the flames that leapt out of the gap between the crumpled bonnet and the front fender.

Aiming the nozzle, he pulled the trigger. The fire retreated, beaten into temporary submission. Moving forward, with a sweeping motion, Tom covered as much of the engine as he could with the foam. As soon as the cylinder started to splutter, he threw it aside and spun back towards the cabin of the car.

Kayla was still there. She hadn't done as he'd asked. Far from it, she'd taken his place in the rear of the car and had finished lowering the driver's seat. She was struggling to move Andy.

'I don't know how long that will hold.' He grabbed her by the upper arm, tugged her aside then slid in to take her place. 'We have to do this now.'

'We really need more hands,' she said, for the first time sounding anxious.

'We haven't got them. Come on, Kayla. Don't fold on me now.' He threaded his hands under Andy's armpits and locked his fingers across the man's chest. 'I'm going to pull him out. You try to ease his legs as they come free.'

'Got it.'

'Let's do it.' He grinned at her and could swear the corners of her mouth moved in a quick response.

'Andy? This is going to be uncomfortable but we need to pull you out of the car now.' It was the best he could do to prepare the victim for what had to be done.

'P-please. Get me out. D-don't leave me here.'

'We won't, mate.'

Tom moved back, taking the man's weight, feeling the resistance and straining past it. Andy groaned. Tom had to steel himself against the agony in the sound. If he left Andy here, there was every chance the man could die in the car.

Kayla had grabbed the thick newspaper from the passenger seat and she used it to support Andy's lower leg as his limb came free. In a move like a circus contortionist, she climbed onto the driver's seat, then over and through the back door, the whole time cradling Andy's injured ankle in the makeshift splint.

Between them, they carried Andy across the road.

'Behind my vehicle, Kayla. It'll give us some protection if the car goes up.'

They lowered a shivering Andy to the ground. Tom opened the back door of his vehicle and took out a blanket. 'Here.'

'Thanks,' Kayla said as she tucked it around Andy's body. 'I need my bag.'

'I'll get it.'

Tom paused for a second as she bent over her patient, getting straight back into the job, her fingers on Andy's wrist. 'How are you feeling, Andy?'

She was a real trooper, brave and resourceful. Damn, that was attractive. His heart swelled. He was…proud of her.

She looked around, one eyebrow shooting up as though she was surprised to see him. 'My bag, Sergeant?'

'Coming right up.' He smiled wryly, feeling chastened and deservedly so. She distracted the hell out of him.

He loped back to the wreck and grabbed her medical kit. The still-strong smell of petrol, coupled with the sizzle of foam on hot metal, was ominous. His prevention measures were still holding but he didn't know for how long. He turned and ran back.

'Here.'

'Thanks.' She reached for the bag as soon as he put it beside her.

'I'll call it in,' Tom said, reaching into the cabin of his four-wheel drive and grabbing the radio handpiece.

'It's Senior Sergeant Tom Jamieson, Dustin Police.' He turned to watch Kayla bandaging a more stable splint on Andy's leg. Her long, clever fingers were quick and efficient. She moved with such grace and competence as she went about her business that Tom was hard pressed to take his eyes off her.

He swallowed and dragged his mind back to his report. 'I need fire and ambulance to a single-vehicle accident on the Valley Highway, west of Dustin. About ten kilometres out of town, nearest intersecting road Reece Lane.

'We've got one injured male, approximately forty-five, possible broken ankle. Doctor on scene providing first aid now.'

He looked over the bull bar of his vehicle towards the wreck. 'The situation is extremely hazardous. One full foam extinguisher has already been discharged to control fire in the motor vehicle's engine. It could reignite at any time.'

'Sergeant?' Kayla barked behind him. Tom turned to see her stripping the blanket off Andy. Her patient was clutching at his chest, his face twisted into a ghastly grimace. Then he collapsed, his arms slumping to his sides.

Kayla leaned over the now inert body, her fingers groping for a neck pulse.

'He's arresting. I need your assistance, stat. Get the resus mask out of my bag.' Kayla's hands were already in the middle of Andy's chest, the heels pumping down hard. 'Hurry.'

Tom let go of the handpiece and dropped to his knees beside the medical bag.

'That's it,' Kayla said as he lifted out a clear plastic mask with a pale green bag attached. 'Over his mouth and nose. Tilt his head back slightly. A solid puff now. And another.'

Tom did as he was directed.

'Good. Two breaths each thirty compressions. I'll count.' She kept up the rhythmic pressing.

It was the first time Tom had seen chest compressions

performed on a live patient and it was a much more brutal process than he'd realised.

'Get ready.' Kayla's voice snapped his attention back. 'Twenty-eight, twenty-nine, Thirty. Again now.'

The radio dangling at the side of the car crackled. 'Sergeant Jamieson? Are you still receiving, over?' Tom ignored the tinny voice as he held the mask and squeezed the bag, forcing the air out into Andy.

Turning, he grabbed the radio, clicked the button and barked, 'Here, Dispatch. The accident vic is having a heart attack.'

Press. Press. 'Twenty-seven, Twenty-eight.'

Tom dropped the handpiece and got ready.

'Twenty-nine. Thirty, now.'

As soon as he'd done his bit, he snatched up the handpiece again. 'We're doing CPR.'

'Roger, Sergeant. Ambulance and fire are on their way. I'll update them. Over.'

'Twenty-nine. Thirty, now.'

The seconds crawled by, turning into minutes as they moved in a bizarre choreography. He rapped out short staccato snips of information on the radio then returned to pump air into Andy's lungs. Kayla placed her fingers on Andy's neck then returned to her compressions.

She worked tirelessly, her slender arms taut, hands linked. With each compression, her hair bobbed on her shoulders, swinging with her exertion. Light caught on the wheat-coloured strands. Tom was intensely aware of her every move. She was a competent, assured expert. If Andy died it wouldn't be because of anything that Kayla failed to do for him.

Three minutes.

Five minutes.

Kayla laid her fingers against Andy's neck, felt the

reassuring bump in the carotid artery. 'Okay, we have a pulse.'

Out of the corner of her eye, she saw the policeman sink back on his heels and lift the handset. 'Dispatch, the victim has a pulse.'

Kayla felt an odd shiver as she let the deep, calm voice wash over her. She shook her head. She was tired, her muscles trembling with fatigue in the aftermath of the adrenalin-charged situation. The tremors were nothing to do with a deep, dark, baritone voice.

The unit crackled. 'Thank you, Sergeant. They should be with you shortly. Standing by.'

She looked at the profile of the man who'd been helping her. Dustin's police sergeant. The strong jaw with a shadow of whiskers on his cheeks. He looked stern and forbidding with the black T-shirt clinging to his chest and sculpted biceps. Much as she loathed large, muscle-bound men, she had to be thankful he'd been here tonight. She'd never have got Andy out of the car on her own.

She swallowed and turned her attention back to her patient. She tucked Andy's arm along his body and reached across for his other one. 'We should turn Andy into the recovery position.'

There was a faint wail of sirens in the distance, creeping closer.

'Going to be sick,' Andy slurred.

'We need to roll him,' she said urgently. 'I'll support his neck, you roll him towards me. My command, on three. Got it? Okay. One, two, three.' Kayla fired out the order as she held Andy's head.

And then the sour smell of vomit as Andy disgorged his stomach contents over the knee of her trousers. She swallowed the gag reflex that threatened. 'Okay, let's settle him so I can clean him up. Gently, gently.'

'Wha's happen…?' Andy struggled to move as she slipped a folded towel under his head.

'Just stay still for me, Andy.' She kept her hand firmly on his shoulder, held him steady as she spoke. 'You've had an accident. We're getting help for you.'

The sirens were closer.

'The cavalry's on its way,' Tom murmured, his rich, gravelly voice sliding over her.

'Amen to that.'

She looked up to find shadowed eyes on her.

And then he smiled. A simple curve of his mouth and his face was transformed. Sergeant Jamieson was a very, very attractive man. Kayla's heart squeezed hard.

Too much man for her to handle, whispered a confidence-sapping inner voice. Too much, too big. Too hard.

Andy moved under her hand. With relief, she wrenched her gaze away from the disturbing man opposite her patient.

CHAPTER TWO

THE smell of smoke drifted on the still air. Tom leaned sideways to look around the end of his car. Flames licked around the front tyre of the wreck.

As he got to his feet, the Dustin fire truck slid between him and his view of the fledgling fire. Thank God. He felt the tension ease across his shoulders.

A paramedic ran up to join Kayla as the ambulance backed slowly towards them. It stopped a couple of metres away and the second medic came around to open the back doors. Tom stood and moved back to give them more room. He watched a moment as Kayla meshed smoothly with the men, working to stabilise their patient.

Feeling superfluous, he crossed to the back of his four-wheel drive to take out the camera, tape measure and notepad. With his gear in hand, he walked around to the other side of the fire truck. The team had the wreck and surrounding area well doused with foam.

'Tom.' Dustin's fire captain, Jack Campbell, nodded to him then turned back to look at the crumpled car. 'How's your vic?'

'Looks like he'll make it, thanks to Kayla.'

'Lucky she was on hand.'

'Yeah.' Tom stared at the wreck, remembering the

frenetic light and sound show in the seconds before the crash. 'Even luckier she wasn't involved in the accident.'

'What happened?' Jack's voice was sharp with concern.

'I need to have a good look at the tyre marks and take her statement.' Tom lifted his shoulder. 'But I'd say she did some pretty fancy driving to avoid a collision. It'll have to be confirmed but indications are that the driver is alcohol-impaired.'

Jack grunted his disgust.

'Yeah.' Tom sighed heavily. 'I'm going to take some photos, make a few measurements for my report. I won't get in your way.'

'Sure. I called Dennis. He's on his way with the tow truck.' Hands on hips, Jack pointed his chin at the wreck. 'We're under control here but we'll hang around to make sure there are no flare-ups when the car's pulled off the tree trunk.'

'Thanks.'

Tom moved away and began snapping photographs from different angles. Inside the car, he took several pieces of the broken whisky bottle, making sure he got a clear shot of the label.

From a vantage point to one side, he made a quick sketch of the scene, placing the cars. On a walk along the road with his torch, he identified the skid marks—Andy's coming onto the main road from the lane; Kayla's where she'd braked and swerved to avoid him.

He could see quite clearly how the incident had unfolded. The tyre tracks told the story. Thick black rubber lines on the sealed road segued into gouges in the gravel verge before spiralling back onto the tarmac again. Just traversing the two vastly different road surfaces in a *straight* line was enough to bring many motorists to disaster. It was nothing short of a miracle that her little car hadn't rolled with the massive forces it had been under.

By concentrating on his job, he could prevent himself from thinking about how close Kayla had been to injury or death. He laid out the measuring tape then jotted in distances on his sketch. With everything he needed for his report, he glanced over the road as he wound the tape up.

The paramedics were wheeling Andy to the back of the ambulance. Kayla was turned away from him, bent double as she wiped a towel down one leg.

Tom inhaled deeply then let the air out through his pursed lips in a silent whistle. The unimpeded view of her shapely bottom in the soft draping material of her trousers was very fine. Very fine indeed.

He wrenched his gaze away, looked down at the equipment in his hands. He wanted to talk to her…sensibly. Which was going to be a tough assignment if he couldn't rein in his physical response.

He gathered his thoughts. They'd made a connection here tonight and he wanted to build on that, not give her any chance, any excuse, to draw back. He'd seen a different side to her as she'd dealt with Andy. Brave, resourceful, competent—and he liked it. A lot.

Holding fast to those thoughts, he refused to succumb to further masculine appreciation of the view as he crossed the road.

'Kayla.'

She straightened abruptly—staggered slightly.

'Oh…no.' Her words were a small, useless protest as she slowly pitched forward.

Tom took the last two steps to her side, catching her to his chest. 'Steady, I've got you.'

'Sorry, sorry,' she mumbled. 'D-don't know what happened… Must have…stood too quickly.'

She didn't resist as he stepped her over to a small tree stump and lowered her to sit. He bent over her and pushed her head between her knees, acutely conscious of the soft, warm skin of her neck beneath his fingers. After a minute, she struggled against his pressure.

'I'm all right. Thank you, Sergeant.' Her voice sounded strangled.

'Tom.'

'Anything. Whatever.' He felt her convulsive shudder as she turned her head towards him, her eyes closed. 'Please. All I can smell is the vomit on my knee.'

'Oh. Sorry, I forgot.' He released her, his grip supporting her as she sat up straight. Silky strands of hair teased the back of his hand. She took a quick breath and swallowed audibly. 'Just sit a minute.'

He kept a hand on her nape as he called to the paramedic who had just backed out of the back of the ambulance and was closing the doors. 'Gaz? Can you take Kayla back with you for a once-over?'

'Sure, no problem.'

Beneath his palm, he could feel the delicate shifting of muscle as Kayla shook her head.

'That's not necessary, Sergeant. I—'

He looked back at her. 'I think it is, Kayla. You were a hair's breadth from being involved in a nasty accident tonight. And the name is Tom.' If she called him Sergeant one more time tonight, he'd plant a kiss right on that luscious mouth and completely ruin her opinion of him.

'But I need my car.' She looked mutinous, her silver eyes glowing with irritation.

'And I'll see that you get it,' he said as he stood. 'For now, I'm impounding it.'

Her mouth opened.

He bent, slipping one arm around her shoulders, the other under her knees and scooped her up. Her mouth snapped shut on a small squeak as she grabbed at his shoulder to steady herself. He smiled grimly. His hands were on Kayla and he couldn't do a thing about it. Torture. He looked down on the curve of lashes on her cheek, the gentle swell of her breasts…the fist in her lap. He'd take no bets on where she'd like to plant it.

He was a masochist.

'Open your front passenger door for me, Gaz.'

'Sure thing, Tom.' Gary grinned as he opened the door wide.

Tom shovelled his armful of warm woman onto the seat, wondering if his reluctance to let her go was obvious to anyone other than him.

God, he had to get out of here before he made an idiot of himself. He stepped back quickly and cleared the congestion from his throat.

'Buckle up, Doc,' he said as he shut the door.

Kayla's narrow-eyed glare should have sizzled his skin. At least her anger had brought some colour to her pallid cheeks. A little hectic but colour just the same.

Tom pivoted and strode over to where Jack Campbell was rolling up the hose. The bonnet of the car had been wrenched open and the engine was now well doused with fire-retardant foam.

'Kayla okay?' asked Jack.

'She says so.' Tom avoided his friend's shrewd eyes. 'I've sent her back with the ambos for a check over.'

'And she was okay with that?'

'Sure. Why wouldn't she be?' Tom set his jaw and ignored the laughter he could see in Jack's face. 'I'll get one of your guys to drive her car back to the hospital when we go, if that's okay?'

'Sure. Might as well be me. I want to roust Liz out. She should have been home a couple of hours ago.'

'Good luck with that.'

'Yeah.' Jack chuckled.

Kayla sucked another deep breath into her oxygen-deprived lungs. Her diaphragm had frozen from the moment the sergeant had lifted her. Making a conscious effort to ease her tension, she uncurled the fists in her lap. Her short practical nails had dug into the soft tissue, leaving small red dints in her palm.

Even with his disturbing presence gone, she could still feel his touch. Hard enough when it had just been his hand on her nape, strong fingers clasped gently on her neck, the rasp of his calloused skin while he'd been holding her head down. Being clasped to his chest, surrounded by his warmth and strength…the awareness of her female softness against the hardness of his muscular frame had overwhelmed her.

The honest, earthy scent of him, a smell that owed more to a hard day's work than scientists testing essences in a laboratory, seemed to call to her in a way that was disturbing, primitive. She'd always liked men to be well groomed, wearing a subtle, musky aftershave. Yet no one she'd dated had ever affected her as profoundly as this man in his snug jeans and a simple black T-shirt.

Thank goodness he didn't realise he was responsible for her light-headed state. Or at least partially responsible. If she'd eaten a proper meal before leaving Melbourne, if she hadn't straightened from her bent position so quickly. If he hadn't crept up on her, spoken her name so unexpectedly. Panic had made her head jerk upright, had flooded her system with an explosion of contrary stimuli. Instead of doing anything sensible, she'd nearly pitched face down at his feet. Would have if he hadn't caught her.

Which brought her full circle back to being held in his arms. She shivered.

What was it about his brand of masculinity that left her dizzy with all sorts of chaotic feelings? Whatever it was, she didn't like the feeling of vulnerability. There were so many strikes against him. A career police officer, strong and hard. Controlled and used to controlling. She had to find a way to cram the sergeant back into the mental box she'd managed to keep him in for the two months she'd been living in Dustin.

He'd said she should call him Tom. She didn't even want to *think* about him that personally…intimately. Ridiculous though it was, if she thought of him as *Tom*, he'd become too real, a man she'd have to deal with. As Sergeant Jamieson, he was a police officer, someone she could keep at a distance. She was only here for another four months. Surely she could lock her unruly reactions down long enough to get through that.

She rolled her head to look at him where he stood with Jack Campbell. Both were long, lean, athletic men. Two of a kind. Yet she'd never felt threatened by Jack. He was a honey. She knew he and Liz had had their problems but they'd come through them and now their marriage was stronger than ever. They were a family, one adorable daughter and another baby on the way.

Sergeant Jamieson was a different proposition altogether. He had hot eyes. At the few social occasions she'd attended, she'd felt him watching her. He'd never put a foot wrong, but in her mind he was disturbing. Radiating a hunger that she didn't want to think about. For things that weren't his, things he had no right to. She shivered again.

He made her feel utterly conscious of her vulnerability as a woman.

She mentally shook herself. It didn't matter what he wanted. What *she* wanted was what counted. And she didn't want any man in her life at the moment.

And definitely not someone like Sergeant Tom Jamieson.

CHAPTER THREE

TOM fell into step with Jack as they walked towards the bright lights at the hospital entrance.

'Here are Kayla's keys.' Jack held out his hand.

'Thanks,' Tom said, spotting his quarry as soon as he stepped through the sliding door into the emergency department.

Tall and straight in the shapeless green theatre pants and top, Kayla still looked entirely too appealing. Her pale face turned towards them. When she realised it was him, an interesting shade of pink bloomed along her cheek bones and her eyes darkened to stormcloud grey. He might have flattered himself that his appearance had that effect— except for the ferocious frown that pleated her forehead a split second later.

'Uh-oh, looks like you're in the dogbox, mate,' murmured Jack beside him as they walked towards her.

'Hey, Kayla.' Jack stooped to kiss her cheek.

'Hello, Jack.'

'Is Liz around?'

'She's in the tearoom with her feet up. I think she'll be glad to go home.'

'That's what I'm here for. Catch you two kids later.' Jack grinned at the two of them and winked.

Tom watched the expressions flit over her face as her

eyes followed Jack. Then suddenly she turned to face him, her silvery eyes impaling him, her mouth firm.

'My keys, please, Sergeant?'

He juggled them in his hands, tossing them from one to the other. 'Have you been cleared by your doctor... *Doctor*?'

'Yes, of course.'

He tilted his head and considered her. 'So, your near collapse was because...?'

Her lips thinned and for a moment he thought she'd refuse to answer. He almost relished the opportunity to lock horns with her.

'Low blood sugar. Tiredness. Getting up too quickly. I prescribed myself a cup of tea and grilled cheese on toast while I waited for you to return my keys.' She held out her hand. 'And now I'd like to go home to bed.'

Tom's fingers clutched the keys as he bit back a tempting retort. She did *not* mean anything by her comment. It was *not* an opening or an offer. If he was a gentleman, he would definitely let that slide through to the keeper.

He cleared his throat and dangled the keys. 'In that case...'

As she reached out, he caught her hand, gently turning it over and depositing the keys on her palm with studied care. He curled her fingers over them one at a time as he held her eyes with his.

'Thank you.' She tugged lightly and when he didn't release her, she narrowed her eyes at him. 'Was there something else...Sergeant?'

'Yes, there is. Kayla.' He let his tongue linger over the syllables of her name. 'You get a good night's sleep.'

He felt her hand twitch in his, saw a flare of awareness in her eyes. And something else. A starkness, a vulnerability. Surely she wasn't afraid of him. He released his grip and her hand dropped to her side.

'Thank you, Sergeant.'

She turned away, walking quickly, her movements oddly jerky as though she was having trouble co-ordinating her limbs. As though she couldn't get away from him fast enough.

He wasn't used to having that sort of effect on women. He knew, without conceit, that he was reasonably good looking. Kayla Morgan was indifferent, immune. No, more than that—she seemed to find him downright distasteful. Damn it, she didn't know him well enough to feel that way about him. It rankled, made him want to get in her way, be hard to ignore.

Hands on hips, he watched until she was several metres away then he called softly, 'Kayla?'

The stiff stride halted. 'Yes?'

He waited, the silence stretched. She pivoted to look at him with obvious reluctance. 'What did you want?'

There it was again, that hint of defencelessness, of desperately masked fear. It reached out and touched him. Made him want to gather her close, shield her from whatever was troubling her. Which was difficult because he seemed to be the main cause of her stress right now. How could he protect her from himself?

'Come and see me at the station this week. I need you to make a statement about the accident.'

'Oh. Yes.' She swallowed, relief patent on her face. 'All right.'

'Goodnight.' He jammed his hands into the front pockets of his jeans.

''Night.' And she was moving away from him again. A couple of steps later she stopped. He could almost see an internal battle being waged as she looked over her shoulder then turned to face him. 'I should thank you for your assistance tonight.'

'Should you?'

'Yes, I should,' she said firmly, squaring her shoulders. Her bearing reminded him of his nephew's attitude when he'd had to apologise for a serious transgression. Courage, trepidation and determination not to flinch from an unpleasant task. No prizes for guessing what, or who, was the distasteful thing in this case. 'You were great at the accident. Thank you, Sergeant.'

'Happy to help…Doctor.'

With a quick nod, she spun around and moved away, without hesitating this time.

Why was he doing this to himself? Kayla was giving him red lights all the way. Yet he felt compelled to keep pushing, to try to get close.

She was confident and competent when doing her job, but so vulnerable and prickly with him when dealing with him on a personal level.

He watched until she moved out of sight without looking back then he huffed out a breath. He'd thought she might look back at him, give him some indication that she knew he was still standing there. A vain hope.

He hunched his shoulders. Perhaps he should back off, let it go. Kayla was Liz's friend. Liz would skewer him if he upset her. The whole thing was complicated.

'Earth to Tom?'

He turned to find Liz watching him, curiosity and concern in her eyes. He wondered how long she'd been standing there, what she'd read on his face. She glanced along the corridor to where Kayla had disappeared.

'Jack was looking for you,' he said quickly into the brief silence.

'He found me. Tony just collared him about something

so I came on ahead.' She paused. 'We stabilised your accident victim and sent him off to Melbourne. I organised
that blood test for his alcohol level, too.'

'Good, thanks.'

'Tom…about Kayla…'

'What about her?' He tried to sound casual but knew
he hadn't succeeded by Liz's troubled expression.

'Tom, I love you very dearly and I'm telling you as a
friend… Kayla's not up to your weight.'

'I don't know what you mean.'

'Don't you?' she said dryly. 'I've seen the way you look
at her. And not just today.'

'Well, she's not looking back so you can put your mind
at ease.'

'Perhaps.' Liz looked along the corridor again. 'Kayla's
my friend, Tom.'

'I know. I'm just having a hard time picturing the two
of you as pals. You seem like an unlikely pair.'

'She came to my rescue when a charming date spiked
my drink. I was in first year at uni and pretty green. Kayla
stood up to him and took me to hospital. She looked after
me, Tom, even though we didn't know each other.' Liz's
eyes examined his face as she spoke. 'She didn't have to
get involved and yet she chose to. She was a better friend
to me that night than all my so-called close friends.'

He rubbed his jaw. This picture of the valiant, loyal,
caring Kayla was incredibly attractive. All the qualities a
man could ask for in a potential life partner.

'Why is she here in Dustin?'

'You know why she's here.' Liz patted her protruding
stomach and looked smug. 'She's working while I'm on
maternity leave.'

'But you're not on leave yet.'

'True.' She tilted her head and looked up at him for

a long moment. Her eyebrows rose. 'Why don't you ask her?'

He grimaced. 'I would if she wasn't so damned prickly. She *Sergeants* me to death and treats me like I've got her under bright lights for interrogation.'

'You can be intimidating.'

'Nah.' He smiled at her. 'I'm a SNAG.'

She gave him a droll look. 'I've yet to meet anyone less like a sensitive new-age guy than you. Except maybe Jack.'

Tom laughed. 'Then I'm in good company.' He waited a beat then said, 'So how about it? What's her story?'

Liz looked at him thoughtfully. 'You know I won't tell you that. But I will tell you that it suited both of us for her to come to Dustin early.' She smoothed her hand over her stomach, a small smile on her mouth. 'And when my time comes, I know I'm in safe hands with Kayla.'

He grinned as he saw Liz's husband approaching. 'Not getting Jack to play midwife for this one?'

'He's on standby. But even he admits he'll be happy to take a back seat for the arrival of future Campbells.' She grinned up at her husband as he slipped his arm around her waist. 'Won't you, darling?'

'Believe it. You, my sweet, are confined to town for the rest of your pregnancy. A maximum of two kilometres from the hospital at all times.'

'Uh-uh. There's the camp draft next weekend. You promised.'

'Only because Kayla's going. And only because it's within my fail-safe ten-kilometre radius from the hospital.'

The look that passed between his friends was one of such pure delight that Tom's heart squeezed. He wanted a woman to look at him like that, as though he was the most important man in her world.

And not just any woman.

He wanted it to be Kayla.

Kayla tugged the front of her shirt, suddenly wishing she'd worn something more substantial than her favourite red shirt. She'd never realised how low the front was, not that it showed cleavage but the respectable square neckline showed an alarming amount of her décolletage. All that bare skin suddenly seemed outrageously provocative. The short, cap sleeves left her arms bare and somehow vulnerable.

And it was red. Sure, it suited her. She'd worn it because red was the colour of confidence and she needed all of that commodity she could muster for this interview. But the colour also screamed, *Look over here, look at me* in a way that she'd never appreciated before.

If it weren't for the fact that she was actually standing on the veranda of the police station, she'd have fled home to change her blouse for something black that covered her from hyoid bone to scaphoid. She looked around surreptitiously and, sure enough, there was a security camera at the corner of the roof line. Great, now she probably looked like she was about to commit a felony.

She'd put off this moment as long as she could. The simple task of making the statement had grown into a task of monumental proportions. All she was doing was giving her version of events, for heaven's sake. A formality. It wasn't as if the accident was her fault. She'd been sober, driving carefully, and her quick evasive actions had prevented an even more serious situation.

As for Sergeant Jamieson…he was just a man. Doing a job. He wouldn't bite. He probably wouldn't even be the person she'd have to deal with so she was getting herself into a lather for nothing. She needed to get a grip, tell the person taking her statement what had happened, answer a few questions. Simple.

She took a deep breath, straightened her shoulders then pushed open the door of the police station.

'Hey, Kayla.'

'Penny. Hi.' Kayla grinned at the neatly uniformed woman on duty behind the counter. The tension in her stomach began to smooth out. She could talk to Penny, give her statement, get on the road to Melbourne. She didn't need to see the sergeant. Reprieve!

'I hear you've got a new fan.' Penny smiled.

'Fan?'

'My niece. Suzy MacIntyre. You saw her the other day.'

'Oh, of course. She's a delight.'

'Isn't she? She was telling me all about her visit to see you. And how brave she was about her injection and the jelly-bean she chose and the cute little animal stamp you gave her. You know she wouldn't let poor Sarah wash it off for ages. They had to bathe her and wash around it.'

'Oh, dear.'

'Now she wants to come back to see you. She said she'd even have another injection if she had to.'

Kayla chuckled.

'Anyway, you probably haven't come by to listen to the ramblings of a proud aunty.' Penny clicked her fingers. 'Oh, I bet you're here about Andy's accident last week.'

'I'm always happy to listen to proud aunty tales. But, yes, I've come to make a statement.'

'Tom won't be long. He's just on a phone call at the moment. Want a coffee?'

'No, thanks. Do you think...well, could I give you the statement?'

Penny looked doubtful. 'Tom was very specific about wanting to see you himself. Which is a bit unusual really for something so routine.'

'It'd be a shame to disturb him.'

'Uncommonly thoughtful of you, Kayla.'

The deep voice made her jump. Spinning to her left, she met the sergeant's knowing dark gaze. Heat swept her from head to toe and she felt as though she'd been caught planning something criminal.

He smiled at her. 'I'm free now. All yours, in fact.'

The skin over her cheek bones was scorching as every particle of heat concentrated in her face. If only it was enough to combust her on the spot.

The dark, narrow-eyed stare raked over her already sensitised skin. 'You're looking better than when I last saw you.'

The personal comment allowed her to pull herself together. 'Really, Sergeant?'

'Tom. No need to stand on ceremony around here, is there, Penny?' He smiled warmly at his constable and Kayla's thought processes stuttered to a halt.

He looked back at her. 'Want to come this way?'

No. She swallowed and forced her jellied knees to move her forward. The tension in her gut returned with an iron fist, making her glad it had been hours since she'd eaten.

Her heart set up a tattoo of great thumping beats as she followed him along a short corridor. She worked to compose herself, using the techniques that had served her so well for years when dealing with the large threatening males in her life. The usual methods weren't working.

'Grab a chair.' He moved behind the desk to open a filing cabinet and take out a pad.

She perched on the edge of the seat and concentrated on the items on his desk. It was all very tidy. Orderly piles of paper, a container of pens.

Long fingers appeared in her line of vision, selected one of the pens and clicked it ready for use.

'Tell me in your own words what happened last Sunday night, Kayla. You were returning from Melbourne?' His smooth, velvety voice invited her to respond.

'Y-yes.' She marshalled her thoughts and began to describe the accident.

He made notes as she spoke.

'So you didn't see the lights of the car coming down the side road towards you?' His dark eyes lifted to her face.

The question brought her up short.

'No. I was…um…distracted.' On that fateful night, she'd spotted him. In her mind's eye, she could remember the tall, still figure beside the police vehicle. She'd wondered what he was doing out there in the middle of the night. Heat crept up her neck and it was all she could do not to put her hand to her throat to try to hide the self-betrayal. 'I had glanced in the side mirror. The—the right-hand one on the…' She stopped. 'Right side.'

She was giving too much information, too much detail. Making herself sound like an idiot. Worse, she was drawing his attention and surely making him wonder what she was hiding.

Just as well she'd never contemplated a life of crime. Giving one tiny statement under Sergeant Jamieson's piercing eyes was turning her into a gibbering wreck.

'And then what happened?'

'I—I looked back and the other car was suddenly there, at my left-hand passenger door. I braked hard and swerved to the right side of the road. My car spun when I hit the gravel.'

He led her through several more questions, then she watched as he finished making his notes.

'Okay, that seems straightforward. I'll just get you to read through this and sign if you're happy with what it says.'

'Okay.' She took the pages. The short, terse sentences in his powerful, energetic script seemed to leap off the paper at her. She blinked and forced herself to concentrate. 'I just sign at the bottom?'

'Yes. You can use my pen.'

The pen was still warm from his fingers. She leaned the paper on the edge of the desk to scrawl her signature then handed the papers back to him.

'So that's it?'

'Pretty much.' He looked at her. 'How about a coffee?'

'Coffee?'

'Yes. I wouldn't expect you to drink the station coffee if that's what you're worried about.' He smiled but his eyes were dark, unreadable.

'Oh, I'm sure it couldn't be as bad as hospital coffee.' She stopped, bit her lip. He'd think she wanted to stay for coffee in a minute. 'Thank you, but, no. I need to get on the road. I've got a long drive.'

'Going to Melbourne for the weekend?'

'Yes.' She gathered up her belongings and decided she'd get her car keys out when she got to her car.

His face was perfectly calm but there was an acuteness about the way he looked at her that made her wonder what he was thinking. Perhaps all policemen cultivated that impression of predatory patience. Waiting to see what might be revealed if they waited long enough. 'Visiting family?'

'Yes. No. Sort of.' Her fingers tightened on her bag.

He raised his eyebrows.

She opened her mouth then shut it. He couldn't possibly be interested in knowing this was her best friend's last weekend in Melbourne before she returned to the far-flung reaches of North West Australia.

His curiosity was a policeman's ingrained habit and she was like Pavlov's dog. A steady stare from an imposing male wearing dark blue epaulettes and it seemed she was still ready to rush into explanations. Her father had trained her well.

Growing up, she'd tried to tell herself it was a sign of his affection that had made him grill her and her sister. But she'd slowly realised it was an uncanny ability to sniff out the tiniest hint of trouble or rebellion.

A fantastic ability in a policeman.

Utterly crushing in a distant, regimented father.

In the end, she'd realised he'd been determined to crush any tendency his daughters might have harboured towards behaving like normal teenagers. Christopher Morgan had been a man with places to go, in line for promotions. No time for messy family dramas and misbehaviour. No taint of gossip would touch him through his family.

She suddenly realised she'd been sitting in the sergeant's office for far too long, staring back at him. She shot out of the chair. 'Well, I won't let you keep me.'

'Won't you?' He stood more slowly, his eyes hooded, a faint smile on his mouth.

She felt the heat rush into her cheeks when she realised what she'd said. 'I mean, I won't keep you.'

He inclined his head. 'I'll walk you out.'

'There's no need. I can find my own way. Thank you, Sergeant.'

'Tom.' His fingers fastened around her arm.

She looked at him blankly, her mind consumed by his touch on the tender skin of her inner elbow.

'My name is Tom.'

'Oh. Yes. Of course.' She looked at him helplessly.

'Say it, Kayla.'

She swallowed. The way he said her name sent a shiver down her spine. Almost as though he was tasting the syllables, trying out the feel of it in his mouth. At the L-sound, she'd been able to see the tip of his tongue touch the edge of his top teeth.

'Say it,' he repeated when she remained silent.

'Tom.' Her throat had difficulty making the sound and it came out raw and husky. She'd worked so hard not to even think of him by his name, and now he'd made her say it. She felt something akin to despair. Now he was real, now he was a man, not a uniform.

He nodded. 'That wasn't so hard, was it?'

He opened his office door and ushered her across to the exit with that gentle but inexorable hold. Her feet moved her along beside him, across the veranda, down the steps to the side of her car. His fingers slid lightly across her elbow joint and finally released her.

He waited while she fumbled in her bag to find her keys to unlock the door. Then he leaned forward to open it for her. 'Drive carefully, Kayla. See you when you get back next week.'

Not if she saw him first. She slipped into the seat and managed to slide the key into the ignition.

'Bye, S—' She gulped the rest of the word when his eyes narrowed. 'Goodbye, Tom.'

He towered in the opening, one hand on the roof and the other on the door, as though he might say something more. But in the end all he said was, 'Bye, Kayla.'

He stepped back and shut the door gently.

As she stopped in the driveway to check the way was clear, she caught sight of him in her rear-vision mirror.

Thank goodness she drove an automatic car. It would just be the last straw to grind the gears or bunny-hop out onto the road under his watchful eye.

She didn't quite know what to make of Tom Jamieson.

But one thing was certain: he was a serious handicap to her enjoyment of Dustin.

CHAPTER FOUR

FROM his position in the corridor just outside the hospital cafeteria, Tom watched Kayla through the glass window and listened with half an ear to his sister's plans for the coming weekend. Kayla turned from the counter and threaded her way through the tables.

'Tom!'

'What?' He looked down at his sister's indignant features.

'You haven't heard a thing I've said, have you?'

He arched an eyebrow. 'Mum's still jet-lagged after travelling back from England on Tuesday and you're concerned about her overdoing it at the barbecue on Saturday night,' he said smugly and glanced back into the cafeteria as he spoke. Kayla had selected a seat by the window. 'You've arranged for Dad to get the meat and everyone else to bring salads and sweets.' He looked back at Charlotte, who gave him a narrow-eyed glare. 'Am I right?'

'Do you know how irritating it is when you can do that?'

'What? Prove I've been listening?'

'Mmm.' She craned her neck to look into the cafeteria. Tom had an overwhelming urge to block her line of sight to Kayla. 'What's so interesting anyway?'

He was saved from answering by the piercing beep of

Charlotte's pager. 'Damn. Got to run. See you on Saturday night, then.'

'Sure thing.'

Thankful for the narrow escape, he pushed open the door and headed towards Kayla. A moment later, her head came up, eyes darting around the room as though she'd sensed imminent danger. No mistaking the dismay on her face as her gaze settled on him. He suppressed a sigh. Nothing had changed—he was a sucker for punishment. Continuing towards her, he set his mouth in a grim smile. Her instinctive intention to bolt was plain. He wondered for a moment if he'd get some early cutting practice for the weekend camp draft—perversely, the thought made his smile broaden. Kayla sank back in her chair—he could practically see each muscle relax as she realised that flight was not an option.

She'd managed to avoid him for a couple of days, once in the supermarket and the other time at the library. And she hadn't returned the message he'd left her but that wasn't a surprise because he'd made it clear the message was private, not official. Perhaps he'd have to resort to something official to get a response.

A roadworthy check, a breathalyser set up outside the hospital just for a chance to talk to her. She was reducing him to a sad state.

But not today.

He tightened his grip on the bag he carried. Today, he had a cast-iron reason to see her. And plenty of time, too, since he knew she'd only just started her lunch break.

He stopped beside her table. 'Kayla.'

'Sergeant.'

He let that slide as he pulled out the chair on the diagonal from her and sat down, setting the bag on the floor. 'You're a hard woman to pin down.'

Her brows arched over darkly lashed grey eyes. 'I wasn't aware that I needed pinning.'

A glorious procession of X-rated images sprang unhelpfully into his mind and he could feel an unfamiliar warmth mushrooming in his face.

Hell, he was blushing.

He never blushed.

'You don't…er…need pinning.' He coughed to clear the huskiness from his vocal cords, all the while aware of her faintly perplexed expression. 'I've been trying to catch up with you.'

'I know. I got your message but it didn't seem urgent. Is there a problem with my statement about the accident?'

'Nope. No problem with that.'

'Good.' Her soft mouth pursed briefly and then she made a production of looking at her watch. 'I really should be getting…'

She trailed off as the cafeteria owner slipped a plate in front of her and then a cup of coffee. Tom stifled an urge to laugh at the comical look of guilt on her face.

'Hey, Tom,' said the woman with a smile. 'Can I get you anything?'

'A coffee would be great.'

'Black, no sugar, coming right up.'

He turned back to look at Kayla. 'Tsk, don't you know it's bad form to lie to a policeman?'

A strange spasm crossed her face. Pain? Then she lowered her eyes. 'Yeah, I do, as it happens.'

His interest sharpened but he left the questions unasked. Instead, he filed her response away with all the other things he wanted to know about her.

'I'll let you off this time.'

'Gee, thanks.' The sarcasm was unmistakeable as she lifted her eyes back to his.

He frowned and let his gaze roam over her face, watched with interest as she fidgeted and a tinge of pink crept into her cheeks. 'You know, if I was a suspicious man, I'd think you were avoiding me.'

She tilted her head to give him a considering look. The corner of her mouth crimped for a moment and then she said, 'You're a policeman. Suspicion is in your job description.'

'Okay. Good point,' he said, biting back the laugh that threatened. She had a quick wit and he was damned if bandying words with her wasn't wickedly good fun. Hoping to provoke another exchange, he reached over and snagged a chip off her plate. 'Eat up. Don't mind me, I've already eaten.'

'Not enough by the look of it,' she said as he blew on the chip.

'Always room for a chip or two.' He popped it in his mouth.

'In that case, do feel free to help yourself,' she said, her tone withering as she picked up her knife and fork.

He grinned and grabbed another. 'I hear you're going to the camp draft this weekend.'

She narrowed her eyes at him. 'Yes. I am.' She sounded reluctant to part with the details.

'With Liz and Jack?'

'Yes.'

'Looking forward to it?' he said, making a mental note to check with Jack to see if they intended to stay out at the grounds over the weekend. They did usually but with Liz being pregnant they might opt for the comfort of home and just drive out during the day.

'I'm sure it'll be interesting.' She pushed the grilled fish around on her plate then cut a small portion off the end. 'What was it you wanted to see me about?'

'I've got some gear for you from Penny. Boots and a hat.'

'Oh. I was going to pick it up from her tonight.'

He shrugged. 'I was coming this way so I offered to drop it off to you.' *Which was a long way from the truth. He'd practically had to prise the bag out of his confused constable's fingers.*

'Thanks.' She laid the knife and fork on her plate.

'My pleasure.' He looked at her substantially untouched food and frowned. 'Not hungry? You should eat more. There's nothing of you.'

More colour flooded into her cheeks and the grey eyes sparkled with irritation. 'Thank you for that professional assessment, Sergeant.'

'Tom. And it's not a complaint. What there is of you is a very nice package.' He knew he was out of line but something about seeing her mouth open in a perfect oval of outrage was irresistible. Baiting her like this was probably doing little to help his cause, but he couldn't seem to help himself. 'I wouldn't like to see you fade away while you're in Dustin.'

'Highly unlikely.' She gave him a fulminating glare from stormy grey eyes. 'Unless you're going to make a habit of dropping by to pilfer my lunch.'

'If that's an invitation, I accept.'

'It's not.'

'Shame. Well, much as I'd love to, I can't stay and chat. There's work to be done.' He pushed himself to his feet and lifted the bag onto the chair. 'Your accessories for the weekend. See you, Kayla.'

Not waiting for an answer, he walked towards the exit. A quick glance in the mirrored glass on the wall showed Kayla watching him leave. Perhaps he should check his shirt for scorch marks when he got back to the station.

He suppressed a grin. At least he could get under her skin. Not his first choice of reactions but it did mean she wasn't completely indifferent to him.

What had that been all about?

Kayla frowned. Since the accident, she seemed to have had more to do with Tom Jamieson than for the entire time she'd been in Dustin prior to that.

She watched the door shut behind him then shifted her gaze to the bag on the chair beside her.

The knots in her stomach unravelled enough to allow a gurgle of hunger to escape.

She looked back at her plate and after a moment picked up the utensils. Stupid to let good food go to waste because the sergeant was so disturbing. Doggedly chewing a mouthful, she tried to banish him from her mind by thinking about the last patient she'd seen before lunch.

A sixty-year-old male, heavy smoker with a long-standing cough. He'd wanted a quick pass through the office and a script for antibiotics but she hadn't liked the wheezing sounds she'd heard in his lungs on auscultation. He hadn't liked her insistence on him having a chest X-ray.

Kayla sighed. She seemed to be bent on annoying the men who came into her orbit today. The expression in the sergeant's deep chocolate eyes had swung between frustration and puckish humour.

Except for those few moments when she could swear he looked embarrassed. He didn't strike her as the sort to be easily disconcerted. Her own system had been so jangled by his presence, she couldn't remember what they'd been talking about.

Her eyes slid back to the bag from Penny.

The weekend. Would Tom be at the camp draft? Her

appetite abruptly evaporated and she had to force the food down her throat.

She reached for her coffee and took a swallow. She'd agreed to camp out at the grounds with Jack and Liz. Her first experience in a tent. She wasn't sure if she was dreading it or looking forward to it. Either way, having Sergeant Tom Jamieson around would only complicate things. He was a hard man to ignore when he got in her face.

She lifted her cup, then, as a sudden suspicion leapt into her mind, she froze with it halfway to her mouth. Surely he wasn't putting himself in her way deliberately.

No. Why would he?

She huffed out a sigh of impatience. In a minute, she'd be chewing her fingernails or twirling a hank of hair like a fourteen-year-old anguishing over the way a boy had looked at her.

So what if Tom Jamieson was there at the weekend. She'd just avoid him.

Easy. Now, if only she could get him out of her thoughts.

Picking up the fork again, she stabbed another piece of fish.

Who'd have thought she'd get such a kick out of the camp draft? Kayla grinned. The dust, the horses, the energetic noise of it, she loved it all. The people of Dustin were putting a touch of country into the city girl.

She looked down at herself and her good humour deepened. The dusty brown cargo pants, her most casual pair of trousers, and the long-sleeved cream shirt were her own. The scuffed elastic-sided boots on her feet and the felt hat perched on the seat beside her were on loan from Penny. Mandatory fashion wear for attending a camp draft event, she'd been told. When she'd dressed to drive out here this morning, she'd been self-conscious in her unfamiliar trimmings. Now they looked just right. She almost felt like the genuine article.

From her seat under the trees, she had a good view, although her position was on the opposite side of the arena to most of the action. People had stopped to chat through the morning and she'd gleaned helpful snippets of information.

She knew that right now the next competitor was in the small penned area known as the *camp* with a group of cows…*no, not plain old cows. For camp drafting, they were known as beasts.*

Tom Jamieson was judging this section of the competition. She'd lost count of the number of people who'd told her that. As if she needed to be told. Her eyes strayed again to the man on the large, sleepy-looking brown horse standing patiently beside the double gates of the camp.

Tom.

He sat in the saddle, loose and relaxed, with his attention on the action in the pen.

She dragged her gaze back to the gates, which would open any moment. The selected beast would bolt through with a hopeful rider in hot pursuit. Then with skill and perhaps a dollop of luck, the animal would be persuaded to gallop a figure-eight pattern around the saplings positioned in the arena.

The gates opened, but luck wasn't with the competitor. His beast evaded him, darting to its left and making a beeline along the fence.

After a few moments, the disqualification whistle sounded. Tom's horse perked up at some invisible command and cantered forward eagerly to herd the errant bovine towards the attendants. With a feeling of despair, Kayla watched the way Tom's body moved with the loping

horse. That sinewy masculine strength moving in graceful partnership with the muscular animal beneath him
appealed to a very basic corner of her psyche.

And it shouldn't.

She wanted to howl with frustration. She'd never had
such a gut-wrenching response to a man before. The wicked
brew of sensations left her reeling.

Why now?

Why him?

He was so unsuitable. Large and physical. Controlling.
And a policeman. Three strikes.

She preferred her men to be medium-sized, medium-
tempered and, after her recent experiences, anything *but*
a career police officer.

The loudspeaker cracked to life. 'And that's the end of
the novice section. We'll take a small break. Could competitors for the next category make sure they're mounted
and ready? Thank you.'

Tom's head swivelled in her direction. His broad-
brimmed hat sat low over his eyes, making it impossible
to see his features, but that didn't stop a tiny shiver of
awareness from lancing through her stomach. Stupid. He
wasn't looking at her. Probably had no idea she was even
there.

She picked up her hat, jammed it on her head and got
to her feet.

She had to get away, give her system a chance to equili-
brate. With Tom out of sight, she'd have more chance of
banishing him from her mind. She turned away from the
arena and strode across the packed-earth path beneath the
trees, enjoying the crunch of dry leaves and twigs.

Jack had taken Liz back to their camp to put her feet up
a while ago. Hopefully, he'd have some water heating for a

billy tea. There! She'd leave Dustin with a new vocabulary as well as some wonderful memories.

She let her arms swing with each step as she sucked in another lungful of warm, morning air and savoured the clean sharp tang of eucalyptus oil.

Each exhalation seemed to clear away more of the fog of sadness and anxiety that had plagued her for the last six months. The betrayal of her fiancé and unceasing disapproval of her father seemed distant, unimportant things in this magical place beneath the gum trees. Even the worries about her sister eased.

In their stead, a marvellous sense of freedom. And a confirmation that she'd made the right decision by coming here to do the locum for Liz. The kilometres between the small country town and her family down in the city helped her to see how suffocating and unhealthy her relationships with them had become.

Ultimately, she would do what she could to heal the rifts with them. But for now she was content with her plans. After she'd finished in Dustin, she was moving on. Remote area medicine. On her weekends off, she'd already done some of the courses that would stand her in good stead, help her to qualify for a position. She was waiting on one final enrolment. With luck she'd pick up a place earlier if there was a cancellation.

No going back to the city. Dustin was the stepping stone to the rest of her life.

She was doing what was right for her, not what was expected.

The simplicity of being in this rural valley was like a balm to her spirit. The steep, treed hillsides of the natural basin, towering gum-leaf canopies, water gurgling over large rocks in the river that curved around the edge of the large flat floor. It was beautiful. Nature's sounds and smells.

Breathe. Enjoy the moment. For today, she was here. In this place. In this particular moment.

It was all good.

Her eyes caught sight of the tents behind her car and her new-found calm abruptly evaporated.

All was good...*except* for the local police sergeant.

When she'd arrived that morning, Jack had proudly shown her the tent he'd set up for her. Another well-prepared person was camping very close. Obviously, a competitor because there was a horse float and a makeshift corral of electric tape. She'd put her bag in on the camp stretcher. Then, and only then, had Jack casually mentioned the tent next to hers belonged to Tom Jamieson.

A wave of chaotic heat swept up from her toes as she remembered the moment.

How was she supposed to avoid the man when she was practically sleeping with him? Sure, they were separated by thin layers of waterproof nylon.

And a few feet of air.

Hardly any sort of barrier at all. She'd hear him when he moved in his tent, in his sleeping bag.

She swallowed.

He'd hear her.

She'd wanted to demand that Jack dismantle her tent and set it up somewhere else. Preferably on the other side of the river, the other side of the basin.

The other side of Australia! A small snicker of laughter escaped her.

She'd even mumbled some stilted half-sentences about moving but Jack had looked at her as though she'd lost her mind. Little did he know how close he was to being right.

She was powerless to control her physical reaction when Tom Jamieson was near her. The tiny shivers that spiralled out of her stomach to every part of her body, clogging her throat, cramping the function of her lungs. Sending her heart into tachycardia. But she could make damned sure he never guessed the struggle she was having.

Cool.

Calm.

Collected.

Her watchwords for dealing with Tom Jamieson.

A loud equine snort jerked her out of her mental pep talk.

A sudden prickle of awareness shivered across her skin. With a feeling of inevitability, she stopped and turned. At eye level was a black mane on a gleaming brown horse. But more disturbing, a pair of lean moleskin-covered legs astride the large creature. A man's hand held leather reins in a relaxed grip, a second hand rested on the thigh nearest to her, long masculine fingers splayed across taut navy fabric.

She'd been thinking about Tom and now here he was as though she'd conjured him up.

She looked up into his smiling face and her heart did a slow somersault before quivering behind her sternum like a jelly. At this rate she'd need to call the paramedics for defibrillation. Everything about this moment would be imprinted on her memory. The curve of his lips, the creak of the saddle, a pleasant animal mustiness from the sun-warmed horse.

Damn.

She was a city girl. Sales at big department stores made her pulse career out of control. Not moments filled with these earthy scents and sights and sounds.

Nature had an evil sense of humour.

CHAPTER FIVE

'ARE you following me, Sergeant?'

'Tom.'

'Are you following me...Sergeant *Tom*?'

He laughed, the corners of his eyes crinkling attractively. Her traitorous heart gave a quick leap. She set her lips, ruthlessly suppressing the smile that wanted to form. If she wasn't careful, he'd think she was bantering with him, encouraging him. The last thing she needed.

His laughter faded and he leaned confidingly towards her. The fabric of his pale blue chambray shirt pulled at the shoulder, moulding to the muscle beneath. He rested a lean, tanned forearm on the front of the saddle, his hand dangling at eye level. She frowned, resisting the impulse to step back.

His eyes made a leisurely examination of her face and then he said, 'Yes.'

She squinted at him, her mind scrambling to make sense of the word. The small silence snapped at her nerves. 'Yes, what?'

'Yes, I am following you,' he clarified.

'Oh.' Her voice came out as a feeble squeak. She cleared her throat. 'Why?'

'When I saw you heading away from the arena, I guessed you'd be going back to camp for a cuppa.' His voice purred along her auditory pathways as she stared at the small satisfied smile curving his mouth. 'I thought I'd join you.'

'Don't you have things to do? Official duties?' She looked back towards the arena in the hope that a task might materialise for him. 'Judging or something?'

'Not right now.' The warmth in his eyes made her pulse jump. 'And, besides, I wanted to talk to you.'

She took a deep breath and recited her mantra again.

Cool.

Calm.

Collected. Was it too much to ask of her cavorting insides? Apparently, it was, because her heart kept chiselling at her ribcage.

'What did you want to talk to me about?' She managed to fix him with a steady look.

'Anything and everything, Kayla.' There it was again, that lingering verbal caress of her name. 'I enjoy crossing swords with you. There's a certain spice to it that I can't seem to resist. You interest me. I want to know what makes you tick.'

'You must be a very busy man if you're this curious with everyone.' She couldn't prevent the tinge of asperity that had crept into her voice.

'Ah, but I'm not this curious with just anyone.' When he paused, she felt her stomach tighten in anticipation of what he'd say next. 'Only the people I want to know better. Like you.' He gave her a sly smile. 'And members of the criminal fraternity, but that's part of the job.'

A small bubble of laughter escaped catching her by surprise. 'You're a typical policeman, aren't you?'

'I am. Does that bother you?' His gaze sharpened with predatory interest as he straightened in the saddle. The horse shifted restlessly beneath him but Tom didn't take his eyes off hers.

She shrugged. 'Why would it?'

'Tsk. Never answer a question with a question. It's one of those things that makes us typical policemen suspicious.' His eyes narrowed and she wondered what he read in her face because when she didn't say anything, he murmured, 'Policing is a job, Kayla, not a personality trait.'

'I know that.' She felt oddly raw, unprepared to hear the questions she could see forming in his mind. Marshalling her thoughts, she said, 'You said you wanted to talk to me?'

'I do.' He kicked his feet out of the stirrups and in the next instant he'd landed lightly on the ground beside her.

Impossibly close.

She took a small surreptitious step in retreat as he passed the reins over his mount's head. Holding them loosely in one hand, he turned to face her and swept his arm towards the tents. 'Shall we?'

So much for her escape. She turned and walked beside him. The sooner they got over to Liz and Jack, the sooner Tom's company would be diluted. Surely the impact on her senses would diminish with others around.

But it wasn't to be. When they arrived at the van, it was deserted.

'How about getting the billy on while I put Ziggy away?' He pointed to the neat cooking set up she'd seen earlier. 'Milk's in the esky. Mugs are on the rack. Sugar and teabags in the box.'

'How prosaic,' she murmured. 'You don't throw a scoop of loose tea into the billy with a handful of eucalyptus leaves?'

His lips twitched. 'We can try that another day if you

like. For today, teabags are easier. I take mine white with one.'

She nodded and crossed to where a blackened pot with a spout sat on a small portable gas cooker. A peek inside the billy revealed plenty of water so she lit the burner.

Everything was very orderly and in a short time she'd gathered the things she needed. With the water heating, she looked over to where Tom was working beside the float. He had the saddle off Ziggy and was brushing the glossy brown coat. The horse lowered his head and blew loudly through his nostrils. It sounded like a snort of contentment. The care Tom took with the big animal touched her.

Helpless to resist while he had his back to her, she ran her eyes over his frame. The muscles in his broad shoulders rippled and bunched with each long, powerful sweep of his arm. His light shirt followed the contours of his torso as it tapered to his trim waist and narrow hips.

After a few moments, he turned aside to put the brush in a carrier nearby and bent to pick up Ziggy's nearest front foot. The horse turned its head to rest its muzzle on Tom's lumbar region. There was a sweetness and trust in the gesture that brought an unexpected lump to her throat. As Tom worked his way around to each foot, she realised that Ziggy was obligingly lifting each foot for attention. Man and horse were obviously a well-established partnership.

When Tom had finished, he straightened, ran a hand over the horse's haunches then walked across to the corral. Ziggy ambled after him and Kayla realised the animal wasn't tethered. Tom unhitched a section of tape. The horse walked over to a pile of hay on the ground and took a mouthful. After a detour to check the bucket, Tom let himself out of the makeshift yard and turned towards her. His long legs began eating up the short distance between them.

She swallowed and snapped her attention to the cooker in front of her where steam was now rising out of the narrow spout. Glad to have something to do with her hands, she picked up the pot and poured hot water over the teabags she had ready.

In her peripheral vision, she saw Tom open a couple of folding chairs as she added a splash of milk to both brews.

With the teaspoon poised over the sugar, she asked, 'Heaped or flat?'

'Heaped.'

'Need sweetening?' She stirred the liquid.

'Some might say so.' He gave her a lopsided grin then leaned down to pick up the drink. 'Thanks. Grab a seat.'

She lifted her own mug and moved to join him. They relaxed into the chairs and the silence between them stretched. To her surprise, it was undemanding, almost comfortable. Sounds around them filled the void. Ziggy's steady munching, the clip-clop of hooves as a competitor trotted past, lowing of cattle. An empty stock truck clattered through the grounds to the other side of the arena.

'I saw you arrive this morning,' Tom said.

'Did you?' She blew on her steaming drink and took a small sip.

'Of course. I'm a policeman. We notice things.'

'Ah, yes.' Thank goodness he hadn't been at the tents to see her reaction to the camping arrangements. She hated to think what conclusions he might have drawn from her appalled expression.

'What do you think of the camp draft?'

She sent him a sideways glance under her lashes and, tongue firmly in cheek, she said, 'As far as I can see, it's a glorified excuse to chase around after a cow.'

'Bite your tongue.' He laughed and the sound rolled over her deliciously. 'It's not a cow. It's called a *beast*.'

'So I've been told.'

'And we don't *chase around* after it, we *control* it.'

'Mmm, control. I understand.' She nodded. 'So camp drafting is a sport for men who like to control things?'

'Hardly,' he said with a chuckle. 'Half a ton of beef on the hoof can be a tad stroppy.' He took a sip of tea. 'As for being in control—who doesn't like things to go their way?'

'True. Very true.' She looked down at the scuffed toes on her boots and contemplated that she was enjoying being here with him, just talking. Her system had started to settle. Her heart no longer thrummed in the desperate, unsustainable beat that felt like it would break out of her ribcage. Now it was a more pleasant, alive feeling. A hum of vitality and energy. Perhaps she'd been tackling the issue of Tom Jamieson all wrong. Maybe she needed to stop avoiding him and see *more* of him instead. Desensitise herself with small doses often.

She turned the option over in her mind, examining it for flaws.

'For instance,' he said breaking into her thoughts, 'I'd like to understand why you react to me the way you do.'

Her stomach dipped as she eyed him warily. So much for enjoying the conversation. She had a feeling he was about to prod her back out of her complacent thoughts.

When she didn't say anything he tilted his head to one side and contemplated her. 'At first, I wondered if it was because you didn't like me.' He didn't sound annoyed, just…meditative.

'Did you?' She took another quick sip to moisten her suddenly parched mouth.

He swirled his mug and stared into it as though an

answer might be hidden in the hot tea. 'But then I decided that couldn't be the case.'

'You—you did?' She was unwillingly curious.

He lifted his eyes to focus on her; intelligence gleamed in his piercing look. He nodded slowly. 'I realised you don't know me well enough to dislike me.'

'Oh.' Not a question, but definitely something that required an answer of some sort. She fingered the handle of her mug as she debated what to say. After a moment, she slid a look at him. 'Does that mean if I get to know you, it will be okay to dislike you then?'

He grinned his appreciation at the way she'd evaded a direct comment. 'No, that's not what I mean at all. *When*, not *if*, you get to know me, I'm sure you'll be charmed by my wit and sparkling personality.'

'And your modesty. Don't forget that.' Her biggest problem was that with his humorous approach he *was* charming her.

'You bet. Faint hearts and fair ladies.' He paused for a moment. 'Would you agree you're an open-minded person, Kayla? The sort who judges people on their merits?'

'I try to be.' But she knew she hadn't been fair with him. She had a feeling he was about to call her on it.

'Then why have you been giving me the cold shoulder?'

'*Trying* to give you the cold shoulder,' she corrected, with a rueful smile. 'I've been spectacularly unsuccessful.'

His lips twitched but other than that she could see he was waiting for an answer. She sighed. She'd give him one, but it wasn't a good one.

'It seemed the best way of handling you.'

'Why?' he asked softly.

'It's the way I deal with the unknown. I keep it at a distance.'

'I've seen you meeting Jack and Liz's other friends for the first time. No sign of frost then. Only when I'm around.'

So it hadn't been her imagination. He had watched her at the social events. She rolled the body of her mug between her hands. His perception was unsettling. 'That's what I mean. *You* are the unknown. You're not my...type.'

'What type am I?'

Sexy, dangerous, masculine, threatening? Overwhelming? Larger than life? Much more man than she could handle? Impossible words and phrases paraded through her mind. She couldn't say any of them. 'Large. Dominant. In the police force.'

'That's the third time you've brought up my job. Interesting. You don't seem the sort who'd have run foul of the law to build up that sort of prejudice.' She waited for him to draw the inevitable conclusion. 'So maybe your experience is a more personal one.'

Her hands were suddenly clammy against the stainless steel of the mug. She tried to think of something to change the subject.

'Someone you went out with?'

'Yes,' she said reluctantly.

'Close?'

She tightened her fingers around the mug. 'We were engaged.'

'Past tense.' After a moment he added, 'But perhaps not very past tense.'

'No, not very.'

'I'm sorry,' he said softly, and tears prickled at the backs of her eyes. She'd thought she was all cried out over Keith. She *was* all cried out—it was Tom's sympathy that was undoing her.

'Don't be.' Her voice was husky with the choky feeling in her throat. 'It was for the best.'

'How long before you came up here?'

'A couple of months.'

'Rough?'

'Yes, it was at the time.'

'Tell me his name. I have connections. I'll have him busted to constable.'

She laughed despite herself, grateful to him for lightening the moment so her incipient tears could recede. 'Tempting, but not a good idea. Besides…I think his connections are better.'

'Really?'

'Mmm.' She pursed her mouth then told him the rest. 'He was marrying his boss's daughter.'

'His boss's daughter?' He sounded thoughtful. 'Using my superior powers of deduction, I'll take a stab and say your father's in the police force.'

'Impressive, Sherlock.'

'I think I can do better. Morgan? That wouldn't be Assistant Commissioner Christopher Morgan, would it?'

'It would.'

She held her breath, waiting for his reaction. Would he be overawed by her father's rank, the way Keith had? Would he see her as a way to fast-track his career?

Tom was silent for a long moment and then he laughed— a genuine sound. 'Yeah, I guess his connections are better. Still, he must have blotted his copybook with your father when you broke it off.'

'Not really.' The support from such an unlikely source pierced straight to her heart. The truth was, far from Tom's assumption, her father thought she was a feather-brained female by breaking it off with his rising star. Now Tom, a man she hardly knew, was standing in her corner. No questions asked.

She'd been a convenience for Keith—one that had become inconvenient when she'd confided in him about her brother-in-law's pass. Even in private, he hadn't been able to be a rock in her time of need.

'Your dad took his side?'

'My father didn't know the whole story behind the break-up.'

'And you think that's okay?'

'Not okay.' She shrugged. 'But unless he knew all the facts, how could he make a decision about whose side to take?'

'You're his daughter, his family. His allegiance should be automatic.'

Should it? It hadn't ever worked that way in her family. She was silent for a long moment. 'You are a nice man, Tom Jamieson.'

He made a hissing sound of disgust through his teeth. *'Nice?'* His mouth curved and his eyes glinted with humour. 'Well, it's a long way from charming but it's a start.'

A small snort of laughter escaped. She bit her lip to smother the unfamiliar sound.

Looking pleased with himself, Tom stretched his legs out in front of him and crossed them at the ankles. She swallowed, all desire to laugh instantly subsiding.

'What were your other two objections to me? Large and dominant?' Tom asked. 'I can't do anything about *large* except to say I would never hurt you physically, Kayla. Never.'

There was nothing but truth in his warm brown eyes. She ducked her head. 'I believe you.'

'Then that just leaves dominant. Is that such a problem?

You're pretty bossy yourself. You didn't have any trouble telling me what to do at Andy's accident. Or ignoring what I wanted you to do.'

He was whittling away her objections, gently, thoroughly, leaving her naked, without protection.

'You wouldn't want a marshmallow man.' He sat forward again, his voice pitched low and intimate. 'You'd walk all over him.'

She stood and walked to the kitchen set up to relight the billy. She had to do something with her hands and making a second cup of tea seemed as good as anything. 'Did you want another cup of tea?'

'No, but I would like you to stop avoiding me, Kayla.'

She turned back to face him. 'I'm not sure where you're going with this. I've agreed that you're nicer than I expected. I'll even admit to the possibility that a warm, sparkling personality might lurk behind your rugged, law-enforcement-officer exterior. What more can I do?'

'Come to my family's barbecue tonight. We always get together on the Saturday night of the camp draft weekend.'

She shook her head. 'I can't gatecrash a family tradition, and besides, I'm here with Liz and Jack.'

'They'll be there. All comers are welcome. There's nothing exclusive about a Jamieson get-together. You'd have ended up coming across with them anyway.'

'Oh.'

He walked across and put his empty mug into the wash bucket. 'This just means you'll be there with me.'

'Then I suppose it would be okay. Where is it?'

His mouth twitched. 'Over the other side of the arena.'

'Okay.' She lifted the lid on the teabag container and got one out. 'Liz and Jack will know.'

'They do.' He looked down at her and said softly, 'But make no mistake here, Kayla. I'm asking you to come with *me*, so I'll come and pick you up.'

'But it'd be just as easy for me to walk over with them, wouldn't it?'

'A gentleman always picks up his date from her front door,' he said lightly.

She scowled. 'It's a tent.'

'From her tent flap, then.' He grinned. 'I want you to walk over with me, Kayla.'

'Oh, very well.' With fumbling fingers, she fitted the lid onto the canister. Picking the container up, she clutched it to her chest like a shield and turned to face him. '*But* since you're so insistent on that, I have some demands of my own.'

His eyelids drooped slightly, giving him a deceptive, sleepy look that was belied by the slow, sexy smile that touched his lips. 'Tell me your demands and I'll do my best to satisfy them.'

Her heart kicked hard and scalding heat crawled up her neck, cell by cell, into her face. *God, what did he think she'd meant?* She longed to bring her hands up, press them to her cheeks, hide them from his gaze. Her fingers tightened on the canister, the plastic lip digging into her palm.

'Ground rules,' she blurted. 'I mean I want to set ground rules.'

His smile faded. 'Ground rules?'

'No…funny business. Strictly friends.' Marvellous. She sounded as gauche as a teen going on her first date.

'Of course.' He nodded gravely, his eyes guileless as they held hers. 'Best behaviour. Nothing you don't approve of.'

'Just as long as we're clear.' She tried hard to concentrate on his words, feeling there was a trap there but not able to concentrate her mind to identify it.

'Crystal clear. Don't look so worried. It'll all work out, you'll see.' He grinned, a natural friendly expression not loaded with innuendo this time. She wondered if she'd misjudged him earlier. 'I'd better get back to the arena to help out.' He lifted his hand and stroked her cheek. 'I'll see you later.'

'Okay. Yes. Good. See you.' The skin on her cheek tingled from his tiny caress.

She watched him walk away, her eyes straying over the broad shoulders and straight back, the long legs. Her physical and emotional reactions mocked her. Clammy hands, racing pulse, abdominal gymnastics. How could she ever think she could desensitise herself against someone like him?

He was a sexy man with a brand of masculinity her feminine weakness yearned towards.

Blast him.

She had to shore up her defences, try to contain her vulnerability. She was only here for another four months. Too short to explore anything even if she wanted to. Not that he'd asked her to… She had to remember, she had plans. Places to go, things to do. A rebellion and a search for herself as much as anything.

Nothing that involved Tom Jamieson.

Nothing that involved *any* man.

Tom wanted to gentle her as he would one of his young foals, imprint her with the idea that he was someone she could trust, that he was someone she could let close, someone who wouldn't betray her. Or ask more than she could give.

But maybe he was lying to himself…wasn't he already

asking more than she wanted to give? She wanted to deny the chemistry between them and her defences were well honed.

He'd made steps this morning, dispelled much of the chill between them but none of the sexual tension. Her astringent sense of humour had him on his toes to keep up with her. She was an interesting combination of good humour and vulnerability when she relaxed her guard.

Liz had been right when she'd warned him that Kayla had been hurt. Tom clenched his jaw, feeling his teeth grind under the pressure. The men in her life obviously hadn't appreciated her special blend of strength and sensitivity and honour.

Assistant Commissioner Morgan was her father. Hard to imagine him being a parent. Must have been tough, being his kid. The man was a straight arrow, incorruptible, uncompromising and well-known throughout the force for his rigid, by-the-book approach to everything. For his job that approach was commendable.

For raising a daughter…perhaps not quite so good. How did a child respond to that sort of environment? Perfectionism? Self-reliance? There was a key to understanding Kayla.

And he really, really wanted to understand her.

He remembered her flushed face when she'd been laying down the law about tonight. Clutching those teabags in front of her like some sort of talisman to ward off invaders. He had no problems with her ground rules.

Not that it would stop him from prodding at the boundaries. But he'd always respect her. She had nothing to worry about.

For now.

He'd worked with horses all his life and had a horseman's appreciation for the finer details of the chase. Of when to apply pressure to a wary creature and when to back off to get a filly to come to him willingly.

But once she did, she was going to be his.

CHAPTER SIX

BACK at the arena, Kayla sat on one of the folding chairs in front of the first-aid tent and listened to the commentator announce the scores.

The latest young competitor had had a disappointing run and now his beast trotted in brief, glorious freedom around the edge of the arena. Mounted attendants converged on the animal to usher it efficiently towards the race at the other end of the enclosure.

Kayla swept her gaze over the riders absentmindedly and then continued to scan the area. A fizz of dismay and resignation rippled through her stomach as she realised she was searching for a *particular* tall, lean figure.

Tom Jamieson.

God, what was wrong with her? Tom wasn't around—she should be *glad*, not trying to find him. Sure, they'd talked, settled some of her wariness. But that didn't make them best buddies. And it was certainly no reason to be visually stalking him like a...camp draft groupie—if there was such a thing. The cup of tea they'd had together had been pleasant...fun, even...but it still didn't mean she was going to seek him out.

Tom had said he enjoyed crossing swords with her. She was honest enough to admit there was a perverse enjoyment in their tension-riddled contact. As though she was flying too close to the sun, flirting with something perilous yet irresistible.

Though, to be fair, he hadn't put a foot wrong. It was the way he made her feel inside. He didn't have to do anything—just be himself. That aura of reckless danger radiated from him.

In her heart, she knew she was no match for him. The courage it would take to keep up with a man like Tom Jamieson was beyond her grasp.

She stood and moved restlessly around the tent, running a distracted eye over the supplies.

A burst of static from the loudspeaker system cut into her. 'The last rider into camp before we break for lunch is Ryan Collins on Misty Lady.'

A collective gasp from the people on the small spectator stand nearby drew her attention back to the arena. She crossed to the fence as the stewards opened the double gates. A brown and white steer burst out of the camp, closely pursued by a slender rider on a grey horse. The fearless boy seemed younger than the thirteen she knew he must be to compete in the camp draft. Lanky, with an uncoordinated look, the way his arms were pumping to urge his horse to go faster.

Unimpressed, the steer began to duck and weave, looking for a way to escape. Kayla's heart leapt to her throat as the horse plunged to the side. The sudden move caught the rider by surprise and she could see his frantic grab for the saddle. For a moment she thought he might recover but in the next second he was tumbling, all long legs and arms, to land, hands first on the sandy surface. Kayla darted back to the tent to grab the medical kit.

Her eyes fixed on the still, sprawled figure in the centre of the arena, she dashed towards the nearest gate. One of the spectators had it open for her.

'Thanks.' She threw the word over her shoulder as she ran. A man vaulted the fence further around the perimeter and in a dozen strides was beside the now-struggling child.

Tom.

Tossing his hat carelessly to the ground, he sank to his knees and reached out to help.

By the time she took her last few steps, the boy was sitting up and cradled against Tom's bigger, stronger body.

'M-my arm hurts.' The boy struggled to suppress his sobs but the tear tracks streaked through the dust on his pale cheeks. He clutched his arm to his body, his face screwed up with pain.

'I know, Ryan,' Tom said, his voice gravelly with sympathy. 'Here's the doc to patch you up.'

The boy's moisture-drenched dark brown eyes blinked at her warily.

'Hey, Ryan. I'm Kayla,' she said as she knelt beside the pair, noting Tom's tender, supporting embrace. His eyes, when she met them briefly, mirrored Ryan's anguish.

Turning her attention back to her patient, she said 'Let's have a look at what you've done to yourself, shall we?'

'It hurts t-too much.' He hunched away, curling his face into Tom's shoulder, protective of the injured limb and wanting to prevent her from touching it. 'Uncle Tom?' The plea stark with fear.

Uncle Tom? Suddenly the family resemblance between the two was obvious—those thickly lashed, deep brown eyes, the wavy, nearly black hair. Ryan was the spitting image of how a young Tom must have looked.

'Ry, you need—' Tom began in a tortured voice.

'It's okay,' Kayla interrupted gently, touching Tom on the hand as she addressed Ryan. 'We can have a look at the rest of you for a minute, can't we, Ryan? Is your arm the only bit that hurts?'

He nodded, still huddling into Tom. 'I th-think so.'

'What about your head? Did you hit it when you landed?'

'N-no.'

'That's good.' She smiled at him. 'Will you let me undo your helmet for you?'

He uncurled a little and tilted his head so she could reach the chin buckle. She gently removed the protective cap.

'I'm just going to touch your neck and back. I want you to tell me if anything hurts. Can you do that?'

'Y-yes.' Some of the tension eased across Ryan's shoulders now that he realised she wasn't going to insist on handling his arm immediately.

Kayla pressed gently down his slender neck. 'How's that feel?'

'O-okay.'

'And here? Any pain?' she asked. She worked around his shoulders and upper arms, acutely aware of the way Tom shifted his grip on his nephew, anticipating her moves, making it easier for her to continue her examination.

'No. It feels okay,' said Ryan.

'Good.' She sat back on her heels and kept a hand on his shoulder as she did a visual assessment of his cradled arm. There was swelling, which meant the delicate bones at his wrist were obscured compared to his uninjured arm. But no blood, no obvious bone displacement, good colour in his fingertips. All positive signs. 'Tell me about the pain in your arm. If I said ten was really, really bad and one was hardly hurting at all, how does yours feel?'

'M-maybe an eight. Or—or a nine. B-but I don't want an injection.'

'No injections.' She met Tom's eyes briefly in silent communication before looking back at Ryan. 'Do you have any medical problems, Ryan? Asthma? Anything else? Do you take any medicine regularly?'

The boy shook his head.

'He's as fit as a fiddle,' Tom said, reading her message and adding his confirmation to Ryan's silent answer. 'But you're a bit accident-prone, aren't you, matey?'

'Yeah.' A faint sheepish grin creased Ryan's drawn face. 'That's what Mum says, too.'

'Great. I have something that will help with the pain before we take a look at your arm.' She dug out an inhaler and quickly charged it with liquid analgesic. 'You need to pop the end in your mouth and suck air through it.'

She read the child's reluctance to let go of his injured limb. 'How about we get your uncle to hold that for you? You just use it whenever you need to.'

Tom adjusted his support of his nephew so he could take the assembled unit. The murmur of the crowd filtered into her consciousness while she waited for the boy to take a couple of good, deep breaths.

'Ryan, I'm just going to take your pulse on your sore arm and then touch your fingers, is that okay? We won't move it yet. I promise.'

'Okay.' Ryan sucked hard on the inhaler and his eyes followed her movements as she curled her fingers carefully around his wrist to feel for the radial pulse. As she expected, the beat was strong and steady, if a little rapid.

Lightly running her fingers over each of his digits, she said, 'Can you feel me doing that?'

'Yes.'

She turned to the kit, located the inflatable splints and chose the size she needed. 'We need to put a splint on your arm to hold your bones still, Ryan. It'll help with your pain. This is what we'll use.' She showed Ryan the opening. 'See, it's a tube. I'll slip your arm in and then I can pump it full of air until it's a nice, firm bubble. Can I do that for you now?'

The boy bit his lip, looking up at the man holding him for guidance. A lump formed in Kayla's throat at the naked affection in Tom's face as he gave Ryan a smiling nod. With the encouragement, her young patient took a deep breath, tears springing to his eyes as he said, 'Okay.'

'You're being very brave.'

'Thanks.' Ryan hiccupped then said, 'It was pretty dumb, though, huh, Uncle Tom? Falling off like that.'

'Nah, happens to all of us, Ry,' Tom said. 'You've seen me come a cropper. Remember when Ziggy bucked me off in the ditch?'

Kayla slid the splint over Ryan's hand and carefully worked it along his forearm as Tom talked.

'Y-yeah, you stunk,' said Ryan with a watery chuckle.

'What happened?' Kayla asked.

'Uncle Tom landed head first in the water.' Ryan wiped his cheek with the palm of his uninjured hand, smearing the dust and moisture into a muddy smut.

'Yeah. I was putrid, wasn't I? Even after I showered, the smell stayed in my nose.'

'M-mum wouldn't let him come inside until he'd hosed off.'

'Which wouldn't have been so bad, except it was the middle of winter and the water was cold.'

'Poor Uncle Tom.' Kayla smiled at Ryan before she flicked a glance at Tom.

His answering smile promised retribution. 'I can tell how sorry you feel for me.'

'Oh, I do.' She swallowed and made the final tweak to position the splint.

'At least, y-you didn't cry or anything.' Ryan must have suddenly compared his uncle's accident and the aftermath to his own performance and found himself wanting. His voice was unsteady again as he said, 'D-don't tell Hannah that I bawled, will you?'

Kayla squeezed the bulb of the splint pump and air began to fill the clear plastic sleeve.

'I won't.'

'Promise? Only g-girls cry,' Ryan said as he watched the splint inflate. 'I d-don't want everyone to know.'

'It's okay to cry, Ryan,' Kayla said gently. The boy gave her such a look of horrified disbelief that she bit the inside of her cheek to stop herself from chuckling. 'It's true. No one should be ashamed to have a good cry if they need to.' She flashed a pointed glance at the tall man cradling the boy. 'Should they...Uncle Tom?'

His amusement was clear in the twitch of his mouth. 'Kayla's right, Ry,' he said to his nephew, but his warm brown eyes lingered on hers.

With an effort, she dragged her gaze away and checked the firmness of the air splint.

'*You* don't cry,' Ryan said, twisting his head so he could look up into the man's face.

'I don't cry where you can see me, kiddo,' Tom said softly. 'There's a difference.'

Kayla's heart melted as he surprised her yet again with his sensitivity. She'd expected him to mouth a quick platitude. Instead, his answer was meaningful, filled with a touching honesty and a wealth of personal experience behind the admission. *What would bring a man like Tom Jamieson to the point of tears?*

'How's your pain level now, Ryan?' she said, pulling her attention back to her patient.

'Better. Yeah.'

'Good. Let's fix you up with this sling,' she said, threading a fabric triangle under his arm then leaning forward so she could tie the ends at the back of his neck. 'I'll organise a stretcher and we can get you out of here.'

'I can walk.'

'But you're—'

'I want to. Please.' His eyes beseeched her before turning to Tom.

'I'll help him, Kayla,' Tom said softly. 'He'll be okay.'

She pursed her lips for a moment then nodded. Both male faces lit up with identical expressions of relief. Suppressing the urge to shake her head at them, she closed up the medical kit. Hoisting the strap onto her shoulder, she stood by ready to assist, but Tom had everything under control. He braced Ryan with loving care and got the boy to his feet. Ryan straightened and Kayla scrutinised her patient's face.

'How do you feel?' she said. 'Not light-headed? Sick?'

'No. I'm good.' Ryan squared his shoulders and stepped forward. On either side of him, she and Tom hovered like anxious guardians, matching his pace.

A cheer went up from the crowd. Ryan's pale cheeks flushed with quiet pride as he lifted a hand in acknowledgement.

Ten minutes later, Tom had Kayla and Ryan tucked into the back seat of his four-wheel drive and was heading for Dustin.

At the intersection, he braked and turned his head to check his precious cargo. Kayla's head was bent towards his nephew, a swing of straight golden hair hiding her profile. She reached up and brushed it back, tucking it behind her ear as he'd seen her do often. She was smiling at Ryan. Her body was curved towards the boy, ready to anticipate his needs. She adjusted the seat belt for him and murmured something. Ryan looked up and smiled. The trust in his nephew's expression made Tom's chest tighten.

He cleared his throat. 'Everything okay back there?'

'Yes,' two voices chorused. Kayla lifted soft grey eyes to meet his.

Tom faced the front again, checked the way was clear then pulled out onto the road.

'Uncle Tom?'

'Yes, Ry?'

'Mum's on duty this morning. Will she look after me?'

'Probably. I've spoken to her so she knows we're on the way.' He glanced at Ryan in the rear-vision mirror then across to Kayla. 'My sister, Ryan's mum, is Charlotte Collins.'

'The radiographer?'

'Yep.'

'Will I have one of those plasters that everyone can sign?' Ryan said, sounding hopeful.

'You will.' Humour laced Kayla's voice.

'Cool. That's better than David. He only had a sling when he broke his collarbone.' There was a small silence. When Tom looked up again, Ryan was yawning. 'When will I be able to ride again?'

'Well, let's get you fixed up before we say for sure,' Kayla said, gently. 'You'll need the plaster on for six weeks and then we'll see. How is your pain now?'

'Okay. I'm tired,' he mumbled through another yawn.

'Why don't you close your eyes?'

A few minutes later, Tom glanced up to see Kayla had her arm around Ryan. His nephew's head rested on her shoulder.

Tom swallowed hard. The picture sent a shaft of pure emotion arrowing so strongly to his heart, it bordered on pain.

She'd handled his nephew flawlessly in the arena, no frustration with his reluctance to have her examine his arm. Just a smooth segue into other checks until Ryan had the confidence to let her near the painful injury. She was fantastic to have around, taking charge, easing difficult moments in an emergency.

He loved the way she'd been so sensitive, quickly grasping Ryan's need to walk out of the arena on his own two feet. Tom had been able to tell she hadn't been happy about it, but she'd understood it was important.

He liked working with her. They made a good team.

A damned good team.

An achy warmth expanded through his chest. The more he knew Kayla, the more he wanted to know.

As Kayla had expected, Ryan's arm had a classic greenstick fracture. A minor manipulation while he was under heavy sedation reduced it. And then she'd put a cast on his forearm.

Now back in the care of his mother, Ryan had immediately tried to extract a promise from the frazzled woman that she'd take him back out for the camp draft barbecue as planned.

'Maybe. We'll see how you are in a couple of hours,' Charlotte prevaricated.

'We'd better head back out to the flat, Charlie,' Tom said with a glance at his watch.

'Of course.' Charlotte turned to Kayla. 'Thank you both again for looking after Ryan.'

'No problem, Charlotte. Everything should be fine with

his arm now but let me know if you have any concerns,' Kayla said.

'I will, thank you.' Charlotte put her arm across her son's shoulders and he snuggled into her side without any self-consciousness. 'Good luck, Tom. And listen, I don't want to see you in here later.'

Tom grinned. 'Yes, boss. See you, Ry.'

'Let's go, Kayla.' He took her arm and Kayla was aware of Charlotte's eyes darting between them curiously.

'Sure. Bye, Ryan, Charlotte.'

Tom shifted his hand to the small of her back and the warmth of his touch through the light cotton of her shirt was all she could think of until he was holding the door of his vehicle open for her.

She clambered into the front passenger seat and watched him walk around the bonnet to the driver's door. His sister's parting words suddenly popped into her mind.

'Why did Charlotte wish you luck?'

'For this afternoon,' he said as he reversed out of the parking space.

Oh. God. She swallowed. 'You're competing in the camp draft?'

'Of course.' He put the car in gear and spun the steering-wheel. 'Are you going to watch?'

'No!'

He glanced at her, raising his eyebrows at her instinctive response.

'I...don't know,' she said, moderating her tone. 'Maybe.' Her heart lurched. *Probably.*

'In medieval times, you'd have given me a token to wear to show your allegiance.'

'Would I?' she said dryly. 'Wouldn't that depend?'

'On?'

'On whether I...um...favoured you.'

'And do you?' His voice flowed like honey over her, leaving heat sweeping through her.

Oh, heavens. Too much, too fast. Too terrifying.

'Well, I certainly don't want to see you skewered on the end of a lance or a cow horn, if that's what you mean.'

'Chicken.' He laughed. 'You're dodging the issue.'

'Not at all,' she said smoothly. 'Back in medieval times, I'd only have to boil a few newts' eyes in my cauldron. Whether you got well or not would have been foretold in the entrails of some poor unsuspecting chicken. These days, it's my job to stitch up any messy aftermaths.'

'Speaking of aftermaths,' he said, his voice soft and sincere, 'you were wonderful with Ryan today. Thank you.'

'He was a trouper.'

They spent the rest of the short journey chatting companionably. She had the feeling Tom was *managing* her, dictating the tenor of their conversations. A little push here, a relaxing topic there.

It had to be her imagination—why would he bother?

'I'll see you shortly,' Tom said as he dropped her at the arena.

'Sure.'

She walked slowly over to the stands, casting a brief look over her shoulder to see him driving slowly over to their camp. He was going to pick up Ziggy so they could compete. She still wasn't sure if she wanted to watch, but how could she not?

As each successive competitor was announced, she felt sick with apprehension until she knew it wasn't Tom's turn.

'Next in camp is Tom Jamieson.'

Her heart froze.

She watched as Tom and Ziggy ambled into the penned

area and stood relaxed at the end for a signal from the judge.

Tom looked over at her and winked, his teeth a flash of white in his face. Her fingers curled into fists and she held them tight in her lap. She was relieved to see that, like all the riders before him, he wore a helmet.

With his back leg cocked, Ziggy stood looking half-asleep. Tom was running his eyes over the cattle at the other end of the fenced area. Kayla knew enough now to know he was choosing his beast. She glanced at the small milling herd, wondering which one looked most cooperative. They all looked the same—large and black with broad, wet noses and big, suspicious eyes.

'Okay,' said the judge.

Tom straightened, gathering the reins. Ziggy's demeanour changed instantly, his ears flickering back and forth. Tom's eyes focussed and he moved forward. Still relaxed but with obvious intent. Almost stalking.

Ziggy's step had a controlled spring and the horse seemed to know which of the animals Tom had chosen.

Slowly, slowly, Tom and Ziggy rode through the group. There was no panic, they seemed to just be moseying around.

And then, suddenly, one of the beasts was free at the gate end of the camp, separated from the others by Tom and Ziggy.

In a desperate attempt to rejoin its herd, the beast tried to bolt along the fence.

But Ziggy was ready. The big horse dived at the wooden barrier, cutting off escape.

Kayla gasped, pressing her clenched fists against her mouth, mashing her lips against her teeth. Surely Tom would be flung off against the rails. But, no, he and Ziggy worked in a fluid dance as the beast dodged and weaved.

There was no way they were going to let the animal evade them. Backwards and forwards. Backwards and forwards. Kayla realised her feet were shuffling in an effort to help.

'Gate.' Tom's voice clipped out the command.

The attendants flung open the double gates at the front of the camp.

The beast charged through with Ziggy in hot pursuit.

Side by side, they rounded the first peg. Man and horse slowed, changed sides to manoeuvre the beast into position for the second peg. And then a huge spurt of speed. Sand flung up from Ziggy's hooves as he curved the animal into the run for the second peg.

Right, right, right.

The horse's shoulder nudged the animal along the desired path. Kayla's heart pounded in her throat. For a moment it seemed as though the beast would resist. And then a yield. The figure eight was completed at a flat gallop.

Down the centre of the arena.

A final turn.

And then through the gate.

The whistle sounded and Kayla leapt to her feet to join with the applause.

A perfect run.

As the excitement of the moment drained away, Kayla realised her joints felt like cooked noodles.

Just as well there was nothing between her and Tom. Or she'd have to give the man a piece of her mind. How dared he scare her like this? Treat his life with so little regard?

CHAPTER SEVEN

'So WHAT's with you and Tom?' Liz's voice floated into the tiny caravan bathroom where Kayla was freshening up for the barbecue.

Her hand jerked and a thick black smudge of mascara appeared on her cheekbone. She softly huffed out a breath and twitched a tissue from the box.

'Nothing.' Using a dab of face cream on the tissue, she scrubbed her skin clean. 'There's nothing with us.'

'But he asked you to the barbecue with his family.'

Kayla's stomach lurched. 'Isn't it like an open house?'

She stared her reflection with dismay. The pink-cheeked woman staring back from the mirror looked...excited, radiant.

Brimming with expectation...but for *what*? This wasn't a real date—it was more of a truce.

She took a deep breath down into her diaphragm to still the swooping sensation. *All comers welcome*, that's what Tom had said.

'Well, yes, it is,' Liz said.

Relief tinged with something less well-defined flashed through Kayla.

Liz went on, 'But he's coming back to pick you up, not

entrusting you to Jack and me for directions.' There was a small silence. 'That seems significant.'

'He probably has to come back to get ready anyway since his gear's here.' But if that was the case, wouldn't he already be here?

Significant. Kayla closed her eyes. Tom had called it a date but she'd avoided thinking of it that way. Having Liz attach importance to it gave unwanted weight to his interpretation. She took another deep breath then jammed her few toiletries back in the bag.

'Thanks for the loan of your bathroom,' she said, changing the subject as she clicked the door shut behind her.

'You're very welcome.' Liz sat on the bed with her feet up, one hand rubbing the mound of her stomach.

Concerned, Kayla frowned at her friend. 'Are you okay? Not having pains, are you?'

'No, nothing like that.' Liz sighed. 'I just feel like I've been pregnant for ever and I can't believe there's only one baby in here. It's starting to feel like I'm going to give birth to a teenager.' Her bottom lip pouted for a moment and she wriggled her bare toes. 'And my feet are sore.'

Kayla sat on the end of the bed. 'Poor thing. Shall I give you a foot massage?'

'That wasn't a hint. Really. But...' Liz said, then moaned as Kayla worked her thumb into the arch of one foot. 'Oh, I'll take it. Thank you.'

'Do you think the baby might come early again?'

'Yes.' Then she sighed. 'But maybe it's just wishful thinking. And for goodness' sake, please don't tell Jack or he'll bundle me home and tie me to the bed.'

'Sounds like it has possibilities.'

A strangled snort of laughter spluttered out of Liz. 'Not in my current state but...maybe down the track.' She sighed blissfully as Kayla moved to the other foot. 'Thanks. I was feeling sorry for myself.'

'You should take it easy.'

'Maybe. Kayla…about you and Tom…' Liz trailed off.

'There is no *me and Tom*, so whatever you're worried about, stop it,' Kayla said gently, as she concentrated on the ball of Liz's foot.

'Okay, but I just wanted to say that Tom really is a darling.'

'I'm starting to realise that the sergeant's rugged, manly exterior hides a certain brusque charm.' Kayla eased Liz's feet back on the bed then stood.

As she walked towards the bathroom to wash her hands, she heard Liz getting up.

'It does. He's got a heart of gold,' Liz called as she went down to the kitchen area. 'And you'll like his family. His parents are lovely.'

Kayla's hands froze for the tiniest second on the bar of soap. *Tom's parents*. Her tension ratcheted up a notch. Well, of course they'd be there tonight. He'd said it was a *family* barbecue. Had he considered that when he'd manoeuvred her into this date? She had to believe that he had, so what did that mean, if anything?

She hung up the towel and stepped into the doorway to the kitchen as there was a commotion at the door. Jack poked his head into the van. Two-year-old Emma clung to his neck, all big brown eyes and a froth of glossy brunette ringlets.

He pursed his lips and let out a shrill wolf whistle. 'Two hot babes. What do you think, Emmie?' He grinned at his daughter. 'Your dad is the luckiest man on Welshman's Flat this weekend.'

'Luck-ee.' Emma touched his face.

'Just the usual *babe* for you, darling,' drawled Liz. 'The *hot* one is waiting for Tom.'

Kayla's gut did another quick roll.

'Is that right?' Jack's blue eyes swung back to her. 'Well, well.'

She gritted her teeth, willed her cheeks not to flood with hot colour and waited for Jack to comment about Tom coming to collect her.

Thankfully, his gaze shifted again to Liz and softened. 'I'll just make do with the most beautiful woman in the world.' He flashed his wife a cocky grin and waggled his eyebrows.

'Smooth, very smooth, Jack Campbell.'

Love shone out of every teasing word between Liz and Jack, every heated glance they exchanged. More than love, they truly *liked* each other.

An extraordinary kaleidoscope of truths held Kayla motionless for a moment. Things she'd known intellectually suddenly seemed to reach a visceral level of believability.

Marriage could work.

A large, strong man *didn't* always rule his family with a cold, hard fist.

He didn't have to be regimented to the exclusion of affection.

A large strong man could be sensitive, caring…

Like Jack with Liz and Emma.

She swallowed.

Like Tom had been that morning with Ryan.

Remembering the way he'd cradled his nephew, empathy etched on his face, love clear in the tender way he'd handled his injured nephew. No question of leaving the care of the child to others, he'd been right there, taking care of transport, waiting at the hospital to make sure everything had gone smoothly.

Her chest tightened uncomfortably. He was so different from the men in her family, her father and her brother-in-law. Tom was brave and honest about his softer emotions.

Oh, God, he was more honest than she was. With her background, she felt ill equipped to deal with a man like that.

'What time is Tom coming to pick you up?' Liz's question pulled Kayla out of her reverie.

'About six.' She glanced at her watch. 'Are you ready to go now?'

'Just about.' Liz turned to her husband. 'Darling, I need you to grab some things for Emma.'

'Sure.' He stepped up into the van.

'Let me get out of the way,' Kayla said, moving along the narrow kitchen area.

As Jack made room for her to pass, Emma leaned out from her position in her father's hold, her little arms wide, confident of her welcome. 'Kay-lah. Hold Emmie.'

Kayla stopped to slip her feet back into the boots she'd left at the door. 'Want me to take her while you get the gear?'

'Yeah, thanks.' Jack passed his daughter across.

Kayla took the toddler, settling the child's weight on one hip as she negotiated the steps to the ground outside.

'You're going to have a little brother soon, Emma,' she said, twirling gently. 'What do you think about that?'

'Good. I help,' said Emma and smiled.

'I'll bet you'll be a big help.' Helpless to do anything else, Kayla grinned back at the girl. Her heart filled with a deep, unexpected yearning. 'You know, if I spend too much time with you, I'm going to end up clucky.'

'Cluck-ee.'

'That's right.'

Voluptuous chuckles gurgled in Emma's throat. 'Kay-lah. Cluck-ee.'

'Uh-oh,' she said ruefully at the word association. 'I think I might regret this. How about we find you a different word to play with, you little syllable sponge.'

'Sly-able.'

'Syllable.' Kayla squeezed the child in a spontaneous hug. 'That's a nice safe word, isn't it? Syllable.'

'Sly-able.'

'Close enough.' Kayla chuckled, her heart melting. She *was* clucky but the matching requirements, a man and a marriage, were a long way in her future. Still, she felt as though a tiny door had been cracked open in her entrenched rejection of the idea. Jack and Liz had unwittingly helped her see possibilities.

Tom's image slid into her mind and sent her heart ricocheting around her ribcage.

God, she'd only just allowed herself to think abstractly that strong men weren't all bad news. No way was she ready to start thinking about a specific man.

She had plans. If there was one thing she'd learned from her father it was the value of having plans, setting goals and achieving them.

She'd learned a lot about herself in the weeks she'd been in Dustin. Especially in the last two weeks—and, disturbingly, most of it through her contact with Tom. When she left here, she'd be grateful to him.

As Tom approached the camping area, he spotted Kayla near the door of the van.

Anticipation tightened his muscles. He slowed to a halt,

forcing a breath deep into his lungs, willing himself to relax.

Kayla.

His date.

She was a visual feast, long and slender and willowy, with little Emma bouncing on her hip. A fitted pale blue top moulded to her breasts, hugging the narrowness of her waist before flaring over the swell of her hips. Navy slacks clung to the slender curves of her legs and buttocks. Unable to resist, his eyes skimmed down to her gently swaying hips, to Emma's chubby little leg wrapped monkey style around Kayla's waist. She carried the child easily, stronger than her slender frame implied. Her upper body was tilted slightly to one side, a cantilever to accommodate the little girl's weight. The posture was appealingly elegant.

Oh, hell. He blew out a long breath, glad she hadn't spotted him yet. Glad he had a moment to get his reactions under control. He'd promised to be on his best behaviour tonight but it wasn't going to be easy.

He wanted Kayla.

Badly.

She turned to speak to someone in the van and he could see her face was relaxed and happy.

Suddenly, Emma saw him and gurgled with excitement, her little hands waving. Kayla turned and he was surprised to see a quick rush of pink to her cheeks.

Such a contrast to the take-charge medical professional who'd handled Ryan earlier today. This Kayla looked self-conscious. But it was the way the laughter in her face faded that made his mood plummet.

That was the look he wanted to banish. The wariness, that visceral reaction, the instinctive closing down, preparation for something unpleasant.

He could see the moment she pulled herself up, making the effort to relax.

One day soon, he wanted to see a completely different look on her face in greeting. Something welcoming, warmer...*no, damn it*, hotter. He wanted hotter.

'You're here,' she said faintly.

'In the flesh.'

At his words, her gaze dropped to his chest, flicked across his shoulders. She looked uncomfortable. He took a deep breath and her eyes skittered away. A stilted silence descended and he felt as callow as a teenager on his first date. He cleared his throat. 'So, are you ready to go?'

'Oh, I hope you don't mind but I, um, thought it'd be nice to walk over with Liz and Jack.'

'Nice? Or safe?'

'Both perhaps.' She fixed him with a wily look as she tucked a strand of honey-blonde hair behind her ear. 'But, then, I don't need to worry about safety, do I? You promised to be on your best behaviour.'

'So I did.' He swallowed. *And I will be—best behaviour...if it kills me.*

'Good,' she said, her face settling into an expression of serene satisfaction.

Tom wanted to reach out, touch her, rattle her again.

Best behaviour, he thought with a touch of desperation. Was the assignment beyond him after all?

Emma reached up to touch one of Kayla's hooped earrings.

'Emmie, hon. I'm attached to that.' She winced and tilted her head to relieve the pull.

Emma's face suddenly screwed up in distress.

'I think she's caught her finger. Let me help.' Tom stepped nearer and bent to the task of freeing the toddler's fingers. As he worked, the feathery ends of Kayla's blonde hair brushed across his knuckles and her fresh, delicious fragrance filled his head. He had to force himself to concentrate when all he really wanted to do was bury his face in the soft skin at the nape of her neck.

After a moment, Emma was free and she switched her attention to him, patting his face. His fingers fumbled to catch the jewellery as it slipped from Kayla's ear.

'It's come out. The catch must have unhooked,' he said, straightening. 'Do you want me to take Emma while you refasten it?'

'Oh, thanks. That'd be great.' She sounded as breathless as he felt.

He tucked the earring into his shirt pocket and held his hands out to Emma. 'Going to come to me, mischief?'

Emma held her hands out and began jiggling on Kayla's hip. 'Yes. Up.'

Kayla bent close to make the transfer easier. Tom slid his arm around the toddler, conscious of Kayla's warmth. When he brushed her midriff, she gasped. Her wide, startled eyes flew to his. He looked down into the crystalline grey irises as dark awareness flared in her inky pupils. He was dimly aware of Emma's arms latching onto him as he stared helplessly, his breath frozen in his chest. Then Kayla blinked and looked away, releasing him from the spell. Elation and hope swelled in his heart, making him giddy. She *was* just as affected by this charge between them as he was.

On impulse, he leaned down and quickly pressed his mouth to Kayla's soft, warm cheek.

'You look lovely,' he murmured.

Fabulous, delicious…edible. But, then, he knew he'd think she looked pretty good in a chaff sack…even better in nothing at all. An ache of need spread through his gut.

'Thanks,' she said, a tiny rough catch in her voice. 'Could I have m-my earring please?' She held out her hand.

He reached into his pocket for the bauble and deposited it on her palm.

She turned away, tilting her head so she could guide the earring back into place. Her hair swung in a silky curtain to hide her face.

'Kay-lah.' Emma wriggled then looked at him expectantly.

'Yes, that's Kayla.'

'Oh, no.' Kayla twisted back to give the toddler a despairing look. 'No, Emmie, hon, remember your new word for today is syllable.'

With delighted giggles, Emma clapped her hands. 'Kay-lah. Cluck-ee.'

Tom's tension evaporated abruptly. He grinned broadly and looked back at mortified Kayla as fresh colour flooded across her cheeks.

'Kay-lah. Cluck-ee.'

'Is she, now?'

Kayla groaned. 'You know she doesn't have any idea what she's saying. She's playing with words and sounds. Unfortunately, those two words have taken her fancy.'

'Bad luck,' Tom said gently.

'Yes.'

His heart lurched at the way her mouth pouted slightly. 'It could be worse.'

'I'm trying to imagine,' she drawled, fixing him with a disbelieving look.

'Oh, definitely. Much worse.' He collected his wits. 'It could have been a swear word. When Ry was about Emma's age, he came over to my place with his dad and went home saying *buddy*. Charlotte thought it was cute until she realised he was actually saying...er—' He stopped and glanced at Emma, who was fingering the logo on his T-shirt. He'd better spell the word just to be on the safe side. 'B-L-O-O-D-Y.'

Kayla chuckled and her eyes sparkled. 'Okay, yes. That is bad.'

'Cluck-ee,' Emma chirped looking from one to the other smugly.

'But so is this.' Kayla huffed out a sigh. 'Everyone who hears her is going to think I'm...'

'Wanting to start a family?' He struggled to keep his voice light. The thought of Kayla's belly round with child made his stomach curl with hunger.

'Yes.' Kayla sent him resigned look under her lashes. She looked so adorable, so desirable. The tension in his gut cranked up another notch.

He was starting to fit her into the mould of the woman he wanted to keep. Was it too soon for that? His head was telling him, yes, it was too soon...but his heart was telling him to go for broke.

Kayla walked beside Tom, acutely aware of his every stride.

Emma was balanced easily on his hip. He hadn't relinquished the toddler; instead he'd offered to carry her. Kayla wished she could put his domesticity down to a misguided attempt to impress but she knew it would be unfair. He was too relaxed, Emma was too comfortable, too familiar with him for it to be a rare event.

Tom Jamieson was genuine. Kayla's heart gave a painful squeeze. *Strength and tenderness all wrapped up in a ruggedly attractive package.*

She was charmed and dismayed in equal measure. His treatment of Ryan and Emma pierced her careful safeguards, leaving her feeling unsettled, susceptible. She was really seeing him, being forced to put aside her preconceived ideas about who he was.

How odd that this weekend of competitive rough-and-tumble sport should showcase such extraordinary sensitivity. The sooner it was over the better. Back in the hospital flat, in town and working—that was what she needed so she could get some perspective.

'Cluck-ee.'

Kayla rolled her eyes to find Tom's amused gaze on her.

'She'll find something new soon.'

'Promise?' She managed a smile. 'Though perhaps you're right. I shouldn't complain. The next thing she latches onto might be worse.'

'With a bit of luck, you won't have to worry about her chattering tonight. With all the fresh air and running around today, she must be worn out. She'll be out like a light after tea.'

As though she'd understood his words, Emma yawned hugely and her head drooped onto Tom's shoulder, her thumb in her mouth. Tom tilted his head and laid his cheek on the snuggling toddler's hair. Kayla's heart melted. She tried to imagine her own father carrying Maddy or herself the way Tom held Emma.

The picture wouldn't come. If her father had a softer side, she and Maddy had never seen it.

Tom's short dark hair was damp and sleek, and she realised he must have found time to bathe between helping to set up for the evening and coming to collect her.

No shave, though. Dark stubble shadowed his jaw. It looked good on him. She'd felt it when he'd bent to kiss her on the cheek. Along with a soft warmth and a hint of moisture with the brush of his lips. She raised her fingers to her face, remembering. For the tiniest, maddest moment she'd wanted to turn her head, feel that pressure and heat on her mouth.

With his free hand, Tom reached out to capture hers and she forgot all about Emma's word obsession. Pleasantly rough skin slid over hers until they were palm to palm. It had been years since she'd held hands with anyone and she'd forgotten how much she enjoyed it. The few men she'd dated had considered themselves too sophisticated for the simple public gesture.

In this peaceful bush setting, she felt suddenly over-whelmed by a wave of contrasting stimuli. The size and brawny strength of the man beside her, his undeniable masculinity…and yet his poignant gentleness.

And then there was the example of her friends. Jack, so tall and strong…and yet his tenderness with Liz and Emma.

It wasn't…right. It wasn't…the way things were between men and women, between men and children. Her experiences hadn't prepared her for the possibility of beauty and softness in the interactions of strong males with those physically weaker than themselves.

Tom's hand on hers acted as an anchor while she struggled to deal with her impressions.

'All right?' he murmured, as though he sensed her turmoil. And his acute sensitivity to her in this moment just made it worse.

'Of course.' Her throat was raw, her voice rough. She managed a tight smile.

Just as well Tom had reiterated his promise to be on his best behaviour. It was her own impulses that she was starting to worry about.

CHAPTER EIGHT

KAYLA suppressed a quiver as Tom's breath whispered over the tender skin of her ear. 'Prepare yourself to be welcomed into the Jamieson family fold,' he murmured.

'This is *all* your family?' she said, looking around at the laughing, talking crowd. Several children were happily playing a chasing game in and around the standing adults and a group of men holding cans of beer had gathered to commune around a barbecue.

'Lots of them. Don't ask me where everyone fits. Mum knows. Friends, too. The camp draft Saturday night barbecue is something of a tradition.'

A slender brunette who'd just hugged Liz looked in their direction and a huge grin immediately lit her face.

'Remember, you only have to give name, rank and serial number,' Tom said, his voice filled with laughter as the smiling woman hurried towards them. Liz and Jack trailed behind her.

Kayla speared Tom with a short glance. 'Worried I might say something to embarrass you?'

'Nope.' His fingers squeezed hers as he pitched his voice for her alone. 'Worried someone might say something to scare you back into the shell I've winkled you out of.'

'You make me sound like a hermit crab,' she muttered.

Tom's chuckle rumbled in her ears before he said, 'Hi, Mum.'

'I've been keeping an eye out so I didn't miss you two arriving. You must be Kayla.' The dark-haired woman stepped forward, her arms wide in welcome. For a split second as Kayla felt Tom release her hand, she wanted to cling to him. The next she was scooped into a hug. 'You're even more gorgeous than the photo Liz showed me.'

'Kayla, meet my mother, Rosie. Mum, as you've guessed, this is Kayla.'

'I can't tell you how much I've been looking forward to meeting you, my dear.' Rosie held her at arm's length and sent her son a quick look filled with mischief. 'Even more since my son told me he'd asked you as his date for tonight.'

There was that word again. *Date*. Kayla swallowed and pinned a smile on her face. 'It's lovely to meet you, Mrs Jamieson.'

'Rosie, I insist. We're delighted to have you join us tonight. How are you enjoying your time in Dustin so far?'

'Very much, Rosie. It makes a nice change of pace from the city.'

'We're lucky to have you filling in for Liz's maternity leave and I hear I have you to thank for patching up my grandson this morning.'

'Oh, of course. Ryan.' Kayla nodded. 'How is he?'

'Good as gold. He was right here a moment ago. Oh, there you are,' the older woman said as Ryan materialised at her side.

'Hi, Kayla,' the boy said, looking up at her shyly.

'Hello, Ryan.' She smiled at him. 'You got to the barbecue after all.'

'I had a sleep this afternoon so Mum said it was okay.'

'How is your arm?'

'Good, 'cept I can't ride.'

'So you want to get back on, then?' Kayla couldn't hide her surprise even though a quick glance at Tom suggested this was to be expected.

'Of course.'

'He's a tough little nut. Aren't you, Ry?' said his grandmother as she ruffled his hair.

'Yeah.' Ryan looked as though he'd been paid the highest compliment.

'Reminds me a lot of someone else while he was growing up.' The look Rosie gave her son was filled with equal parts of affection and exasperation. 'Tom gave me more than his fair share of grey hairs. He still does. They're always your children, Kayla, no matter how big and competent they get.'

Kayla's chest tightened unexpectedly at the words. What would it have been like to grow up with someone so firmly in her corner as Rosie obviously was for her children and grandchildren.

'What about Mum?' Ryan asked.

'Her, too. The stories I could tell you.'

'But you'll resist because we don't want to send Kayla hightailing it back to Melbourne, do we, Mum?' Tom said. 'We need her.'

His tone shivered down Kayla's spine. He almost sounded...possessive. The idea should be utterly repugnant but instead she felt a quick, unwelcome stab of feminine curiosity.

'True.' Rosie laughed undaunted by her son's warning. 'But she might like to know what she's letting herself in for.'

Did Rosie mean in Dustin? With the Jamiesons?

Or with Tom? Her heart squeezed painfully.

She was glad Jack chose that moment to come to collect Emma so that Tom was occupied transferring the sleepy toddler. She needed a moment to take a deep breath, pull herself together without his too-perceptive eyes on her.

'Come and get it!' one of the men near the barbecue called out as he transported a laden platter towards the food table.

'Oh, yes, do. Go,' Rosie said, making ushering movements towards the table. 'Food disappears quickly around here.'

'Come on.' Tom captured her hand and tugged her forward. He handed her a plate and a serviette-wrapped set of utensils.

'Kebabs?' Two appeared on her plate. 'Chops? Rissoles? Salad?'

Tom moved with her around the table, efficiently loading up her plate. He did it so naturally she found herself unable to object. 'Let's grab a seat.'

He steadied her while she stepped over the bench then put his plate on the table to save his spot. 'Can I get you something to drink?'

'A small red wine would be lovely.' She watched him walk away. Being cared for the way Tom was looking after her as his date was a new experience. It was both wonderful and unsettling.

'Be right back.' He left his jacket on the seat.

A moment later, a girl bounced onto Tom's jacket and said, 'Hello. Ry said you're the doctor who fixed his arm?'

'That's right. I'm Kayla.' She turned her attention to the feminine version of Ryan. 'Are you Hannah?'

'Yep.' Hannah grinned showing a neat set of orthodontic

braces. 'Ry let me sign the plaster already. I was the first.'

'Lucky you,' Tom said, returning with a couple of glasses. He leaned over Hannah to put them on the table.

'Yep, he's pretty good. For a boy.' Hannah grinned at her uncle then turned her ingenuous blue eyes back in Kayla's direction. 'He said it hurt a lot when he fell off but that he didn't cry.'

'Your brother was very brave,' Kayla said.

'Hannah, come and get your dinner, please,' Charlotte called from the food table. She waved to Kayla and said, 'Hi, Kayla, glad you could join us. Hannah, any time today would be good, please.'

Kayla waved back, watching a reluctant Hannah do her mother's bidding. 'She's going to be a heartbreaker when she gets older.'

'I think Charlie's hoping that contempt for boys stays with her for another ten years.' Tom climbed over the seat. As he settled beside her, his thigh brushed hers, sending a crazy fizz of sensation over her skin. 'You protected Ryan. I half expected you to give Hannah the line about tears being nothing to be ashamed of.'

Kayla cleared her throat. 'For a start, it's not a line. And, secondly, I figure it falls under the heading of patient confidentiality.'

'I'm glad.' He twisted towards her and smiled, his eyes warmly approving. Heat came off his body in waves that enveloped her. She stared at him helplessly as he spoke. 'Han's a sweetheart deep down but she's hiding it under a thick layer of holy terror at the moment.'

Someone called his name and he turned away. Kayla blew out a small breath of relief. Being the focus of Tom's attention was not getting any easier. The man had some serious chemistry.

Other friends and family members joined them at the long table and the conversation became general. His family were fun, lively, affectionate and friendly. As she chatted, Kayla tried to convince herself that she'd imagined her response to Tom. But almost as though he understood what was going on in her mind, Tom turned to touch her. His hand lingered on her shoulder while he asked her to pass the salt, then stroked down to the small of her back as she leaned forward to get it.

'Thanks.' His fingers closed over hers briefly as she tried to place the container on the table in front of him.

Nothing objectionable, just enough to ensure all her senses were tuned to him.

Every time he spoke.

Every time he shifted on the bench seat.

Her very cells seemed to be anticipating the next time he might touch her.

'Kayla?' Her name spoken in a soft girl's voice was accompanied by a light tug on her sleeve. She turned to see Hannah, her elbow on the table and her face propped in her hand.

'Yes, Hannah.'

'Are you in love with Uncle Tom?'

Kayla blinked at the child, feeling a rush of heat running into her cheeks. She sensed Tom's stillness beside her and she didn't dare look in his direction. The gathering twilight would help to hide the betraying colour—she hoped.

'I'm sure he's, um, very loveable, Hannah,' she said, selecting her words carefully. 'And I bet you love him very much.'

'Yes, but he's my uncle so I have to.'

'Right.' Kayla met the still-questioning blue eyes. 'You see, I've only just met him, so it's too soon to know.' She only just stopped the *yet* that was ready to trip off her tongue.

'But you like him, right?' the child persisted, and Kayla had a sudden sympathy for Ryan wanting to keep his tears a secret.

'Yes, I like him. He's a nice man.' She heard Tom's soft chuckle. 'But if he's not careful, that could change.'

'Why would it change?' The girl frowned.

Kayla suppressed a sigh. 'I'm teasing you, Hannah.'

'Oh.' Hannah nodded, her expression plainly saying she'd never understand the vagaries of adult humour. 'Good. You're the first girlfriend that Uncle Tom's had for ages. Nana said ever since—'

'Dessert's up, Han,' Tom said. 'I heard Aunty Doreen was bringing her peppermint and chocolate pavlova,' Tom said. 'You don't want to miss out.'

The child was gone in a flash.

'Great magic trick, *Uncle Tom*.' Kayla slid him a disgusted look. 'Pity you didn't perform it five minutes earlier.'

'But I was learning so much. A man's gotta do what a man's gotta do.' He reached out and his fingers brushed her hair back over her ear in a slow caress that left her breathless.

'Not when he's promised to be on his best behaviour,' she murmured.

'Ah, yes.' His hooded gaze was darker, sharper, holding her captive for a moment before sliding down to her mouth. A sharp stab of longing shocked her. 'You could always release me from my promise.'

Her heart slammed into her ribs as she wrenched her eyes away from him to look around the table. Everyone else was talking as though nothing out of the ordinary had happened. It was only her world that had been shaken.

'I could.' She reached for her glass. The liquid sloshed as she picked it up. 'But I don't think I will.'

'But you want to. Admit it,' he said, his words laced with sinful temptation.

Damn it. He was right.

Her mouth was drier than the dust on the dirt road. God, what had made her think she could indulge in repartee with Tom and get away with it.

'Name, rank and serial number, didn't you say?'

His delicious, low chuckle hummed across her senses.

Tom looked over to where Kayla was helping pack away the last of the dishes. Jack and Liz had returned to camp much earlier with little Emma snuggled up fast asleep in a sleeping bag.

Kayla had insisted on staying to help, mucking in willingly with the clean-up. He wondered if she realised the consequence of that—she'd have to walk back to camp with him.

Alone.

Tom swallowed. Him and Kayla.

Just the two of them.

Best behaviour.

Dating Kayla required strategy. Like camp drafting. Rush in too soon and he risked spooking his elusive quarry. The trick was to balance patience with decisive action at the right time and right place. He was a champion camp draft rider. He only hoped he had the strength and sensitivity to apply patience and pressure at the right times and places with Kayla.

He suppressed a chuckle. Would Kayla appreciate his analogy for their fledgling relationship? He thought she might with her quick, wicked sense of humour. He enjoyed it...he enjoyed her. His gut tightened.

He dropped the tied rubbish bag into the bin and turned back towards the barbecue area in time to see Kayla throw her head back to laugh at something with his mother. She appeared to have enjoyed herself tonight with his family. And that was important to him. He loved his family.

He walked slowly back towards the two women.

He hadn't brought anyone home to meet his family for years. Not since he'd been shot. No wonder Hannah had picked up on the family scuttlebutt. His then girlfriend had dumped him while he still lay in hospital, tubes threading through his body. Marissa hadn't wanted to stay at his bedside to play nursemaid to an invalid. He'd had a lucky escape there, in more ways than one. Her defection hadn't surprised him...and it hadn't hurt him either. Except for his pride.

A band of tension circled his chest. He had the feeling Kayla could hurt him badly.

But he was going to make his move anyway.

Did that make him a fool? He frowned.

'Thanks for your help, Kayla.'

'My pleasure, Rosie. I've had a lovely evening.'

'Ready to go?' His question came out more harshly than he'd meant and both women looked at him in surprise.

'Yes. I'll just get my jumper,' Kayla said.

He consciously eased the muscles across his shoulders. 'I've got it here.'

'Goodnight, Kayla,' his mother said. 'I'll look forward to seeing you again soon.'

'Goodnight, Rosie.'

''Night, Mum.'

He settled his hand in the small of Kayla's back, feeling

her body heat through his palm, the rub of her clothing at each step a small torturous friction

Silence closed around them, only broken by the soft rustle of dry leaves beneath their feet. The lamp he held played over the ground around them. Diffused light enclosing them in a golden bubble of intimacy.

'Penny?' he said, reaching out to capture her hand.

She chuckled softly. 'I was just thinking that all this is so different from the things I usually do on a night out.'

'Different good or different bad?'

'Oh, different good, definitely. I really did have a great time. I wasn't just saying that.' Her teeth glinted briefly in the pale oval of her face. 'Your family is wonderful. Special.'

'I think so, too.'

After a moment, he said, 'What sort of things are a usual night out for you?'

'Nothing very dashing. Juggling a social life can be hard when you work odd hours. But I like the occasional movie, maybe a light opera. Maybe a bike ride along the Yarra.'

With her fiancé, probably. Tom clenched his jaw. He didn't ask. He didn't want to know.

Tonight, *he* was the man here with Kayla in the dim light, surrounded by towering gums. It was his fingers curled around the fragile bones of her clever healer's hand. He felt ten feet tall.

'I enjoy meeting friends for dinner,' she said. 'Or having them over to my place.'

'Are you an adventurous cook?'

She laughed and he thought he detected an underlying note of bitterness. 'You must have realised by now, I'm not an adventurous anything.'

'Not true. You've uprooted yourself to come to Dustin.

You've attended your first camp draft. You've survived an evening with the Jamiesons.'

'Mmm, when you put it like that, I'm positively intrepid.' Her laughter this time was light and the teasing, joyous note rippled across his senses, making him smile.

'You are,' he murmured.

A low whicker greeted them as they reached the edge of their camp.

'There,' he said. 'Even Ziggy agrees.'

'Straight from the horse's mouth?' She chuckled as her footsteps slowed then stopped at her tent. 'Ziggy recognises your voice.'

'Yeah.' Tom rubbed his thumb over her knuckles. 'And he likes his chances of another biscuit of hay.'

'Are they good? His chances?' Her voice was soft.

'Better than average.' He looked down at their still-clasped hands. 'I'd planned on giving him something else before I turned in.'

'Well, I'd better let you get on with it.' There was the tiniest tremor in her words.

'Kayla?' He stepped closer to her, felt the heat of her body reaching out to his. 'I'm going to step out of line.'

She looked up at him. He felt the small shudder that shook her. 'Are you?'

'Yes.' He ran his finger tips up her arm. 'What are you going to do about it?'

'N-nothing.'

Lifting his free hand slowly, he cupped her face, feeling the soft skin against his palm, the cool silk of her hair across his fingers. She tilted her head, offering her mouth to him.

He could feel the tension in her, watched as her lips parted slightly and she bit down on her bottom lip for a tiny second then released it so it plumped back up.

He leaned forward slowly, gave her time to stop him. Her eyelids drifted shut. Over the thunder of his heart, he heard her quick, shuddering breath.

And then his lips touched hers, pressing gently, and everything else became irrelevant. The sensation was electric, exquisite. He rubbed his mouth across hers slowly, backwards and forwards. The sweet softness gave under the pressure, inviting, making him want more than he should on a first kiss.

Eyes shut, he savoured the explosion of taste. Delicious. Exciting. He was drowning, drenched in need.

Her fingers wrapped around his wrist. Flexing once, twice, as though she was debating whether to tug his hand away. But in the end she just held him as though anchoring herself.

He drew her bottom lip into his mouth with gentle suction and ran his tongue over the succulent flesh. Then reluctantly let it go.

Pulling back slowly, he struggled to surface. Kayla didn't move for a long moment, her mouth still offered up to his, swollen, inviting. Unbearably tempting.

Her eyes opened. He heard the shaky breath she sucked in, saw her breasts rise and fall. He clenched his jaw with the effort of not plunging back to take more. He wanted to drop the lamp he held, bury his fingers deep in her hair, use both hands so he could tip her head and take their kiss to a whole new level. Pull her under into the tide of excitement that was raging through him, threatening to sweep him away.

But he had to resist. He wasn't in this for a quick tumble. He wanted more, wanted it all. This was for keeps. The thought crystallised. She was what he wanted for his future.

Reining back his lust, he pressed a kiss to each corner of her mouth and stepped back.

'Let's get you into your tent.' His voice was hoarse.

'M-my tent?' She sounded as dazed as he felt.

'Yeah. While I still remember my promise to behave,' he muttered as he bent to unzip the door. His fingers fumbled with the tab but after a moment he had it open so he could usher her in. 'There you go.'

'Th-thanks.' She bent and stepped into the tent. 'Goodnight, Tom.'

With a sense of desperation, he quickly zipped the door closed before he could disgrace himself by begging. With his fingertips touching the nylon lightly, he closed his eyes and swallowed hard. His mouth still throbbed from her kiss. 'Goodnight, Kayla. Sleep well.'

Not waiting for a reply, he turned to walk towards the float and Ziggy's hay supply.

Kayla had kissed him. Progress. Elation and frustration coursed through him. He'd achieved more than he'd expected, less than he'd wanted.

Ziggy whickered again as Tom snipped the hay band. He tossed a biscuit of hay into the corral.

With one last look towards Kayla's tent, he unzipped his own nylon igloo and crawled inside.

He stripped and climbed into his swag. Eyes open, he rolled over, looking in the direction of Kayla's tent. Was she snuggled into her sleeping bag now? Unable to resist torturing himself a little, he tried to picture her. Pyjamas? Naked? He swallowed as a cold sweat broke across his skin.

Bad idea.

He turned to lie on his back. He wanted to get her into bed, desperately. But more than that, he wanted to look after her, cherish her, erase the sadness he sensed in her.

She presented a tough, capable exterior—and she was all those things. But underneath there was a sweet, vulnerable woman.

A city girl who fitted in with his town, his family. And, most of all, with him.

CHAPTER NINE

KAYLA woke the next morning to the snap of twigs and the smell of wood smoke. When she opened her eyes and saw the faint glow of light through dark blue nylon, it took her a moment to remember where she was.

She lay for a moment, listening to masculine voices talking softly. A low masculine chuckle sent a shiver down her spine.

Tom.

He'd kissed her…she'd let him. More than that, she'd *wanted* him to. Her heart lurched as she lifted her fingers to touch her lips. His mouth on hers had been quite simply mind-blowing.

For all her fine thoughts that she couldn't get involved, it had been Tom who'd called a halt last night.

Footsteps moved away and the voices faded then stopped altogether.

Hiding out in the tent was appealing but not realistic—she needed to face Tom some time today. Training of a lifetime said it might as well be sooner rather than later. Cool air hit her skin as she wriggled out of the sleeping bag. She grabbed her clothes and pulled them on, then ran a brush through her hair. When she got home tonight, she'd enjoy a nice hot shower. Perhaps that was one of the attractions of camping—returning to the benefits of civilisation gave them a disproportionate decadence.

She unzipped the tent and clambered out into a pale misty morning. Light slanted in ethereal golden beams, catching on the smoky fogginess and silhouetting the trees. Sounds of campers stirring at the sites around them was dampened by the mist. The musical chink of metal hitting metal, a hushed voice, horses neighing.

A small distance away from her tent, a fire crackled. A billy was just starting to steam and a big black cast-iron pot sat in coals at the edge.

The scene delighted her with its natural innocence. She stretched and grinned, feeling an unfamiliar sense of peace settle over her. The air she inhaled smelled of smoke and earth and eucalyptus and...horse. She liked the basic raw-ness of it.

Who'd have thought there was a corner of her that would enjoy camping? Not that she'd had to do anything useful herself, she thought, huffing out a small laugh. Jack had set her tent up and Tom's family had fed her last night so she could hardly congratulate herself on being intrepid and resourceful. Still, she was...having fun. Frivolous, naive, unsophisticated fun.

Tom came back into view from behind the horse float and the lovely calmness evaporated abruptly. She felt her smile falter as he walked towards her.

'Good morning, Kayla.' He lingered over her name as though savouring a particularly interesting flavour. She suppressed a quiver. Warm intimacy glowed in his eyes as though they shared something special.

Which they had...

Her eyes moved to his mouth and she had to consciously stop herself from moistening her lips.

'Good morning.' The sound was little more than a croak. She cleared her throat.

'I've got coffee on,' he said. 'Can I tempt you?'

'Yes, please.' She winced. With the direction of her thoughts, *tempt* seemed to be the perfect word for everything about Tom Jamieson.

He moved over to the fire and hunkered down to lift off the pot. There was something very potent about the way his moleskins pulled taut over his buttocks and clung to lean, straight thighs. From the chunky navy jumper that moulded to his broad shoulders to the well-worn leather boots on his feet, he exuded a vital masculinity. She'd never have predicted that she could be susceptible to the cowboy image. But she was. Oh, God! Was she ever!

He straightened and handed her a mug.

'Thanks.' She took the drink, wrapping her fingers around the warm china and trying to collect her scattered wits.

'Sleep well?'

The simple question reminded her of the long minutes that she'd lain awake, straining her ears for every little sound he'd made. Torturing herself with her imagination, wondering what every little rustle might be. She felt her cheeks warm.

'Very,' she croaked, then cleared her throat. 'All that fresh air knocks us city slickers around.'

He tilted his head and slid her a teasing look. 'Need some exhaust fumes to re-tox you?'

'That's right.' She chuckled, feeling her tension subsiding.

He bent back over the fire and tapped the cast-iron pot with his fingertips. 'How does breakfast of damper with baked beans, eggs and bacon sound?'

'Wicked. Irresistible.' Saliva filled her mouth. 'About

a million miles away from the healthy balanced meal I usually call breakfast but I'm game.'

Her reward was a big smile.

She swallowed. 'Do you want a hand?'

'Have you cooked over a campfire before?'

'First-timer camper, I'm afraid. Never a Girl Guide.'

'In that case, grab a seat and supervise this time.' He picked up a pair of leather gloves and a small shovel and began spreading glowing coals out from the fire. 'Next time, maybe we'll get you more hands on.'

Next time. There wouldn't be a next time, but it seemed churlish to point that out. Even more confusing was the way her heart squeezed with a pang of strong regret that there *wouldn't* be another opportunity.

She shook off the feeling. Sure, the camping weekend was turning into an unexpected treat—but part of that was probably the novelty of it. And the novelty of Tom—he'd challenged her out of her usual reservations and she was still struggling to find her equilibrium.

Liz joined her. While Jack arranged the chairs so his pregnant wife was sitting with her feet up, Emma crawled onto Kayla's knee.

'This is the life, don't you think?' Liz gave her an impish grin as Jack turned to join Tom at the fire.

'Sitting around a campfire?' Holding her hot drink out to the side so Emma couldn't spill it, Kayla brushed her hand over Emma's curls.

'Yes, there's something about roughing it that makes the man in your life take over domestic chores and demonstrate his survival skills.'

Kayla was helpless to stop her gaze from straying to Tom. He was breaking eggs, one-handed, into a bowl suggesting he was no stranger to cooking.

The man in your life. Not that he was the man in her

life… She didn't want a man in her life right now but if she did…

'And the view's not half bad, is it?' Liz murmured.

Heat scorched across Kayla's cheeks, momentarily frying her thought processes as surely as the bacon that was sputtering in the pan. She couldn't meet Liz's eyes. 'They work well together, don't they? Jack and Tom. Do the three of you do this often? Camping, I mean?' Smooth change of subject. Yep, no way was Liz going to notice that. Kayla stifled a sigh. Dustin's police sergeant was turning her into a jabbering wreck, hardly able to string a sensible sentence together, and she didn't have the faintest idea of how to regain her customary poise.

Tom moved over to the other side of the fire and crouched at the pot with the beans. The murmur of Kayla and Liz talking in the chairs nearby was nearly drowned by the sizzling bacon. He stirred the bubbling beans and flicked a glance towards the women. Emma had settled on to Kayla's lap, looking right at home. Warm longing wrapped around his heart, making it hard to breathe.

He realised Liz was watching him with a thoughtful look. Would she feel obliged to give him another warning about Kayla? He didn't feel as though he deserved one but there was no doubting her protective instincts. His intentions were honourable, though given half a chance he sure would like to take some dishonourable shortcuts.

He looked down into the beans.

'The damper's ready and so's the bacon,' Jack said, interrupting his reverie.

Tom nodded and checked the temperature of the second pan. 'Eggs coming right up.'

Time to get his mind back on the meal. He had some ideas for social gatherings this week, nothing too obvious that Kayla would baulk at. A little patience here, a little pressure there. Already she was starting to look at him with less instinctive wariness after their talk yesterday. Great strategy as long as he could keep himself reined in.

Kayla enjoyed the second day at the arena, glad her professional services weren't required. A couple of minor falls resulted in nothing more than injured pride for the competitors involved. Before the afternoon was over she'd been invited to the post-camp draft celebration at the pub, a darts tournament to watch Tom's father play on Wednesday, his mother's birthday on Thursday and to Tom's traditional Friday night marinara get-together.

Her social calendar looked suddenly exciting…and full of opportunities to see Tom.

Friday evening arrived and Kayla followed Tom's directions. Past a white weatherboard house, a small dip with a grove of gums and then, on the left, brick pillars and wrought-iron gates.

She turned in and accelerated cautiously down the long driveway. Horses grazed in the paddocks to either side, including Ziggy from the camp draft in the paddock nearest the house.

Her car was the only one in the gravel circle in front of the big, old house. Her stomach swooped and she took a deep breath into her diaphragm to relax the tension. The others would arrive soon, so she wouldn't be alone with Tom for long.

Gathering up her bag and the bottle of wine she'd bought, she slipped out of the car and looked at the house. Wonderful wide verandas encased the three sides and two large chimneys in the roof hinted at cosy fire-heated rooms on wintry nights. There were signs of work in progress on the primer-coated window-sills and a couple of sawhorses at one corner of the veranda.

The door was open but she rang the doorbell anyway.

'Come on through,' Tom called from somewhere deep in the house. 'Straight down the hall, the kitchen's on the left. You can't miss me.'

'Okay.' She walked along the hall, glancing in the rooms off to each side. Comfortable furniture in the lounge, a big king-sized bed in another room.

He stood at the stove. With his back to her, she took the opportunity to look her fill for a few precious seconds. Short dark hair, broad shoulders hugged by a white T-shirt, his long, lean body. Whipcord muscles in his arms working as he lifted the pot. A tea-towel wrapped around his waist and tucked into the waistband of his low-slung jeans.

Her gaze tracked down until she reached his bare feet on the black and white tiles.

'Hi. I was starting to think you'd got lost.'

She dragged her eyes up to meet his. 'Hi. I was just...' *Ogling you.* No, that would never do. She searched for a different topic. A rich tomato aroma wafted to her. 'Something smells wonderful.'

He gave her a wide smile. 'Mmm, I hope it's dinner.' He picked up a spoon from the bench and dipped it into the pot then turned and walked towards her. 'Taste.'

The sauce-covered spoon hovered at her mouth with his hand cupped underneath to catch drips. He looked at her expectantly and after a tiny hesitation she leaned forward to sample. The flavour was every bit as full bodied and fabulous as it smelled. 'Delicious.'

He leaned down to kiss her, his tongue stroking delicately along her bottom lip. His cheeks creased with a smile when he pulled back. 'Mmm, not bad at all.'

Her pulse raced at the heat in his eyes.

'You don't think it needs more salt?' he said, and she struggled to make sense of his words. 'The sauce?'

She shook her head, unable to speak.

'Okay, good.'

When he turned away and walked back to the stove, she managed to drag a deep breath into her lungs, feeling almost light-headed with relief.

'Make yourself at home.'

'Thanks,' she said, glad her voice didn't betray any of the internal shaking she was feeling. She glanced around the room, taking in the modern adaptation of an old-style kitchen. Weathered Baltic pine cupboards and hutches, wide polished benches. An old, ornate cast-iron wood stove in the wall, copper hooks with pans and other utensils hanging from a rack over the bench. 'I brought a white wine since you said it was marinara.'

'Thanks.' He took the bottle and put it in the fridge to keep chilled.

'Can I help?'

'Sure. Do you want to set the table? I've got everything laid out.' He waved at the neat stack of cutlery and crockery on the island bench. 'I just hadn't had a chance to finish.'

Then she noticed that there was two of everything—plates, glasses, cutlery. 'I thought you were having lots of people over for dinner.'

'Not tonight. There's salad already made up in the fridge and dressing too.'

'So it's just the two of us?'

'Yes.' He slanted a surprised look at her as he picked up a dish mounded with thick golden straps of uncooked pasta. 'Is that a problem?'

'Yes. No. Maybe.' Tension tightened her jaw as she

looked at him. 'You said it was a tradition for you to have friends over for marinara on Friday nights.'

'It is. This week, I'm having one special friend over. You.' He turned away to the pots and said casually, 'Once I put the pasta and the marinara on to cook it won't take long.'

Kayla chewed her lip for a moment then shrugged and picked up the plates. It was obviously her misunderstanding and she wasn't going to turn around and go home now. He hadn't put a foot wrong and she didn't feel unsafe with him. She did feel unsettled, on edge, but not in any way threatened.

At the table, she saw he'd put out two plain utilitarian white candles. The makeshift holders, empty fruit juice bottles, were a sweet touch and somehow more seductive than if he'd been able to produce formal candlesticks.

Tom brought over an ice bucket with the now opened bottle of wine. He poured wine into the glasses then handed her one and chinked the lip of his against hers. 'Cheers.'

'Cheers.'

'Nice. Good choice,' he said after a quick sip. 'Everything's ready. I just need to drain the pasta and bring it over. Sit.'

She watched him move around the kitchen. Confident and graceful, a man at home in his skin. He made a very appealing picture...far too appealing.

She lowered her gaze to the table. 'You've left the matches here—shall I light the candles?'

'Yes, please.' He lifted the mounded bowls and walked towards her.

'That looks like real home-made pasta,' she said as he put them on the table.

'It is.' He used a pasta ladle to pick up a scoop of spaghetti and transferred it to her plate. From the other bowl he lifted a generous serving of the sauce. 'Only the best for my marinara.'

'Who made it for you?'

'Made it myself.' There was a small secret smile playing around his mouth.

'You *made* the pasta? *Real* pasta?'

'Yep.'

She gave an uncertain laugh. 'Right. Jamieson is obviously a good, solid Italian name.'

He raised his brows and gave her an affronted look, which was spoiled by the way his dark brown eyes sparkled with mischief. 'I'll have you know that my grandmother is Italian. I learned to make pasta from an expert.'

'Okay, okay.' She held her hands up in a mock surrender. 'I apologise. You've done an amazing job.'

'Thank you.' He rewarded her with a big smile. After filling a bowl for himself, he slipped into the seat across the table from her. 'Dig in.'

She twirled the pasta onto her fork and lifted it. The strands melted in her mouth. 'Oh. My. Goodness.' She took a second mouthful. 'Mmm, I think I've died and gone to heaven. This is seriously delicious.'

He grinned. 'Glad you like it.'

'Like it? I love it.' She took another mouthful. 'You are deservedly famous for your spaghetti marinara.'

Tom watched her eating the food he'd prepared. Her genuine relish gave him a good feeling. Even though he knew it had been hard for her once she'd realised she was his only guest for dinner, she'd still decided to trust him enough to relax anyway. That was a huge step and he had to be careful not to abuse that. He could tuck his needs ruthlessly back into line. Tonight was about laying more groundwork. Just as well he was a patient man.

'Tell me about growing up with a deputy commissioner for a father,' he said.

'Wow.' She stopped and blinked at him. 'There's a leap into a tough topic.'

'I want to know about you. How else will I learn if I don't ask the hard questions?' He grinned at her. 'I should also point out that you've avoided the question so that tells me a whole lot, too.'

'Now you're scaring me.'

He picked up his wine and took a sip, letting the silence grow.

She shrugged and looked down at her plate. 'Dad was working towards his promotion when I was growing up. Of course…like anything, it had good points and bad points. He tried to run the household like a mini police academy. Not altogether a success.' She gave him a small smile. 'On the other hand, by the time I left high school I was good at self-discipline, delayed gratification, problem-solving and goal-setting.'

She huffed out a small self-mocking laugh. 'And my boyfriends were *very* well behaved. I was always home before curfew, no octopus hands, no love bites, no whisker burn, no rumpled clothing.' Using her fork, she twirled spaghetti onto the tines and took a mouthful.

'Does that count as a good point or a bad one?'

She finished chewing and swallowed. 'Excellent question. I'm not sure. I think maybe it stunted the development of my feminine wiles.'

'Believe me, honey,' he murmured, as he speared a prawn then looked at her, 'those have developed just fine.'

She regarded him for a moment then with the tiniest movement of her shoulder she said, 'Maybe.' Her gaze dropped to her plate.

It was obvious she didn't believe him. Kayla was beautiful, courageous and competent. Confident, too—except for a large blind spot about her own value. Surely, a father's job was to give his children belief in themselves and their abilities?

The way his own father had done for him.

The way he wanted to do for his children.

Tom swallowed his mouthful of food and turned the conversation to more general topics. He sensed Kayla's relief and he was rewarded when she relaxed again and opened up more. Her warm laughter rolled over him. He set himself to tease yet another delightful peal out of her.

As he looked his fill, he reflected that he could easily get used to her sitting on the other side of his table...sleeping on the other side of his bed.

At the end of the evening, he followed her home. He waited at the front door while she unlocked it. When she turned back to face him, he moved forward, placed both hands on the brick wall behind her, one each side of her head. She turned her face up for his kiss. His lips sank onto hers, feeling her open to him as he enjoyed her softness, her taste. More. He needed more. His libido strained at the curb bit.

He pulled back and swallowed hard. 'If you're smart, you won't ask me in.'

'Why not?' Her voice was low and husky, delicious.

'I'm in danger of growing tentacles.'

'Tentacles?'

'Like an octopus. Hands everywhere.'

'Oh.' She gave a small nervous laugh. 'Excellent advice, then.'

'Yeah, it is. Go inside and lock the door.' *Quickly.*

As though she'd felt his urgency, she ducked under his arm and slipped through the door. 'Goodnight, Tom.'

Only when he heard the latch snick did he straighten and walk slowly off the porch. With all the self-control he'd been exercising lately, he was going to be eligible for sainthood. But it was worth it.

Kayla listened to Tom's footsteps. Sly images had formed in her mind at Tom's words. How would it be to have his hands on her...everywhere? They were playing with fire and they had to stop. She was glad they'd agreed to be friends—but anything more was impossible. She had to tell him, had to explain why nothing could happen between them.

CHAPTER TEN

LATE afternoon the next day, Kayla stopped at the supermarket's refrigerated shelves and studied the selection. The succulent prawns reminded her of Tom's traditional marinara dinner last night. She smiled wryly. She'd half expected him to make a move while he'd had her in the privacy of his home. She'd been prepared, all her defences at the ready, but he'd disarmed her with the care he'd take over dinner. Even with her vulnerability he hadn't stepped out of line.

He'd followed her home and left her on her doorstep after an earth-shattering kiss that had left her close to whimpering. Why hadn't he pressed his advantage? She frowned as another thought occurred to her.

Damn it…she was being manoeuvred as surely as one of his camp draft steers. A little pressure here then none at all when she'd been expecting some. All the while, she'd enjoyed herself, basked in the Jamiesons' readiness to accept her, lapped up Tom's easy companionship because he didn't ask more than she was prepared to give. The camp draft and dinner at the pub to celebrate afterwards, his father's darts tournament, his mother's birthday, the traditional marinara dinner last night.

He was clever. She couldn't help but admire his seduction by stealth. She'd enjoyed every step of the process but it had to stop. They couldn't, mustn't, get any more involved. She had plans.

'I'd prefer a nice juicy steak myself.'

She jolted as a deep masculine voice rumbled in her ear. The plastic-wrapped chicken flew out of her hands. Tom leaned around her, his hand on her shoulder and caught the packet easily on its trajectory back to the supermarket's refrigerated shelf.

'Hello, Kayla.'

'Hi, Tom.' Her mouth split in a wide involuntary smile that refused to be dampened.

He looked pleased as he leaned down to press a quick kiss to her mouth. Her heart stuttered to a stop then raced into a madly erratic gallop.

'Could I have my shopping back, please?' She was proud of how calm she sounded given the hectic things her pulse was doing.

He handed the packet to her. 'You'll need a bit more than that if you're inviting me for dinner at your place.'

'Really?' She rolled her eyes at him and pushed the trolley along to the dairy section. 'Now I see the catch with letting you cook dinner for me last night. You expect me to reciprocate.'

'Caught me out.' He grinned.

She grabbed a tub of plain yoghurt. 'Well, I will—'

'I'm free tonight.' The eagerness on his face was hard to resist.

'I will have you around for dinner,' she said as though he hadn't interrupted, 'with the other people I owe invitations to.'

'You could start with just me tonight.'

'I could. But I don't think I will.'

'Notice too short? You're doing something else?'

'Nope.' She stared sightlessly at the shelves as they

meandered past them. At this rate, she was going to get home with none of the things on her list. 'I don't think intimate dinners for two are a good idea.'

'Why not?' He put his hand over hers on the trolley handle.

She stopped and looked at him. 'Because it's asking for trouble.'

'What do you mean?' He tipped his head to one side, his brown eyes intent.

'I'm sure you don't need me to spell that out.'

'You know I can behave myself. Haven't I been good?' His gaze slipped down to her mouth and she knew he was thinking about the kisses they'd shared at the end of each evening.

She looked at the food in her trolley. With the heat radiating from her cheeks, it was a wonder the chicken wasn't grilling right in front of her.

'Mostly,' he said softly.

She refused to think about the *mostly*. He *had* been the perfect gentleman all week. But that didn't make him any less threatening to her. His kisses had been restrained but they still made her feel more than she'd ever felt before. He pushed at her boundaries just by being near her. If he asked for more, she wondered if she'd have the strength to keep saying no. 'You were.'

But she couldn't keep playing with fire or she'd end up roasted. She was moving on in a few months—she needed to keep her eyes on her long-term plans.

'Then how about a meal at the bistro? Plenty of people around. I want to talk to you.'

She tightened her hands around the handle of the trolley. He was right—they did need to talk. There were things she needed to say, too, things to clarify. Meeting on neutral ground at a restaurant would be the best place to do that. Less complicated.

'Kayla?'

She realised her eyes were focussed on Tom's lips. Wrenching her gaze back to his, she said, 'All right.'

He blinked. 'You will?'

'You asked me, didn't you?' she said dryly, oddly satisfied by his scramble to keep up with her abrupt change of mind.

'Yeah, I did, but you looked so intense there for a moment I didn't expect you to agree.' He grinned.

Kayla had to quell a little bubble of treacherous pleasure. He was so sure of himself, it was nice to see him thrown, just a little. 'Yes, well, you're right...we do have things to discuss.'

'Uh-oh. I'm not so sure I like the sound of that.' He looked at her quizzically. 'Should I be worried?'

'Probably.' She couldn't suppress a small smile.

'Oh, Tom, Dr Morgan.' Kayla turned to see a pleasant-faced, plump woman beaming at them. 'I'm so glad to catch the two of you like this. I wanted to thank you. You and Tom saved my Andy's life a couple of weeks ago. At the accident on the main road.'

'Mrs Smyth?' Kayla said.

'Mary, please.'

'Mary. I saw Andy had been transferred home the other day.' She mentally reviewed the patient notes, recalling a stent had been successfully fitted in one of his coronary arteries. 'How is he?'

'He's so much better. We've got an appointment to come and see you next week so you'll see for yourself then. It sounds crazy, and you'd never wish it on anyone, but that accident and his heart attack might be the best things to have happened to our marriage. A real wake-up call for him, for both of us.'

'That's wonderful.' Kayla smiled warmly. 'I'll look forward to seeing the two of you.'

'Anyway, I'm sorry to interrupt. But spotting you together was such a good opportunity to say thank you.' She smiled knowingly, her gaze ping-ponging between her and Tom. 'Anyway, you two have a nice evening.'

Kayla gritted her teeth.

'Thanks, Mary. We will,' Tom said.

'Be careful or you'll really have the grapevine thinking there's something going on,' Kayla said, when the woman had moved on.

'There is.'

'Yes, but...' She huffed out a breath. 'Never mind. What time shall I meet you?'

'I'll pick you up.'

'No,' she said firmly, wanting to circumvent any problems later. 'I might get called out or you might, so I'd prefer to have my car.'

For a moment she thought he was going to argue, but then he nodded. 'Seven o'clock?'

'Okay.'

'You've still got my phone number?'

'Yes.' She gave him a carefully bland look. 'Let me finish my shopping. I'll see you in an hour and a half.'

'See you then.' She watched him walk away, her eyes straying over the broad shoulders and straight back. He moved with a powerful masculine grace, sexy in ways she didn't have any defences against. She reminded herself of all the reasons why getting involved with Tom was a bad idea. Coming to Dustin was just *one* step that she intended to take away from her old life—not the *only* step. Getting involved with anyone was not in her plans—no matter how tempting that *anyone* was.

Tom was such a powerful, compelling man that a woman could get lost in his shadow. Something she didn't want for herself. She'd only just extracted herself from her family's influence, especially from her father's dominance.

Tom turned at the end of the aisle and looked back at her. A jolt like electricity ran through her from head to toe. How much better for her self-respect if she'd moved off as soon as he'd walked away. Instead, he'd caught her loitering beside the breakfast cereals, staring after him like a little lost soul. It was her own fault if he thought she was interested.

He raised his hand in a salute. Sighing, she lifted hers in reluctant acknowledgement.

Oh, yes, he tied her up in nice little knots.

Blast him.

Where was she?

He should have insisted on picking her up. But she'd wanted her car. Miss Independence. Not that he wanted a clinging vine but he hoped it wouldn't be too long before she'd at least accept some things from him.

Tom looked at his watch again and blew out a breath. *Okay, so it wasn't quite seven yet.* God, he'd never been this keyed up about a date in his entire life. To make matters worse, in Kayla's eyes this wasn't even a date—just an opportunity to talk.

He looked around at the door and there she was, speaking to the waitress.

Kayla. One kind of tension eased, only to be replaced immediately by another.

Her fitted dark green top moulded to her breasts, hugging the narrowness of her waist before flaring over the swell of her hips. A multicoloured swirling skirt draped to mid-calf.

He'd always thought short skirts were sexy but Kayla's modest outfit stirred his senses more than any expanse of bare flesh would have. For the first time, he understood why the Victorians considered exposed ankles to be provocative.

His pulse bounded as he imagined his fingers closing like a bracelet around the narrow part of her shin then running up the soft skin. Under the hem of her skirt, over the roundness of her calf, the smoothness of her thighs...

Oh, hell. He blew out a long breath, glad she hadn't spotted him yet. Glad he had a moment to collect himself.

He wanted her.

Badly.

This week of caution and restraint had him champing at the bit. But it was worth it. Kayla was relaxing around him, laughing with him, teasing him. When he'd caught her in the supermarket earlier, her immediate reaction had been a spontaneous smile that had warmed his heart.

The tension between them now was all simmering attraction. He was positive. He was enjoying this slow seduction, enjoying her, the company. Even enjoying the frustration of not getting his own way, having to pursue her, work for her. Taking his time was worth the prize.

She turned and walked in his direction. When she got closer, he rose and held out the chair adjacent to him.

'Thanks.' She smiled at him and slipped into the seat.

The next few minutes were taken up with placing their order.

'What did you want to talk to me about?' Kayla said, her beautiful voice slightly husky.

'Nothing serious until after we've eaten. Better for the digestion.'

'All right. We'll talk about other things.' She straightened her cutlery in a small nervous movement that he found endearing. 'Have you always wanted to be in the police force? Is this what the ten-year-old Tom Jamieson saw himself doing?'

He chuckled. 'My ten-year-old self was a thorough ratbag and if he'd thought about it, he'd probably have seen himself on the other end of the long arm of the law.'

'Really? What saved you from yourself?'

'My parents and the senior constable who worked here at the time conspired to scare me straight.'

'What did you do?'

'Nothing good.'

The silence stretched and her eyebrows rose.

'You know I'm going to annoy you until you tell me,' she said.

'Yeah, I kind of got that feeling. You might not respect me in the morning.'

'Try me.'

A dozen suggestive responses danced on his tongue but he suppressed them all, took a sip of his drink and settled for the truth. 'My cousin and I broke into an uncle's place and liberated some alcohol and cigarettes. Rather a lot of alcohol and cigarettes.'

'Ah.'

He grimaced. 'We made ourselves very, *very* sick.'

'Nasty,' she murmured.

'It was. Our parents made us work on our uncle's place gratis for the Christmas school holidays. Rory and I have both been model citizens ever since.'

'I'm sure.' Her eyes twinkled at him.

The discussion moved on to his work and carried them through the meal. Tom enjoyed telling her about his work, relished the perceptive questions she asked and her insights into human behaviour. In no time at all, the waitress had come back to clear their plates.

In the small silence that followed, he watched Kayla's long fingers stroke the side of her glass.

'Go out with me,' he said, completely forgetting the speech he'd prepared to put his case.

Her eyes lifted to his and he read the conflict there. 'No.'

'Kayla...this chemistry between us isn't something that comes along every day. Aren't you curious about where it might lead?'

'No.' Her response was quick and short. Was she trying to convince him...or herself?

'Are you denying the attraction is mutual?' Let her try, he thought, remembering their kiss, the response he'd felt in her mobile lips.

'I'm not denying it...but I—I don't want to take it any further.'

Frustration welled up and so did poorly chosen words before he could stop them. 'I'm asking you out on a date, not to leap into bed.'

Her mouth dropped open in a perfect oval of surprise. He shut his eyes and dragged a hand down his face.

'Thank you for clarifying that.' Her voice sounded strangled.

'Bloody hell...why don't I cut my tongue out now?' He could feel the heat crawling into his cheeks. 'All right. I admit it. That thought has crossed my mind, too. What can I say?' He forced his mouth into a wry grin, hoping it might disarm her. 'I'm a man.'

Her eyes were coolly amused. 'Your honesty is... refreshing.'

'Refreshing?' He leaned his elbows on the table and

looked at her. 'Is that code for I've completely blown my chances?'

'No, not at all.' She reached for her glass and circled the base on the coaster.

'That's a relief.'

'Your chances were blown before you started.'

'Okay, excellent.' He rubbed his jaw. 'So they haven't got any worse, then.'

There was a small stunned silence and then she laughed. A good sign, considering how far down his throat he'd jammed his foot. He grinned.

After a moment, she sobered. 'I'll level with you, Tom. I can't see the point of getting involved with anyone in Dustin.'

'When you put it like that, a lot of things are pointless, aren't they?' He gave her a long look. 'You might only be here for a short time but that's no excuse not to get involved. With the community, with people.' He reached across the table and laid his fingers over hers. 'With me.'

Her throat moved in a swallow and she watched him steadily. He could see the denial in the pewter depths of her eyes. Desperation spurred him on.

'You're already involved. Look at Mary and Andy. You've profoundly affected their lives. You're friends with Jack and Liz. My mum and dad love you—my whole family loves you. Wherever you go, whatever you do, you'll be involved, whether you like it or not.'

'Yes, I agree as far as the job goes, but it's still temporary. I'm leaving Dustin once Liz's maternity leave is up. I'm only here for the six months. Eight months tops.'

'If you're worried because it's a short stint, we'd find a way to work out the logistics when you go back to Melbourne.' He wasn't ordinarily a fan of long-distance relationships but there were ways around it. Melbourne was only a couple of hours away.

'I'm not going back to Melbourne.'

'Then there's no problem,' he said quickly. 'Stay here.'

She shook her head. 'I'm moving on, Tom. Going north.' Her smile felt like more of a grimace, stiff and unnatural. His enthusiasm and the sincerity behind it had caught her unawares. 'I need to sort myself out, find out what I really want. I've always been good old reliable Kayla. Study hard, don't rock the boat, fill in, help out, don't let anyone down, don't have any inconvenient emotions. I'm rebelling. It's only a decade and a half overdue. No more doormat for me.'

'I don't want to wipe my feet on you, Kayla. How you are in a relationship is a choice. Your choice. If I behave like an idiot, you tell me. You don't let me get away with anything now while we're friends. That won't change if we go out.'

His words held an appealing logic. She had to steel herself against the seductiveness of it.

He leaned forward and reached across the table to take her hands. 'Make me part of your rebellion.'

'What?' She stared at him. 'No.'

'Why not?' His face was alight with enthusiasm.

'Several reasons. Dustin is a small town and you are an important public figure.' She looked at his hand, at the thumb stroking over her knuckles in a long, lazy stroke. 'You can't just run around having affairs.'

'I'm entitled to a private life.'

'But that's it,' she said. 'In Dustin, it wouldn't *be* private.'

'It's still my concern. Tell me what else I'm fighting against here.'

She frowned. 'I'd be using you.'

'It wouldn't be using me if I know and I'm willing.'

'But what if you get hurt.'

'I won't break.' A muscle rippled in his jaw. 'Maybe I'm prepared to take my chances.'

'Maybe I'm not prepared to let you.' She swallowed and lifted her eyes to his. 'Besides, you might hurt me and I'm not prepared to risk that either.'

'Ah.' Humour twinkled in the deep brown eyes that watched her steadily. 'So rebelling safely, then.'

She laughed but even she recognised there was no humour in the sound. 'I guess you caught me out. I can't change everything at once.'

'You're set on this, aren't you?' In the other room, a band struck up couple of notes. Before she could answer, he stood, recapturing her hand. 'Enough talking. Come and dance with me.'

The fast, catchy beat thrummed through her as they entered the larger room. Rock and roll. She loved it.

Tom spun her, controlling her as though she were a top. She laughed with delight and gave herself to the moment, trusting him to catch her. And he did, always, effortlessly.

One song, two. Breathless and energised, she lost count. He led, she followed. It made her feel alive, hedonistic. Utterly feminine.

Good dancers make good lovers.

Her feet nearly stumbled as her outrageous dance teacher's words slipped into her mind. Tom covered her gaffe, easily pulling her into his flank for another embrace. The move had never seemed so laden with sensuality. She'd done it dozens of times, hundreds of times…but she'd never been so conscious of her body, of her partner's body. The physicality, the sensuality of the dance.

Pressed hip to hip, thigh to thigh. His arm around her, strong and firm. His dark eyes burned down into hers, suddenly predatory as though he could see the question in flaming scarlet letters in her brain.

What sort of lover would Tom Jamieson make?

Her mouth was dry, her heart fluttering frantically, knocking against her ribs in a panicked beat.

And then he was spinning her away and she could tell herself she'd imagined those heated seconds.

She refused to meet his eyes directly again, focussing anywhere else on his face. His mouth, the feral smile. Did he understand what she was doing? She would insist they take a break after this song so she could gather her tattered composure.

And then he was lifting her, the world tilted crazily for a second and then she was back on her feet, twirling away, only to be snatched back and dipped as Tom arched her over his arm.

The music stopped. She blinked up into hot chocolate eyes.

Applause and whistles filtered through her hazy thoughts.

He set her back on her feet and caught her hand in his as he grinned and sketched a brief bow to their audience.

Tom had controlled her easily, effortlessly, masterfully.

And she'd revelled in every moment of it.

'Let's have a coffee and then I'll see you home,' he said as the band announced they were taking a short break.

Catching her lip, she waged a silent battle. Common sense told her she needed to head home. She glanced at her watch. 'I'll take a rain-check on the coffee as it's nearly ten o'clock. Thank you for dinner and the dancing. It was wonderful.'

'I'll see you home.'

Her heart skittered. 'There's no need. I have the car.'

'I know. I'll follow you.'

Sensing the futility of arguing, she nodded. The sooner she got home, the sooner she'd be out of his disturbing orbit. She drove home, aware of his vehicle behind her for the brief journey.

His headlights loomed in her rear-vision mirror as she turned into her driveway. Keys ready, she got out of her car.

He met her on the path, taking her arm and walking her to her front door. He'd left his motor running, the steady chug of the diesel engine the only sound.

As she slid the key into the lock, she felt her hair being brushed aside, felt warm breath on her neck. Shuddered as his lips pressed to her nape, feeling the marrow in her bones turn to jelly.

'We could be good together, Kayla,' he said softly. 'I haven't given up the idea of pinning you down.'

She turned, wrapped her fingers around the strap of her shoulder bag to stop them from reaching for him. 'I'm not some hapless camp draft steer you can run around pegs in the arena.'

He leaned on the door, his hands bracketing her head. 'Honey, you'd be a heifer, not a steer and, trust me, I'd bypass the arena and take you straight to the branding yard if I could.'

It took a moment for his murmured words to sink in and then laughter bubbled up from somewhere deep inside her.

'I don't think I've met anyone quite like you, Tom Jamieson.' She wiped moisture from beneath her eyes then lowered her hand to clutch her bag.

'I guess that's good.' His grin faded quickly. 'I like making you laugh. You should do it more often.'

He tilted his head and captured her lips. Just the barest touch of his clever mouth, warm, undemanding, almost waiting. She needed to step back but instead she felt herself begin to tremble, her breath coming in short, desperate gasps. Only then did his hands move to her face, to tip her head so he could deepen the kiss.

She was vaguely aware of a small thud as she dropped her bag and brought her hands up to cling to his shoulders. His arms came around her, scooping her even closer.

And then it was over.

He stepped back, lifting a hand to cup her jaw, his thumb stroked lightly across her mouth, making her aware of how swollen and pouty her lips felt. 'I won't give up, Kayla.'

'You should.' Shivers spiralled out of her stomach to every part of her body. 'Goodnight, Tom.'

She watched him go. The temptation to ask him in was nearly unbearable. She had to severely curtail the amount of time she spent with him before she did something they'd both regret. He made her feel things she'd never felt with a man before. A craving for his touch, his scent, his presence.

Being responsible had never seemed a heavier burden than it did right this minute.

CHAPTER ELEVEN

'GOOD morning, Hilda,' Kayla said cheerfully. She glanced at the waiting room as she joined the nurse at the emergency room status board. A woman was sipping from a mug with her arms around one child while a second sat sucking his thumb beside her. They all looked grubby and dazed. 'Looks like we're busy.'

'Kayla, you're early.' Hilda gave her a brief smile and pushed a stray hair back from her forehead with the back of her hand. The usually immaculate nurse looked subdued. 'Things are just settling down now. This is the first chance I've had update the board.'

She could hear a deep, harsh coughing from the cubicle area as someone struggled to draw breath, then a man's raised, agitated voice.

'Fill me in. Who's our priority?'

'We've got smoke inhalation victims from a house fire. The Martin family. Tony's with the father now. The youngest child has been sedated and ventilated for airlift down to the Children's.'

'That's the rest of the family in the waiting room?'

'Yes, they've been checked over. The grandmother is on her way to pick up the kiddies. It could have been much worse if Tom Jamieson hadn't been passing their house.'

'Tom?' Kayla glanced at the board, her skin prickling

with apprehension. His name wasn't there. Relief settled like quivering jelly into her knees.

'He was the hero of the day.'

Was? *Was?* Kayla's heart stopped then lurched into motion again with a sickening, fluttery beat. Suddenly, *not* having Tom's name on the board *didn't* sound like good news.

'He woke the family, got them out and then went back in for the kiddie we're transferring.'

She was grateful when Hilda continued but she wanted to shake her and demand information about Tom. His name set up a persistent tattoo in her mind and she didn't trust herself to speak.

'The father went back in so Tom had to pull him out, too.'

Oh, God! Tom!

Kayla uncleaved her tongue from the roof of her dry mouth. 'Is he all right?'

'He's not good. That's him you can hear coughing.'

At least he's alive. Relief shuddered through her in a profound wave, leaving her shaky and weak. She put her hand on the wall to steady herself—as soon as she could trust her legs she was going to find him, see for herself that he was all right.

Hilda shook her head. 'The crazy things people do under pressure. His wife thinks he was after his coin collection.'

'Tom. I meant is Tom all right?' Kayla's throat felt raw and she was surprised when Hilda didn't seem to notice the croaky rasp.

'He's a bit knocked about but he seems okay. He's in cubicle three, waiting for Tony to finish.'

'I'll take a look at him now.'

'Oh, would you? That'd be great. I've been doing obs.'

She glanced at the watch pinned to her uniform. 'He's due for another lot now.'

'I'll do them.' She walked on wobbly legs towards the area, barely holding her shudders of reaction in check.

She'd turned him down last night because of her fear of making a mistake, of losing control of her plans. He, on the other hand, was fearless, putting himself on the line, throwing himself, his precious life, into a dangerous situation.

All he'd asked her to do was to take a chance, go out with him. She'd drawn back, hesitant, afraid.

She felt barely able to contain the brew of conflicting emotions bubbling inside her. Anger with him for putting himself in danger and yet so achingly proud of him at the same time. He embraced life, the danger and mess and pain of it.

While she played it safe from the sidelines.

Sure, she planned on travelling north to work in remote areas. But in her usual careful way, she'd tried to ensure nothing deflected her from her course, nothing got untidy along the way.

As Tom had teased last night, she was even *rebelling with caution*. It suddenly seemed like a sad indictment of the person she was.

She slipped into the cubicle through the gap in the curtains.

Tom was sitting up on the bed, leaning back on the pillows, eyes closed. She was glad of this moment before he noticed her, so she could devour him with her eyes. She wanted to run to his side, slide her hands over every inch of him to make sure he really was all right. Hot tears gathered, pressing for release, but she blinked them back.

In a moment she would have to click into professional

mode and work through his clinical examination but for a few precious seconds she could just look.

One leg bent with his forearm braced on the knee and his hand dangling. The other soot-smudged hand rested on the sheet, the clip of an oximeter attached to his finger.

His pale blue uniform shirt hung open. The fabric was pockmarked with tiny cinder holes. On the sleeve, the upper arm badge was smeared with black, as were the white chevrons of his dark blue shoulder epaulettes. A long, ragged tear on the front panel just over Tom's ribs showed traces of blood. Where the edges of the shirt parted, a corner of gauze pad peeped out.

She must have made some small sound because his eyes snapped open and the dark-lashed brown gaze zeroed in on her. She felt as though she'd been zapped by a defibrillator. His whole demeanour changed.

'Kayla,' he rasped, his red-rimmed eyes sliding past her. 'What are you doing here?'

She made a superhuman effort to pull herself together. 'I've come to check you over.'

'I was expecting Tony.' He sat up, swinging his legs off the bed.

'He's busy.' She picked up his chart from the end of the bed and concentrated on his obs. BP slightly elevated, pulse normal, oxygen saturation normal. Shallow laceration. Calmer now, she hung the clipboard back on the rail.

'You get me instead.' She glanced at his face, noting the dirty smudges down one side. 'Is there a problem?'

'Hell, yes, there's a problem.' He scowled.

Her stomach swooped at his fierce look. When he didn't go on, she said, 'And that would be?'

'I want your hands on me, Kayla, but not in any damned professional capacity.' He unclipped the oximeter.

'Tom, you need—'

'You're not my doctor,' he said roughly as he stripped off the nasal cannula then stood in his socked feet and pulled the edges of his shirt together. 'I'm serious.'

'So am I.' She put her hand on his arm, felt the muscle twitch beneath warm skin. 'You're not going anywhere until you've been thoroughly checked over.' When he just looked at her silently, she said, 'And it doesn't make me your doctor. Tony is the attending and I'll make sure he sees you and confirms everything I'm telling you.'

An unpleasant waft of stale smoke filled her nostrils, reminding her why they were there. 'Please, Tom, get back up on the bed.'

'As long as this isn't going to cause you any ethical dilemmas. If it will, you tell me now.' He gave her a narrow-eyed stare. 'I'll discharge myself rather than have you use it as *another* excuse to avoid what's between us.'

'Crabby when we're not well, are we?' she teased gently in an attempt to lighten the moment.

'I mean it, Kayla.' He was obviously in no mood to be cajoled into co-operation. 'Tell me if this is going to be a problem.'

'There's no dilemma.'

'What does that mean?' he growled.

'It means treating you now won't make you my patient. God knows, I wouldn't want anyone so difficult,' she said, goaded. 'And it won't change how I think of you.'

'Not quite what I wanted to hear but it'll do for now.' He gave her the slow, lopsided grin through the sooty daubs on his face. The poignancy of it pierced straight to her heart.

She swallowed hard and dredged up the tattered remnants of her exasperation. 'So sit down, shut up and take your blasted shirt off.'

'Great bedside manner, Dr Morgan.'

'Glad you like it. Less lip and more action from my patient would be even better.'

'Yes, Doc.' He moved slowly as though he ached.

'Let me help,' she said, reaching to peel the grimy garment carefully off his shoulders.

'If I'd realised running into a burning building would make you want to take my clothes off, I might have done it weeks ago.'

'Funny man.' She congratulated herself on her detachment as he pulled his arms out of the sleeves.

'Do you feel short of breath?' she said, feeling the constriction in her own breathing as he sat on to the edge of the bed, his shirt bunched in his hands.

'No.'

'Headache? Nausea?'

'No.'

She examined his eyes, peeling back the lids, all the time aware of his steady regard. Nose and throat—all the mucosal tissues were pink and healthy.

'Now I know how a horse feels, having a soundness check. Do I pass muster?' He lowered his voice. 'Will you want me? I won't cost you much.'

'Coming on to your doctor is poor form,' she said, hoping her desperation didn't show in the clipped words.

'But you're not my doctor.'

'Let's pretend I am for this exercise,' she muttered. Her hand was *not* going to tremble. She wouldn't let it. 'It'll make it easier on both of us.'

She unhooked her stethoscope from around her neck and put in the earpieces. 'I'm going to listen to your chest then I'll look at the laceration over your ribs. Just breathe normally for me.'

He gave her a quizzical look as she lifted the diaphragm

and stepped beside him. The steady *lub-dub* of his heart was somewhat above normal rate—but, then, so was hers right now. After all *he'd* been through, it wasn't unexpected.

She closed her eyes and listened intently at each auscultation point for any abnormality in his lungs, any signs of fluid accumulation in the delicate respiratory tissues.

She reached around to his back and pressed the diaphragm into place, ignoring the toned muscle and warm skin beneath her fingertips.

'Okay, that sounds good.' She straightened and removed the stethoscope. 'Any tightness or pain when you breathe?'

'No. Just my ribs when I cough.'

'Let me take your shirt and I'll have a look now.' She held out her hands and he parted with it reluctantly. For the first time she noticed a long, narrow midline scar.

'You've had abdominal surgery.'

'Yes.' He obviously wasn't going to elaborate.

'How long ago?'

'A couple of years.'

'No ongoing issues?'

'No.'

She snapped on a pair of gloves and bent to peel back the dressing on his laceration. The wound was a shallow gouge, with bruising just starting to develop around the edges. But it was the small circular scar lower down, with its smooth centre and puckered edges, that held her rooted to the spot.

'You've been shot.'

'Oh, that.' He shifted, almost a wriggle as though he was embarrassed. 'Yeah.'

'How did it happen?'

'The usual way.'

'You've got a smart mouth, you know that?' She compressed her lips into a thin line, holding herself tightly in check. He could have been killed this morning. He could have been killed by this bullet. And all he could do was make light of it. His flippancy was the last straw. She wanted to smack him...she wanted wrap her arms around him, stop him from putting himself in harm's way.

But most of all...worst of all...she wanted to kiss him.

She took a deep, steadying breath and checked his back. No blemish. Not a through and through, then. A catalogue of the underlying structures flowed through her mind. A little higher or lower or further to the right and the outcome might have been very different. 'Is this related to your laparotomy?'

'Yes.'

'What damage did you sustain?'

'I lost a bit of large intestine apparently. I don't miss it.'

'You were lucky.'

'Yeah, I was,' he said softly.

She turned her attention to the recent damage.

'Take a deep breath for me, please. Any pain?'

'A bit.'

She reached out to press lightly on the ribs around the area. 'What about now?'

'Yes,' he hissed out through clenched teeth.

'I'm sorry. You've got some nasty bruising, if not a fractured rib.' She straightened. 'How did it happen?'

'Don fell on me when I was helping him out of the house. He was pretty groggy by the time I got to him. I landed on a lump on the floor with him on top of me. He's a big bloke.'

His laconic understatement told her more than anything

else how fraught those moments in the burning building must have been.

'Did you hit your head when you fell?'

'No.'

'Okay. Lie down on the bed, I just want to check your abdomen and then we'll send you for an X-ray.'

As soon as she touched him, she felt his quick breath in. 'Just breathe normally. Don't hold.'

'Right. Breathe normally,' he muttered.

'That's better.' She moved her hand along the soft tissue below his ribcage, palpating gently.

He groaned.

'That hurt?' She froze, her fingers poised lightly on the upper abdominal quadrant. No guarding and it felt normal, but his response indicated otherwise.

'No.' He sounded strained, as though his teeth were clamped together. 'Have you finished?'

Lifting her hands and steepling her fingers, she said, 'So, no tenderness at all?'

'None.'

She frowned at him, noting the slash of red across his cheekbones. His gaze was fixed on the ceiling, his mouth set in a straight, hard line as though he was angry.

As Kayla turned away, she suppressed a sigh. 'I'll organise a dressing for that and then we'll get you down to Radiology.'

She worked in silence, irrigating the wound then drying the surrounding skin.

'After the X-ray, can I go?'

'I want you to stay here for a few hours so we can keep an eye on you,' she said as she squeezed some antiseptic ointment onto a non-stick dressing pad.

'No chance,' he said gruffly.

She taped the dressing in place and stifled the urge to

berate him. Stripping off her gloves, she said, 'Let's get you X-rayed and then we'll see, depending on the results.'

'*Tony* will see,' he corrected.

She tipped her head in acknowledgement. 'Tony will see. If it's clear, you should take it easy for the rest of the day. No exertion. But you must come back or call an ambulance if you start having difficulty breathing, any headaches or nausea. Or if the hoarseness in your voice gets worse.'

'Got it.'

She made notes on his record sheet. 'Stay here. I'll arrange the X-ray and then get Tony to come and have a word.'

'Thanks, Kayla.'

She nodded and stepped out of the curtained cubicle. She straightened her shapeless hospital-issue white coat and took a deep breath. He was fine.

Fine. There was no need to have him admitted and put under twenty-four-hour observation. It would be a waste of resources.

And he'd never agree.

The hospital would never agree to having him forcibly detained for his own good, either.

But it was what she wanted to do.

Tom watched the curtain close behind Kayla, then tipped his head back onto the pillow and shut his eyes.

The sounds of the emergency department filtered into his consciousness. The deep hacking cough of the man he'd rescued, the subdued murmur of staff. A beeper sounding.

Today's Kayla was all business in her white coat of armour with her stethoscope and clinical detachment. The silver-grey eyes had been steady and assessing. Her touch gentle but impersonal. Hard to take when he yearned for so much more.

No sign of the woman whose lips had burned under his and shaken him to the core. No sign of the magical, fluid creature who'd been so sweetly responsive to his lead on the dance floor less than twenty-four hours ago.

He'd looked for a glimpse of caring, for something personal over and above her professional manner. But apart from that fleeting moment of dismay when she'd identified his old bullet wound and a couple of small slips where her irritation had showed, she'd been cool and efficient.

He'd been nothing more than a job to her.

Last night, she'd told him in no uncertain terms that he was wasting his time. But he'd still come away with her kisses on his lips and felt hopeful.

Now he just felt tired and battered. Dispirited. His ribs hurt, the skin over them stung—but worst of all was the ache in his heart.

Later in the morning, Kayla saw Tony at the desk.

'Have you heard how our house-fire victims are?' She picked up the results of the biochemistry work-up she'd requested on a diabetic patient.

'Father and son both on ventilators but they're stable.'

'And Tom?' She'd already checked his X-ray but perhaps Tony had picked up something she'd missed.

'Tom?' Tony sounded vague, his mind obviously on the file he was reading. 'He's fine. I discharged him after checking his X-ray.'

'No problems, then?'

Her boss looked up from the folder in his hand, his shrewd eyes fixing on her. 'Like what?'

'Nothing in particular,' she said, wishing she hadn't persisted. 'His rib was very tender, I just wondered.'

Tony shrugged and went back to his reading. 'Heavy bruising. I went through his home care. Which I gather you'd already covered.' He flipped the page. 'And I told him to come back at the first sign of any problems—which you'd also covered.'

'Good. Thanks.'

His lack of concern should have been reassuring. She didn't need to follow up further, didn't need to go out to Tom's place to check up on him.

But she wanted to...

CHAPTER TWELVE

KAYLA slowed to a halt at the front of the burnt-out house, her stomach clenching. Tom had been in there while hungry flames wreaked their havoc. He'd gone in twice, *twice*, heedless of the risk to himself to pull out the occupants.

A cold chill shivered down her spine as she stared at the charred roof struts poking out of gaping holes where the roof tiles had fallen in. The front entrance was an open, smoke-stained mouth with broken windows like sightless eye sockets on either side. She could see all the way through the blackened interior of the house to the rose glow of sunset-etched plants in the back yard.

Jack had told Liz the smoke detectors hadn't had batteries. The family was lucky to be alive.

And so was Tom.

She swallowed the nausea that threatened to rise up her throat.

Her pulse thumped in a quick rhythm. Each beat mocked her interest in the house as the procrastination it really was.

She was afraid.

Tom seemed so sure of what he wanted. Her stomach swooped sickeningly. He pushed her out of her comfort zone just by being himself. What if he expected more than she had to give, more than she was capable of?

She swallowed. She couldn't let herself think about that now. Tonight she was here to check on his recovery, cook him dinner, make a gesture. Not seduce him.

He was right. She was in Dustin, she was involved with the town. With him. But she could choose the level of the involvement.

With one final look, she put the car in gear. Tom's place was further along on the outer fringes of the township. She'd only been there the once, on Friday night…only a couple of days ago. But the way she felt, it could have been a lifetime ago with all that had happened since.

She parked on the gravel in front of Tom's house and gathered the handles of the shopping bags with trembling fingers.

He'd said he liked steak so she'd bought eye fillet and vegetables. And sticky date pudding. She chewed her lip. Had she brought too much? Overdone it? She blew out an impatient breath and scrambled out of the car. The bags weren't heavy but with each step closer to the house they seemed to gain unbelievable weight. If she kept this up, she was going to paralyse herself with doubt.

She marched up the steps to knock on the front door before she could change her mind.

Keep it light. Keep it light. Keep it—

The door opened and suddenly Tom was there.

Her heart ricocheted around her ribcage before lodging in her throat as she stared at him. Powerful shoulders and arms were left bare by the navy singlet that moulded to his torso. She could see the outline of the dressing she'd applied to his ribs earlier. Faded blue jeans rode low on his hips.

'Kayla.' His voice, still slightly hoarse from the smoke he'd inhaled, was flat.

She jerked her eyes back up to meet his narrow-eyed

stare. He looked moody and his mouth had firmed to a thin uncompromising line.

She swallowed. He was fine, more than fine.

But he was far from pleased to see her. She hadn't really expected that. An unpleasant band tightened around her heart. Perhaps she should have called first.

'I came to see how you were.' If anything, he looked even grimmer. *Keep it light*. She held up her shopping bags as though they were offerings to appease. 'And I brought dinner. You cooked for me the other night—I thought I'd return the favour tonight.'

He moved aside silently.

She walked into the foyer and waited while he closed the door. His face was unreadable as he held out his hands for the bags.

'Oh, no. They're not heavy,' she said, clutching the handles. Her smile felt uncomfortable; a desperate, flimsy disguise for her fear of rejection. 'I'll…take them through to the kitchen if that's okay?'

'Sure. Why not?'

Her smile faltered. So far from the welcome she'd hoped for but at least he'd let her in. The temptation to turn tail in the face of his gruffness was nearly overwhelming. He didn't want her there—he couldn't be any clearer. She would make him dinner and leave as quickly as possible.

'Right.' She turned and began to walk.

Although he moved silently, she was aware of him every step of her journey along the wide hall. She knew the moment he stopped at the kitchen doorway while she continued across the room.

She moved behind the island bench. Having Tom nearby seemed more manageable now that she had the barrier between them. She lifted the bags on the bench and pulled out the carrots, greens and onions. 'You said you preferred steak so that's what I've brought. Do you have a barbecue?' She glanced over to where he stood with his thumbs hooked into the belt band of his jeans. 'Or should I do it under the griller?'

'I've got a barbecue.'

'Well, don't light it yet.' Not that he'd offered. Unhappiness knotted her stomach as she looked down at the vegetables on the bench. The sooner she got on with this the sooner she could go. She squared her shoulders and, with determined brightness she said, 'I've gone for comfort food.' She looked around while she spoke then glanced at him. 'Is it okay if I raid your drawers for a peeler?'

He shrugged, looking cool and disinterested. 'Raid them for whatever you like.'

She found a small peeler then set to work on a carrot. The silence was unbearable. She had to fill it—even if it was with ramblings. 'I'm going to make a stir-fry. I hope you like asparagus. I couldn't resist it. The supermarket had a fresh batch.'

The flow of words took on a life of their own now that she'd started. She shrugged mentally as she heard herself start about the sticky date pudding for desert. If he wasn't going to contribute or deflect her ramblings then he'd just have to make of it whatever he liked.

She paused for a breath, searching for another topic.

'Why are you here, Kayla?' He sounded tired.

Her heart lurched. She should have known once he did break his silence, he'd cut straight to the chase. He was going to make her work for this. She could feel her courage slipping away.

'I told you, I came to see how you are.' She flashed him a quick smile. Desperate to keep working with her hands, she twisted around to rummage in the drawer for a knife. 'So how are you?'

She straightened and turned. A small gasp locked in her throat. Tom stood a scant foot from her. Her fingers clenched around the handle of the utensil she held.

His darkly lashed eyes moved over her face then slipped downwards. She followed his line of vision to the paring knife she held in front of her as though she was preparing to defend her honour. He reached out to unfurl her fingers.

With the blade safely on the bench, he folded his arms. 'Are you asking me as a doctor? Or a friend? Or something else?'

'A f-friend.'

Tom clenched his jaw to stop the pithy word that sprang to his tongue.

She was here as a friend with her food and succour and medical expertise.

All he wanted was her.

Just her. Plain and simple.

And so bloody complex.

He curled his fingers into fists. 'Well, *friend*, you didn't pick a great time. I'm not feeling all that…friendly at the moment.'

She winced and looked away. A flash of vulnerability in her eyes cut straight to his heart and he regretted his sharp tone.

'Then…how about as a woman who h-has changed her mind?'

His unruly heart skipped a beat before common sense insisted he was probably misunderstanding her. 'Changed her mind about what?' he asked evenly.

'Getting involved.' Her words came out haltingly as though she was forcing each one off her tongue. 'With. You.'

His whole body shook with the need to reach out to grab her. Jerking away, he stalked across the room. Hell. The woman he craved was standing here in his kitchen, apparently offering herself to him on a platter. *But why now?* He didn't like the answer that presented itself.

He turned back to face her. 'Is this some sort of warped hero-worship thing?'

Her mouth dropped open. 'No! Of course not.' She made a small negative movement with her hands then clasped them in front of her. 'I mean you are a hero but that's not why I'm here.'

He watched her, not trusting himself to get closer. 'Then why now?'

'You're not going to make this easy, are you?' She put her hands on the bench behind her as though to steady herself. He could see her tension in the way each finger gripped, her skin stretched white across each knuckle. She stared at the floor, gnawing at her bottom lip as though to gather courage.

He ran a hand over his face—he wanted her but he didn't want her coming to him as some sort of misguided self-sacrifice. It wouldn't be right. Besides, he wanted her to want *him*. Just him, not some heroic version she thought he was.

'All right.' As though she'd made a decision, she looked up. Grey eyes burned into his with a dark intensity that took his breath away. 'Right from the first time I laid eyes on you, you scared me to death. I'm afraid of the way you make me feel.'

He could feel the heat burning in his face. This was the third time she'd made him blush. 'How do I make you feel?'

'As though I'm out of control.' The tip of her tongue made a quick, nervous sweep of her lips and he felt his system jolt. 'You're larger than life and I...don't know if I can handle you.'

'Handle me?'

Her eyes clung to his. 'I've never felt anything like this and it terrifies me. Y-you terrify me.'

'God, Kayla,' he groaned. He was torn. Half of him wanted to take her in his arms, reassure her, seduce her until she accepted the magic of the chemistry between them. The other half of him wondered if his long-term plans would be better served by halting her flow of words until he had the composure to deal with her confession. 'What am I going to do with you?'

The colour came and went in her face. 'Nothing, by the sounds of it.' She huffed out a small self-mocking laugh that ended in a hiccup. 'You've changed your mind, haven't you?'

'Changed my mind? No, I haven't changed my mind,' he rasped. 'I've been frustrated for the entire two months, three weeks and roughly six days since you arrived in Dustin.'

She blinked. 'R-really?'

'Oh, yeah.' He smiled ruefully, still not trusting himself to go near her.

She caught her bottom lip between her teeth for a moment. 'W-well, where does that leave us, then?'

'I know what I want.' He speared his fingers through his hair, continuing the thrust until his hand reached the back of his neck. 'I don't know what you want and I'm worried you don't know, either. I know I suggested I could become part of your rebellion. But you refused me last night, Kayla. The only thing that's happened since then is the fire.'

'I know.' She looked at him steadily. 'Finding out you

were in the emergency department this morning gave me a shock. Made me realise how fragile life is.' Her throat moved in a swallow. 'How important you are. And how right you were last night. I am involved here in Dustin.'

'But I—'

She held her hand up. 'Please, Tom, let me finish. I want to be braver. I want to take some chances, do some things spontaneously.' She looked at him, her eyes dark pewter with emotion. 'I want…you.'

For a second he was frozen, his body paralysed by the intensity of his emotion. Then, in four strides, he was across the kitchen to scoop her face into his hands. 'I don't know if is the right thing but, heaven help me, I can't resist you.'

Her breathing changed, a tiny hitch…the most sexy thing. 'I'm glad. I've never thrown myself at a man before.'

'Is that what you're doing?' He kissed the corner of her mouth. 'Then I'm glad, too.' Another small peck in the centre of her mouth. 'A smart man would catch you and keep you.' Tom nibbled the cushion of her lower lip. He pulled back and looked down into her shining quicksilver eyes. 'I'm a smart man, Kayla.'

'Please. Kiss me again.' Her voice was a husky murmur, entrancing. Her lashes lowered as her eyes drifted down to his mouth. As potent as a touch. 'Let's worry about right now.'

Alarm bells jangled but not enough to still the need rising through him with a savagery he'd never felt before. He couldn't help himself. She was here, saying the things he wanted to hear. He couldn't say no. Couldn't.

Her hands clutched at his waist, then burrowed under his singlet to slide up. The feeling of her fingers on his skin was bliss.

He sucked in a deep breath and she stilled. 'Oh, your rib. Did that hurt?'

He could have laughed. Was she serious? 'Honey, trust me when I tell you that I'm feeling no pain right now.'

'Yes, but as your doctor—' He pressed his thumbs gently to her mouth, refusing to let her finish that sentence. He wanted her to see him as a man, not a patient. The soft, warm lips yielded beneath his touch.

'Not my doctor,' he said hoarsely as the tip of her tongue touched the sensitive pads of his fingers.

She smiled slowly and gave him a knowing look. 'Then as your lover-to-be, who happens to be a doctor, I feel honour-bound to point out that you're full of dopamine and other feel-good chemicals. You might be sorry you exerted yourself later.'

'I'll never regret this.' He touched his lips to hers. 'Never.'

CHAPTER THIRTEEN

'I THINK you might be a bad influence,' Kayla murmured. Beneath her ear, Tom's heart beat a rapid tattoo that synchronised with her stuttering pulse. She lay boneless, half-sprawled across his chest, so completely exhausted and relaxed she wondered when she'd be able to move again.

Or if she'd ever want to. She smiled at the fanciful thought of staying right where she was—listening to the rhythm of a man's heartbeat. Not just any man—specifically Tom Jamieson.

'Bad influence? Who? Me?' His fingers traced lazy patterns up and down her arm.

'Yes, you.' She inhaled his fragrance—hot, male and musky. Delicious. 'I don't think I've ever felt so...wicked.' She paused. 'I think I like it.'

'Stick with me, honey. I'll show you everything I know.' Rich amusement threaded through his voice.

She brushed her hand through the dark hair on his chest, enjoying the feel of it on the sensitive skin of her palm. 'Promise?'

His arm tightened, holding her even closer as his laughter vibrated through his torso and into her body. 'And you were worried about being able to handle me.'

She swallowed, gathering her courage. 'I—I think I'll take you up on your offer if it's still open.'

'I'll be happy to oblige.' His voice rumbled under her ear in instant agreement. Her heart skipped. A small pause and then he said, 'Which offer was that?'

She tweaked a couple of chest hairs in a light tug, feeling half foolish, half annoyed. 'How can you say you'll be happy to oblige if you can't even remember what it's about?'

'Ouch.' He captured her fingers and carried them to his lips. 'Hey, if it involves you and me together, how can I lose?'

He sounded so sincere and certain. The unexpected, unconditional support caught her on the raw.

'Nice recovery,' she said huskily around the hot lump that had formed in her throat.

'I thought so.' After a small silence, he said, 'What have I committed to?'

She took a steadying breath. 'To being part of my Dustin rebellion.'

'Oh, yeah.' The warmth in his voice made her toes curl. 'I'm at your command.'

She propped herself up on one elbow and looked down at him. 'You sound like you're about to offer me three wishes.'

His fingers curled around the back of her neck. 'Honey, you can have as many wishes as you like.'

He tugged her mouth down to his.

'Can I have that in writing?' she said, feeling his lips curve under hers.

He caught her lower lip gently between his teeth for a moment. 'You'll have to take it on trust.'

She pulled back, averting her eyes from his. His words were teasing but they instantly doused the glow that had warmed her heart.

She could feel his gaze on her profile, could sense his

curiosity about her withdrawal. To distract him, and herself, she ran her hand across his flat belly, felt his sharply indrawn breath as his muscles contracted beneath her fingertips. She traced the thin flat laparotomy scar then detoured to the nubbly little scar near his flank.

'Tell me what happened.'

'It was a carjacking.' His voice was gravelly. He cleared his throat. 'One in a series of attacks. The guy waited in railway car parks, preying on young women as they came out of the station to their cars.'

'I think I remember,' she said slowly, searching her memory for the details. 'He made them drive to deserted locations then raped them and took their cars.'

'That's right. He was getting bolder. The violence of his attacks was escalating.'

'He shot the off-duty policeman who stopped him.' She looked into the steady, dark eyes watching her. 'That was you.'

'Yeah. I was lucky. He had a point two-two air pistol.'

She raised her eyebrows. 'That's lucky?'

'Solid pellet, no fragmentation.'

'You could still have been killed,' she said severely, to cover the fear that cramped her stomach. How could he think about the technicalities when his life had been at stake?

'But I wasn't.' He brushed her hair back, tucking it behind her ear.

'You're a hero.' A blush swept across his cheekbones, fascinating her.

He shook his head. 'Just someone doing what they had to at the time.'

'It's more than a lot of people would have done. Same with the house fire this morning.' She examined his face, feature by feature. The regular, lean, good looks hid a lion's heart. 'You're a very special man.'

'I'm not sure where you're going with this, Kayla.' Dark eyes glittered intently up at her as he tilted his head on the pillow and frowned. 'But I'm not special. Cut me and I bleed. I hurt just like any other man.'

A spiral of icy discomfort twisted through her gut and she had to look away.

Regardless of his modesty, he was courageous, physically and emotionally. So open and loving and family orientated. She was none of those things—for all that she had envied her friends with close family. Was there something missing in her, some integral ingredient, that meant she had to be on the outside?

And where did that leave Tom? Would she hurt him before they were done? She had to be careful that didn't happen.

'What's wrong?'

'Nothing.' She smiled, feeling the stiffness of her face. 'Hey, I promised you food.'

'Kayla—'

She moved away to scramble off the other side of the bed. 'Mind if I use your shower?'

'Sure.' He propped himself up on one elbow. 'There's a clean towel in the cupboard beside the door.'

'And the bathroom?'

'Across the passage.'

As she walked to the door, his eyes were irresistibly drawn down her trim back, the curve of her waist, over the flare of peach-shaped buttocks to long legs.

His pulse revved but he tamped down the stirrings of male interest.

Had she just run out on him?

He rolled off the bed, feeling his bruised ribs protesting

the movement. Not so painless now, but he wouldn't change a thing about the last hour. In fact, given half a chance, he was ready to do it all over again.

Perhaps in the shower…

But when he got to the bathroom, Kayla had finished. The towel wrapped around her body was secured sarong-style above her breasts and covering way too much skin… but he could work with it.

She met his eyes in the mirror. 'All yours.'

'Yes, please.' He stepped behind her, pressing his mouth to her nape. Satisfaction poured through him at her shiver.

'I didn't mean that.' Her throaty voice made him want to growl.

'Maybe you should have.' He reached out and caught the towel. 'Kayla?'

She didn't resist as he turned her to face him. When he bent to touch his lips to hers, she brought her hands up to frame his face. He contemplated the logistics of making love in the shower cubicle, the idea growing on him by the second.

The next moment he was free, a damp towel dangling from his hand.

'Don't dawdle,' she said over her shoulder as she waltzed out the door towards his bedroom. 'I'll go and finish preparing the vegetables.'

On the surface, she was all beans and business but he couldn't help wondering if it was clever camouflage for something that had upset her. He tightened his grip on the towel, tempted to follow her and pin her to the bed until he got to the bottom of whatever it was.

'I'll get you to turn on the barbecue plate for the steak when you come out.' Kayla's voice floated cheerily across the hallway.

He shook his head, telling himself he must have imagined that moment of coolness. Stepping into the shower cubicle, he reached for the taps. He washed quickly making sure he kept the dressing over his ribs as dry as possible. It was waterproof but he figured the less he disturbed it for today the better.

Back in the bedroom he pulled on a clean pair of boxers, dragged on his jeans, then padded along to the kitchen.

When he reached the archway, the domestic scene stopped him in his tracks. Without a trace of self-consciousness, Kayla was talking to a black and white cat sitting on the floor beside her.

Oh, yes, this was what he wanted, every day for the rest of his life.

This woman.

In his home.

In his heart.

He tucked his hands in his pockets as he walked across the tiles. 'I see Jerry's chatting you up.'

'His name's Jerry? Wasn't there a cartoon…?' She trailed off.

'*Tom and Jerry.* Naming him was Dad's idea. Too many comics when he was growing up.'

She chuckled.

'He's not usually this friendly.' Tom moved behind her and placed his hands on her waist, trapping her at the bench. 'You've charmed all the males in this household.'

'I think it's much more prosaic than that. I think the males here like their chances of getting what they want.'

'Uh-huh.' He nuzzled into the side of her neck. 'What are the chances?'

'Zero until after dinner.' She was proud of how steady her voice was given the quivers that zinged along her nerve pathways. His lips on her skin were electric. Before she could stop herself, she'd tilted her head, giving him better access to her nape. 'M-maybe we can renegotiate then.'

His hands flexed on her hips. 'I bet I could change your mind.'

'No bet.' She twisted out of his grip. In a smooth movement, she scooped up the plate that held the steaks and thrust it towards him. 'Be useful. Go and cook. Got to keep your strength up.'

'Good point.' He gave her a slow, wicked smile. 'How do you like your steak?'

'Medium.'

She blew out a long, shaky breath as he moved away. With him safely outside, she raised a hand to her sternum. Her flesh trembled with each hard beat of her heart. Turning back to the bench, she stood staring at the vegetables. She was out of her depth but the temptation to keep trying to stay afloat with Tom was overwhelming.

'Problem?'

She jumped, her heart lurching out of rhythm. 'No. No problem. Are you…?' Her mind went completely blank for a long moment. 'Um, have you got any soy sauce?'

'In the pantry in the corner.'

'Great.' She reached for the door handle. 'I don't suppose you have a wok?'

'You'd be wrong. It's in the cupboard under the sink.' He peered under the island bench and after a moment held up a bottle. 'Red wine?'

'A half-glass would be nice. Thanks.' The vegetables would only take a couple of minutes. She put the pan on a moderate heat then turned back to face Tom.

With a few expert twists of his wrist, he had the cork removed from the bottle. He moved with grace, economy and confidence. She liked watching him—more than was sensible. The sturdy wrists. Firm, well-muscled biceps, not too bulky. Forearms lightly covered with dark hair. The plain silver watch strapped above his left wrist shouldn't have been sexy...but it was.

He set the bottle aside with the glasses to breathe. 'I'll go and turn the steak.'

Glad to have something to do, Kayla tipped the vegetables into the wok, stirring the heat through them.

A short time later, they were seated at the table. The same makeshift candle holders glowed in the centre of the table.

Tom poured wine into the glasses then handed her one and chinked the lip of his against hers.

'A toast to rebellion,' he said, smiling at her mischievously over the rim of his glass.

Her cheeks warmed.

'To rebellion.' She lifted her drink and took a sip.

'I'm glad you came to check up on me tonight. Thanks,' he said softly.

The warm gratitude in his eyes made her want to fidget. She slid the casserole dish across the table. 'My pleasure. Help yourself before it cools down.'

Tom picked up the serving spoon, added a scoop of stir-fried vegetables to his plate and turned the conversation to more general topics. He sensed Kayla's relief and he was rewarded when she relaxed again and opened up more. Her warm laughter rolled over him.

As he looked his fill, he reflected how well she fitted, with him, with his life.

It was much later when she pushed back her chair and picked up the plates. 'We'd better clear up. How about I wash since I don't know where things go?'

He liked it that she sounded as regretful as he was that there was no excuse to linger at the table.

'Sure.' He picked up the serving dish and glasses and

followed her to the sink. 'I'm going to my cousin's engagement party on Saturday night. Want to come?'

'Your cousin? Didn't I meet him and his girlfriend at the camp draft barbecue?'

'Jonathon and Natalie,' he confirmed.

'Sounds like fun. I'm working during the day but as long as everything's under control it should be okay.' Her voice was muffled as she rummaged under the bench. She came up with an ancient pair of dish-washing gloves he didn't know were there. 'I can take a change of clothes to work with me.'

'Great.' Congratulating himself on how well his casual approach was working, he went back to the table and snuffed out the candles. 'What about next week?'

'What about it?' she said over the running water.

'Here's how it works.' Back in the kitchen, he snagged a clean tea-towel from a drawer. 'Me plus you plus relationship equals me wanting to see you as often as possible.' With his hands busy wiping a glass, he studied her profile, trying to read her reactions. 'Every day would be good but I can be flexible.'

'Oh.' She washed the steak knives and put them on the drainer. Her lips pursed. Not a good sign. 'Next week, I'm studying because Saturday week I'm going down to Melbourne to do a course.' She lifted a plate out of the soapy water and slotted it into the rack, then hesitated. 'And I'll be staying down there.'

'You can study here.'

'Study here?' She glanced at him, as she stacked the second plate, her eyes filled with humour. 'With you around? I don't think so.'

'I can control myself.'

'Yes…well…maybe it's not you I'm worried about,' she muttered.

He threw the tea-towel on the rack and reached for her. 'You can't say things like that and expect to just stand there, washing dishes.'

She squeaked as he scooped her up, suds flying. Pain stabbed him in the side and he couldn't suppress a small grimace.

'Your ribs—' she began, her silver eyes shadowed with concern.

'Are fine as long as you stay still,' he said.

She frowned, but other than that she didn't move a muscle. 'They're not. I can see you've hurt yourself. Please, put me down.'

'Not on your life.' He turned and started for the door. 'I've got you where I want you.'

'Where are you taking me?'

'Back to the bedroom.' He smiled in anticipation.

'Tom,' she protested on a half-laugh. 'What about the rest of the dishes?'

'They'll still be there tomorrow.'

She held her green-covered fingers up. 'Then what about the gloves?'

'Maybe I like you in rubber.'

'Kinky.' She chuckled. The sound was delightful.

'Okay, so maybe not dishwashing gloves.' He turned and walked the short distance to the bench. 'Take them off.'

'Ooh, you're doing masterful.' She obediently dropped the gloves on the bench. 'It suits you.'

'You bet. Now you put your arms around my neck.'

She wound her arms around his neck and stroked his skin. He nearly moaned.

'Turn out the lights,' he growled as he stopped by the doorjamb.

In the bedroom, he pinned her to the bed. 'Now I've really got you where I want you.'

Where she belonged.

It was too soon to tell her that, of course, but he could show her, worship her with his body. Prove to her that they had something special.

After a magical hour of exploring each other, testing their limits, he wrapped her in his arms. Perfect. With her legs entwined with his like this, she had no chance of running out on him. As he drifted off to sleep, he smiled. He was looking forward to waking her up in the morning.

He woke slowly, in the filtered dawn light, aware of a pervasive sense of well-being. The warmth of a body was pressed to his torso.

Kayla. She was still here.

He reached down to stroke her awake.

Fur!

He sat bolt upright and pain stabbed him sharply in the side. Smothering a curse, he held a hand to his injured ribs and stared into Jerry's yellow eyes.

Kayla was gone.

Hours ago by the feel of the rest of the bed. The only warmth was that under Jerry's contented furry self.

Tom scowled. Kayla had run out on him after all.

If she thought that was acceptable, then she had another thought coming.

He threw back the covers and rolled out of bed. He had places to go…and a certain person to see.

CHAPTER FOURTEEN

As soon as he entered the kitchen, he saw the note propped up on the counter. So she hadn't *quite* done a runner on him. His simmering frustration eased a fraction.

He picked up the note, hoping for something to salve his bruised heart. Her writing, the little there was of it, was neat and controlled—like Kayla herself. Each beautifully formed letter sloped the same way. The words themselves were simple, concise. Bland. No acknowledgement of what had happened between them, nothing about their earth-shattering connection.

He smoothed the note on the bench, his eyes narrowing. Not even a damned X to signify a kiss.

Just that she'd see him tomorrow. It was something…but it wasn't much. It didn't come close to what he wanted.

He huffed out a breath, cautioning himself to be patient. She'd taken a huge step by coming to him last night, being prepared to admit that she wanted him. He had to take one careful step at a time. But if she thought leaving a note meant she was completely off the hook until tomorrow night, she was very much mistaken. A lazy smile spread across his face.

Later today, he'd find a way to see her—even if it was just briefly.

* * *

All the chairs in the emergency department were empty when Tom walked through the entrance that evening. Probably the lull before the evening rush. Good, he wouldn't be interrupting her.

'Hi, Hilda.' He leaned on the counter. 'Is Kayla about?'

'She's on a meal break while we're quiet.' The matronly nurse gave him a kind smile as though she could see through his casual demeanour. 'She shouldn't be long.'

'Down in the cafeteria?'

'As far as I know.'

'Thanks. I'll try and catch her there.' Anticipation hummed through his body. With luck, she'd be there alone.

He spotted his quarry at the sink, rinsing her mug. His gut tightened. A quick sweep confirmed the rest of the room was empty. Eyes focussed on Kayla, he stalked silently towards her.

When he was halfway across the room, her head whipped around sharply as though she sensed his presence. Her face lit up with a smile and his pulse leapt in response.

He wondered what she saw in his expression because a moment later her smile faltered. A wash of delicate colour swept across her fair skin. She turned to face him, clutching the mug in front of her breasts like a shield.

'Tom?'

'Kayla.'

He planted his hands on the bench either side of her and bent to capture her mouth. She tasted of coffee and dark chocolate. Tantalising. Sensational. He took his time, savouring the flavours, lingering over the warmth and softness of her lips. He heard her breath catch then quicken.

By a superhuman effort he kept the caress leisurely,

ignoring his body's demand to plunge deeper. He tightened his grip on the bench, felt the fine tremors in his muscles from the self-control he exerted.

He drew back slowly and looked down into her wide eyes. The pupils had expanded into huge pools of black rimmed by quicksilver. 'Good morning.'

She blinked. 'Morning?'

'Yeah. I've been saving that for you *all* day.' His voice was rough with betraying emotion but he didn't care. 'Ever since I found you'd gone when I woke up.'

'Oh.' Her eyes flicked away and then back to him. 'I left you a note.'

'I saw it but it's not quite the same. Besides, there was no kiss in your note.' He deliberately slid his eyes down to her mouth. 'I had to rectify that oversight.'

She made a tiny sound, almost a whimper, as he leaned down to kiss her again.

Her lips clung to his but when he lifted his head, she stuttered, 'Y-you have to stop. I'm working.'

'I know. I'll get out of your hair now that I've finished making my special delivery.'

'R-right.' She looked adorable when she was flustered. 'Thanks.'

'You're very welcome.' He ran a finger across the cushion of her lower lip, feeling the faint dampness. The touch was a mistake, cranking his hunger almost beyond tolerance. He had to leave before he disgraced himself and begged her to let him stay with her tonight. 'Maybe you'll stay around to collect the next good-morning kiss in person. Not that I object to hunting you down to deliver them.'

He managed a smile. 'Goodnight, sweetheart. I hope you're not too busy tonight. I'll see you tomorrow.'

Kayla swallowed.

'See you then,' she rasped, barely able to recognise her voice.

He strode across the room, long legs eating the distance. Kayla caught her bottom lip between her teeth. Watching him move, watching everything about him, was a wayward pleasure that she didn't think would ever pall. From the short, dark hair on his well-shaped head, the broad shoulders stretching his plain white T-shirt, to the snug-fitting blue jeans. She'd never been so acutely conscious of a man's body before. Making love with him last night hadn't taken any of the edge off her awareness—if anything, it had made it more intense.

He stopped at the door to look back at her. The cocky smile that touched his lips sent her heart rate careening again.

As soon as he disappeared, she let out the breath that had frozen in her lungs and slumped back against the bench. A belated check of the room showed that no one had witnessed the scene. Tom knocked her sideways, making her forget her usual caution.

She shook herself mentally and turned to put her mug in the staff cupboard. Making a quick detour to the bathroom on her way back to the department, she checked her appearance. She looked the same as ever. No indelible scarlet stamp across her features that said *Tom Jamieson's lover*. The only clues anything out of the ordinary had happened in her meal break were her pink cheeks and uncontrollable smile. She set her mouth but the fatuous curve kept breaking through.

Hilda looked up as she re-entered the department. 'Did Tom find you?'

'Yes, he did,' Kayla said, her mind scrambling. She needed to think of something to say to change the subject.

No way could she stand here and chat casually about Tom Jamieson. Her mind stayed unhelpfully blank.

'I see he's had no ill-effects after yesterday's events,' Hilda said.

Kayla stared at her blankly, heat spreading up through her body. Her affair with Tom couldn't be public knowledge…it couldn't. A wave of nausea cramped in her stomach.

Hilda raised her eyebrows then said, 'After the house fire.'

'Oh. Mmm.' Kayla sucked her lips in and clamped them between her teeth. If she opened her mouth, the first sound out was going to be laughter, and she didn't trust it not to be liberally tinged with hysteria.

'The wee one and his father are both off ventilators now. It was a close call.'

'Yes, it was.' The urge to laugh abruptly subsided in a shiver as Kayla remembered the burnt-out husk of the house and Tom's rescue of the family. He was a hero.

'Anyway, I've got a nasty set of tonsils in cubicle three for you,' Hilda said briskly. 'And a lacerated hand in two. Nineteen-year-old male, put his hand through a window.'

'Okay. Thanks.' She took the files, relieved to have something concrete to do.

If she and Tom went out, talk would be expected in a small town like Dustin. But that was different from everyone knowing that she was sleeping with him. She was an intensely private person so how did she feel about that being public knowledge?

How would Tom feel about it?

'You're very quiet. Is something wrong?' Tom glanced at Kayla as he steered along his driveway after his cousin's engagement party.

'No, I'm just pleasantly tired.' She paused then said, 'Jon and Natalie are lovely. They're good together.'

'They are.' Could he hear wistfulness in her voice—or was it only wishful thinking on his part?

He switched off the engine and unbuckled his seat belt. Turning towards her, he casually laid his arm across the back of the seats. He sifted his fingers through the gold silk of her hair. 'Want to make out in the car?'

She laughed and rolled her head to look at him. Light from the front porch caught in her eyes, showing the delicate spokes of silver radiating out from the pupils. 'You're a real romantic, you know that?'

'I'm taking my job as co-conspirator in your rebellion seriously.' He rubbed his jaw with his free hand. 'I can't help you with the whisker burn because I shaved earlier but I can definitely manage a love bite.'

'I'll pass on the whisker burn *and* the love bite but I'm very impressed with your dedication to your role.' She batted her eyelashes at him and grinned cheekily. 'I'm sure you've got other good ideas.'

'Yeah.' He cupped her jaw and ran his thumb across the soft, warm skin of her cheek. 'Stay.'

She turned her head and kissed the palm of his hand. 'Of course.'

'No, I meant stay the whole night. I want to wake up with you beside me.'

'Oh.' The smile faded from her eyes and she looked at him silently. 'I don't know if that's a good idea.'

'Why not?'

'I'm… It seems too hot and heavy for where we are. And I'm only here for a short time.'

'You've told me.' He examined her face, looking for a weakness, some indication he wasn't being a complete fool. They had something special, something worth giving a chance. He weighed his words with care. 'Let's get some things straight. We *are* hot and heavy. This might be a rebellion but it's also a relationship.'

'For the time I'm here.'

He clenched his jaw, feeling the grind of his molars as he held back the temptation to push. 'For the time you're here. Exclusive. Dating no one else.'

She was silent for a long, torturous moment. 'Aren't you worried what people will think?' Her sombre grey eyes held mixed emotions, the foremost being concern. For him.

'They'll think I got lucky.' He grinned but she didn't respond. His stomach dropped.

'I'm serious, Tom.'

'Why would they care?'

'You…have an important position in a small community.'

'And your point is?'

'People look up to you. Surely it's even more vital for you to maintain your reputation now than when you worked in the city.'

'How would you staying the night with me affect that?'

'You think I'm being ridiculous.' She chewed on her lip. 'I…guess…worrying about how things might be perceived is ingrained.' She stared through the windscreen but he had the feeling she wasn't seeing anything. She was too wrapped up in her thoughts.

Tom waited.

'It seemed to be the most important thing when I was growing up. Dad… Mum's life revolved around Dad so she worried about how our behaviour reflected on him, his chances of promotion. After she died it seemed even more important to keep up appearances.'

'So you're worried about what people will say 0about you?'

'I don't know. Maybe.' She laughed but there was no humour in the sound. 'What does that say about me? A rebel afraid of losing her reputation. Has to be paradox, doesn't it?'

He thought he saw the shimmer of moisture on her eyelashes before she turned her head away from him. 'Kayla. Don't.'

He tugged her into his arms. After a tiny moment of resistance she melted there and feeling her cuddling close felt so right.

'People won't think anything about you and me. Even if they did, I don't give a damn,' he said. 'I don't want some hole-in-the-corner affair with you. If you have any doubts about that, tell me now and I'll take out a full-page ad in the *Dustin Gazette*.'

'Okay.' Her voice was thick.

'Okay, you'll stay the night or I should take out an ad?'

'Okay, I'll stay the night.'

He'd take it. He wanted more, he wanted her to say she'd stay for ever but for now he accepted she was giving him what she could. And it was a damned sight more than he'd expected a few weeks ago.

He could help her, give her room. She was so used to living her life within parameters set by someone else. Rebelling was new to her. For now she needed to feel in control of her plans. He needed to be patient until she was ready to adjust her plans to find a place for him. He could do that.

Tom was like an addiction, Kayla thought. The more she saw of him, the more she wanted to see. She'd missed him during the weekend away on her course, had been impatient to get back to Dustin to see him. It was made worse by the fact that she'd spent every night that week at his place, studying. He'd been great—annoyingly so. When she'd been tempted to play hookey, he'd sat her down at the table and gone out to his workshop so she'd had no excuse to stop studying. Two nights away from him while she'd been down in Melbourne at the course had been awful. It had been his suggestion that she go back to his place on the Sunday night and he'd given her a key to the front door.

He'd made her greedy. She wanted to see as much of him as she could.

She didn't want to think about her plans for now or about the limited time she had in Dustin. Surely the shine on the relationship would have worn off by the time her contract was up. In the meantime, she wanted to revel in the things she was learning about him and about herself.

Surely it wasn't so unreasonable.

CHAPTER FIFTEEN

KAYLA slotted the key into the front door. The pleasant smell of eucalyptus smoke on the frosty air promised warmth inside. Tom had the fire going. Bless him.

A shiver seized her as she entered the foyer and shut the door behind her. Delicious heat curled across her chilled skin. She smiled her pleasure as she stripped off her jacket and hung it on the hallstand. This unprecedented late spring cold snap was brutal, a real taste of winter. Snow flurries had made dazzling white starbursts in the headlights. Beautiful but potentially deadly.

Tom had wanted to travel into town to pick her up after her shift. She'd refused but the gesture had touched her. She wasn't used to such a nurturing approach from men in her life. Having grown up within a rigid set of her father's guidelines, she'd learned not to expect softness, consideration. No cosseting at all.

And here was Tom ready to pamper her as much as she'd let him. His powerful drive to look out for people, for *her*, was as bewildering as it was beguiling.

Her emotions see-sawed back and forth about it. Part of her wanted to bask in his treatment, become accustomed to his brand of spoiling. But another part of her said it would be weak, a step towards losing independence.

She sighed, pushing away the troubling thoughts. For now it was lovely to be home.

Home! *Home?*

She put out a hand to steady herself as the floor seemed to rock beneath her feet. When had she started to think of this as home? This was Tom's place. She didn't belong here. Regardless of how welcome he made her feel.

She took a deep breath and tried to calm the twist in her stomach. When she had steadied, she switched off the front porch light then walked along the hall towards the gentle glow coming from the lounge.

Tom was there, asleep on the sofa. She'd told him not to wait up for her but he had anyway. An open book rested on his chest, rising and falling with each breath.

She tiptoed across to look down at him and her heart squeezed painfully.

He was beautiful in a masculine, angular way. Lean cheeks, square jaw, a strong nose. Dark stubby lashes formed a thick fringe along his closed eyelids. His head had rolled slightly to one side, his mouth relaxed in sleep.

His mouth, so clever and versatile. Firm, commanding lips that demanded a response…soft, teasing lips that seduced a response.

She shivered, not from the cold this time. It was so tempting to bend down, press her mouth to his, taste the tenor of his kisses tonight. He'd make love to her with a generous, tender expertise. The thought made her pulse race. Being with him was spectacular in a way she'd never experienced before.

She would always be glad to have been a part of his life—even for this short interlude. The knowledge that her time here was limited sat in her chest like an unpleasant weight. She pressed her hand to her sternum. Leaving him was going to be harder than she could have predicted.

Somehow, over the last couple of weeks, she'd almost ended up living at Tom's place. Perhaps they needed to ease back, see less of each other.

As though he'd read her troubled thoughts, his forehead pleated in a small frown. Perhaps a case at work was bothering him. He was the sort of man others depended on. Responsible, trustworthy. He expected people to bring their problems to him...welcomed it, even. With every last ounce of strength and intelligence, he did whatever he could to help.

He'd have been a good pioneer, resourceful, tough and brave. She smiled at the idea then bent to lift the book off his chest. A second later her wrist was caught by his fingers in a gentle but unbreakable grip.

Her heart leapt into her throat. She snapped her eyes up to meet heavy-lidded eyes so dark they were nearly black.

'Caught you red-handed.' His voice was a sexy, throaty rasp. He took his book from her hand and dropped it carelessly over the arm of the sofa on to the floor. One expert tug and he'd tumbled her into the narrow gap between his body and the cushioning. It was like lying next to a furnace. 'Mmm, now I'm going to have to punish you.'

Still breathless and disorientated from her rapid change of position, she gasped, 'Any excuse.'

'Is that a complaint?' His lips feathered across her temple.

'Only that you're talking too much,' she said, pushing her turmoil further into the back of her mind. She was here now. With him. Winding her arms around his neck, she touched her fingers to his bare nape.

He reared back to grab her hands in his. 'God, woman, your fingers are like blocks of ice.'

'I know.' The warmth of his palms began to seep into

her fingers. 'But you're so lovely and warm. I want to snuggle up.'

His weight settled back on her. 'Marry me and you get automatic snuggle rights.'

She froze, the thoughts she'd been having earlier crashing back with a vengeance. 'Tom—'

'All right, you drive a hard bargain.' His mouth closed over hers as he tucked her hands under his jumper. 'You can have snuggle rights anyway.'

All thought of protesting evaporated as his body heat, then his love-making transported her to a place without doubts, filled only with ecstasy.

But much later, in bed, when Tom enfolded her into his warmth, his body spooning against hers beneath the light quilt, her mind returned to her concerns.

'Tom?'

'Mmm-hmm.' His voice rumbled, half-asleep.

'You are happy with the way things are between us, aren't you? You understand it's temporary? I can't stay in Dustin.'

'Mmm.' His hand slipped around her waist, fingers splaying for a moment across her stomach then relaxing as he said, 'I understand what you told me.'

'Okay.' An odd ambivalence shook her. She should be glad… she *was* glad. At least it meant she didn't have to worry about him being hurt…and if she was more involved than she'd anticipated, then that was her problem. Not his. She could let herself have this time to store up memories to sustain her when she moved on. 'Okay. That's good.'

Tom deepened his breathing, relaxed his body consciously. He blinked in the darkness, inhaling Kayla's sweet fragrance. Feeling her body pressed along his, the backs of her thighs aligned with the tops of his, her spine against his stomach and chest. The warmth they created so much more than they'd make individually.

Together they were so much more than they were alone. Couldn't Kayla see that?

He'd hoped time would convince her but tonight he'd rushed. His quip about marriage, the long-term plan, prematurely exposed. The comment had slipped from the deepest recesses of his relaxed mind straight onto his tongue.

Marriage. A wife, a partner to share his life with, to make a family with. Things he'd promised himself since he'd woken up in the hospital recovery suite after surgery for the gunshot wound. His need had been a slow burn in the last two years…these last few weeks with Kayla had turned it into a raging inferno.

Had he blown his chance with the unguarded words?

She was such a valiant, determined spirit. Driven to prove herself against some standard he couldn't comprehend, she was unnecessarily hard on herself. He was in awe of her already. She had nothing to prove to him. But that was the problem. She had everything to prove to herself. It remained to be seen whether that would mean sacrificing what they had.

He wouldn't let her go easily, be a gentleman about it. He was prepared to bare himself, to let her see his heart and soul.

He'd do whatever it took because he was playing for keeps.

Look out, Kayla, he thought as he tumbled into sleep.

Moments before the alarm went off, Tom felt Kayla slip out of his arms. Still half-asleep, he wondered why she hadn't turned and wrapped her arms around him as she'd got into the habit of doing in the mornings. A heartbeat later, he remembered last night.

Through narrowed eyelids, he watched her leave the room. The shower came on and a short time later he heard her pad down to the kitchen. Stifling a sigh, he rolled over and pushed back the covers.

He had a bad feeling about this morning.

Clean clothes in hand, he headed for the bathroom. The steamy room smelled of her. A combination of soap, shampoo, moisturiser and Kayla. One more part of her presence he'd become used to around the place.

By the time he got to the living area, Kayla was standing in front of the wood heater, a mug in one hand.

'Good morning,' he said, stopping in front of her. He wrapped his fingers around hers and lifted the mug to his lips to take a mouthful of her coffee. 'Mmm, that's good. I love it that you take your coffee the right way.'

Her eyes flickered over his bare torso, a quick flare of interest in the pewter. 'I've got yours ready, I just need to pour it.'

'Thanks.' He grinned and released her.

Kneeling at the hearth, he opened the damper before releasing the catch on the door so he could stoke the fire. A spark landed on his forearm and he brushed it away casually before it could burn.

'You're asking for trouble with all that bare skin,' Kayla said from just behind him.

'I'm trying to impress you with how tough I am.' He stood and took the drink she offered. 'I thought it would improve my chances of getting you back to the bedroom.'

The smile she gave him was tentative, her eyes tinged with sadness to his hypersensitive mind. 'You have a one-track mind.'

'Pretty much.'

Her knuckles gleamed as her fingers tightened around her mug. 'Tom, we need to talk.'

'Uh-oh. The four words a man doesn't want to hear from the woman in his life,' he said, trying to lighten the moment, but she just watched him sombrely. He stroked a finger down her cheek. 'Hon, we've only just got up. What can be so serious at this hour?'

'We are.' Her mouth turned down in a grimace. 'We're serious, Tom. And we said we wouldn't be.'

The temptation to contradict her was strong but it wouldn't be honest so he shrugged. 'So we broke the rules.'

'But it means that I'm not being fair.' She perched on the edge of one of the armchairs. 'What you said last night made me wonder... You think this is going somewhere, don't you?'

Hell, yes. He settled for a noncommittal 'Well, it might.'

She shook her head. 'It won't, Tom. I'm sorry but it can't. I told you I have plans. I need to see them through. They're important, worthwhile and I need to prove I can do this.'

He crossed to the sofa they'd made love on last night and sat near her, his knees nearly touching hers. 'Who do you need to prove it to, Kayla? Your father? Your ex-fiancé?' He watched tell-tale emotions flicker through her expressive silver eyes. 'You don't have to prove a damned thing to anyone.'

'I have to prove it to me.' Her mouth trembled but her voice was firm.

'Okay.' He dragged a hand down his face, thinking hard, trying to decide a different tack. 'Then what's wrong with plans that allow for some flexibility? Changing a plan isn't a hanging offence. We're good together. Admit it.'

'Tom—'

'We're better than good, we're great.' He clenched his fingers into fists to keep himself from reaching for her.

'Because it's still new, Tom. We're in the honeymoon phase. We're both putting our best foot forward. I'm not staying for the next phase.'

'No pipe and slippers. Message understood.' Blood pounded at his temples.

'You *said* that before.' She stared into her coffee, tension obvious from the set line of her shoulders. 'But now we're getting in too deep and we have to stop.'

'So we'll stop. We won't get in too deep.'

Her haunted grey eyes came back to his. 'No, I mean we need to stop seeing each other now, before we get hurt.'

He rubbed his chest, feeling the pain. She was dumping him. The go-slow plan was out the window…he might as well let her see just how bad he was in.

'You think it's that easy. You've put your cards on the table. Now it's my turn.' He pulled in a deep breath and looked her full in the eye. 'I love you, Kayla Morgan. I would die for you before I would hurt you.'

She looked stricken. Not the look he wanted to see on the face of the woman he'd just bared his soul to. His heart kept beating despite the desperate chill that invaded his chest.

He clenched his jaw, wondering if he had the courage to tell her the rest. But he'd come this far… 'I've let you call the shots in our relationship when all I wanted to do was march you down to the church and tie you up with rings and signatures and legalities.' His throat felt raw. 'This is the lifetime deal for me.'

Begging words paraded through his brain, desperate deals to keep things going. He shut his mouth to stop them from escaping and making him more woeful than he had to be.

'Oh, Tom. I'm so sorry.' She reached out to touch him, her fingers not quite steady.

He twisted away from her. 'That's not a good idea right now, Kayla,' he said. *Pity.* He couldn't bear it. 'Unless you're going to give me something more than sympathy.'

'I—I…' She stopped, unable to say the words he so badly wanted her to say. 'I'm sorry. I can't be what you want.'

'You *are* what I want.' He stood, took several jerky paces away. His frustration at not being able to reach her was like a tightly wound spring needing release. 'Just you being yourself. Nothing more. I'd give anything, do anything, if I could help you to believe that.'

'You make it sound like I need rescuing but I don't, Tom. I know what I have to do.' Kayla looked at Tom's rigid back. Although he hadn't raised his voice, she could hear the tension, the pain, he held in check.

She'd hurt him. The last thing she'd wanted to do. She'd hoped that by being honest with him from the beginning they'd be able to stay heart-whole.

Now she could see how she'd deluded herself. Tom loved her and he'd shown her in so many ways. Because it had suited her, she'd ignored the warning signs. In him. In herself.

They were never supposed to get this serious. How had she let it happen?

She looked at him, at the pain she'd caused, and it was nearly enough to make her buckle. She felt like her heart had been cut out. How she ached to go to him, to offer him whatever it took to make take his pain away.

But she was confused and to weaken would mean hurting him even more.

She was right to end it now. She couldn't steal any more moments from him. He deserved better. He deserved the things he wanted.

Her hand shook as she put aside her half-finished coffee. 'I'll go and get my gear.'

Hardly aware of what she was doing, she went to the bedroom and gathered all her belongings. Tears blinded her as she struggled with the zipper of her carry-all. She stopped, pressed the heels of her hands to her eyes and counted. Control. She had to get herself under control so she could face Tom before going.

She went back to the lounge. He was still standing where she'd left him. He'd looked so shattered. More than anything, she wanted to put her arms around him. But after what she'd done, she had no right to comfort him. And that would only make it worse.

'I'm sorry, Tom. I've made a hash of this. I didn't mean to.'

'I know.' He looked at her, his heart, unashamedly, in his eyes.

She swallowed hard. 'I hope you find what you need.'

'I have.' The small crooked smile he managed tore at her. 'But she doesn't need me.'

'Tom, please...' Her throat threatened to close over.

'What did you expect, Kayla? That I'd make it easy for you?' He shook his head slightly. 'I'm sorry, honey. I'd do a lot of things for you but that's beyond me.'

'Goodbye, Tom.' She turned away quickly, blinking hard as she made her way to the door. Down the steps to her car. Her hands shook so much she had trouble getting the key into the ignition.

She drove carefully, glad of the numbness that allowed her to concentrate on the road. But as soon as she pulled up at her flat, sensation returned with a vengeance. Her heart felt raw, flayed. Her hands clenched on the steering-wheel as sobs erupted from deep within her, racking her until she was exhausted.

Moving like an old, old woman, she collected her bag and let herself into the flat.

She'd made such a mess of things, hurt Tom cruelly when all he'd done had been to treat her well.

He loved her.

She sagged against the door and slid down until she sat on the floor. Fresh tears scalded her eyes.

How could she bear knowing she'd caused him such pain?

CHAPTER SIXTEEN

Tom juggled his handhold on the heavy wardrobe and craned his head around the end of the unit. 'I thought this was supposed to be empty.'

'It is. It's solid cedar,' Liz said.

'I'm starting to think it'd make damned good kindling.' Jack grunted as they manoeuvred the awkward bulk.

'You're nearly there,' Liz said. 'Just a bit further. That's it. Oh, perfect, thank you.' She stood back and beamed, her hands folded over her bulging stomach. Tom looked at her gingerly, wondering exactly when the baby was due.

'Now, will you have a rest, please?' Jack said, sounding close to the end of his tether.

'Okay. As soon as I've made you two a cup of coffee.'

'No. Now. Tom and I will make the coffee. Put your feet up. That's an order.'

'All right, boss.' She and Jack grinned at each other, their faces softening with such overwhelming love that Tom felt like an intruder in the moment. His heart squeezed painfully. This was what he'd wanted with Kayla, what he'd been so sure would be in their future. He'd been wrong.

'Scoot.'

'I'm gone.' She grinned.

Jack frowned at the empty doorway after Liz had left

the room. 'Not planning to take Kayla far afield tonight, are you, mate?'

'Not tonight,' Tom said. *Not any night for the foreseeable future.* The agony of it battered him. He clamped his jaw. 'Why?'

His friend rolled his shoulders as though to release the tension there. 'Liz is in the first stages of labour.'

'What? Now?' Aghast, Tom stared at his friend. 'Shouldn't you do something? Boil water? Go to the hospital?'

'If I had my way, she'd be chained to a hospital bed right now,' Jack muttered, then shrugged. 'She says it's too early. Come on, let's make that coffee.'

Tom followed him into the kitchen.

A split second later, Liz appeared, an odd look on her face and her hands clutching her stomach. 'Change of plans, darling.'

Jack was beside her in a flash. 'Now? Is it now?'

'Yes. Time to go to the hospital.'

'I'll drive. We'll take my car,' Tom said, digging his keys out of his pocket as Jack scooped Liz into his arms. 'It's in the driveway ready to go.'

'Wait,' she said, as Jack strode towards the door. 'I need to ring Kayla and I want my bag.'

'We can ring on the way,' Jack said. 'I'll come back for your bag later.'

'No. I want it now. There's no need to panic. I'm not going to drop your son on the front veranda,' Liz said. 'Please, darling.'

'I'll ring Kayla while you get the bag, Jack,' Tom said, picking up the handset on the bench and punching in Kayla's number.

'Hell. All right.' Jack lowered Liz gently onto a chair. 'Stay,' he said, then stalked out of the room.

'Hey, Liz, sweetie.' Kayla's husky voice, warm, loving and calm, flowed down the phone line like honey and Tom's pulse leapt painfully. 'I've been expecting your call. Are you ready to come in?'

His unruly heart clamoured regardless of the fact that all her sweet reassurance wasn't meant for him.

'Kayla, it's Tom,' he rasped.

'Tom?' There was a fraction of a second of stark silence on the other end of the line. He could almost feel her shock, hear her thoughts spinning, but before he could reassure her, she said, 'Is Liz all right?'

'She's in labour. Jack's just getting her bag and then we'll be on our way.'

'Okay. Ask Liz what stage.' Her voice was steady, unhurried. 'Have her waters broken?'

'Kayla wants to know what stage you're at and if your waters have broken.'

'My waters haven't broken and the contractions—' Liz stopped abruptly, her face screwed up as she puffed. 'Two minutes apart and getting stronger. Near transition.'

It was all he could do to subdue the dismay that mushroomed through him. They'd done the theory of delivering babies but he'd never imagined having to use the rusty knowledge. He relayed Liz's information. 'She says she's not far off transition, whatever that means.'

'It means don't panic but don't dawdle either.' He could hear the smile in Kayla's voice. It curled into his ears like a caress. She was strong and calm on the other end of the line, instilling her confidence over the phone. Not that Liz needed it. But he did. 'Tell Liz the room is all ready and I'll see her soon. Drive carefully, Tom.'

'I will.' He thumbed the off button as Jack came back into the room. 'Okay, give me the bag, you get Liz. Let's go.'

Tom curbed his impatience on the short drive to the hospital. He was torn between wanting to floor it with emergency lights blazing, sirens blaring, and wanting to make the ride as smooth as possible for his precious cargo.

Most of all, he wanted to be *there*, with Kayla and her expertise.

As he drove, he listened to his friend's murmurs of reassurance coming from the back seat.

At the emergency entrance, he could see Kayla at the door with a wheelchair. He felt his tension leach away, only to be replaced by the profound sadness he'd lived with for the last week. Despite the grinding physical ache that cramped in his chest, he couldn't take his eyes off Kayla. She looked beautiful, perhaps a little pale.

'I want to walk,' Liz insisted as she clambered out of back door. 'I need to walk. Jack?'

'Right here, darling.'

'Let's get you set up in the birthing room.' Kayla ushered them through the door, looking back at him with a sweet smile. 'Thanks, Tom. You did good.'

The quick words of gratitude, the way her beautiful grey eyes had clung to his with soft warmth and approval, filled him with an odd painful pleasure.

The door shut behind them. He'd done his bit, he could go home now…should go home.

But he didn't want to. There was nothing, *no one*, waiting for him there. Seeing Kayla tonight underlined the emptiness he felt.

He sighed and climbed into the driver's seat. Perhaps he'd park the vehicle, stay a bit longer in case Jack and Liz needed him.

* * *

Less than an hour later, Kayla smiled at her friends huddled together, their new baby boy cradled lovingly.

'I'll leave you three alone to get acquainted. If you need anything at all, the buzzer's there. Just ring.'

Jack and Liz looked up, their eyes damp. 'Thanks, Kayla.'

'Thank you for letting me be here.' She smiled through the tears brimming in her eyes. 'All of you did a great job.'

Turning away, she let herself out of the room quietly. Her heart was so full. The miracle of birth was always profound, but today it had affected her even more than usual.

She stood with her fingertips resting on the wood of the closed door. In a moment of crystal clarity she realised this was what she wanted. A future with a man she loved, with Tom. He'd offered her a place in his heart and she'd been too afraid to grasp it.

But now she knew what she had to do. Urgency gripped her and she hoped against hope that Tom would still be in the waiting room. Not taking the time to change out of her scrubs, she hurried along the corridor. She'd made a mistake and it was time to face it, own it. And make what amends she could.

The damage she'd done might be irrevocable but, re-gardless, she had to tell Tom how she felt. She had to put her heart on the line and take a risk.

Tom loved her...or at least he *had* loved her. She needed to ask if he'd give her a second chance.

Her footsteps slowed as she scanned the room of patients waiting to be attended to. Tom wasn't there. Disappointment punctured her, leaving a brutal, unhappy void in her stomach. She'd pinned so much on being about to see him straight away.

'Are you looking for Tom?' Hilda asked from behind the desk.

'Yes.' Kayla felt her chin tremble as she looked at the kindly nurse. 'Is he still around?'

'He's only just walked out.' Hilda nodded towards the door. 'You can probably still catch him if you hurry.'

'Thanks.'

As soon as she was out of the door, Kayla broke into a run towards Tom's four-wheel drive.

Eyes closed, he was sitting behind the steering-wheel. She knocked on the glass of the driver's window. His eyes flew open then widened when he saw her.

The window was down in a trice and he barked at her, 'Jack and Liz?'

'They're fine. Fine. All three of them.'

He seemed to sag. 'Thank God.'

'I'm sorry. I didn't mean to scare you like that.' Now that she'd tracked him down she felt oddly tongue tied. She put her hands on the doorframe, wrapping her fingers over the edge of the open window. 'Tom, I... Can we go somewhere to talk?'

A muscle along his jaw flexed and she read rejection in his eyes. Pain tightened her chest.

'Kayla—'

'Please,' she whispered, gripping harder and willing him to hear her out.

He sighed out a breath. 'Okay. I'm listening.'

She hesitated then swallowed. 'Can I...can I get in?'

'Of course.'

She walked around to the other side of the vehicle as she tried to gather her thoughts. Suddenly Tom was beside her, opening the door.

She turned to face him, looked up into his dear, dear

face. Suddenly his features blurred and she blinked hard to bring him back into focus.

'I'm sorry for hurting you the way I did, Tom.'

'I know. It's not your fault. You tried to warn me.' A sad smile touched his lips. 'I just didn't want to hear because I was so busy with my own plans.'

He was trying to make it better, easier for her. He was baring himself again and it was her job. A hot tear streaked down her face.

'Stop. Please.' She laid her fingertips to his mouth. 'I'm doing this all wrong.'

He lifted a hand and stroked the moisture from her cheek. Covering his hand with hers, she turned her head and placed a kiss in the palm.

'Kayla—'

'I love you, Tom.' She felt a jolt run through his body as the words rasped in her throat. She'd said them, they were out there. It was as if a huge weight had been lifted from her soul. Saying the rest would be easy now. 'I want to be with you. I'm sorry I hurt you and I know you might have changed your mind.'

'Changed my mind? Are you crazy? Not in a million years. I love you so much it hurts.' He freed his hands and she found herself crushed to his body. 'God. Say the words again so I know I didn't imagine them.'

'I love you, Tom.'

He squeezed her hard and she revelled in the embrace. Tremors shook them. Did they come from him or her? It didn't matter. All that mattered was they were together.

His lips found hers. She dived into the kiss, not holding back any part of herself, relishing how much sweeter and even more perfect the feel of his mouth on hers was now that her emotions were stripped naked.

He pulled back, brushing her hair back and looking

deep into her eyes. 'Your plans. What about your plans, Kayla? Honey, you're so passionate about them.'

'A reason to avoid life and pain and messy emotions and the scary out-of-control way you make me feel. I don't want to avoid that any more. I still want to make plans but I want to make them with you.'

'I've got some plans of my own.' He pressed her back against the fender of the vehicle.

She laughed. 'I already know what one of them is.'

'Yeah.' Colour flared along his cheekbones. 'Well, we'll get to that. But we've got some more important things to settle first…make an honest man of me.'

'As soon as you like.'

'Family?'

'Oh, yes. I can't wait until we start working on that plan. I love you, Tom. Take me home.'

Medical Romance™

ST PIRAN'S: PRINCE ON THE CHILDREN'S WARD
by Sarah Morgan

Children's doctor Tasha O'Hara's new job is looking after a sinfully gorgeous, injured Mediterranean prince. This isn't just *any* prince, but heartbreaker Prince Alessandro Cavalieri. Alessandro's definition of No Physical Activity *definitely* goes against doctor's orders…and it's becoming impossible for Tasha not to succumb to temptation!

HARRY ST CLAIR: ROGUE OR DOCTOR?
by Fiona McArthur

Harry St Clair does a good job persuading people that the devil-may-care rogue is the real him, but midwife Bonnie McKenzie isn't fooled! The real Harry St Clair is one of the best doctors in the southern hemisphere. The real Harry St Clair is buried under the weight of his devastating secrets—a weight he no longer has to carry alone…

On sale from 3rd June 2011
Don't miss out!

Available at WHSmith, Tesco, ASDA, Eason and all good bookshops
www.millsandboon.co.uk

Meet the three Keyes sisters—in Susan Mallery's unmissable family saga

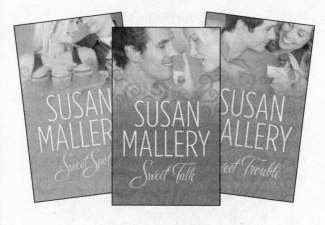

Sweet Talk
Available 18th March 2011

Sweet Spot
Available 15th April 2011

Sweet Trouble
Available 20th May 2011

For "readers who can't get enough of Nora Roberts' family series"—Booklist

www.millsandboon.co.uk

Everybody loves a royal wedding!

AND WE HAVE FOUR...

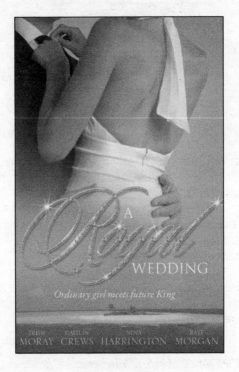

OUT NOW!

2 FREE BOOKS
AND A SURPRISE GIFT

We would like to take this opportunity to thank you for reading this Mills & Boon® book by offering you the chance to take TWO more specially selected books from the Medical™ series absolutely FREE! We're also making this offer to introduce you to the benefits of the Mills & Boon® Book Club™—

- **FREE home delivery**
- **FREE gifts and competitions**
- **FREE monthly Newsletter**
- **Exclusive Mills & Boon Book Club offers**
- **Books available before they're in the shops**

Accepting these FREE books and gift places you under no obligation to buy, you may cancel at any time, even after receiving your free books. Simply complete your details below and return the entire page to the address below. You don't even need a stamp!

YES Please send me 2 free Medical books and a surprise gift. I understand that unless you hear from me, I will receive 5 superb new stories every month including two 2-in-1 books priced at £5.30 each and a single book priced at £3.30, postage and packing free. I am under no obligation to purchase any books and may cancel my subscription at any time. The free books and gift will be mine to keep in any case.

Ms/Mrs/Miss/Mr _____ Initials _____

Surname _____

Address _____

_____ Postcode _____

E-mail _____

Send this whole page to: Mills & Boon Book Club, Free Book Offer, FREEPOST NAT 10298, Richmond, TW9 1BR